WEREWOLF STANDOFF!

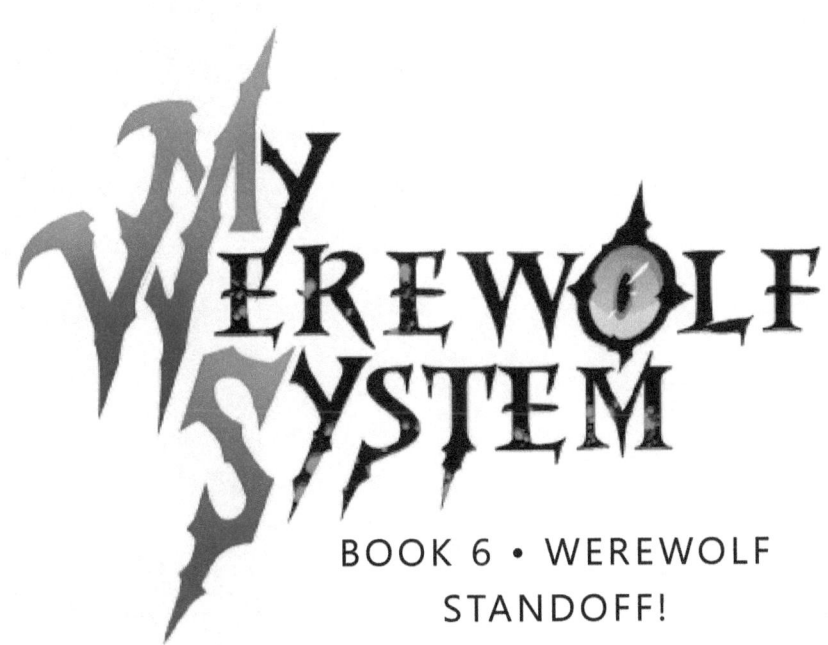

BOOK 6 • WEREWOLF STANDOFF!

JKSMANGA

Podium

Copyright © 2026 by Kawin Jack Sherwin

Cover design by Husa

ISBN: 978-1-0394-8005-6

Published in 2026 by Podium Publishing
www.podiumentertainment.com

Podium

WEREWOLF STANDOFF!

CHAPTER 1

THE TRIO ACTS!

Numba was a student of the Altered Fighting Academy. Originally, he had gone into the academy planning to stay separate from everyone, wishing to do well to help his father progress even further in his business. He never thought he would make friends, nor did he ever imagine that the situation back home would take a sour turn.

Somehow, beaten, unsure what to do, he had pleaded with the one person he could trust in the academy: Gary Dem. He had asked him for help, and now he felt kind of stupid for doing so; after all, what could one person do, who was only a student?

Numba had been told that he was to stay in the hospital one more day. His wounds had mostly healed up, but they wanted to make sure that nothing else was wrong before he continued his regular activities. This was a fighting academy, so just being well enough to walk wasn't good enough.

The others had eventually left: first Gary, and then Izzy and Ian left together. One would think that they were a couple based on how much time they spent together, but it was clear to Numba that Izzy had certain feelings for someone else, which was why he didn't say who had actually stopped the students that had attacked him.

Why were they together? And both walking at the back of the academy? Suddenly, a few lewd thoughts entered Numba's head, which caused his face to go slightly red.

Gary said they knew each other, but I wonder, could they possibly be dating?

While he was thinking this, there was a slight knock on the door. It was quite late, but he assumed one of the others had something that they had forgotten to say.

"Come in!" Numba called out.

A delicate, smooth-skinned hand pushed open the door, and he saw gray hair flowing down. One of the people he had been thinking about seconds ago now stood right in front of him.

"It's a pleasure to meet you, Numba Cardenez. My name is Xin Clove; I believe we met during the debut match," Xin said politely as she gave a little bow.

Immediately, Numba bowed back.

"Yes, I remember you, but please, there is no need to be so formal with me. You were the one who saved *me* back there. So please don't bow," Numba replied, bowing down several times.

Xin couldn't help but giggle, and Numba's heart started to throb.

"Well, I can see why you fell for this girl," Numba said. "But I would never do anything to get in the way of the two of you. I wish the best for both of you."

"I actually came to speak to you," Xin said as she approached the bed. "About the students that attacked you. I have reported them to the teacher, who will have a review with the professors as to what to do with them.

"They will look into this matter further, but I wanted to just tell you that you will be safe. I have a bit of sway with the teachers, being the number one student, and I can safely say that you won't be getting in trouble." She smiled.

Numba had been worried about what would happen to him for fighting outside the school. Although the academy was the last of his problems, he was happy to know that at least this was off his mind.

"I have something else to tell you, something that the teachers don't know," Xin explained as she looked to her left and right. "The one who ordered the attack was a student named Sty. A student usually doesn't have the power to force others to risk getting kicked out of the academy, which means someone else was involved, most likely. I thought you should at least know that much."

This confirmed Numba's suspicions: that the ones behind everything were the Scatterbugs. Beating up Sty or confronting him about it wouldn't do anything, though, as this was a matter between their groups.

"Thank you, Xin, and thank you again for the help. I hope things go well for you," Numba said, then whispered, "and I wish you good luck with Gary."

After Xin left the room, there was a lot for him to think about: leaving the academy altogether and then heading back to help his dad.

Even though his father said it was pointless, sitting here doing nothing was also pointless.

When the next day arrived, Numba was still in his hospital bed; the lessons had come to an end, and Numba had been cleared to leave as well. As he left his room, he was surprised to see two people waiting for him.

"Look at you, you look as good as new!" Ian shouted, punching him in the arm.

As for Izzy, she was looking behind Numba into his room.

"It's good to see you. Is Gary with you?" Izzy asked.

"No . . . why?" Numba raised an eyebrow.

Ian and Izzy looked at each other.

"Because Gary didn't turn up to one lesson today. We thought he came to see you and maybe stayed with you the whole day," Izzy explained.

The three of them went to Gary's room, but after five minutes of knocking there was no answer.

"So he's not in his room, and he didn't turn up for lessons. Unless he's taking a big dump, I don't think he's here, guys." Ian shrugged, looking for an explanation.

Numba stormed off to Professor Humfree's office, knocked once, and burst into the room, with Ian and Izzy close on his heels.

The room looked more like a library than a professor's office, as the walls on each side of his desk were filled with books.

"Professor Humfree, we can't find Gary Dem anywhere. Did he request time away from the academy?" Numba asked.

The professor was a little startled, but he knew who Numba was because of the special lessons he had been taking, and he also knew that Numba was close to Gary.

"Hmmm . . . yes," Humfree answered, stroking his beard. "Last night, he requested time away from the academy. Although it is none of my business, I will say this. If he didn't tell you why he was taking time off, then perhaps he had a reason?"

Numba already knew the reason. After what happened yesterday, it couldn't be a coincidence.

"No way! Do you really think Gary left to help Numba's situation? That's crazy! I thought he was going to ask his gang for help, not go himself!" Ian said.

"Well, I mean if the gang said they wouldn't get involved, you know what type of person Gary is," Izzy replied. "Most likely he decided to take matters into his own hands. I know Gary is strong, but I think he might be underestimating their power a little bit."

The professor was carefully listening in to the panicked students' conversation. Unfortunately, it wasn't the first time something like this had happened. In an academy where groups from all sorts of places converged, it was more common than one might think.

The worry was written all over Numba's face, and he remembered Gary's last words, talking about how they were an alliance and how they were going to help him.

He's doing all this just because I helped him during that assessment. You idiot, you already paid off that debt a long time ago, there is no need for you to do anything! Numba thought.

"We . . . we are an alliance," Numba finally said. "Professor, please may I ask for immediate leave from the academy? I don't know when I will be back, but I have some family issues to take care of."

"Numba!" Izzy said, grabbing his arm. "There is no need for you to get involved in this. If you stay in the academy, they won't be able to touch you, but if you go outside, there are no rules out there."

Numba shook Izzy's hand off.

"I have to."

"Then I'm coming with you!" Ian shouted. "Like you said, we're an alliance so we need to do this together, and we can just talk Gary out of this crazy idea."

Izzy shook her head, but in the end she gave in and smiled.

"You two are idiots, which is why you will need me to look after you."

All three of them asked for leave from the professor, for the same reason.

"Okay, I will take note of that," Professor Humfree said. "And I expect to see you all come back to the academy soon."

CHAPTER 2

THE DEAL IS DONE

In the Wolf's Pool Club the air was heavy. Harry Cardenez, the owner of Cardenez Electronics, was still on his knees. He no longer had his head down, as he was waiting for the decision of the Howlers.

In the middle of it all, a phone call delayed that decision. Will couldn't believe the audacity of the guy in the fox mask, who didn't seem much older than himself. To answer a phone call of all things, unaware who was on the other end!

Kai didn't say much, other than a few nods here and there, as the other person appeared to be doing most of the talking.

"Don't worry, that shouldn't be a problem. In fact, it seems like this was something that was meant to be," Kai said as he looked over to the kneeling adult. "See you soon."

With that, the call ended and Kai set the phone on the desk. He placed his hands together and smiled. This time he wasn't covering the bottom half of his face, which made Harry and the others wonder what news he had just received.

"Mr. Cardenez, it looks like you haven't run out of luck just yet," Kai revealed. "I like that, which means the momentum is on our side. The Howlers will agree to help you."

When Harry heard this, his eyes lit up, but Will's reaction wasn't the same. Because even with the help of a Tier 3 gang, how much hope did they really have? There were already two Tier 3 gangs attacking them, with a Tier-2-gang wall behind it all. They would need to sacrifice a lot, and without convincing other gangs to come to their aid, there was no guarantee that they would be able to fend off these attacks. Will's heart was hurting imagining just how much that would cost.

"However, as you are perfectly aware, the conditions have changed," Kai added. "We will help you not only weather the storm but even get back at those guys, in exchange for . . . fifty-one percent. Not just of Cardenez Electronics, but of every venture you undertake in the future and in other cities. Fifty-one percent means that we will have a say about what cities you expand in and where the business is going."

In a way, this was similar to the deal the Scatterbugs had proposed. Kai was asking for exclusivity by making sure they would have the majority vote for all future decisions, giving them final say in any business. However, it was a larger chunk compared to the Scatterbugs.

"You . . . you . . . you're taking advantage of us in this desperate situation!" Will couldn't hold his tongue any longer. Kai's terms meant giving up control of the company. If they had to give up such a large piece of the pie, how were they supposed to rope in other gangs?

"So?" Kai said nonchalantly. "I think you should let your boss do the talking, as he seems to understand what my offer entails. Based on the gangs you are dealing with, the Howlers are taking a huge risk. This is essentially a gamble. After all, we will have to quite literally go to war for you to obtain fifty-one percent of the Cardenez company. Should we fail, the Howlers will be no more, and I'm talking about actual lives, not some company. Tell me, who do you think is taking the bigger risk here?"

In truth, Kai felt like he could have asked for a bigger percentage of the company. He could tell how desperate Harry was. No other gang would be crazy enough to accept such a deal. Even he was on the fence until Gary called.

That call just happened to be the nail in the coffin. In the end, Kai was making the best of the situation. He didn't know how to run an electronics company, and he already had enough on his plate. As long as he could veto major decisions that might harm their interests, he was fine with it. Besides, demanding a larger chunk of the company would make the other side lose their drive.

Why would someone work hard for the company owning just ten percent of it, while someone else got ninety percent?

This was best for both of them in the end.

"You . . . have given us a very fair deal," Harry said as he stood up from his kneeling position. "I'm thankful that you have considered our situation. I promise you that we will not just stand by and let you do the work. In this partnership we will also do our best to protect our interests. If I have to pick up a bat myself, I will get rid of the gangsters trying to take over my company!" he shouted fiercely, tensing his fist.

I can tell . . . this is it! Kai thought with excitement. *This is the power of a leader. Bringing him to our side will help us grow! This is exactly what we need right now. If we allow him to proceed with his ambitions, we can get to the top together.*

Kai stood up and held out his hand. "Olivia, call our lawyer and let's sort out the contract right here and now."

Olivia silently pulled out her phone while Kai and Harry exchanged a firm handshake. A deal had been struck, but they needed to make it official.

When the lawyer came, the documents for the deal were drafted up. Before the contract was officially signed by both parties, Will looked it over. He wasn't just Harry's personal assistant, but also a law school graduate in charge of negotiating terms for the company.

While the lawyers were talking things over, Harry and Kai sat face to face.

"I know it may be a bit late to say this now, but the Scatterbugs . . . they are a big group, it will be tough," Harry said.

"Don't worry, I did my research. They've come to us before, so we needed to know how bad it would be if we offended them by refusing. It's funny, one might even call it fate, that you came back to us. After all, you didn't know about the offer, you didn't accept ours, and now we are back here." Kai smiled.

"Is . . . this okay?" Harry asked. "I mean, you are doing this without your leader present. He was the person I met before. I'm sure you would need to ask him, and I would like to apologize for what I said last time."

"You don't have to worry about that. I can assure you he supports this. Perhaps you will be able to meet him sometime soon, and you can thank him in person then."

Their conversation was interrupted by the sound of Will slamming down the thick contract against the table behind them.

"Look right here, what is this?" Will pointed.

"Is something wrong?" Harry asked.

"Yes, sir," Will replied. "The contract. It states that forty-one percent of the company will go to the Howlers Limited corporation."

At first Harry raised an eyebrow. Forty-one percent! Was Kai trying to see if he was willing to accept such terms? He would never be that nice.

"Then it says that ten percent will belong to the Gary Dem Foundation. Why would we give ten percent to a stranger? On top of that, if there was a major decision, then this person would be able to sway it to one side or the other."

Again, Harry was confused. For one, why were the Howlers willing to give ten percent to a stranger? This was actually better for Harry. As long as the Cardenez company got him on their good side, they could either buy him out and take back control of their company at some point, or persuade him to make decisions that were in their favor rather than the Howlers'.

"Ah yes, you see, the Howlers have a lot to thank him for. He's been a sort of . . . I guess you could call him an angel investor of sorts. A lot of improvements in Slough have been due to his money, and he supports the Howlers greatly. We owe him a lot, which is why we decided to repay him by including him in the deal.

"Either way, isn't that better for you guys? This way we Howlers don't have majority control," Kai pointed out with a smile.

Will was perplexed because what Kai was saying was true, but judging from the smile it was as if he was hiding something. Why would they do this? Of course, they didn't know that Gary Dem was also the leader of the Howlers.

This was the start of Kai's grand plan of spreading the name of Gary Dem, hidden business tycoon who worked closely with the Howlers.

"Okay . . . if you are fine with it," Will said.

The contract was brought to the desk, and the parties signed on the dotted line. It was now set in stone.

Kai stood up and clapped his hands.

"All right, the deal is done. Now that we own part of the Cardenez company, we need to protect what's ours, right? Olivia, prepare everyone!"

CHAPTER 3

THE ALLIANCE GATHERS

Three large black vehicles were heading out of the town of Slough, one more than what had entered. Their destination was Brighthum, the Tier 3 city where Cardenez Electronics resided.

The new addition was the car in the center, a long limo driven by none other than Tyler. He was nervous about the whole thing as he tightly gripped the steering wheel and looked into the camera on his dashboard.

The divider between the driver and the passengers had been closed to give those in the back their privacy. Nevertheless, Tyler was able to see what was going on through the screen on his dash, so he snuck a few glances from time to time.

Man oh man, every time we leave the city I get nervous. Especially when the others wear their masks, since it almost always means we are headed for a fight. It doesn't help that there are strangers in the car, Tyler thought as he shifted his focus back to the road.

In the car were the core members of the Howlers, wearing their uniforms and masks: Marie, Austin, Innu, Olivia, and of course Kai. But they weren't alone in the car; Harry and Will had decided to ride with them rather than take the cars they had arrived in.

"I have to admit that I'm quite surprised you've decided to come back with us," Harry said.

"Well, your situation is quite dire. Besides, I'm only doing what we would do if we had signed the original deal. There's no point in having a percentage of your company without the factories that you have built up," Kai replied.

There was a lot of tension in Will's hands, indicating that he had a lot he wanted to say at this moment.

"The Freaks . . . are an elite force that work for us," he said. "They have the power to stop the other Tier 3 gangs from attacking. The problem is that we have two major factories and a few small ones as well. "Because of the constant attacks from the other cities, either the Freaks are spread too thin, or we fail to move quickly. I worry that the people you brought here are not enough."

Will was sure that the Howlers had many members to keep control over Slough, yet they had only brought a handful.

Kai responded, "I can tell what you're thinking. Our enemy has us outnumbered, so we have to be careful with how we use our members. Right now the Howlers are preparing. There is a chance that once they find out we have decided to side with you, they'll attack us in retaliation, either directly or by sending proxies as in your case. So our members need to be prepared to defend our town as well.

"However, I feel like that is unlikely. Either way, they will be ready when the real war against Notsburg begins. For the time being, I can assure you that we will have enough fighters to deal with these Tier 3 gangs who are bothering your workers."

Kai's words sounded confident, but looking at the number of gang members, Will didn't share his confidence. Judging by their bodies and the sound of their voices, they all seemed quite young. Only two seemed to be adults: the person they called Olivia, although he was unsure whether her name was real or fake, and the large man with the pompadour hairstyle.

Will was worried that Harry was putting too much hope into this group. During the entire drive, Kai's attention remained glued to his phone as he was typing a text to someone.

"If I'm correct, one of the factories is in Whitley, while another is in Hightown?" Kai asked as he continued to type, not even looking at them.

"That is correct," Will replied. "We don't know when the attacks will come, but those two gangs have proven quite capable in coordinating their attacks to launch at the same time. On top of that, their numbers are getting larger with each attack, and they have switched to a hit-and-run tactic. Because of it, the Freaks are tired and are accumulating injuries. It's only a matter of time until they destroy everything in the factory."

"Okay, that makes things simpler, then. We will head to Whitley right now," Kai said. "We will focus on protecting Whitley; don't worry about the other factory."

Now Harry was concerned. "If they attack the other factory with no support, the Freaks there will not be able to hold. Are you trying to say one is better than none?"

"You should trust him a bit more," Olivia blurted out. She was the first person other than Kai to speak to them. "If you want to save your company, anyway. That's all I'm going to say."

The three cars finally entered Brightum. Because it was a city rather than a town, it was around twice the size of Slough with many districts and quite a few cars on the road. Kai was already looking at the structures, which weren't well built.

Because of the way the highways and roads were laid out a long time ago, transport was lacking and they were stuck in traffic even now. It made sense, with the size of the city and this level of traffic, why it would take them so long to get from one factory to the other.

With all the overdeveloped buildings in small areas, there weren't many places for them to build large factories. Ideally the city could do with an underground subway system to allow faster travel and less traffic, but that wasn't a luxury that a Tier 3 city could afford.

Eventually, after going through the city, they came out on an open road, where they could see the large factory up ahead. It was so large that to walk around the whole thing would take at least an hour.

Kai could see why the factory was so hard for them to protect. However, he saw some clever play at work. Surrounding the factory were broken abandoned cars, which acted as a sort of makeshift wall. Standing on top, as well as in front of the cars, were hired guards, gang members, and assorted Freaks.

The wall of cars was a good hundred yards away from the factory itself. As they approached, everyone started to stretch, and it was safe to say that the strange appearance of the Howlers had caught the eyes of the guards around the factory.

"Why are they looking at us so weirdly?" Innu asked as he locked eyes with one of the guards. "I mean, they have the Freaks that are dressed up as clowns, right?"

"Yeah, I'm just thankful that I never made us wear something like those clown suits. I understand that it's like a symbol, a uniform that people remember and that strikes fear into the enemy, but why clowns of all things?" Kai said.

"That should be obvious," Austin said seriously, folding his arms. "Clowns are scary."

He spoke in such a deadly tone that no one knew whether it was a joke, and they were too scared to comment.

"Speaking of," Tyler called out as he leaned on the car. The three cars were parked within the hundred-yard circle, between the factory and the wall of cars. "Shouldn't I wear a mask? You know, to hide my identity."

"What for?" Olivia said. "What benefit would someone possibly have from targeting our driver?"

This made Tyler sulk somewhat, because he felt like his position in the gang was replaceable.

"Tyler," Marie called out, smiling underneath her mask. "You're a great driver. Usually I get carsick in cars, but with you driving I never do! I wouldn't want anyone else."

Tears of joy nearly leaked from Tyler's eyes. He had never met anyone so sweet, and Marie looked like an angel to him at that moment. If she weren't in the gang, Tyler might have quit a while ago.

Right now, the group was waiting patiently for something to happen: an attack or some type of messenger to appear. After about twenty minutes, the gates opened for another car. Harry and Will looked at each other in confusion, as they weren't expecting any guests.

When the car stopped, three young students emerged.

"Numba!" Harry called out.

CHAPTER 4

THE GROUPS MEET

The Howlers were baffled at the sight of the three new arrivals. They were sure that the whole city should know by now that this was a dangerous area; a person would only come here if they knew their life was on the line.

"What are a bunch of students doing in a place like this?" Innu blurted out.

"Should we really be the ones saying this?" Marie whispered at his side.

Although it hadn't been long since all of them had dropped out of school, the teenagers sometimes forgot that without the gang they too would be regular students. It was quite clear from Harry's reaction that these three weren't just brave passersby.

"Numba," Harry said softly at first, but then his eyebrows started to furrow so much that it looked like they were touching each other. "What are you doing here? Did you decide to disobey your own father?"

He rushed toward Numba, startling Izzy and Ian, who stood beside him.

"Hey, if the old man attacks us, we can at least defend ourselves, right?" Ian asked his childhood friend.

"No, you doofus! Remember, this is Numba's father, and he's an ordinary human whereas you're an Altered!" Izzy replied back.

"I told you to stay at the academy! I told you to live your life there! Do you think your father can't handle things on his own?" Harry shouted at his son.

"I'm involved in all of this, Father!" Numba shouted back. "I've been a part of this ever since the day you took me into your family. How am I supposed to live a life in the academy when I know all of this is happening? I could . . . I would never forgive myself!"

The old man stopped about three yards away. Izzy and Ian were hiding behind Numba, who was surprisingly standing his ground.

"Father, it's not just you . . . they have already targeted me back at the academy. And not just me, but my friends as well. I have personal issues with them. Let me help you!" Numba locked eyes with his father.

Neither one looked away. It was as if they were the only two people on the concrete.

After a good minute or so, Harry smirked as he pondered out loud, "Just where did I go wrong in raising you?"

"You didn't," Numba replied. "You gave me the perfect life and I just want to repay you for it."

"You have grown a lot since the academy. It looks like you've gone through more things than I can imagine." Harry sighed. "I'm assuming the two behind you are your friends from the academy? All right, since you're already here, I'll place you under Gib in the Freaks; you are to support him and follow his lead!"

One of the men dressed as clowns with large red noses came over. Gib had two bats on his back, but rather than being made out of wood or metal, they were gray with black handles. They were Anti-Altered weapons, albeit a basic one with a slight electrifying power.

The Howlers were too far away from the students to hear much of what was said apart from a few angry words here and there. Only Kai and Olivia, with their enhanced hearing, heard it all.

"That person's name . . . I see why you took a liking to him, Gary; in some ways he is like you. A new business and loyalty from three Altered. I would say if things go well here, we're well on our way to the top."

While the others followed Gib, Harry and Will were talking to the managers of the factory. They were trying to get a handle on the situation with employees leaving. They needed to come up with a plan to reinstate confidence and also discuss how much production was behind.

As they followed Gib, Ian and the others noticed a group of people standing by a high-end car, all wearing strange masks and dressed in black and gold.

"Man, what is with your family?" Ian asked Numba. "I mean, I thought the clowns were strange, but now we've got these Freaks in masks as well."

Izzy kicked Ian's shin, causing him to jump up and down, rubbing his leg, even though she was freaked out as well.

"Those guys aren't part of my family. I don't know who they are. Did the gang get some help, Gib?" Numba asked.

"Yes, young master," Gib answered. "Your father managed to receive help from a neighboring town called Slough. These people are a gang who call themselves the Howlers."

They stopped in their tracks and looked at each other. Gib wondered what he had said that was so confusing.

Immediately, Ian put his arms around the other two and made them huddle up into a circle.

"Hey, I'm not going crazy, right? That clown just called them the Howlers, from Slough? Isn't that the same group that Gary told us he was from?" Ian asked.

"You're right, but I had no clue that my father was going to ask them for help. I guess this must have happened while we were in the academy," Numba replied.

"From what you told us, though, the ones responsible are the Tier 2 gang the Scatterbugs. Any gang would be crazy to help you out. Sorry . . . I know that was a bit rude, but you know what I mean. Does this mean Gary actually managed to convince them to help?" Izzy asked.

They all looked over at the Howlers again. None of them had the same hairstyle or hair color as Gary, nor did their body types match. At the same time, they realized that the number of people from the Howlers was incredibly low.

"If Gary did ask them, then where is he? I mean he left before us, so he should be with them," Ian said.

"I hate to say this, but it looks like the Howlers sent a token force because Gary asked them. They want to keep Gary on their good side because he's talented," Izzy guessed. "So they say they sent help, but really it isn't much. I think it's a good thing that we came in the end."

They broke their huddle and continued to follow Gib with a smile, but Numba couldn't help looking at the people in the masks. For a group that Izzy thought had been sent to be cannon fodder, they looked quite brave.

At the same time, was it true that Gary had been kept back by his gang, told that he wasn't allowed to come to help out?

Thank you, Gary, for at least trying. I bet you did whatever you could to help us . . . so I will do the same, Numba thought.

They eventually reached their post, at a small gap in the wall of cars. These small gaps appeared throughout the wall, to allow their members in and out, a few at a time.

The numbers did not appear to be in their favor. As they waited, Numba had a few more words to say.

"We came here to stop Gary from doing something stupid . . . but I have decided that I will be staying here, even if Gary isn't here," Numba explained. "I have to help my family no matter what, but for you guys it isn't the same. This isn't your family. If any of you are in danger at any point in time, then please just get out of here."

Izzy and Ian did not reply; instead, Ian went to Gib and whispered something in his ear, and Gib called out to one of the other members of the Freaks.

"What did you ask for?" Izzy asked.

"You'll see."

A short while later, the Freaks had come back, with some clothes, makeup, and red squidgy noses for the two of them.

"With these disguises, our parents will never know we were in-volved," Ian explained. "Let me know if you need any help."

After they had changed into their costumes Ian couldn't stop laughing at how ridiculous Izzy looked, but his laughter was cut short by an announcement.

"They're coming, everyone get ready!"

CHAPTER 5

PROTECT THE FACTORY (PART 1)

Harry's factory was currently well guarded, at least more so than the others, for several reasons. For one, a couple of his Freak group members always stayed with him.

Since he was at this location, about eight members of the Freaks were nearby. At the same time, it was the larger factory of the two. In all honesty, if Harry had to save one of the two factories, he would choose this one simply based on its size.

However, the problem was that both factories were getting hit with the same amount of force by two different gangs.

I can't be thinking about the other factory right now. We have to put all our efforts into protecting this one! Harry had made up his mind, and he knew he couldn't afford to distract himself right now.

"Give me a report on the enemy numbers!" Harry demanded.

"I have received messages stating that this time, the number of attackers appears to be in the hundreds. Several cars and motorbikes have been spotted at the scene. This is the biggest attack from them up until now," Will said, his hand trembling nervously.

Along with the eight Freaks, about twenty guards were stationed around half of the building, having moved toward the direction where the attackers were coming from.

Since the factory was outside the central part of the city, there were only really two directions they could attack from: from the main city roads or, more likely, from over the hill, where they could approach from the countryside.

There was more land on that side, and it was harder for the guards to spot the enemy if they came from that way.

Harry thought, *Even if we have the Howlers on our side, their numbers are more than double compared to ours. Not to mention, our people are tired from the constant fighting as well, including the Freaks. Is this their final push to finish us off?*

"Stop the advance, do whatever you have to stop the advance, and somebody get me a damn weapon. We will fight and take care of these guys until we meet the Scatterbugs ourselves!" Harry shouted, rolling up his sleeves.

"Wow, your dad really is a scary man," Ian gulped, seeing Harry's enthusiasm.

"He's not scary," Numba replied matter-of-factly, "he's just passionate about these things."

The Freaks moved out of the small gaps between the doors of the cars, while the regular guards stayed behind the wall, waiting for the enemy to come in. Gib, the leader of the Freaks, turned around to all the others.

"Let us take out as much as possible, and then we will leave the rest to you." Gib looked at the three students, indicating that those words were meant for them as well.

The sound of revving motorbikes braking as they screeched to a halt echoed in the air. Multiple cars and motorbikes had driven over the grassy fields and were now congregating on the gray concrete.

They had stopped, not wishing to collide with the barrier and the guards in front of them. Just as the reports had indicated, there appeared to be about a hundred thugs, carrying all sorts of weapons.

One large man with a tank top, black pants and a golden tooth stood in front of the others. They hadn't rushed forward to attack just yet.

"Today is the day we finish the job!" the man clamored, raising a hand on which he wore a set of brass knuckles. The others cheered loudly, and the sound of a hundred people enrapturing was quite deafening.

There was no breather for them as they all charged in, with those on the motorbikes leading the pack. One of them went straight toward Gib, brandishing a crowbar.

The attacker swung the crowbar, but Gib ducked under it, hitting the man in the stomach; his motorbike continued forward without him before it skidded across the ground and crashed into the wall of cars.

It was an explosive start to the fight. The men surrounded the Freaks, but their reputation preceded them and they held off their attackers even though they were outnumbered.

Swinging their weapons, they began the counterattack. They had great stamina; whenever they hit someone, it knocked them out or took them out of the fight. However, in the end, they weren't invincible.

Gib was struck in the ribs by a chain, and as he flinched, the man with the brass knuckles delivered a powerful uppercut to his chin. It was a blow that would have knocked out most adult men, but somehow, Gib was able to hold on.

With the Freaks slowing down, the other gang members were able to run around them and get to the gap in the cars.

"No wonder my boys couldn't finish you off last time." The man smiled, showing his gold tooth. "Well, it's a good thing I personally decided to come this time. I have to say that after this, we will never have to worry about a day in our lives again, and you can rest in peace as well, ha ha!"

The man lifted Gib by the top of his curly head of hair and readied his knuckleduster once more.

But before he could swing, an explosive bang resounded as if a heavy weight had hit the ground. Then, as the gold-toothed man turned his head, he took a heavy hit right in his stomach. Intense pain instantly clutched him as his ribs cracked from the impact, and he was sent crashing into his own men, then landed unmoving on the ground.

"Is that a . . . clown with horns?" The man lifted his head before passing out.

Gib looked up, and standing in his attacker's place was none other than the young master of the company. In a clown outfit, of all things, with horns sticking out of his head.

"You have done what you can; head back to the factory and recover yourself. Leave the rest to us. If you don't follow this order, you're fired," Numba said.

Gib nodded while trying his best to remain calm.

"You're getting a bit ahead of yourself; you're not in a position to make those decisions yet."

CHAPTER 6

PROTECT THE FACTORY (PART 2)

Everyone, including the guards working for the Cardenez group, saw the Freaks take on the attackers. This was not the first time the gang had attacked them. The Freaks had always seemed so strong, able to stop them before they could do too much damage to the factory.

However, today was the first time that they witnessed the Freaks on the short end of the stick, struggling to prolong the battle. Not only had a considerably larger number of gang members come to attack them, but they also seemed to be a cut above the thugs that had come last time. All the Freaks understood the gravity behind the battle, and thus they were giving it their everything.

Unfortunately, courage alone couldn't decide a fight. The guards watched the Freaks get beaten, hit, and kicked over and over again, but despite their worsening wounds, the clown-dressed gang members continued to fight. At this moment the guards asked themselves how they could just stand behind the walls and do nothing.

It wasn't right, which was why they decided to act. The guards abandoned their orders to wait and deal with the leftovers as they had done previously; instead they rushed out through the barrier they had built and attacked the gang members who surrounded the Freaks on their last legs.

Fortunately, they weren't on their own, as a few others dressed similarly to the Freaks had arrived on the scene. Two gang members had swung their bats toward the guards, only to have them be wrapped by a strange extended appendage and held in its grasp. Before they could react, another large tentacle-like vine, the same kind that had wrapped around their weapons, hit them in the stomach and sent them flying through the air.

Then another one wrapped around a Freak's waist and lifted him up. "I'll take him back to the factory! Don't fight here, you guys; get back behind the barrier as soon as you can!" Izzy shouted, ordering around the guards. While she appreciated the gesture, it was obvious at a glance that they were more of a liability than actual help in this gang fight.

Izzy was using her unique Altered form to fight, and as she headed back to the others, she immobilized a few more attackers on the way, protecting the barrier.

At the same time, not too far away, another Freak was being protected by a person dressed as a clown. Several gang members were on the floor bleeding from their hands, and others had even dropped to their knees out of fear.

Meanwhile, Ian in his clown getup had several spikes sticking out from his body. They were more like the small bristles of a hedgehog, and several holes had already formed in his clothes as they retracted back into his body.

"I'm sorry, my fellow clown friend, but it looks like I ruined this set of clothes."

The Freak, who looked to have a broken leg, couldn't help but laugh.

"Just get me out of here, and I'll make sure the boss won't chew you out for it," the clown replied. Ian was happy to hear that and gave his ally a hand and shoulder to lean on, before he headed back to the barrier just like the rest, followed by Numba and Gib.

Inside the factory, the medical staff was already busy treating the incoming patients. Unfortunately, there were only a handful of them. Money could only go so far in convincing someone to risk their own life, especially since it was guaranteed that the factory would turn into a dangerous area.

After making sure that the injured Freaks were taken care of, the three Altered students quickly returned to the fray, but the situation had changed. The rival gang members had entered through the gaps in the cars, and although the initial plan of attacking them as they came through had worked at first, eventually they were overpowered.

Seeing this, Numba exploded from his position, striking a man so hard that he flew back and hit a car.

"Get the fuck away from our company property!" Numba roared. With the three Altered fighting within a hundred-yard radius of the factory, they were able to hold off the gangs pretty well.

Harry, seeing all this, had to blink twice, placing his hand on his chest. "You . . . I can't believe it. This factory is being saved right now . . . and it's all thanks to you. I don't know what I did to have someone like you in my life," Harry said.

These were strong words coming from the president, and it was the first time Will had heard him compliment his son in such a way.

Far back from where the gang members were attacking, a middle-aged man with long hair was leaning up against the car with his arms folded.

Three Altered? Now that is a surprise. Did the Cardenez family hire them? I didn't think anyone would support them in this situation. Surely they should know the Scatterbugs are behind this. Maybe this is something I should report, the man wondered to himself as his hand went toward his phone.

The man wasn't the only one watching everything from the back. Kai and the other members of the Howlers had yet to join the fight. So far, they had stayed in the shadows, he to observe, the rest waiting for him to give them the go-ahead.

Kai thought, *Those Freaks are more impressive than I thought. They might be on the same level as the Underdogs' Cheetah Squad. The Scatterbugs must have never expected that a simple company would be so hard to take over, but that just shows Harry's strong mindset. He is definitely someone we want on our side.*

As for those three, they are all highly skilled Altered. I guess that's what I should expect from AFA students, but they are particularly talented, and that girl seems to have a good head on her shoulders. Without any major changes in this fight, the Cardenez group might actually make it out of this without the need for us to intervene.

Well, we can't just let things end like this, not without letting them know what we're capable of as their allies. I wouldn't want to give them a reason to weasel out of our deal.

Kai turned around to the others, who all seemed restless. It was taking everything they had to hold back from joining the fight.

"I know that all of you are eager to get involved, but it was important that you saw what those guys are capable of. They are nothing like us, and the group behind them is even worse. You've seen it for yourselves, these people hurt others without a second thought.

"Some of them have taken lives just for fun. If these people find out who we are, or if we give them the chance, they will pay us back tenfold. I want you to imagine not what they would do to you but what they would do to those you care about, what they would do if they manage to get a hold of your family! Do you understand?" Kai shouted.

Numba was busy fighting, but he could hear Kai's voice. The Altered was doing well, but fighting like this had exhausted him and he wondered if the Howlers would ever do something. At that moment, a man on a motorbike drove through the gap, heading straight for the Howlers.

"I want you to all fight without holding back!" Kai ordered.

As the man on the bike came closer, Austin accelerated and clashed with him. The man swung down his crowbar on the bull-masked teenager's shoulder. Surprisingly, it did nothing, leaving no injury. At the same time, the bike crashed right into Austin and stopped in its tracks.

"I understand!" Austin replied as he lifted the front of the bike into the air with ease, causing the man to fall off, and hurled it into the incoming rival gang members.

Numba was ready to deal with a group of attackers in front of him when a bike came flying from the side. It hit a group of six of them, knocking them off their feet and crushing their bones.

He turned to see the masked figures walking their way.

"You've done enough, now it's our turn. I promise we'll get rid of all of them for you!" Kai said as he ran forward, his hands transforming with a tuft of gray fur.

CHAPTER 7

THE HOWLERS JOIN

The Howlers finally decided to join in, and the first act of one of their members had caused nearly the entire group to stop fighting. The tall guy in the bull mask had not only performed a superhuman feat by lifting a heavy, large vehicle, but he had furthermore chucked it a far distance at an incredible speed.

Harry and Will rubbed their eyes to make sure they were seeing right, and while all attention was on Austin, Kai lifted his transformed hand in the air. "This factory and the Cardenez group as a whole belong to the Howlers! An attack on them is an attack against us!"

Kai rushed to the closest rival gang member, grabbing him by the head and slamming him down on the concrete. This act of violence ended the momentary peace, and his fellow gang members rushed at the fox-masked aggressor with their weapons drawn.

One swung a bat toward Kai's head, but was met with the swing of an axe that sliced the weapon in half.

Before the person could act, a kick to his head spun his body before he landed on the ground.

Innu continued his attack, avoiding swings and hits from the invaders. One of his axes buried itself in a gang member's shin causing him to scream in pain.

Remember Kai's words: we can't let these guys go. Letting them off easy is also out of the question, else they won't just come for us. I care about Kevin and Suzan too! Innu thought, as his weapons supplied him with another boost of energy.

More members were running through the gaps, but before they could make it through, they were hit by a bolt that electrified them on the spot. Marie had become quite the decent archer as she continued to fire at spots that would disrupt more of them coming in.

"Oh, I thought . . . you were like me," Tyler said.

"I used to be, but when you hang around these guys, you inexplicably tend to find yourself in situations like this. I know that I'm not as good as them in a head-on fight, so I try to keep up with them in my own way, though I'm told that I'm too shabby with my pair of daggers these days," Marie smiled.

All Tyler could do was smile, as he wasn't sure whether she was joking. Suddenly everyone heard a loud scream, because the most brutal member of the Howlers wasn't holding back at all. Olivia had wrapped her whip around one of the large man's hands. Using her werewolf strength, she lifted the man in the air, causing his shoulder to pop.

Unfortunately for him, that wasn't the end of it. His body swung toward her, and she slammed a transformed werewolf fist deep into the man's stomach, causing him to cough out blood all over her, tainting her mask, which revealed her shiny blue eyes.

The fight continued, but the invading gang members were ignoring Numba and the others, forced to focus on the biggest threat in front of them. The Howlers, however, were proving capable of dealing with everyone coming their way.

A chain swung right at Kai, and he used his claws to rip right through it. The injured Freaks had come back out after being partially treated, thinking that they might be needed to help out in the fight. All they could see were several unconscious gang members bleeding on the ground, many of them either dead or not far from it.

"I think we were wrong about the Howlers, sir," Will said. "Rather than too few, I would say they sent out far more than were needed to deal with our problem. How can a Tier 3 city have . . . I don't even know how many of them are Altered at this point."

It was a hard thing to determine because the only ones who had visibly transformed were Kai and Olivia. The others were displaying powers that seemed beyond what a normal human was capable of, but not necessarily enough to identify them as Altered.

"I think we all underestimated them," Harry concluded.

The AFA students stood there watching, like the Howlers had done in the beginning. They were looking for ways to help out, but eventually the area became mostly clear. There were still gang members on the other side, but they were having trouble getting in.

"*This* is the gang Gary belongs to?" Ian blinked a few times, still finding it hard to believe. "He told us he was from a Tier 3 town, right? How is it possible for any town to have so many Altered and not be known far and wide?"

"I know," Izzy agreed. "Any one of them should easily be able to secure a place in the AFA and do well, so what's stopping them? Why did they decide to sponsor someone like Gary and send him as their sole representative?"

Numba was focusing on something else. *Gary managed to secure us help from some strong people. He really is a great friend.*

Like Ian and Izzy, he had assumed that the few members of the Howlers had just been sent here as a show of solidarity. However, the fact that a gang had sent out more than one Altered meant the other side was treating this seriously.

A Tier 3 gang shouldn't have many Altered to begin with. It just showed how much importance his gang must place on him, and it made their enemies all the more intrigued to find out just what type of group the Howlers were.

Two gang members swung their bats toward Kai, who transformed his arms, growing more gray fur as his forearms bulged. He swung them out, breaking both of the bats and, a second later, swiped his claws right toward their necks, causing them to spurt blood and killing them on the spot.

When their bodies fell, Numba was looking directly into Kai's blue eyes. It reminded him of a similar transformation he had witnessed, but he didn't share his realization with the others, although it was a hard thing to miss.

The transformations of Kai and Olivia into their Altered forms looked incredibly similar to Gary's. Was this merely a coincidence, or was there more to it?

CHAPTER 8

SENDING A MESSAGE

Taking another look at Kai, Numba saw that not only was he similar to Gary, but aside from the fur color there were certain similarities between him and Olivia. It was more than just the mere appearance of the werewolves, though; it was the ferocity behind their attacks.

"You noticed it as well, right?" Izzy asked. "It's not unheard of for there to be Altered who are similar to each other, but there are still variations between them, as if they were distant cousins. Those two and Gary seem to be more closely related, like they are somehow siblings.

"What's even stranger, if there was an Altered form that was known to be this strong and multiple solutions of that type were sold, it should have cost an insane amount of money. Not something that Tier 3s like us could afford, gang or not.

"The only possibility I can think of is that someone made a huge gamble on mystery solutions. There's no way of knowing what type of Altered you will become, but it's next to impossible to find those on the market.

"Two of those Wolf Altered might have been a coincidence, but three of them means something is going on. Something that we don't know about. It makes me think that the Howlers have someone bigger backing them, or maybe even whoever is backing them has found a way to extract more than one solution out of an Altered fossil."

Izzy had not only summed up Numba's thoughts on the matter but had even given him a lot to think about. The last option was unlikely, but if it was true . . . it might become a breakthrough and usher in an age of Altered!

Since it was obvious that they were no longer needed, the AFA students reverted to their human forms as the fight came to an end.

All of the gang members who had crossed the barrier of cars had been beaten up. As if that weren't enough, Olivia was using her whip to pick up those who were injured, passed out, or dead and was throwing them over the wall.

Her allies could only imagine the horror the invaders would feel when they saw their friends chucked over, a complete mess. It certainly had the effect that Olivia was going for as the few remaining members outside had decided against fighting their way in.

"We can't just let them go this easily, can we? Bull!" Kai said with a smile.

Harry, the guards, and the AFA students were baffled. *Easy* was the last word they would use to describe what had happened to the invaders. That was when Austin went to the barrier of cars and lifted one over his head—with his great strength and in his full Altered form that made him look like just a regular human.

Okay, no way that guy is a regular human. He must be an Altered as well! Ian stared in amazement, wondering if he could even do such a thing in his fully transformed state.

With the car above his head, Austin jumped up on top of the car below. He could see the ten or so gang members who were running away for their lives. The Minotaur Altered hurled the car into several of the men, preventing them from moving today or ever.

Austin had strong resolve in the beginning when he knew what type of life he would need to live, and he too accepted the weight of Kai's speech. The Howlers had regathered but were still transformed in their uniforms and masks. None of the members looked to have suffered so much as a scratch.

"The Howlers have saved us," Will uttered in disbelief, pinching his cheek to see if all of this was a dream.

"No, they haven't saved us yet. There is still much to do, but they have given us a chance to keep what is ours!" Harry replied.

No longer was there fighting or other gang members rushing in to attack. For a second they all felt safe.

Standing at the back of the concrete base, where the attackers had come from, was the man with long black hair, who just shook his head at the scene, with his phone in his hand. As soon as he saw Austin throwing the car at his men, he hit speed dial.

"Boss, I'm sorry to report this, but the attack was a complete failure. We weren't able to touch the factory. They have gotten a group called the Howlers to help them out, and they brought along an Altered."

Everyone had clearly heard Kai's words, and the man had made a note of it all, as well as of Kai standing on top of the cars and looking out toward the man still in his transformed state.

"There's an update: the reason they are so confident is that they have at least two Altered in their midst."

The man had to pull the phone away from his ear because of the person shouting on the other end. When the shouting was over, he heard only deep breathing.

"Fine, we will show them an ounce of our strength, is there a leader of some kind?" the voice at the other end asked.

Kai gave a friendly wave and took a deep breath.

"You there, tell your boss that if he dares to touch our turf again, we'll be coming for him next!" Kai yelled out with a deep howl at the end. His voice easily reached everyone there.

"Yes, I think there is a perfect person to target. I imagine if we get rid of him, they will all start to crumble," the man on the phone reported.

On the other side of the call, the boss set the phone down on the table, which was slightly cracked from having been punched earlier during the call.

"Midwak, I have a special task for you."

"Yes, sir," a man in a Hawaiian shirt replied, stepping forward, his eyes starting to glow with a slight tint of yellow.

CHAPTER 9

ANOTHER FACTORY

Some of the gang members that had been chucked over the wall were able to move after a few minutes.

On the order of the long-haired man at the back, they were told to gather their men and return to their city or town with the cars they had brought with them.

There was a chance that the Howlers or the Cardenez family wouldn't allow this and would finish off the gang members completely, but they did have a heart, and Kai believed they had done more than enough to deter the other gangs from doing the dirty work of the Scatterbugs. In the end, one's life was more important than anything, and that included money.

Eventually the gang members left in their cars, heading back to where they had come from. Everyone breathed a big sigh of relief.

"Please sit, sir, you must be exhausted," Will said, as he pulled a pop-up chair seemingly out of nowhere.

Harry took the seat, wiping the sweat from his forehead. The entire time, even when it looked like the group was on the upside, he had been nervous.

"The factory, the business, is saved for one more day at least."

The Freaks and the guards had gathered to give them an update on the situation. In the end, the guards were told to head inside to inform everyone that the place was safely protected and they could continue their work with no worries.

Seeing the full fleet of guards all present would give the workers confidence.

"I need to thank you three as well," Harry said, as he looked at the Altered students. "This was none of your business and you could have been hurt. Just because you guys are skillful, don't let your guard down or let it go to your head."

Ian and Izzy knew this was a compliment from the old man, even though it was said in a fatherly type of way.

Just then the group heard footsteps coming toward them, and it was none other than the masked fighters: the Howlers.

The Freaks and the Altered students stood next to Harry in a line, and when the Howlers were close enough, Numba bowed down at a ninety-degree angle.

"Thank you for helping our company out. Thank you for agreeing to help the Cardenez company," Numba shouted.

Harry stood up and the rest of them bowed down as well, all saying at the same time, "Thank you!"

The Howlers' smiles were visible even under their masks. It was nice to be thanked for their work even if it was for beating up a bunch of people.

"As I said before, we are just doing what we can to protect what is ours. We want to show you that working with us is the right choice," Kai explained. "Besides, the one that you should really be thanking is our leader."

Numba had assumed that the one talking now was the leader, but from his words that didn't seem to be the case at all.

"You are correct; I believe the last time we met I greatly disrespected your leader. I should be getting down on my knees and thanking him. Where is your leader?"

Kai smiled.

"Ah, I texted him earlier. I think he should be done soon. Don't you remember how in the car I asked you for the location of both factories?"

Harry's eyes widened.

"Are you telling me that your leader went to the other factory?" he asked.

In all honesty, Harry had given up hope on the other factory and was just happy that the one in front of him was still standing.

"Ha-ha, you guys are more sly than I imagined." Will chuckled. "I can't believe you sent the rest of the Howlers to the other factory with your leader; no wonder so few of you were here."

Kai shook his head.

"I didn't lie, the rest of the Howlers are still back in Slough. Our leader went to the other location himself."

Both Harry and Will began to panic.

"Are you crazy?" Will shouted. "Didn't we tell you before that both factories so far have been attacked with an equal amount of force. Which means if your leader went out there on his own, he would be facing these guys with just a few guards!"

Immediately, Will called the other factory. There was a good chance that no one would pick up, but if they could save their leader, then maybe the Howlers would still agree to help them.

After a few rings, the phone was picked up.

"Report! What is the situation over there?" Will shouted, not even giving time for the other person to speak.

"Sir . . . everything is fine here," the man answered.

"Was there no attack? There might be one any second now, so prepare yourselves," Will said.

"That's not it, sir. We were attacked but a man came and helped us, a man wearing a wolf mask . . . he just finished dealing with them now."

On the other side of the phone, the guard was still in disbelief at what he had witnessed. Unlike at the other factory, there was no barrier made of cars.

When the masked man appeared, he just said one thing to the group.

"I'm from the Howlers . . . don't come close to me or I might hit you."

Moments later an unbelievable scene had appeared in front of them.

Now all that was left was remnants of the fight. Claw marks dug deep into the ground, blood was splattered everywhere, and right now, as they looked at Gary, he was dragging a person by their head across the ground back toward the group.

"Tell them I got one of them that can help us," Gary replied, as he could hear the conversation on the other side of the phone.

Will hung up the phone after the call was over.

"Your leader . . . he dealt with all of them and said he caught one of them."

The Freaks, Harry, Will, and the Altered students all gulped at that moment, as they were just realizing how strong the leader of the Howlers was.

CHAPTER 10

THE COUNTERATTACK

While the people belonging to the Cardenez group were thanking the Howlers for their help, Kai was on his phone, informing Gary about how things had progressed on their end, and his plan in regard to what they should do next. Once done, he gave a polite bow and started to head back toward the car.

Tyler, seeing this, took it as his cue to open the door for the Howlers.

"Wait, where are you going now?" Will asked nervously. Now that he had seen for himself how capable and deadly the Howlers actually were, he was unable to talk with them as harshly as he had done in the past. "I mean, shouldn't we head inside and discuss what to do next? I doubt the Scatterbugs will sit back and do nothing. Perhaps we should invite your leader here as well."

Will was putting on his biggest smile as he suggested this, trying to look friendly, but he obviously lacked experience in faking sincerity.

"There's no need for us to stay here any longer," Kai explained as he turned around. "After today, other gangs will no longer dare to attack you out in the open. If I were you, I would use this interlude to convince your workforce to return. I don't know how much setback you've suffered, but no factory is able to function without its workers."

"As long as I'm alive, I will make sure that our companies won't have to close down," Harry said as he stepped forward, prompting a smile from the fox-masked fellow.

"Good. In the meantime, we'll be ready for the Scatterbugs' response," Kai added. "However, after my earlier message, it won't be you they'll be after. I also doubt that they'll send someone else to do their dirty work after we've stomped over their reputation like this; all the more reason we should hurry back to Slough.

"The plan is simple. After we defend ourselves against their next attack, we will counterattack with our full force. The entire force of the Howlers will move into Notsburg and show them why they shouldn't have messed with us.

"Hopefully, the Cardenez group, the Freaks, and their powerful allies will come to join us in that attack," Kai concluded, looking toward Numba and his friends. For some reason they were happy to be included in that plan, no matter how suicidal it might sound. It was almost as if someone above them was acknowledging them.

Before anyone had a chance to say anything about his plan, though, Kai and the others entered their vehicle and Tyler was off, heading back to Slough.

As suggested, Harry called down all the employees who had come to work these past few days and had stayed with them. He thanked them all profusely, reassuring them that not only had they successfully protected the factory, but after today's performance there was unlikely to be another attack in the future.

He also didn't shy away from mentioning who had helped protect them. Although the Howlers weren't a name that those outside Slough would recognize, Harry wanted them to get them the recognition they deserved. In the future, when they became a household name, many would argue that this was the start of the gang's real journey to the top.

Harry saw that as long as the Howlers could best the Scatterbugs, other companies would come to them, just as he had done in the past, and would gladly offer up half of their business just for the opportunity to work with them.

The day was getting late and eventually Harry and the others returned to the company's headquarters, a large, wide, one-story building rather than the typical multistory corporate office.

"Wow!" Ian exclaimed as he walked through the halls, adorned with ancient vases and paintings worth a small fortune. "Why didn't you mention that your family was super rich? The way you talked about being from a Tier 3 town like mine and Izzy's, I thought that you might be slightly better off, but this is on another level!"

"It's not like any of this belongs to me." Numba shrugged. "Even if I inherit it all one day, what's the point of that much money without the power to protect it? The Scatterbugs hired two gangs and nearly managed to take us out entirely without having to lift a finger."

The three students decided that they would stay under Numba's care until this matter was resolved, no matter how long it took. Harry Cardenez had no problem with Ian and his friends accompanying them, especially since he had been told about how they had helped out his men.

As they were taking a tour around the place, Will suddenly arrived in front of them through the large hall.

"I apologize for interrupting, but I was asked to accompany Numba and his father. I hope you don't mind," Will requested with his dreaded smile again. It was almost as if he was practicing to be a nicer person.

At last Harry, Will and Numba reached Harry's office.

I went against my father's orders. Is he going to punish me for this? Numba wondered. Worst-case scenario, he might be disowned and return to being an orphan once more. If that happened, though, he would be fine with it, not regretting his choice at the time.

Harry said, "We won't talk about what happened in the past. I'm sure you're already reflecting on your actions, so let's focus about what to do going forward. Our next step may decide our future path, and as my heir, it is not only your right to be part of that decision, it is your duty."

These were the nicest words he had ever heard Harry say. Were Harry that type of father, he would have hugged him right now.

"I wish for you to head to Slough. As the man in the fox mask said earlier, the Scatterbugs are most likely to attack the Howlers to enact revenge. Seeing as they have only become involved in this entire mess after partnering up with us, it seems wrong for us to just watch from the sidelines.

"I don't know how much help you being there might actually offer, Numba, but I truly wish for them to regard us as equal partners. Therefore, it is my wish for you to help them fight back against the Scatterbugs. I have to admit that I feel guilty asking you to do this because I can't do it myself, but I saw your strength today."

"Ultimately, the decision is yours."

Without taking a moment to weigh the pros and cons, Numba spoke his mind. "I will head to Slough and help fend off the Scatterbugs."

With nothing else to be said, the Altered bowed down to his father and left the room, but not before seeing the biggest smile on his father's face. He found the others resting in one of the many large living rooms; it had a projector that displayed a large cinema-like screen and a kitchen in the back.

His two friends seemed to have not wasted any time making themselves at home, as they sat back on the sofa helping themselves to a large tray of beautifully prepared food.

"Hey, everyone, I have some news . . ." Numba said, and he explained the plan.

"I'll come along," Izzy said as soon as Numba was finished. "Slough is where Gary is from, right? We originally came to stop him, and we agreed to go together. I understand that you want to go to the Howlers and thank Gary personally, but I have a lot of things to thank him for as well!"

"Yeah, and remember we are an alliance. It's only right that we go slap Gary on the back of his head for leaving us," Ian added. "So let's all go together."

Numba, who hadn't expected to make friends with anyone at the academy, felt like he had a strong group around him.

"All right, let's head to Slough; we will see the Howlers and meet up with Gary!"

CHAPTER 11

THE LAST ONE

It hadn't been long since Gary had set foot in the Wolf's Pool Club, yet he had found himself back here again, and sooner than they expected.

Not only was Gary present, but all of the core members from the Howlers were upstairs playing pool with each other.

Yesterday had been an exhausting event for all of them. Although they had been able to defend the factory with ease, they were silent on the car ride back.

When they got home, they had all fallen asleep immediately. As for Gary, he had given his sister another surprise visit and stayed over.

Nearly all of them had slept till midday, when they had received a message from Gary to meet at the Wolf's Pool Club.

It was closed for the day, with a sign stating that there was a private work event and the whole place had been booked out.

"You should all enjoy today," Kai said, as he threw a small cocktail sausage in the air and caught it in his mouth. "Everyone did a good job yesterday, and we don't know when they will attack again."

There were smiles all around, and the others couldn't stop talking to each other about their skills.

"Hey, Marie, do you think maybe you could show me how to use some of those Altered weapons?" Tyler asked. "I mean for self-defense, of course."

"Sure, I would be happy to. I'm not too busy these days," Marie replied.

"If you want to learn self-defense, then you should learn to fight using your bare hands first," said a deeper female voice, which caused tingles to run up and down Tyler's spine. "If you lose your weapon, then what are you going to do? You should come practice with me."

The boys were smirking at the suggestion; they could just imagine Tyler getting whipped by Olivia every time he did something wrong.

"Gary, you must have gotten even stronger, right? For you to take out all those guys on your own. Are they feeding you some type of special juice at that academy?" Innu asked.

Gary was nervous about answering because, in a way, Innu was right. One of the main reasons for his growth was that he was eating others and the beasts in the special lessons.

"It's a shame we didn't see you fight," Austin said. "I would have liked you to see my Altered form, and hearing about what you did, I would have liked to see it in person."

When Gary had first arrived at the factory, he was only going to help enough so that the others didn't get hurt.

However, he had received a specific quest to take out fifty percent of the attacking forces. This made him act quickly and display more of his powers than he would have liked.

It was no wonder that the others had heard about what Gary had done before he was even able to explain it himself.

In the end, he had received a single Pawn point for completing the quest—which he thought was a bit cheap. But, then again, because of the level of opponent he was going against, it made sense since the job wasn't hard by any means.

As the day went on and the group enjoyed their celebrations, the sky gradually turned dark. Gary stayed mostly by Kai's side as they talked about what was going to happen next.

What was amazing to Gary was that Numba had a relationship with the Cardenez group. He realized where he had heard the name before.

The fact that Kai's plan and Gary's wish to help Numba aligned with each other was perfect.

"I'll be honest, I felt bad asking the gang to help out in a personal matter, so it does make me feel a bit more at ease," Gary said.

Kai replied, "These people have already gone through a lot of trouble. Also, they joined the gang knowing full well that they would do these types of things. If anything, I would like you to be more honest and use us more when you need it. You have to understand that it's because of you that this gang exists."

These nice words made Gary feel like the entire group was stronger and closer together than before, though he felt like he was missing out a little.

"Speaking of your friends, or maybe I should say the friends who were at the other factory along with us, I was surprised that they were all quite skilled. You going to that academy may have improved the gang in more ways than you realize. Also, I was wondering, do they know you're the leader?"

Gary shook his head. "I didn't tell them anything, and I was surprised to hear they were here, to be honest. They think the Howlers are just a group that sponsored me."

"Well, if you trust them, you're free to tell them what you like, but if other students find out who you really are it might cause a problem, maybe even for the academy," Kai replied.

Gary would keep this in mind, as there were already enough people keeping an eye on him at the academy.

Eventually it got late, and one by one, everyone began to head home. Even Marie and her mother had departed, leaving only Kai and Gary alone together.

"You don't have to stay and babysit me. I looked after myself for a long time before I met you. I have a lot of paperwork to do, so you go ahead," Kai said.

They were in Slough and Kai was as strong as any Altered, so Gary felt like he didn't have much to worry about as he left Kai downstairs in the office alone.

An hour later, Kai started to yawn. He looked at the time and saw that it was eleven p.m.—not too late, but the party must have taken quite a bit out of him.

Just outside on the empty street, footsteps stopped in front of the main entrance.

"So this is the place: the Wolf's Pool Club."

CHAPTER 12

THE WOLF'S BREAK

Thanks to his enhanced hearing, Kai was able to make out the sound of someone being at the door, even from downstairs in his office. Wondering who it might be at this late hour, he decided to take a break from the paperwork and find out.

It was only when he was at the stairs that he noticed that the noise didn't belong to a single individual, but a small group. Not fearing for his own safety, the werewolf opened the door.

"It's rare to see visitors at this time of night," Kai said as he got a good look at the three before him. After a slight moment of surprise from suddenly having the door opened from the inside, the visitors immediately bowed down.

"W-we are so sorry for disturbing you late at night . . . sir," a female voice stuttered.

"Don't you think that's a bit much? He looks the same age as us," A boy said, speaking his mind.

At this, the girl kicked him, making the other boy shake his head for ruining their first impression.

"Your friend is right, there's no need to address me as 'sir.' Now, how about we take this talk inside," Kai suggested, trying to keep a smirk off his face over their antics.

Entering the Wolf's Pool Club were naturally none other than Numba, Izzy, and Ian. Will had told them that this establishment was the main meeting place of the Howlers gang.

Like a good host, Kai got the three of them some soft drinks from behind the bar. After that, the blond teenager gestured them to take a seat on the barstools, already having a good guess as to why they had come to Slough.

"As you can see, this place is empty, but something is telling me you aren't here for a game of pool or drinks," Kai said.

"We . . . we heard that this place belongs to the Howlers. Are you part of their group, by any chance?" Numba asked politely.

"Ah yes, I suppose you don't recognize me looking like this." Kai chuckled. He transformed part of his arm in front of them, showing his gray fur. "Well, at least I can be sure now that the masks do their job."

The three weren't gang members, and their groups' interests aligned for the foreseeable future, so Kai didn't mind revealing this much as a sign of goodwill. He knew them to be friends of Gary, and Kai trusted in their leader's judgment of people.

"Y-you're that gray Altered from before!" Ian's eyes widened. "I am so sorry for being rude to you earlier; I thought that was an old man . . . or like an older teenager or something."

"It's okay," Kai replied. "You behaved without taking into account our positions, and frankly I'd prefer you continue doing that. Anyway, you have yet to tell me what brings you over."

Numba's face changed now that he knew that he was actually talking to a high-ranking member of the Howlers.

"We were sent here by the Cardenez group to support you against a possible attack for the Scatterbugs," Numba proudly said. "Although we don't think you will have any trouble dealing with them. We believe that it is not right that the Howlers take on all the risk, that we should have some risk on the line as well."

Kai nodded. If there was a large-scale attack, then of course having three Altered, especially talented ones like these, would always be a welcome help.

"I assume that you came here directly because you wish to meet our leader as well? Perhaps to personally thank him?" Kai asked, and the three nodded in unison.

"That's too bad. Unfortunately, you just missed him. However, I will happily pass on the message."

There was a nervous pause, as the students didn't really know what to do now. They had money for a place to stay, but there was one more thing on their mind. It looked like Numba felt uncomfortable about overstretching Kai's hospitality, so Izzy decided to do so instead.

"Gary Dem," Izzy started off. "He is our fellow student from the AFA. We wanted to ask if you know where he is. You see, we are quite close with him . . . and we wanted to also know if he asked the gang for help. We just hope that he won't get in trouble or doesn't have to do some crazy deal to get you to help him."

Kai couldn't help but smile at this sweet statement. He thought, *How did you manage to win over a bunch of students like this? Gary, you really are a natural leader to attract people to you.*

"Don't worry, Gary has quite the special status in the Howlers, and I'm happy to learn that he has made such caring friends during his stay," Kai said. "Tell you what, if you come here tomorrow, I'll make sure to arrange a meeting with Gary and our leader. Also, if you guys don't have a place to stay, then I can take you to one of our hotels that we have part ownership in; let me just grab my things."

Kai went downstairs, and the three students were happy to know that the Howlers were kind people. They knew that gang members were hard to deal with, but it didn't seem to be the case here.

KRGG

"Did you hear that?" Ian asked, turning toward the door to see the handle moving up and down.

"I think someone is trying to get in," Izzy answered as the door handle continued to rattle.

The next second, the door was kicked right off its hinges and went flying toward the group. Numba quickly stood in the way and knocked the door to the side.

Standing at the entrance was a man in a Hawaiian shirt.

CHAPTER 13

THREE ALTERED UNITE

In the middle of the night, in a place like this, Numba didn't expect to have to fight. Neither did he expect to get a door slammed in his face, and he wasn't too pleased about it. His instincts were telling him to transform, as the person in front of him clearly had no good intentions coming here. The horns grew from his head and his feet were already changing slightly, breaking through his shoes.

"Who the hell is that guy? Why did he do that?" Ian asked, puzzled about the sudden intrusion.

"I don't know him, but we can be sure that he's not a friend of the Howlers based on his entrance," Izzy said, as she started to transform as well. The hair on her head started to clump together, growing larger, turning into six separate hands.

"Should I transform as well? Isn't that overkill against just one guy?" Ian asked. "Besides, maybe this is just some sort of giant misunderstanding?"

"Where are they?" the man in the Hawaiian shirt said. "Where are the people in the masks? I need to get rid of them all."

"Okay, scratch that, he's clearly an enemy!" Ian sighed.

At that moment, the man at the entrance charged toward them. The floorboards underneath his feet broke as he leapt across the entire length of the room, and while he was midair, his eyes started to glow yellow and black , and fur started to grow across his face and arms. He targeted Izzy first; her hair stretched out, aiming for the hands and legs of the attacker as she attempted to wrap him up, which would allow Numba to strike at him with his strongest attack. As soon as she got close, though, the attacker's hands turned into sharp deadly claws that ripped through her hair.

"ARGHH!" Izzy shouted in pain. She was in her transformed state, and although her hair's durability rivaled that of steel, the man had severed it like it was nothing. Unfortunately for Izzy, all those hair extensions had a ton of nerves inside them, making her feel as if someone had pulled out all her teeth.

After slamming through most of the hair strands, the man allowed one of the hair extensions to wrap around his wrist. He then twisted it around a few more times before pulling Izzy forward, lifting her into the air.

"Let go of her!" Numba shouted as he exploded in speed to jump right in front of the man. The Goat Altered delivered an explosive punch right into the man's stomach. The resulting shock wave lifted the man's body into the air, and his grip on Izzy's hair loosened for a bit.

However, the man smiled as he kicked Numba right in the face. The Altered crashed into one of the pool tables, breaking it on the spot, yet after a few seconds he got back up.

"I see that you are quite a strong one," the man admitted. "Out of respect for you brave young fighters, I shall tell you my name. I'm Midwak Convel, the person who will send you to your graves!"

Midwak then quickly jumped into the air once again, ready to land on top of Numba, but just then another person dove right on top of Numba, his back facing away.

Large golden bristles came out of the defender's back. Midwak slammed his hands down onto the bristles, which tore right through his flesh. They didn't pierce his bones, but moved them to the side.

Midwak had still managed to crash into Ian's body, but Ian used all the power he could to avoid crushing Numba as much as possible.

"Ian, what are you doing?" Numba asked.

Blood was pouring out of Ian's mouth.

"My name . . . I'm going to tell that bastard my name!" Ian shouted at the top of his lungs; his back started to shake and so did the bristles.

Midwak could sense that something was going to happen as he pulled both his arms out. Seconds later, the bristles started to shoot out, heading straight toward him.

Lifting his arms in a cross, he covered his face, but the hard, thick bristles still managed to hit him all over his body. Midwak jumped back toward the entrance to the club.

Numba got up off the floor to help Ian, who seemed exhausted after the attack. The good thing was, it looked like Izzy wasn't badly injured either, as her hair had regrown to its previous length, and the three of them stood there looking at the attacker.

"My name . . . my name is Ian! You fucker, you don't even deserve to know my last name! Just remember that I was the one to kick your ass," Ian shouted, his words less convincing as a small amount of blood spilled out of his mouth.

It was then that Midwak let out a tremendous howl as his eyes began to glow. Bristles shot out of his body onto the floor. Right in front of their eyes, the wounds that he had suffered began to heal at a visible pace.

With no use for the shirt anymore, Midwak ripped it off, baring his chest to them all. Now that his wounds had healed, his arms were transforming more than before, covered in fur, and his eyes were mesmerizing with their yellow glow.

"Guys . . . am I going crazy, or are there more and more Wolf Altered showing up recently?" Numba asked, gulping down hard.

"He must be an exiled member of the Howlers. The claws, the transformation, the crazy healing, the physical abilities. We need to work together, because right now it feels like when the three of us were going up against Gary!" Izzy declared, cautioning them to be careful.

Midwak strode toward them with confidence. "You three were just collateral, but I'll make sure to ask my employee for sufficient compensation for all of you. Especially for you, lamb!" A deep smile appeared on his face, which was starting to transform even more, elongating into a snout.

Amid his transformation, a gray blur passed by all three of the Altered, crashing into Midwak. As it did, the other side of the pool club was trashed, and seconds later a large Altered wolflike human lifted the transformed man into the air and slammed him onto the floor.

"Those clothes . . . they're black and gold . . . is that the guy from earlier?" Izzy asked, her mind unable to process all these changes.

Kai's eyes shone blue as he took a step back. A full-blown werewolf, fully transformed, had clomped across the broken pool table parts, his yellow eyes challenging the teenager.

What the hell is another werewolf doing here? Kai wondered.

CHAPTER 14

BETA VS. OMEGA

During their time at the academy, the three Altered students had seen Gary transform his appendages many times. They still recalled how shaken up they had been when they saw it for the first time, yet without realizing it they had grown used to it. So seeing Kai and Olivia do the same during the gang war had not really fazed them.

Thanks to that experience, seeing Midwak to do the same and attack them with his deadly claws and strength had not frightened the trio into inaction. Nevertheless, all of that changed now as they stared at his bestial form. From head to toe, it felt like they were staring at a wall of muscle.

In his full werewolf form, Midwak was around eight feet tall, his head only around a foot shy of touching the ceiling. His razor-sharp teeth dripped bits of saliva onto the floor. Their natural instincts told the three Altered that they should run away, rather than face such a creature.

"They're in full Altered form!" Ian shouted as he pointed at the two. It wasn't just Midwak who was giving them a strange feeling; the blond teenager had fully transformed as well. If it weren't for the fact that they could still see his black-and-gold uniform that had stretched to fit his new size, there was a good chance they wouldn't have recognized him either.

For a moment, nobody moved. Only the heavy, deep breathing of the two werewolves could be heard in the room.

This will be my first time fighting against a werewolf who isn't Olivia or Gary, Kai thought as he continued to observe the intruder. *Unlike with Olivia or Gary, I don't feel any sort of connection to him, so he could be from another pack. I have no idea how old that guy is, but he doesn't seem surprised that I'm also a werewolf. I have no idea what he is capable of, so I need to be careful, especially with Gary's friends still around.*

"You." Midwak pointed with a long finger and a sharp fingernail. "Your eyes . . . you're a beta. You're not worth my time! Bring out your leader!"

The heavy growl in his voice shook what was left of the furniture, and the students couldn't help but gulp. They had to remind themselves to breathe.

"Fine, if you don't want to call him, I'll give your alpha a reason to show up!" Midwak smiled as he charged at the gray werewolf. Once he was within range, Kai kicked toward his face with his werewolf strength and speed.

The kick hit the side of Midwak's arm; he grunted and gripped the leg under his armpit and lifted Kai's entire body, slamming him into the floor.

"W-we have to help!" Numba stammered, exploding forward Although his attention had been on Kai, Midwak leapt into the air and grabbed onto the ceiling with his legs and arms.

His target gone, Numba hit nothing, unable to stop. That was the problem with his Altered form. His explosive power was as much a boon as it was a downside when he missed.

"I don't need you annoying flies anymore," Midwak growled as he jumped down from the ceiling toward Ian and Izzy. Seeing this, Ian prepared to sacrifice himself as he activated his Altered form, standing in front of his childhood friend.

Midwak raised his enormous arm and, at a speed beyond Ian's ability to follow, delivered a heavy backhand to Ian's face, chucking his whole body into the air. Ian looked back and saw the Werewolf standing right in front of Izzy, who was shaking with fear. The girl hadn't transformed, nor had she moved from her spot.

Move! I have to move! Why isn't my body listening to me? Izzy's mind was ordering her feet to do as they were told, but nothing was happening. *Everyone else was able to move, so why can't I?*

53

Opening his large mouth, Midwak bit down on Izzy's shoulder, sinking his teeth easily into her flesh. As the boys saw this, they screamed at the top of their lungs.

Izzy looked at both of them. She only felt a sharp pain in the area. A breeze passed Numba just then, as he saw something else leap up and open its mouth wide.

It bit down hard on Midwak's neck, not letting go and twisting its head.

That's a . . . gray wolf. Numba was baffled as to where the creature had come from. With Altered being an accepted part of society, it wasn't too strange for two people to transform into wolf-human hybrids, but this was undoubtedly a wild animal, a large one at that, which had appeared out of nowhere. Yet it had some strange items of clothing on it as well.

Midwak was forced to let go of Izzy, shifting his attention to the gray wolf. It was on the floor on all fours and ran right toward Midwak, then leapt into the air and transformed back into a werewolf, crashing right into the black-furred giant, piercing his stomach with its sharp nails.

Kai's werewolf form was hovering above Midwak as he knelt on the floor putting pressure on his wound.

"You, Goat Altered, take your friends out of here!" Kai ordered in a growling voice. "You're no help in the fight, and are more of a hindrance. If you want to help, call Gary!"

Midwak lifted his hand off the wound, which had already healed, and pointed his nails at Kai; they flew through the air like projectiles, embedding themselves in the gray werewolf's chest. Kai was bleeding profusely, but the black werewolf jumped up and landed right on top of Kai.

"Just get out of here and look for Gary!" Kai shouted as the two werewolves were wrestling on the floor. "Tell them what is going on and to get Olivia and the others! HURRY!"

CHAPTER 15

A CALL FOR HELP

Numba was reluctant to follow Kai's orders. Who in their right mind would send away three Altered, especially talented AFA students? Sure, the Goat Altered had to admit that the gray werewolf was faring better against Midwak than their trio, but . . . was that really the right thing to do?

When he looked at Ian, who had been hit twice, most likely suffering internal damage, and saw the side of his friend's face swelling up, it became clear that the three of them were not really in fighting condition anymore. Then there was Izzy, whose shoulder was bleeding quite badly. Her clothes had already been dyed red and would have to be discarded later.

I don't want to leave him on his own . . . but I need to look after my friends. They came along with me just to help out, I can't let them die. Numba, his eyes almost closed, ran to his allies because if he could see what was going on, he thought there was a higher chance for him to jump in.

He picked up Ian first, then went next to Izzy, and all three of them headed out the door. The good news was Ian and Izzy, although hurt, were conscious and still able to move. As they ran down the street, they heard loud crashes and bangs behind them, clearly coming from the club. They could only imagine the destruction that was going on.

"Ahhh!" Izzy shouted in pain as she tripped over her own leg and fell onto the concrete; her knees banged against the ground, but the pain coming from her shoulder was hurting far more. "This bite . . . it stings like crazy!"

"Should we . . . go to the hospital or something?" Numba asked, panicked and unsure what to do. He looked around to see if there was anyone on the street, but it had to be close to midnight, and this wasn't really a popular area for people to be at this time of day.

"I'll be okay . . . I can bear with it . . . for now," Izzy said through gritted teeth. It was hurting a lot, but the girl felt like she had only been a burden so far, so she couldn't get in the way again. They needed to help Kai, who had risked his own life to allow them to get away with their lives.

"That guy . . . he told us to find Gary, right?" Izzy asked.

"Yeah, I thought that was strange," Ian said. "Shouldn't we be looking for a member of the Howlers, or maybe try to find their leader? Why would he ask for Gary specifically?"

Izzy thought about it for a while. At first, she thought the attack might have had something to do with the Scatterbugs, but maybe this was something else. Had someone sold the Howlers all of the solution, and now there was a disagreement?

Perhaps the teenage boy was asking Gary not for help, but for him to run away, or know the right thing to do.

"At the moment, we really don't know anyone in the Howlers in the first place," Izzy pointed out. "So the best thing we can do is listen to that guy and do our best to get in contact with Gary."

Izzy was trying to find her phone, but with no luck. Her best guess was that it must have fallen out of her pocket when they were fighting earlier. Ian, understanding what she was doing, searched his pockets. He felt a small prick, and discovered that his phone had been smashed to pieces.

Fortunately when Numba looked, he still had his phone. But when he scrolled through his list he realized something.

"I . . . I don't have Gary's number," Numba said in a quiet voice, earning him strange gazes from the others. "We were without our phones for so long, and we were seeing each other every day, okay? I never thought something like this would happen, so I didn't ask for his number."

"We have to do something!" Ian said, turning to Izzy. "You're the smart one; we have no phone, and we're in a strange town in the middle of the night, so how do we contact Gary?"

Izzy looked worried, and in the end she could only come up with one desperate answer. A few moments later, they were running down the streets of Slough, without any shame, shouting at the top of their lungs, "Gary! Gary, are you out there? We need your help, Gary! Does anyone know Gary?"

It didn't seem to be working, apart from a few people turning on the lights in their apartments, wondering what the commotion was about. Many even opened their windows, shouting at them to shut up, but this didn't stop the trio.

"Howlers! We need your help! One of your leaders is in danger!" Izzy screamed at the top of her lungs. It was a desperate plea, but they needed help.

After running through the streets for a while, shouting Gary's name, they thought it was useless, and they were about to give up and come up with another tactic, until they heard a voice: "You three are hurt."

A young, handsome boy stood in front of them. "Those wounds don't look like they were made by weapons . . . they almost look like bite marks. Were you attacked by an Altered?" he asked.

The three didn't know how to answer. What if they were to call the police? Wouldn't that make the situation worse?

"Gary," Ian blurted out. "We are looking for a teenager, about this tall, green hair."

The young man's eyes lit up. "Gary . . . as in Gary Dem?"

"YES!" Numba excitedly jumped up and down. "Please, can you help us get in contact with him? Better yet, do you know where he might be? One of his friends needs immediate help. It's literally his life on the line!"

The young boy looked at the three of them and their wounds.

"I . . . I don't know where Gary could be right now, but . . . maybe I can help you. Take me to the Altered who did this to you."

CHAPTER 16

SLOUGH GATHERS

The chances of running into someone who knew Gary were low. Sure, he was a member of the Howlers, the gang that controlled the city, but as far as they knew, he was just a member, nothing more, nothing less. Yet their desperate pleas had been heard, and the wounds on their bodies had piqued that person's interest.

What are the chances that this crazy idea actually worked and we found someone who not only knows Gary but can also help us? Izzy wondered. The three of them were Altered from the AFA, so how much help could a random passerby actually be in this situation? Then again, now wasn't the time to ask questions.

"I don't know where he is, but I have his number. Let me text him . . . what do you want me to say, that he's urgently needed at the Wolf's Pool Club, right?" the stranger replied, already sending a text.

"Yeah, that's correct. Can you add that the blond guy is in trouble, and to also inform someone named Olivia?" Ian repeated Kai's request.

"All right, the message is sent. It's best if you guys stay on the path to the Wolf's Pool Club if you hope to run into Gary," the stranger advised, as it looked like he was ready to take off.

"Wait!" Numba shouted. "Why are you heading toward the pool club? Don't you understand that it was an Altered who hurt us? Are you really planning to go there?"

"Yes," the stranger answered, and resumed running off into the distance.

The three stared at the stranger from behind, too injured to follow after him, and if they returned with anyone but Gary or other members of the Howlers, they felt like it would be pointless.

"Hey . . . did we just send a random person who knows Gary to his death?" Ian asked with a gulp.

"I'm not too sure." Izzy replied. "Let's just hope he isn't crazy and actually knows what he is doing."

She kept a close eye on their savior as he ran, and somehow, he was able to run faster than a human could. Was it possible that they had run into another Altered? Just how many were there in Slough?

As Blake approached the Wolf's Pool Club after leaving the trio, he heard loud sounds of destruction. He wasn't out this late at night for no reason. He was searching for information, which was why he had a few items on him.

He pulled out a black mask and put it on. Attached to his back were two red-colored weapons. Underneath his shirt was armor, of the type that only Altered Hunters wore.

If I bring back down another Altered, maybe I can prove to the association that there is no need for them to send me a partner . . .

The three students continued down the street, hoping for the best from the stranger. At least they knew that Gary had been made aware of the situation, but he alone might not be enough.

"We need to look for other members of the Howlers," Numba said. Just then, a figure leapt out from one of the alleyways. It was a woman wearing a tight-fitting uniform in black and gold. However, she wore no mask, and she looked panicked. She seemed to be sniffing the air as she noticed the three people in front of her.

"The smell of blood . . . it's from you," the woman said, seemingly unsurprised about their sorry state.

"Hey . . . she has to be a member of the Howlers!" Ian exclaimed. "I recognize the uniform!"

Ian had also noticed the figure of the woman who could transform into a wolf. The two boys would never forget the curves of her body, and there was also her trusty whip to give her away.

Giving them another look, Olivia Pearl realized that she had seen the three of them not too long ago, having fought on the same side.

"What the hell are you guys doing here, and who injured you to this degree?" she asked immediately.

Without her realizing it, Olivia's eyes started to change slightly and to glow blue, which they had seen on the blond boy as well. At the same time, Olivia started to squint as if she were in pain, and her chest seemed to be hurting.

"Your friend is in trouble; he was attacked by a Wolf Altered or a Werewolf Altered!" Ian shouted. "The one with the fox mask and blond hair; he turned into a wolf and was attacked by another guy who turned into a werewolf. How come there are so many Wolf Altered here?" Ian said, as he came to the realization the others had long since made.

"He needs help," Numba said. "He told us to look for Gary. We met another teenager who texted him a message, but we don't know if he saw it yet, and that guy also headed toward the pool club."

Olivia took in what the others were saying. The blond boy could only refer to Kai, especially since they had seen him turn into a wolf. If he chose to reveal such a thing, it could only mean that he must be seriously in trouble.

In his absence, the two beta werewolves often sparred against each other, and although she would never admit it, after the first few times it became obvious that the teenager seemed to be better suited to fight as a werewolf. Even though she might be stronger, he had always found a way to outsmart her in their matches, so for him to say he needed help . . . Olivia wondered if she alone would be enough.

"Gary . . . I don't have my phone with me, and we don't have the time to look for him. We can get to him after rescuing that guy!" Olivia stated, ready to transform and rush to the club.

Just as they turned, though, from above, seemingly out of nowhere, a large person landed right in front of them. The others braced themselves, as they thought they were under attack. The ground cracked and dust rose. Through the dust, all they could see was a pair of red glowing eyes. All the hairs on their body stood up.

CHAPTER 17

LEAVING A MESSAGE

"Gary!" Numba called out as he recognized the figure.

Gary had noticed the others from above as he headed toward the club in his fully transformed state. He was desperate and didn't care about conserving his energy, but when he saw the others, he thought it best not to frighten them with his full form, so he reverted to Controlled Transformation.

"You're bleeding," Gary said urgently, mostly concerned for Izzy. "What happened?" He was surprised to see the three of them in the same city, especially since they were traveling with Olivia, but their injuries were a more pressing concern. The bite marks on their bodies were large and deep, causing Gary to worry.

"We were looking for you everywhere!" Ian replied. "Did you get the text message from that guy? Is that why you're here?"

Blake sent me a message. Just what is going on today? Gary wondered as he quickly scanned the text message from Blake and saw that it was an urgent request for help. "I just came here because I had a bad feeling, an instinct that told me to hurry over. It was as if something was calling out to me."

"Gary, you don't have time to worry about us!" Numba said in a pained voice. "One of the Howlers members, the blond guy who can transform into a gray wolf, he was attacked in the pool club! The guy who attacked him was able to transform into a black Wolf Altered!"

In response to what he had just heard, Gary's heart started to pump louder and faster. With Billy dead, the only black-furred Werewolf should be Olivia, but the woman was clearly in front of him. For there to be another Wolf Altered, it meant that an actual werewolf had come to Slough. This was very bad news, since the members of his pack were all relatively young, and their experience fighting other Werewolves was all but nonexistent.

"He told us to come and get you and tell you what was going on," Izzy explained.

Without wasting any more time, Gary immediately took off running down the street, transforming as he went. Olivia chased after him, struggling to keep up with his speed.

"Gary, are you just going to charge in there without a plan?" Olivia asked, panting as she tried to keep pace with him.

"What choice do I have?" Gary replied, his voice urgent as he picked up the pace.

Olivia was worried because she knew Kai was strong and had seen the three Altered students fight. They were quite formidable opponents, and she wasn't sure if Gary, who hadn't shown her his strength since returning from the academy, had improved enough to handle the situation. As she watched him vanish from sight, she could only hope for the best.

The three students were unable to make up their minds about what to do next. They had informed Gary, and just like they had feared, their friend had thrown caution out the window and simply run off to help Kai.

"This is why I didn't think it was a good idea to tell Gary." Izzy shook her head. "I knew he wouldn't go to the leader or call the other members, he just rushed in there himself."

"At least he isn't alone. He is with that woman Altered, and there is also the guy who rushed in earlier. With all of them working together, don't you think there's a chance they can do something about that Hawaiian shirt guy?" Ian tried to see a silver lining in the situation.

"Well, I'm going to help as well!" Numba decided as he hurried down the street.

Ian and Izzy looked at each other and let out an exasperated sigh. They had managed to heal slightly from their wounds, not enough to be in any real fighting shape, but at least to the point that they could follow

Numba. They knew that this was stupid and went completely against Kai's orders, but they couldn't just stay away when all their friends were risking their lives.

As they approached the club, they noticed that the windows had all been smashed and there were multiple holes in the building. The destruction had spilled onto the street, with debris and broken glass littering the ground. The once lively and vibrant club now seemed like a desolate and abandoned place.

Ian and Izzy looked at each other with a mixture of shock and worry on their faces. They had never seen such destruction before and couldn't even begin to imagine the kind of power and strength it would take to cause such damage.

Numba, on the other hand, seemed determined and undaunted. He took a deep breath and charged toward the club, ready to face whatever lay ahead. Ian and Izzy exchanged a quick glance before following after him, ready to support their friend and fellow Altered.

"What is going on . . . did they do it?" Ian asked.

There was only one thing they could do. The three of them slowly approached the entrance of the pool club. The door was broken, hanging half off its frame. Still unable to hear anything, they entered the club, and the first thing they saw was blood.

There was blood all over the place. Then they saw Gary standing in the center of the room; by his side were Olivia and a strange man dressed in black armor. They were staring at something on the wall.

The students moved in closer to make out what the others were looking at. All three of them covered their mouths, in shock, trying not to make any sound. Tears started to flow out of Izzy's eyes.

"I'm sorry, Gary," the masked man said. "When I got here . . . he was already like this. The guy who did this to him is gone. You arrived seconds after I did."

Gary slowly approached the wall; his own body functions were out of control. His face, his arms, they were transforming and reverting as he moved forward. It was a true show of his emotions.

Kai was pinned to the wall, hanging by some thick nails. His body had been ripped to pieces, and his blood was dripping onto the floor in a slowly spreading pool.

He was no longer transformed, but back in his human form, riddled with wounds, with the objectively worst one being his mouth, or lack thereof. Parts of his teeth were visible through the muscle, and his ripped-off jaw lay on the floor.

"ARGHHHHHHH!!!!!!!!!" Gary's cries of anger echoed throughout the neighborhood as he stared at the gruesome sight of his friend.

Impaled in Kai's chest was a fingernail with a card attached to it, displaying a picture of a single Hercules beetle, the sign of the Scatterbugs.

CHAPTER 18

SAVE HIM!

It was hard to look at such a sight, yet at the same time they all felt like they needed to. The entire pool club had been destroyed: the glass, the bar, every inch and every corner. It was unrecognizable.

Markings of blood were everywhere, and the same could be said about Kai's body. Deep cuts had been torn through his skin, and he had lost a lot of blood.

The others didn't want to say anything as Gary just stood there. He stared at the whole scene for a few seconds, then suddenly began issuing orders.

"Call the hospital and get an ambulance here immediately!" Gary shouted. "One of you, go get some food, it's vital for him, and I'll take him down!"

Gary rushed over to Kai, pulled out the fingernail that pierced Kai's chest, threw the piece of paper to the side, and got to work pulling out the other nails.

"Wait . . . is he alive?" Ian asked.

He thought there was no chance for Kai to be able to live through such a thing; even for an Altered to survive something like this was crazy. Perhaps a lot of people would think the same, but not Gary.

Because Kai wasn't an Altered, he was a werewolf, and one of the strongest traits of werewolves was that they were resilient; they were fighting warriors who could keep fighting even with missing limbs.

While Gary took all the nails out of Kai's body and lowered him to the floor, Blake called an ambulance and Olivia went running off to search for some raw food. She knew how important it was for his healing to kick in.

Now, seeing Kai up close, Izzy noticed something strange. Although there were many deep claw marks, none had been made deep enough on his stomach to the point where his guts were spilling out. If anything, the most lethal injury was that his jaw had been ripped off.

"Kai, you have to fight, your time in this world is not over!" Gary said, shouting at his friend.

Because of the late hour, the ambulances were able to travel quickly, and they could be heard approaching off in the distance.

The system, you are still a member of my pack in the system . . . If the system is still showing that you are there, then that means you are still alive! Gary thought.

At first, he was panicked and angry like everyone else, and just like the others he thought that not even Kai could survive this. In fact, a werewolf who could do this to Kai would have been able to finish him off, and it would have made sense for him to do so.

After all, was there any reason for a werewolf to attack Kai and allow him to live? Not that Gary could think of, but then the system had come to mind, and that was when Gary made his move.

Olivia had returned with food; with his sharp nails he shredded it as finely as he could. After all, Kai couldn't use his jaw. After it was finely shredded, Gary mixed it with some water and slowly poured it into his throat at an angle.

"You promised me that we would go to the top together. This is an order, you are not allowed to die here!" Gary said.

As the food hit the back of Kai's throat, the muscles moved slightly, taking it in and sending it into his stomach. The food gave him some of the energy he needed. By then the ambulance had arrived and the paramedics came in to load him up.

Gary climbed into the ambulance with Kai, whether they wanted him to or not.

The ambulance rushed to the closest hospital. The paramedics had picked up Kai's jaw to bring along. They weren't too hopeful that it could be reattached, but Gary insisted that they take it anyway, telling them that Kai was an Altered, so there was a good chance that the doctors could do something. When they arrived at the hospital, Kai was taken into the emergency room and Gary was left waiting outside.

"Shit!" he said to himself as he paced back and forth. "What the fuck happened? How am I in the same situation again? I thought, after getting stronger and learning how to use my powers, that I would never be in a hospital again, waiting like this."

Eventually the others arrived; Blake was no longer in his uniform but felt that he should come in. The other Altered had been asked to get checked out, and Olivia was there as well.

"Gary, just sit down for now; there is nothing else we can do," Blake said.

All three of them sat down; the hospital wasn't too busy and the reception staff were having a nice chat with each other.

"What . . . happened? The others said it was a werewolf that attacked Kai? Why?" Gary asked.

"On the way here, we asked the others what happened," Blake explained. "Because the way Kai was nailed up like that was strange, and I wanted to give you as much information as possible.

"I don't know much about werewolves but I do know quite a bit about gangs and Altered. The fact that that werewolf was able to leave Kai in such a state means he didn't just beat him but overwhelmed him with his power.

"Which is why it's confusing that he left him barely alive. The piece of paper that was left behind was from the Scatterbugs."

Gary's body tensed up as he heard these words. Kai had said that the Scatterbugs were likely to attack them, but he never expected them to have a werewolf.

Did this mean that the Scatterbugs controlled a Tier 2 city because of the werewolves they had? Did they have an entire pack?

"Was leaving Kai like that a warning for us to not get involved?" Gary asked.

Blake shook his head. "That's the part I don't get. Killing the messenger sends a stronger message than letting them live. I can only guess that the werewolf left him alive because of a werewolf thing, rather than a gang thing."

Unfortunately, Gary didn't know much about werewolves, because his own situation wasn't very traditional in the first place.

"I know what you're thinking," Olivia chimed in. "But I don't believe the Scatterbugs have a pack of werewolves or are in the same situation as us. In the first place, it's quite easy to find out information on the Scatterbugs' Altered, and there has been no talk of a wolflike Altered.

"However, from the piece of paper they left, it's clear that he was sent by the Scatterbugs, but my last guess as to why he was working alone is because of what those kids said. The werewolf's eyes . . . they were yellow."

Instantly Gary remembered something that Tom had told him. Yellow eyes meant an omega wolf, which was a lone wolf, not belonging to any pack at all. He thought, *So the Scatterbugs have someone like that under their control . . . but it doesn't change anything.*

Just then, a tired-looking doctor came out through the double doors. Gary was getting a serious sense of déjà vu. He was just hoping that the news wasn't going to be the same.

"You are the young man who brought in your friend, correct?" the doctor said, as Gary rushed over to him with the others.

Gary nodded.

"I have some good news for you," the doctor said. "Your friend, he is healing well. His condition has stabilized. However, at the moment, it doesn't seem like he is waking up."

A dreaded fear started to overcome Gary; it felt like a darkness was creeping up his throat, as he spoke.

"Like a coma," Gary said.

"Not quite," the doctor replied. "His brain is quite active and wasn't badly damaged. Everything is healing well, but the healing process in certain parts looks to be taking longer. We have seen some cases with Altered like this before. I think at most it will take a week for your friend to wake up."

Gary fell to his knees right there and then, with his head toward the floor.

"Thank you . . . thank you . . . thank you."

CHAPTER 19

THE LEADER OF THE HOWLERS

The three students from the AFA had decided to get a check-up as well. The doctors seemed to know that they were Altered while treating them, and they assumed that this was a hospital that the Howlers had dealt with before.

It was common for gangs to have relationships with hospitals because a lot of their members ended up going there. At this hospital, Olivia was the Howlers' liaison, giving the doctors direction and informing everyone of any updates.

Kai, Marie, and Olivia knew the most about the Howlers' businesses, and since Olivia had handled a large gang in the past, Kai had always asked her opinion on things, which was why she was taking over now.

At first she thought it was quite a pain; their leader was off at the AFA, while she and Kai were practically running the gang. It was a strange setup, to say the least, but maybe it was the werewolf part of her . . . lately she had been finding it harder and harder to hate Gary in his position.

Izzy had just finished having her checkup; her shoulder had been disinfected and bandaged, and it looked like the doctor had a few words to say to her before she left.

"You're an Altered, so your recovery will be quite fast. There is no need for you to stay at the hospital," the doctor explained. "However, as you may have noticed yourself, the wounds on your shoulders are struggling to heal. They are healing, just at a slow rate.

"Although I seldom get the chance to treat Altered, from the data we do have shared across hospitals, it is a little unusual, but I would say it's nothing to worry about. If the problem persists I would get it checked out, perhaps by the medical staff at the AFA; it is more likely that they would have a better understanding of what is going on."

Izzy wasn't particularly concerned about her wounds. Her body felt fine, a little weak, but that was expected after being involved in a fight for her life. At the moment, she just wanted to know how everyone else was.

When she left the examination room, Izzy saw Ian and Numba waiting for her. Ian's head was on Numba's shoulder; he seemed to be sleeping, with dribble running down the side of his mouth onto Numba's shirt.

She didn't need to ask if Ian was okay, as he was obviously back to his usual self already, but Numba didn't look okay. He was just looking straight ahead; he didn't look at Izzy and didn't seem to notice the pool of spit that had built up on his shoulder.

Eventually, Izzy and Numba made eye contact.

"Hey . . . you still have bandages on you. I thought you would have been healed by now," Numba said.

"It's okay, it's just a precaution," Izzy replied. "What about Gary . . . have you gone to see him yet, or talked about what he's going to do? I'm not sure about the relationship between him and this Kai person, but the two of them seem to be pretty close."

The three AFA students had always been classified as different at their schools, and they didn't make many friends. It was safe to say that Izzy, Ian, and Numba, along with Gary, made up the closest friend group they had ever had.

They had almost forgotten that Gary had a life outside the academy. It appeared that Gary didn't just work for the gang but was a big part of it. Numba was reminded of himself, because it was the same for him.

Hearing Izzy's question, Numba thought back to a call he had just made to his father. He had updated his father on the situation, how the person with a foxlike mask and gray fur had been attacked quite badly, and judging from the note it was certainly an attack from the Scatterbugs.

"I imagined that the Scatterbugs would act, but I would have thought they'd send a full force to deal with the Howlers. That young person was a talented member of the Howlers gang, and he had a good head on his shoulders," Harry said.

"If I were to guess, an attack will eventually come. They have weakened the Howlers quite a bit with this move, and have weakened their confidence. I'm sorry to hear about the situation you have been put in . . . I will leave the decision of what you wish for you and your friends to do in your hands."

Numba thought about it for a while. He was hesitant; an attack from a single person . . . was this something that the Howlers could survive, and what about Gary? Surely he would stay to protect his hometown; there would be no convincing him to come back to the AFA for safety.

"I can tell you're hesitating," Harry added. "But let me tell you one thing. This attack was most likely more of an assassination attempt on the leader of the group. That Kai fellow had made the biggest scene; it was almost as if he wanted them to believe that he was the leader of the group.

"I have a feeling that the boy also predicted that this would occur, but remember, the Howlers still have a leader. Someone that all of those strong people we met, including Kai, choose to follow. There has to be a reason for it."

The Howlers were a strong group; they didn't just have Kai, so it always made Numba wonder where was the Howlers' leader? At a time like this, when one of his members was in the hospital, why hadn't he made an appearance, or decided to do anything?

If his leader was this type of person, then Numba didn't have much hope in the group after all.

When the students walked back to the main reception area of the hospital, the automatic doors opened and a group of people entered.

The three of them paused because they had recognized the black-and-gold uniforms, and although they hadn't seen their faces, they did recognize the body shapes of the others.

Innu, Marie, Tyler, and Austin had entered the hospital. Every single one of them wore a serious look on their face.

"Those guys . . . they must be the ones that wore the masks and were with us at the factory, right? It has to be them," Ian said.

But there was still no sign of the Howlers' leader, which infuriated Numba even more.

CHAPTER 20

IT'S AN ORDER

If the trio had been unsure about the identity of the group of teenagers who had appeared at the hospital, it became obvious enough that they had to be members of the Howlers when Marie asked for Kai's room. A few moments later, they headed in the direction in which the receptionist had pointed.

"Come on, let's go with them and see Gary," Numba said.

"Are you sure that's a good idea? Shouldn't we, like, leave gang business to the gang members? We might be close with Gary, but we don't really know any of the other members. Heck, an hour ago, we didn't even know that Kai guy." Ian wasn't too keen to interrupt their group, especially given the circumstances of their visit.

"We've risked our lives not only by coming here, but we also fought that guy. We did the best we could to help Kai. That should be worth something," Numba argued. "Besides, whatever they're going to talk about, we need to hear it as well. After that, I also have a lot of questions I would like answered, and depending on what those answers might be . . . we might need to find a way to pull Gary out of this gang."

The three started to follow the Howlers down the hallway, but it didn't take long for one of them to notice. Innu stopped and turned around, hearing the footsteps of the Altered trio behind them. It took him a moment to recognize them without their clown makeup.

"Oh, it's you guys," Innu said. "We heard the gist of what happened. It's great that you three were there; otherwise, Kai might have been in even more trouble. We've been told that he isn't in any condition to speak right now, but if you guys want to come in and see him as well, feel free to join us. I don't think he would mind you guys seeing him, not that he can say anything anyway."

It was an unexpected response, because the students just never thought that gang members, especially the ones that they had seen breaking bones so easily, would be so nice. Then again, they hadn't exactly expected the Howlers members to be this young, either.

"Thank you," Izzy answered for the group, since Numba was at a loss for words. The Goat Altered's anger had been building up, but the Howlers' response had caught him off guard.

As they joined up with the Howlers, they heard sniffles coming from the black-haired girl with pigtails. She kept wiping at her face as she got closer to the door of Kai's room.

"You have to be strong, Marie," Austin told her. "We all have to show strength in this type of situation. Remember what the receptionist said: he will leave . . . even if he will likely end up with scars."

The students were realizing how close-knit this gang seemed to be. Expressing these strong feelings, they didn't feel like a gang at all. It was clear how much they thought of Kai as well.

When they entered the room, Marie somehow managed to stop her tears, and Tyler held the door open for the three students. The room was relatively large, but with all of them inside there wasn't much room to move around.

Gary was already inside, sitting next to Kai on one of the few chairs. Olivia and Blake were with him, standing by the wall a short distance from Kai's bed.

The teenager himself was covered with a bedsheet, so the large bandages around his face were prominent, as well as the tubes attached to him. He had stitches all over his jaw, no doubt from the surgery to reattach it.

Although the surgery was apparently successful, there were obvious imperfections. Altered or not, it was practically guaranteed that even if he healed from this, it would leave behind visible scars, perhaps even disfiguring the previously pretty boy.

Those who had just entered the room went to get a close look at Kai; they could hear the monitor, the sound of his heart beating, but they were unable to see Gary's face as he looked down at the floor, hunched over.

The students decided that this wasn't the best time to talk with him, so they stayed at the back with the others, giving the Howlers a chance to deal with the situation.

Seeing Kai's miserable state, Marie couldn't hold back her tears any longer, and her sobs turned into loud crying. There was nothing anybody could say to make her stop, and so it was the only sound that filled the room. After a few minutes, Marie quieted down, and the others silently helped walk her toward the back of the room with the others so she wouldn't have to look at Kai.

The silence felt deafening, and the pressure was tense. A few times Numba opened his mouth to say something, only to close it again, since the timing felt horribly wrong.

"The Scatterbugs." Eventually Gary broke the silence, his head still down. "They're the ones responsible for him lying here. They ordered a hit and went for Kai's life. I'm going to take them out . . . I'm going to take out every single fucking one of them and rip them to shreds, just like they did to Kai!"

Numba could tell from the pain in Gary's voice that his friend was serious and intended to put his words into action. He couldn't help but feel guilty; after all, this entire situation came about because the Howlers had decided to help his father's company.

"I get how you're feeling, but attacking them outright was not part of Kai's plan," Olivia chimed in. "His plan was to defend against an attack from the Scatterbugs, that we would take the fight to them before they had any chance to regroup. This attack on him wasn't that; they will surely come for us soon, and it is always easier to be the defenders rather than the invading force. They're a Tier 2 gang, in a city none of us have ever visited."

Gary stood up and turned toward them, still looking down at the floor with his fists tightly clenched.

"I don't care!" the alpha werewolf growled. "The guy who did this . . . he is hiding behind the Scatterbugs. How can I just stand by and do nothing?"

"Gary!" Numba finally spoke. "I know how you feel . . . I know you're strong, but you can't just attack the Scatterbugs on your own. Going into a city without anyone there to back you up is suicidal."

There was a pause; Ian and Izzy agreed with Numba. They were just too shy to say it in this situation.

"He's your friend, but do you really think all of the Howlers will go on a vendetta just for one guy? Your gang won't start a gang war over one person . . . Please, Gary, just come back to the academy. It will be safe there."

Gary finally lifted his head up, and when he did, his whole face was scrunched up, his teeth were elongated, and his red eyes were glowing as he looked at all of them.

"I'll be going to attack the Scatterbugs tomorrow. Inform everyone in the Howlers that anyone who wishes to come with me should be in front of the Wolf's Pool Club at nine o'clock. This is a direct order," Gary stated.

The Howlers in the room knew what to do. Gary rarely used those words, and it meant he had made his decision, so there was only one response they could all give.

"Yes, boss!" they all replied in unison, bowing their heads.

"Boss?" Numba repeated.

CHAPTER 21

THE LEADER OF THE HOWLERS

After his proclamation, Gary closed the door behind him, leaving behind the Howlers and the AFA trio. Numba's mouth hung wide open as he struggled to comprehend what he had just seen and heard.

Before the Goat Altered had come here, his father had informed him that during the initial meeting between the Cardenez group and the Howlers in Slough, Kai had been next to the leader, a green-haired fellow in a wolf mask.

Given the fact that the first contact both sides had made had been through the blond teenager, Harry had shared his assumptions that the guy in the fox mask had to be something like the second in command. This assumption had only grown stronger once Kai had brought out all those strong fighters to defend the factories.

If what Ian said earlier was true, and Austin, Innu, and Mary were indeed the three masked helpers, it had to mean that they were part of the top echelon of the gang, yet all three of them had just referred to Gary as "boss."

Numba turned around to check his friends' reaction, and their mouths hung wide open as well.

"You heard what I heard, right, Izzy? You're the smart one, so explain to me like I'm five what just happened," Ian said. "Not only did they not tell him off, but they agreed with a 'Yes, boss!'"

"Unless we're all going crazy . . . I heard it as well," Izzy said, taking deep breaths to regain her cool. "It should be exactly what you think. The Howlers may be different, but I doubt any gang would use the title of 'boss' lightly. It's reserved for one person, the actual boss of the gang."

Numba wanted answers, and he needed answers now. How was it possible for someone like Gary to be the boss of an entire gang? He was an AFA student—sure, a very skillful one—but what kind of gang leader would have the time to attend a fighting academy?

"Is it true?" Numba asked the Howlers. "Is Gary . . . is he the leader of the Howlers gang?"

Olivia just looked at them, not saying much. Blake felt awkward, since he had missed the opportunity to get out. He did not really wish to get involved in the whole gang business, but seeing as at least one were-wolf was involved, it seemed wise to find out more about their plan.

Marie wasn't in the right mind to answer, and Austin was too busy making sure she didn't start crying again. So it fell to Innu to answer. "We thought you knew. Was that something that he and Kai were hiding?"

It was true, all of it was true. The students now knew that the entire gang followed Gary Dem, the same person who attended the AFA with them. The confidence he carried, the way he was able to lead people, it was starting to make sense now, but it was still hard for Numba to process, so he fell silent once more.

"How's that possible? Gary is the same age as us. How can he be the head of the gang? How is it possible for him to even rise up that high?" Ian asked the obvious.

In situations like these Izzy was glad for her childhood friend's open way. She wanted to ask the same things, because in her head it made no sense. In the first place, to become an Altered you had to have a big corporation sponsor you. Assuming there would actually be one willing to sponsor Gary, what would they have to gain by overtaking a city or letting him be in charge of a gang? Even if there might be something she was unaware of, how did making him an AFA student fit into all of this?

Everyone had to have your respect, everyone had to think that you were right for that position, but since Gary was so young she could only imagine that he rose to that position or took it over, but she couldn't process how someone would even start to do that.

"We . . . are all friends of Gary's," Marie answered, letting out another sniffle. "Look at us, do we look that much older than he is? Honestly, the way you guys are acting is probably a natural reaction. Seeing it makes me realize how lucky we are to have someone like him leading us, but it's not just him, it's Kai as well.

"It's a long story, but thanks to the two of them, we are in the position we are in today. So if he says he'll help you, he doesn't mean just him; all of the Howlers will go and follow him."

As Numba heard those words, something clicked in his head. It was when he was in the hospital, when he had asked for Gary to help, when he asked him for a favor. It all lined up; at the same time, the Howlers had agreed to help.

"Gary, you really got involved to help me?" Numba was welling up; he felt a large lump in his chest and eventually he couldn't hold the tears back as he fell on his knees and started to punch the floor.

"You idiot, Gary . . . why . . . why would you help me so much, when you have your own things to deal with?"

The Howlers smiled at each other. "You should know the answer to that one, that's just how Gary is," Innu answered with a smile. "So that's why, when he gives an order, we're going to comply."

With that, everyone but the AFA students left the hospital. The three of them sat down in the reception hall to take the time to process everything.

"Man, I really can't believe it," Ian said. "He told us he was part of a gang, but to be the leader . . . well, I doubt we would have believed him even if he had told us. It feels unreal; all those guys seem to be so strong."

"They must really trust each other," Izzy agreed. "If you think about it, they let Gary attend the AFA. I can only guess that Kai was the one running things in his absence. It's the only way it could work. However, can you imagine any one else doing something that crazy? To put your trust into a single person, to not try to backstab or betray him. It seems like they're not your typical gang, and the bond between those two must be pretty close. No wonder Gary was upset."

Numba was thinking back, going over all the interactions he had had with Gary, from the very first assessment to the troubles with Sty and more, even the laughs that the two of them had enjoyed with each other.

Did the revelation that Gary was the leader of the Howlers change any of that? No, all of his reactions were genuine; if anything, the fact that he was the leader of a large group and was still doing those things actually made it more impactful.

"I guess when we made that alliance, none of us but him knew what exactly we were agreeing to, did we?" Numba said, and all three of them were smiling.

"I was going to ask you about your plans for tomorrow, but I guess I already know your answer," Izzy said.

Numba stood up and looked outside.

"Let's get some rest, while we still can. Tomorrow is going to be a big day."

CHAPTER 22

9:00 A.M.

In the future this would be remembered as a very important day for the gang known as the Howlers.

Thanks to Kai's tiered system, it was easy to pass on the message. All Olivia, Innu, Austin, and Marie had to do was inform the people directly below them, who would do the same, until the entire gang knew what had happened and what Gary intended to do about it:

"Taking on an entire Tier 2 City . . . and not just any city but Notsburg and their Scatterbugs . . . I've heard that our leader is reckless, but to this degree? I heard those guys are strong enough that some Tier 1 gangs come to *them* to ask for help."

"I feel you, man. I've seen for myself that our masked bosses are strong, but can we really do this? We're just a Tier 3 gang. If our boss wants to expand, shouldn't we go up against lower-tier places first? This is a big jump!"

"Didn't you get the same message as the rest of us? We don't have to come; it's only for those who are interested in taking part. It seems like this is a personal grudge. According to my superior, they took out Fox yesterday, so the boss wants revenge."

"I'm glad that I won't get into trouble for not coming, then. Still, if they're powerful enough to take him out, doesn't that mean that the Scatterbugs have the power to take out our core members in our own territory? If that's the case, though, and only the core members go out, won't they one hundred percent lose this fight? And then what happens to the Howlers?"

"My guess is that someone else will take over. Anyway, I'm out. No matter how much they're willing to pay me to come, there's no point in joining a losing fight. I still need to be alive to be able to spend it."

Conversations like these were happening all over Slough. Naturally, the news didn't spread only to those in the Howlers, though; it also spread to important figures behind the scenes in Slough. Among them were the leaders of gangs who had been suppressed, and of course a particular mayor who sat in his office.

"Ha-ha-ha, finally things are looking up! If I had known that those bastards would find themselves such a powerful enemy, I would have waited by the side and enjoyed the show!" Ben Clove laughed heartily in his office. "This is perfect! The Howlers will fail, and the Scatterbugs will see that there isn't much for them to gain in Slough. They will leave, and the town will be back in my hands again."

Outside the Wolf's Pool Club, at 8:55 a.m., Gary sat on the few steps that used to lead up to the door. The club was still destroyed behind him. After all, given how late it was when the fight broke out, nobody had reported that the place needed repairs.

Gary was busy putting together some pieces like a puzzle. As the first one to arrive, he had spent his time looking around for salvageable things in the pool club. There wasn't much to find, as the intruder had done a horrific job making sure that their establishment would be out for business for a while. However, he did find the smashed fox mask, and with nothing better to do, he had made sure to find as many pieces as possible.

"There, that should be most of them. Just looking at your mask, I can practically picture you wearing it, Kai, berating me for doing something stupid and reckless again. Well, I can't argue that it will be reckless, but as I recall I'm not the only one in our gang to do reckless things."

Gary grinned as he thought back to how Kai had let himself get captured, on the off chance that he would be put into the same cell as Gary. What's more, when he found out that Gary was unable to do much about his situation, Kai had forced Gary to turn him by nearly sacrificing his own hand.

"You got us out of that situation back then, so by the time you wake up, I'll do what I can to have our situation with them resolved. Once that is done, I'll return your mask, and if you want, you can still berate me afterward."

Eventually Gary saw a car driving toward the pool club. It was the usual limo that the Howlers used for various trips. The door opened and Tyler stepped out, and he opened the door for Olivia, Innu, Austin, and Marie, each one of them wearing their masks. Gary noticed that Austin's mask was different from what Gary had remembered before. Now it had what looked like a bull with a ring hanging from its nose covering his mouth slightly, and also Olivia's was slightly different, looking more like a wolf, although it didn't look the same as Gary's, as it had indented eyelashes.

"It was a gift from Kai; I thought it was only appropriate," Austin explained.

Gary smiled and put the fragments of Kai's mask into his pocket before he put on his own mask.

"Gary," Marie said, "I'll be honest, we're most likely going to be the only ones. Everyone knows that we're going up against the Scatterbugs, and since you told us to write that this was a personal vendetta, even our lieutenants are unwilling to come."

Gary had been afraid that this might be the case, but as a gang leader responsible for the lives of his gang members, he had felt that it was only right to let them decide for themselves. Just when he was about to stand up and get into the car, the Howlers turned around toward the sound of approaching footsteps.

"A smaller, stronger team might be better, anyway," Ian said, greeting them with confidence.

"Before you even try to say that we are not allowed to come with you, let me remind you about what you said before: we are in an alliance, and that's what these alliances are for in the first place!" Numba said. "Besides, Gary, you're a friend, and a good one. You would do the same for me; in fact, you already have done so, so I have to do the same for you."

Gary couldn't argue with those words, and having three more Altered by their side boosted their strength considerably.

"We also made a deal once," another voice said to his left.

"Blake . . . but why would you . . . I mean, you're a . . . are you sure you won't get into lots of trouble if you tag along?" Gary asked.

"What do you mean? From what I've seen yesterday, that was the work of an 'Altered' who came into my town before he fled to Notsburg. In other words, I'm just coming along to do what's supposed to be my job, right?"

Gary knew Blake's skill from when the two of them had fought against a werewolf, and he had no doubt that he had continued to hone his skills.

"I . . . thanks, I'll really owe you one for this." Gary smiled.

Just as it looked like everyone had arrived who was going to, a few more people wearing the black-and-gold uniform started to creep in and fill the streets. It was a good thing that the core members were wearing their masks.

"We want to help as well!" one of the new arrivals shouted. "Slough has changed so much since the Howlers took over, and I don't want it to go back to the way it was before!"

Another called out, "I used to be a member of the Underdogs and they treated us like dirt. You saved us, so it's only right we follow you!"

At least ten people from the Howlers had shown up, but when Gary looked at them, he made a decision.

"Thank you, you truly have shown your loyalty to the gang, and for that you have my gratitude. I won't forget the faces of those who came here today . . . but I can't take you with me; I can't have you risk your lives.

"I realize now that this is something that we have to solve ourselves, because what the Scatterbugs have done to us . . . is personal," Gary said as he walked to the car with the other masked leaders, and they all got in one by one and drove off to Notsburg.

You thought you could end this fight by taking out one person; well, now you have a war on your hands, Scatterbugs, Gary thought as he looked out the window.

CHAPTER 23

SLOUGH VS. NOTSBURG

As usual, Tyler was incredibly nervous as he drove the limo with the core members of the Howlers and the AFA students inside. And yet, though they were heading toward Notsburg, the stronghold of the Scatterbugs, he felt less nervous than during their other trips, mainly because Gary was traveling with them this time. For some reason, seeing the younger teenager always gave him a feeling of safety, reminding him of the time when Gary had stood up for him in his last job.

At the same time, Tyler could see how different the alpha werewolf looked now, how much pain and anger lay behind that face. He wanted to do something to help, even if it was something as simple as driving him and the others to their destination.

The group spent the majority of the ride silently watching out the window as they approached the Tier 2 city. Anyone would think that the plan was mad, going on the offensive with such a small group of people.

"Before he was attacked, Kai shared with me his plans for our potential counterattack," Olivia said. "I'm not too sure how effective it will be, since his plan accounted for him being part of it, but seeing as we have three Altered, it might still work. Kai had come up with a couple of plans, but the simplest one was to go straight for the Scatterbugs' main base and attack them while their defense is down.

"Of course, that plan relied on us taking us their main fighters beforehand, but now we will have to just use the element of surprise to our advantage. From what we found out, the Scatterbugs' forces are spread among multiple casinos, but there is one where the leader resides most of the time.

"A typical gang war isn't exactly resolved in a single day. There will be back-and-forth, small and big attacks all over the city here and there. However, in this situation, the best thing to do is head to the main casino. There will be a lot of Scatterbugs there, but if you want to end it quickly, taking out the leader might be the best shot we'll have."

Hearing the plan, Numba was quite surprised because when he was talking with his father he had said the same thing. The Scatterbugs were a large gang, but therein lay the problem. Once gangs exceeded a certain size, the organizational structure would prevent them from reacting to things quickly.

The best tactic was a full-frontal attack on their leaders and those around them; from there the rest would crumble. Ironically, the Scatterbugs had attempted to do the same thing by taking care of Kai, but that hadn't worked with the Howlers.

Over the silence inside the car, they heard a vehicle revving loudly. Ian looked out the back window and saw a person on a motorbike following them.

"So is anybody gonna tell us why that pretty boy is out there and not in here? It's not like we don't have the space for one more passenger," Ian asked.

"Him?" Innu couldn't help but chuckle because of who was asking the question. "You're right, he's not part of the Howlers, but he's also not exactly an enemy. It might be the easiest for you to think of him as outside help. Sometimes he's on our side, sometimes he's not, the relationship is complicated, though I'd advise you guys in particular to stay away from him."

The students looked confused as they tried to understand what Innu meant, but none of it made any sense.

"I want to know more about this operation," Marie said. "If we go with Olivia's plan, how likely is this to work? Surely before an event like this, Kai would brief you about everything, but now . . ."

Kai's absence was making them lose a bit of confidence, and Gary knew that, yet everyone had come today to accompany him despite knowing the risks.

"I actually don't think what we're about to do is such a bad plan," Izzy said; she had been thinking about it for a while. "They attacked only yesterday. Logically speaking, you should have strengthened your defenses and waited for their actual attack. Nobody will expect you to come for revenge while Kai is still in the hospital.

"Of course, that doesn't mean they will be completely defenseless. They will be somewhat prepared in case of attacks of any nature. So don't expect this to be a complete walk in the park, either. Remember, with the amount of money they have at their disposal, they can easily have a couple of Altered on their payroll as their guard dogs."

It gave them a bit to think about, and at least it allowed the others to envision a little of what to expect.

Entering the city via the highway was relatively easy. There was no checkpoint like there was at the Dark Guild city. Gangs ruled the cities and towns, but they didn't rule the whole country.

Which was why only those with top-level influence were able to do something like that. As they entered Notsburg, though, everyone could soon see the amount of wealth in the city.

Bright lights lit up nearly all the buildings, giant screens were filled with advertisements, and, of course, several casinos were placed all through the city.

"It's like night and day," Marie said. "This is nearly as impressive as a Tier 1 city."

"As a group grows, they venture into different activities and businesses," Olivia said. "All the cities tend to specialize in something that will attract the public to come and spend their money there. So the normal workers try hard to rise up and get a good job so they can afford to move there. This is an entertainment city, one that focuses on the thrill of gambling, so of course it will look good from the outside."

As they continued onward, they spotted their location from far away: a large casino that seemed to be placed in the middle of a lake of all things, with one bridge connecting to it. It had mostly golden lights shining off it, and being the only building there with nothing surrounding it, it stood out like a sore thumb.

The bridge leading up to the casino was protected by barriers, and the car had no choice but to stop. Two guards stood at the booth, and one of the men walked around to the driver's side of the car.

"Hi there, good sir, we have come to your establishment for some nice gambling today!" Tyler said, happily stating their prepared reason for coming.

"This place is only open to VIP customers. Please show us your VIP card, or give us a proof of invitation, else I'll have to ask you to turn around and go to one of the other casinos," the man replied in a professional manner.

Tyler was nervous, as he didn't know what else to say.

"Roll down the window on my side," Gary replied.

Tyler did as he asked and rolled down Gary's tinted window. Seeing this, the guard naturally moved to the window, expecting to recognize the person behind it.

"Please, sir, if you could show us your—"

A hand reached out and grabbed the man's jaw before he could finish his sentence. Gary's grip was so tight that the man was unable to utter another word. Opening the door, while still holding the man's jaw with his hand through the window, Gary got out wearing his wolf mask.

"There is no mercy for any of you." Gary lifted the man off his feet and pulled him through the window, chucking him inside the car with the others. He then quickly leapt up onto the car and jumped across. He broke through the glass window of the guard station, shattering it with a kick that hit the other guard right in the face.

The second man's body crashed into the wall behind him. A few seconds later, Gary walked out of the booth, straightening his uniform.

"No one is to go easy on any of these guys," Gary said. "I will not have what happened to Kai happen to you; I won't give them the chance."

CHAPTER 24

TAKE THE CASINO (PART 1)

Inside the grand casino, that was practically an island, the inner-circle members of the Scatterbugs had gathered. Not all of their members had come here from the other casinos, but most of the crucial and strongest members of the Notsburg gang had come at their leader's behest.

At the very top of the casino, in the penthouse suite, Slith was sitting in his office, wearing a red suit as he played with a black betting chip, twirling it between his fingers and knuckles back and forth. Standing in front of him were all the Altered that the Tier 2 city commanded.

There were twelve in total, including him and Midwak by his side. On top of that, about two hundred staff members in the casino itself worked for the gang. Although they looked like normal guards, dealers, and more, they were all trained fighters.

On a day-to-day basis, they dealt with people who came from gangs and all levels of cities. Their customers often got rowdy when they had been drinking too much or suffered a large loss. Which was why the casino workers had to be strong enough to deal with those that crossed their paths.

If there was one place where Slith felt safe, it was in his own casino.

"You have all been gathered today because it's come to my attention that a gang known as the Howlers might attack us," Slith explained.

The members of the Scatterbugs looked at each other with slight confusion. They had believed this would be some kind of meeting, but not about an attack. Most couldn't even remember the last time someone had been stupid enough to attack them, much less directly at their stronghold.

On top of that, the gang's name didn't ring a bell in any of their heads. If this was a gang that they really needed to worry about, they would call the heads of the other casinos to this place.

"I can see the look on your faces, so let me say that I've gathered you here mostly as a precaution," Slith explained. "The chances are slim, but Midwak is the one who has advised me. I sent him out to strike at them, and it is his professional opinion that these Howlers will be more troublesome than we expect."

Slith turned to look at Midwak. Had someone else been the one to advise him, he would have called this meeting excessive, but so far listening to his most trusted aide had always proven beneficial. It was hard for the gang leader to believe that a Tier 3 town that they had nearly hired for a job could turn out to be such a pain in their side.

Midwak didn't say anything. He just looked at the other Altered, grinning to himself as he thought back to the conversation he had with Kai yesterday.

After the initial attacks, Midwak had proven too powerful for Kai, overpowering the beta werewolf in the fight. The injuries Kai sustained appeared to be too much for his body to recover in a small amount of time. Midwak knew the limits of a werewolf's body quite well, which was why he had decided to shoot out his nails, pinning Kai to a wall.

"You . . . think . . ." Kai began speaking as he was nailed to the wall, barely clinging to consciousness. "I'm . . . afraid . . . of death?"

Midwak looked at Kai, who was lifeless apart from the look in his eyes. He walked up to him, placing his hand up onto his chin, holding his mouth, so Kai was unable to talk.

"Do you think I give a damn about you when you are nothing but a Knight?" Midwak replied. "You still have the smell of a whelp on you, so you probably don't even know what I'm talking about. If there's one thing you should take away from this, then let it be this: being in a pack is nothing special!"

Kai wanted to say something, but Midwak's hand was holding his mouth so tight that he was unable to speak. The omega werewolf was right, Kai had no idea what he meant by calling him a Knight. He didn't care much about this werewolf business; he regarded them mostly as a special type of Altered, though one that came with downsides around the full moon.

"I can see in your eyes that you're not going to give up your leader, but you see, after I'm done with you, your body will *be* the message. All alphas are the same. Their weakness is that they care too much for their pack, and they get hell-bent on revenge when one of their members gets hurt!

"Do you know what will happen after I defeat him? Once an omega beats the alpha, I will become the alpha of your pack. Which means you will have to obey me whether you like it or not! It would be too much of a waste to get rid of you completely.

"Once I become alpha and take over your pack, I will need strong fighters to go up against them. They will regret everything they did to me."

Kai was trying his best to follow; he could hear what Midwak was saying, but because of the blood loss and damage he was unable to think straight, unable to figure out what this werewolf was doing to him.

"I still have a need for you, but I don't necessarily need you in one piece. I think it's safe if we remove this nasty mouth of yours, so you can't say anything to your leader. I doubt you will be able to wake up for a while after this." Midwak said as he ripped Kai's lower jaw off and threw it onto the floor.

After thinking back to what happened, Midwak stood up. "Don't worry, Slith, they will come. I only hope they bring a strong group with him. This will be our biggest step forward, trust me."

Midwak was unable to control his feelings, and his eyes were already starting to glow yellow. Slith had known his battle-hungry ally long enough to be able to tell he was excited.

"Sir!" One of the men standing guard by the door had just been given a report through his earpiece. "Someone has just driven through the barriers and is heading straight to the casino!"

"I told you they would come," Midwak said.

CHAPTER 25

TAKE THE CASINO (PART 2)

The casino was thriving as it would have done any other day. People had dressed in their very best, throwing their money around at the tables with smiles on their faces. At the same time, many VIP members were enjoying their time as they placed bet after bet.

Some of the guests had come from Tier 1 cities after hearing about the luxury gambling establishment from their friends and deciding to pay Notsburg a visit. There were also many scouts from other gangs among the guests, having come here since they didn't believe that a Tier 2 gang with no backers could survive on their own. They were there to see if some other Tier 1 gang was secretly backing the Scatterbugs, and if not, finding out what it would take to convince Slith to work with their group.

As bets were being made, every member of the staff received messages through their earpieces.

"I'm sorry, but due to some unforeseen circumstances, the game right now will be put on hold," one of the dealers said at his table.

"What? You can't do this! I was on a run! Do you want me to tell all my friends that your casino is just a damn con?" a large man with a cigar in his mouth shouted. Soon, though, the man heard the same sentence being repeated by all of the other dealers on the shop floor.

"Let us apologize once more for this. As compensation, you will receive double the amount of chips the next time you cash in," the dealer stated.

The big spenders accepted this apology, which calmed them down slightly. For the casino, it didn't matter, because all the extra money they had just given out would be returned to them.

After all, the guards and dealers had told the civilians about the special circumstances. They were wondering what was going to happen next, and some had gotten up to leave.

"Sorry, sir, but it might be best if you stay inside the establishment," the dealer said with his hand out and a big smile on his face. "We have had to pause for a short while because of some uninvited guests."

The workers started to move to the front of the casino. There were three large swivel doors at the main entrance, yet no one had entered for a while. The casino workers asked all the guests to move behind them, take cover, or stand to the side. They began pulling out their batons, knives, and other weapons as they waited for what was to come. The tension was high in the room; the guests whispered among themselves as they wondered what was going on.

"Should one of us head outside and see what's going on?" one of the workers asked his supervisor. But the supervisor remained silent, and since waiting around like this wasn't in his nature, he decided to head toward the doors.

As he got closer, his eyes widened as he saw something through the glass. He quickly turned around and started to run, but it was too late.

A car smashed through the doors and collided with the man and several guards as well. The other workers quickly ran to help their colleagues, who had been flattened by the impact.

"There's no one inside!" one of them shouted.

"That's impossible! Are you saying that a ghost drove that thing in here?"

Eventually, with several workers using all their strength, they were able to push the car up onto its side. They pulled their injured colleagues out from underneath the car as quickly as they could.

Now with the car on its side they were able to take a closer look at it. There were two deep claw marks and handprints on the side.

"The car . . . it was thrown in," one of them deduced, and just then they all heard the sound of footsteps crushing glass. When the workers turned their heads, they saw a man in a black and gold wolf mask, in a uniform of the same color scheme.

"Tell your damn bosses that the Howlers from Slough are here," Gary demanded.

As he stood there, his imposing presence and sharpened nails let the others know that he was an Altered. It was quite an entrance; seeing a car hurled into the casino and the werewolf releasing his bloodlust made for a scary scene.

"Who the hell do you think you are? Just wait until our boss puts an outsider like you into your place!" one of the workers shouted as he ran forward with a baton. "Anyone who is crazy enough to attack us leaves in a body bag!"

Gary tensed his fist and sent it crashing into the baton, bending it and hitting the man right in the face. His whole body was lifted off the ground and spun in the air, then collapsed to the ground. One single punch was all it took to make a grown man unable to move.

"The rest of the Howlers and I are not leaving this place until we get what we want . . . and, unfortunately for you, I want blood," Gary growled as his eyes turned red.

CHAPTER 26

TAKE THE CASINO (PART 3)

After Gary took out the first person with ease, the rest wore nervous looks on their faces. Although Gary was just one man, the casino staff were reluctant to just charge in recklessly. He seemed a bit crazy. After all, how could one person have so much confidence when he was in enemy territory and surrounded by so many people?

"What are you doing charging in on your own?" a woman wearing a wolf mask complained as she ran in from behind. Two others followed behind her, wearing the same uniform and also masked.

"I told you he was going to do something like this; we just have to go with the flow," Innu said as he pulled out his two red axes from behind and got into a fighting stance. Marie quickly did the same as she saw the sheer number of people in suits facing them.

"Can we . . . do this, just with us?" Marie asked in a whisper.

"You have to have confidence, young one," Olivia said as she brought out her whip and swung it quickly, cracking it in the air. The move radiated strength, and once again the opponents thought they were crazy. Now they knew that the man who had entered wasn't on his own, but had only three other people by his side.

"You're right, and the others will be here soon as well," Marie replied. "We just have to hold off, we can do that."

After Gary had taken out the two guards at the barrier with ease, they knew it was only a matter of time before somebody reported their arrival. Their one advantage was the element of surprise, but it might disappear at any moment.

Which was why Izzy was looking at their surroundings trying to form a plan.

"I think there's something we can do," Izzy said, as she knew there were only a couple of minutes until the car reached the main building. "No one else is going to come to us in this fight . . . but, Gary, let me ask you this: how confident are you that you can take out whoever might be in the casino?"

After a pause, Gary answered, "Anyone but the guy who injured Kai, I should be able to take!"

"Then if you let me borrow Austin, I can assure you that the Scatterbugs will receive no backup, but I have to tell you this, we will be trapped as well," Izzy suggested.

"Do it," Gary answered.

He would put his trust in the AFA students. This way he only had to focus on one thing: the people inside the casino. A short distance from the entrance, Tyler stopped the car sideways on Gary's behalf.

The members of the Howlers burst out, each of them taking out the guards in the parking area and at the front. It was relatively easy; Marie and Olivia were able to take out the ones a little farther away with their Anti-Altered crossbow and whip, respectively.

However, when the others turned around, they were unable to see Gary, because he had already moved ahead of them all, aiming for the entrance. Seeing this, Izzy called upon Numba and the others for help, as well as the person who would be the biggest help: Austin.

"That's it, slowly, and place the car right here!" Izzy ordered.

Austin carried a car over his head with his immense strength and placed it down on the bridge. He had worked quickly with the help of the others. Now they had created a barrier of cars on the bridge.

"I've finished on my end as well!" Numba shouted, pouring the last bit of gasoline over the cars. He had been gathering the fuel from other cars, pouring it over the ones that had been placed as a barrier.

Finally, Ian had returned with a lighter, one that could stay aflame for a short while.

"So what's your plan? Are you planning to blow up the whole bridge to stop the other gang members from getting here?" Ian asked.

"Not quite; cars are harder to blow up than you think. It's not like the movies," Izzy replied. "But we should be able to create a fire big enough to melt part of the bridge structure. If that doesn't work, then there'll be a wall of fire that they'll have to try and get through."

She let Ian do the honors as he threw the lighter, igniting a blaze at an incredibly fast speed. They had to glance away for a second at the explosion of heat.

"Now let's go give Gary some backup," Izzy said with a smile, turning around. They ran toward the entrance, but her smile soon faded. This was a true gamble, as neither side would be able to receive any help, but it was the best that she could do.

Inside the casino, the others had yet to move, and Gary had noticed a message from the system.

New Quest received
You have invaded the Scatterbugs (Tier 2 gang)
Defeat the gang or force them to surrender
Reward: unknown

"I know that it was just one man who attacked my friend, so I'll give all of you Scatterbugs an option!" Gary shouted as he walked toward them. He lifted his hand, transforming it fully in front of them. "Surrender and step aside, so you can live another day, or die by my hand protecting this piece-of-shit gang of yours!"

CHAPTER 27

TAKE THE CASINO (PART 4)

Once again Gary's words startled them. He spoke with conviction. This was truly the last chance he was giving them to leave now without a fight.

"Shut up!" one of the workers shouted. "Look at how many of us there are and how many of them. Remember what the boss said. For each one that is taken out, we will get to keep ten percent of the profits for one month at this place. You will never have to lift a finger in your life if you take these guys out."

The greed seemed to have gotten to them, and they rushed toward the Howlers.

Gary shook his head in disappointment.

"I gave you one chance. I never wanted to go down this route, but now you've forced me."

Gary moved in a flash, appearing right in front of the gang members. One swung his bat but hit nothing but the ground, and Gary grabbed him by the head.

He lifted the man into the air and chucked him toward the others, knocking them off their feet. One of the other gang members tried to kick Gary in his side, but Gary swatted his leg away, destroying his shin in the process.

He then punched the man in front in the chest with a loud crack, sending him flying back into the people behind him. All of Gary's strikes were breaking bones, shattering them so that they would never be functional again.

Gary wasn't the only one fighting, as there were far too many people in the large casino for him to fight all at once, but the other Howlers were faring well. Olivia was using her whip to knock their enemies back and gain distance, but then she shortened the distance by leaping forward and slashing right through a man's chest.

Gary had altered the pack rules, because he didn't want them to hold back.

Innu and Marie were struggling the most in the battle; more accurately it was Marie who was struggling, and Innu was struggling because of Marie. He stayed by her side, swinging his axe down.

He had hit a man right between his neck and shoulder, cutting deep. With the extra strength Innu drew from the axes, he could take out his opponents with ease. Glancing to the side, though, he saw that Marie was in trouble. She was still using her crossbow, and three men had gotten too close to her.

Innu immediately threw one of his axes, and it embedded itself right in one man's head. As the man next to him turned around, Innu leapt in the air and slammed his other axe into his face.

As he touched the ground, Innu pulled the axe from the head of the first person he had dealt with and spun, swinging it down and hitting the third man in the leg.

"Marie, stab him!" Innu shouted.

With their enemies so close, Marie could no longer use her crossbow unless she was able to get into a better position. So she had switched to an Anti-Altered spear, which could be thrust through the enemy, but the tip could electrify them as well.

She thrust the spear but pulled back at the last second, letting the tip only slightly touch the man. His whole body lit up, but she needed to hold it in place for a few seconds before the man passed out.

"Watch out!" Innu shouted, as a man with brass knuckles threw a punch toward her head. Innu had seen it too late and from where he was, it would be hard for Marie to react. Gary was in the middle of dealing with all the others; he was too far away.

Before the knuckles touched her, the man's hand was wrapped by Olivia's whip and yanked off his body, spilling blood everywhere.

"You're going to get us killed!" Olivia shouted. "If you don't have the resolve to kill your enemies, then what are you even doing here?"

Marie was stunned by what could have happened, but even more stunned by the blood that was all around her. Innu came to her side, axes in his hands, ready to protect her.

Just then a man charged in, and with a swing of his axe Innu shoved it into the side of his neck and pulled it out, dropping him to the floor.

"How, Innu . . . how can you kill people so easily?" Marie asked.

"I hate to say this, Marie, but Olivia is right. After everything they did to Kai, how can you feel something for these people? Can you imagine what they have already done?" Innu shouted, as he continued to fight, delivering a kick to a man's thigh and dropping him on the ground.

"When I look at these people, I don't see humans in front of me. It's because of people like this that everyone at the orphanage, everyone who meant everything to me, is gone, and once again, these people are trying to take it away from us. That's how! That's how I'm able to kill these bastards so easily!" Innu shouted.

A large man almost three times his size, suddenly appeared in front of Innu. He swung his axe and hit the man, but it got stuck. He was wearing some type of armor under his clothes.

"I just need to use a little bit more energy to take you on!" Innu shouted, pulling the axe out and getting ready to swing it again, but before he could, a large fist hit the man right in the face, causing him to tumble across the floor, skidding on his face, leaving a smear of blood behind.

"I can't let you have all the fun," Austin said, as he and the others joined in on the fight.

CHAPTER 28

TAKE THE CASINO
(PART 5)

The Altered students along with Austin had all arrived in the main gambling hall. They had quickly transformed and were making quick work of those who were in front of them. Izzy hadn't transformed, but she was still skilled enough to fight.

As the battle went on, though, everyone noticed something. The fighting seemed endless, yet there seemed to be the same number of people as before. On top of that, they weren't regular gang members.

Everyone had to stay vigilant because of the others' skills. If they relaxed or made a small mistake they would pay the price, and having taken a few hits after breaking concentration, they knew this was true.

We can't keep fighting like this. Izzy thought, as she attempted to control her breathing. *Although these gang members are skilled, one can tell that they are just cannon fodder.*

Where are the Altered, Slith, and the one who fought us before? They have to be in this building. I bet they're even watching through the cameras. Are they trying to tire us out? If that's the case, then their plan might very well work.

"They want to tire us out!" Izzy shouted. "Conserve your energy, don't use your Altered forms too much."

Gary had a lot of stamina, but he too was conserving himself, because he knew there was another Werewolf that he would have to do battle against. So he was mostly using his skills to fight, but if he got injured, then he would need more energy to heal the wounds so he could fight in top condition.

Right now, he was in a bit of a pickle.

Hearing Izzy's command, though, Marie thought of something, a way to win this fight, because their current situation reminded her of one in the past.

"We are going to have to do the same as we did against the Pincers!" Marie shouted to everyone. "We need to make a path, and let our leader do his thing."

Olivia knew about this well, because she had taken on Gary on his own; it was a risky move to make. It might mean that Gary would have to face all of the Altered, including the one that had attacked Kai, on his own, but what other choice did they have?

"I will clear a path!" Austin shouted, stomping his feet. The ground beneath them cracked and large bull-like horns grew from his head. Everyone felt the rise in his energy as he charged forward.

Anyone who got in his way was smashed to the side. One gangster with a knife tried to stab Austin in the shoulder, but his knife didn't get very far, as Austin's skin had become incredibly thick, making the blade do next to nothing.

When Austin stopped his charge and turned around, there was a tunnel of fallen men behind him. Quickly seeing an opportunity, Gary jumped onto a gang member's shoulders and pushed off, sending him to the ground and Gary up in the air.

He landed in the tunnel of bodies and sprinted toward Austin, who was standing by the doors that would let Gary into the casino.

"Thank you, Austin," Gary said as he passed through the doors.

Austin turned around and slammed the doors shut. "No one is going through this door without my permission."

After seeing the single charge and the horns on Austin's head, the gang members knew without a doubt that this was an Altered, and some of them turned toward the cameras in the room, wondering if help would ever arrive, because if it didn't arrive soon, nearly all of the workers at the casino would have been dealt with.

After exiting the main gambling hall, Gary noticed how much quieter the casino was. There were almost no people at all, but several gambling rooms lay ahead of him.

The doors were already swung wide open. Whoever had been inside them had already left.

I have to move fast and deal with this. Everyone outside is fighting, giving me this chance, Gary thought as he moved forward.

As he passed the first room, he saw a poker table and nothing else. The chips had been left behind, and so had the cards. There was still no way for him to continue on farther into the casino.

When he passed the second door, an arm swung out, brandishing an incredibly sharp blade.

I wasn't able to smell them. The smell of blood is too strong and is throwing off all my senses, Gary thought.

It was a fast attack, so sudden that Gary wasn't able to completely move away, the blade sliced his forearm. It didn't go deep, because of his fast reflexes. He had now jumped back to the first room.

"I see now that wasn't a blade, that was your body," Gary said.

His attacker was a double-jointed man with blades sticking out from each limb and jointed area. His reach was twice as long as that of a normal human.

"You think it's so easy to come into Scatterbugs territory like this? Well, it's time to slice you up," the man shouted.

Just then Gary heard something behind him; it was vibrating and the sound was getting louder and more aggressive.

"Move!" a voice shouted.

As he jumped into the room, a motorbike roared down the hall and crashed into his attacker. A few seconds later, a man stood in front of the doorway, wearing a solid black mask.

"Leave this one to me. I came here to hunt Altered and it looks like I found what I was looking for," Blake said, pulling out his red dueling swords.

CHAPTER 29

ALTERED-HUNTER HELPER

Although the casino was run by a gang, it nevertheless followed the town's safety regulations, meaning that aside from the one main entrance, it also had multiple emergency exits in case of a fire. In his head, Blake had convinced himself that he was merely using the fight between the Howlers and the Scatterbugs as an opportunity to hunt the Altered who had come into his territory.

To make it clear that he was in no way associated with the Howlers, the Altered Hunter had chosen against traveling with them. He had come here on his trusty motorbike and used the confusion that the Howlers' entrance created to get farther into the building.

Wearing his special Altered Hunter mask, Blake had an easier time locating Altered, and that was what had brought him here. In the hallway with the Altered in front of him, Blake lifted the motorbike so all the weight was on the back wheel, raising the front end, and jumped off.

The bike continued going forward, and he hoped that the person he assumed to be Gary from the green hair would move away. The bike was fast and heavy as it careened toward the surprised Altered. He swung his long, double-jointed arms to the right, digging the bladed parts deep into the frame of the bike.

Sharp serrated edges appeared on the blades, grabbing the bike. As he swung it to the side, the serrated edges disappeared and the bike was flung into the room next to the Altered, crashing into the back wall.

Gary exited the private room and ran to Blake, making sure that it was his friend who had just entered. He was wearing the same type of clothing as on the day they fought Billy, though he had brought along a new set of weapons.

"I know that you're helping us, and I don't mind, but fighting these guys is dangerous; the last thing I would want to happen is for you to lose your life over something that I started," Gary said as he started to transform.

"Do you really think I'm risking my life for you? Did you forget what I am?" Blake replied in an annoyed manner. "My existence means I risk my life on a daily basis. Don't get me wrong, I'm just here to hunt some Altered. Given what you are, you're not someone I need to worry about."

After saying these words, Blake charged forward. He was fast; he was always a talented athlete, better than most, but he wasn't at the Altered level. At the end of the day, although Altered Hunters were strong enough to take on Altered, there was a reason why they hunted in pairs or groups and not alone.

The Altered who worked for the Scatterbugs was faster; he also charged forward and swung one of his arms from above. Before the blow landed, though, Blake threw a punch at one of the elbowlike joints on the attacker's body. It was a strong hit, hacking the entire arm into the doorway.

It's just like last time, I can see the lines in my vision, telling me where to strike! Blake thought.

He swung his other sword toward the Altered's shoulder joint; the blade went through his clothing but not through his body. It felt hard, like he was clashing his sword against a solid plate of armor.

Still, the expression on the Altered's face showed his pain; his whole arm was shaking and he was unable to move his other arm to attack. Before he knew it, three dartlike objects had flown from Blake's strange gloves and hit the Altered.

The three darts lit up slightly blue, electrifying the entire body of the Altered. Meanwhile, Blake aimed his swords right for the neck of the Altered.

He swung with all his strength, and the swords glowed as they hit the enemy.

They didn't quite pierce the skin, but the Altered was knocked off his feet and onto the floor.

"What are you doing? The longer you take to take them out, the more likely you are to lose someone you care about," Blake said, chastising Gary. "As you can see, I'm fine by myself here!"

Gary realized that Blake was right; he had to hurry. He had asked for the help of the others when he had decided to attack the Scatterbugs, so he needed to do whatever he could to end it as soon as possible.

Running past the Altered and Blake, Gary didn't look back as he turned down the hallway going deeper into the casino.

The Altered had somewhat recovered and swung his arms from the floor, aiming for Blake's feet. He moved back, but his left foot was slightly slow, and the Altered's blade slashed through his armored boot and cut his chin slightly.

It was painful, but Blake remained standing.

"Now I know what you are!" the Altered said as he stood up. "You're one of those Altered Hunter psychos. With all that clothing and those fancy, stupid gadgets! Now, why would someone like you work alongside another gang?"

It seemed like a genuine question, but of course Blake had no intention of answering.

So there's a link to the Altered Hunter Association? Is this why they were so confident in attacking us? Well, I guess that just means it's more important for us to take out this Howlers gang, and it will be pretty interesting to know what the other cities think when they learn of this! The Altered smiled.

CHAPTER 30

THE ONE-STAR HUNTER

Although Blake didn't say anything when accused of working with the Howlers, he nevertheless was slightly concerned. True or not, if rumors started spreading that there was some type of connection between the two, things were bound to become difficult for him and the gang. Normal gangs might ignore it, but higher-tier gangs, perhaps even the Kings, might become interested, and Gary and company were definitely not ready for that.

Even worse, the Altered Hunters might also send their men to find out what had led to those rumors and start questioning Blake. Should they find out about Gary and the other gang members being werewolves, it wouldn't end well for them.

I guess this just means that I can't let him live, not that I was planning on that in the first place! Blake thought as he threw his black leather jacket toward the Altered. His opponent sliced it up, but through the large cuts he saw the red blades coming toward him again.

"It seems my words have made you a little angry!" The Altered swung his large arms, and the bladed parts flailed like a whip. They hit the red swords and threw Blake off balance, overpowering him. Seeing another swing from the Altered, he ducked under the blow and pulled back.

Now Blake stood there, still wearing his mask, his forearms bared to the elbow. His thick black gloves covered his hands.

But the Altered glimpsed something on his shoulder.

"A one-star Hunter, huh? Tsk, it appears I was worried about nothing," the Altered said. "If the Altered Hunters really cared about the Howlers, they would have sent a more experienced Hunter! A shame. If you were more experienced, I bet the boss would have paid a nice bonus for your head."

The Altered was the one to charge in this time. He swung his bladed arm around, but midswing one of his double-jointed arms extended slightly. It now looked like his arms had four sections, as if he had two forearms, in addition to his upper arms and the blades.

Blake swung his sword, hitting the arm but not one of the hard round joints, and the bladed part continued to swing in a different direction, as if it had a full range of motion.

The bladed part of the Altered's arm was going straight for his forearm. It cut through his armored gloves and penetrated his skin, eventually hitting the bone.

Arghh! His blades are really sharp, and I can't see the white lines anymore. I'm just fighting with instinct. Blake pulled back before his entire arm got sliced off, but from the other side he saw the other arm swinging toward him.

He barely managed to block the blow with his sword, hitting the bladed part of the Altered rather than the joint. Regardless, the Altered wasn't stopping there; he swung its arms out one after another, throwing attack after attack.

Blake quickly figured out that the best way to block the attack was by hitting the bladed part and staying quite a distance away from the Altered, only there were two problems with this.

If I stay this far away, I can't deal a damaging blow from this distance, Blake thought, analyzing his situation. *Then there's the more urgent problem. My right arm is severely injured. Every time I block an attack, I feel like my bones are shattering. I don't know how much longer I can fight in this state, when it feels like any moment it's going to give in and snap. I can't block for much longer; I need an answer, a way to win this fight.*

The Altered seemed to be enjoying this. It was only a matter of time; sure, the Altered Hunter was blocking all his hits, but there was a difference between the two fighters.

"You Altered Hunters are a pest, but in the end you're only strong humans. You must be getting tired; your body is getting weaker!" the Altered sneered. "You don't need to answer; I can hear your breathing getting heavier even though you've only been fighting for a few minutes!"

It was true that with each hit, Blake could feel his body getting weaker, but the Altered's words made him realize something.

My breathing, it's all out of control! Blake thought.

Usually in a match, even one of this difficulty, he wouldn't tire out this quickly, and one of the biggest teaching points for the Altered Hunters was controlling their breathing in a match.

I must have panicked for a few seconds without realizing it. So what if he's stronger than me? Altered Hunters aren't stronger than Altered, never have been, that's why Dad drilled me into learning to use the special equipment to make up the difference. Fighting as an Altered Hunter has always been about skill, and using your head!

The first thing Blake did as he continued to block the hits was control his breathing, in and out. Taking deep breaths he calmed his heart, and that was when he could see them again, the white lines in his vision that told him where best to cut.

When one of the arms came toward him, instead of barely blocking it with one hand, Blake stepped back, allowing it to skim his chest. It made a large cut, but he needed to be close. Then, holding both of the red swords in one hand, he swung them, hitting the back of the bladed arms of the Altered.

As he did, the weight shifted the whole arm, and the Altered's other long limb came swinging down, slashing right through the first arm. Blood spilled everywhere, and part of the bladed arm now lay on the floor.

With both fists, Blake shot out several more darts, hitting his opponent and shocking his body. The Altered couldn't move for a second, and that was when he saw the masked man running toward him with something strange in his hands.

Blake was holding part of the Altered's own arm. He shoved it right through the Altered's neck, severing the Altered's head and causing it to fall to the floor.

A few seconds later, Blake himself collapsed, heaving deep breaths. When he had recovered slightly, he lifted his head; his whole body was sore, but he could see the rolling head in the hallway.

Another head . . . of all things . . . but at least I did it this time. I defeated this Altered all on my own. Blake crawled to the side and leaned his back against the wall. *Sorry, Gary, but it looks like I'm out of this fight for now. I helped you out as much as I could, and I certainly paid the price, so the rest is on you.*

CHAPTER 31

FIND YOUR SUPPORT

In the main hall of the casino, the civilians had moved to the sides, hiding behind the tables. Most of them had simply come to Notsburg to enjoy some gambling, but who could have guessed that they would end up trapped between two gangs. Even those from other gangs feared for their lives as they hid behind slot machines or ran off into the hallways.

Alas, it seemed impossible to escape the fight. Even if they managed to find a quiet spot, the next moment a burly man would come flying through the air. Those less fortunate ended up colliding with the slot machines, coughing up blood.

It was hard for the onlookers to get a full grasp of what was going on, as the casino was filled with Scatterbugs members who were trying their best to dogpile on top of the invading gang members, yet somehow they were the only ones getting injured, despite their numerical advantage.

"How is this possible?" one of the casino staff members shouted in disbelief. "There's only a handful of them, but we haven't taken down a single one. Are these guys monsters?"

Austin was still standing by the door; his uniform had been ripped and a few Anti-Altered arrows were stuck in his body. A gang like the Scatterbugs would have such weapons in case of an Altered attack, but they didn't expect them to have next to no effect on the large teenager. As the weapons shocked his body, he wasn't startled for even a second. He swung his arm, hitting two men at once, sending them crashing into the slot machines.

"Great job!" Marie cheered Austin on from the side as she thrust her spear, sticking it deep into a man's stomach. During the fight, she had been cut on the arm, and once again Innu had saved her in the nick of time as he swung his axe, hitting her attacker in the back of the head. The cut wasn't deep, but it made her realize that these people were out for blood; it truly was kill or be killed.

Pulling out the spear, she then whacked the man on the side of his head, knocking him out in one blow, but her arms were starting to feel numb. She usually practiced fighting with either her crossbow or her small daggers; her muscles weren't trained to use a spear. A few times she had been close to dropping it.

"You're not ready for melee combat. Just stay close to me!" Innu shouted, his breathing heavy. The Black teenager felt confident after learning that he could draw extra energy from the weapon. Unfortunately, after the first time, the amount of energy he recovered had lessened each subsequent time, until it lost effect. He had expected the weapon to have limitations, but now was an awful time to learn that lesson.

One of the gang members threw a knife toward Innu, who lifted his axe to block it, but another dagger with a sharp blade came flying toward him. At the same time, several knives were thrown at Marie. She needed to make a choice: to thrust her spear and stab Innu's attacker or try to defend herself.

"Don't forget about us!" A burst of power exploded from one side of the room, and a fist hit Innu's attacker right in the face. Meanwhile, several long strands of what looked like hair had grabbed all the projectiles that had been hurled toward Marie and sent them flying back to the attackers.

"Are you okay?" Izzy asked, looking back at Marie.

"I'm fine, thanks. None of them hit me, but what about you?" Marie asked.

It was only then that Izzy noticed she had been injured. There was a small cut on her shoulder. She was bleeding. She checked out her hair, which was very much alive in her Altered form, and found that it was still in place.

I knew something was strange . . . it seems like I really can't control my Altered form properly. Could this be some after-effect from the wound on my shoulder? Was it because of that bite? I guess I need to be more careful, Izzy thought.

"Everyone, duck!" Ian shouted, as he curled his body into a ball.

Everyone looked at him, wondering what he was planning to do, but Izzy had known her childhood friend long enough to guess what he was up to. She quickly did as she was told and pulled Marie down with her.

A second later, several sharp thick bristles shot out from his body, hitting all the gang members who were close by, while Olivia had used her whip to drag one of the gang members in front of her, taking the brunt of the attack.

"Ah . . . I don't know if that was such a good idea . . . I'm starting to feel a little faint," Ian said, as Numba grabbed him from behind. He looked around and saw that there were half as many opponents as before, but in his mind that wasn't a good sign.

All of these guys are weak, incredibly weak. A Tier 2 gang being taken out just by a few Altered? That makes no sense. Which can only mean all the strong ones are inside.

"Hey, cat lady!" Numba called out.

The Howlers were stunned into silence, wondering who Numba was trying to call.

"You can't be talking to me, can you, boy?" Olivia said as she appeared at Numba's side with a man pinned under her arm, his face scratched up and her eyes glowing blue.

"I'm worried about Gary," Numba admitted. "The guy who beat Kai isn't here, and I'm sure there are stronger people inside. I know Gary is strong, but to face them all by himself . . . I'm afraid he'll tire himself out. He'll need you by his side!"

Olivia kicked one of the gang members in the stomach, sending him flying far away, as she heard this.

"Look, we can take care of the ones that are left in here. We're weaker than you, and with your help he has a chance. Just leave us behind and do what you can to take that guy down!" Numba suggested.

Olivia considered the situation before looking back at the Howlers. She wondered when she had started to try so hard for the sake of the gang that had completely ruined her life. Honestly, she agreed with Numba's suggestion, but she was conflicted about helping Gary.

After all, from what she understood, she would be free if he was gone.

"If we leave, you could die," Olivia argued.

"There's a small chance of that, but if you don't follow Gary, the chance of him dying is far greater. And without him . . . aren't we all as good as dead anyway?" Numba smiled.

Furrowing her eyebrows, Olivia was angry that he could smile in a situation like this, but for some reason, it appealed to her.

"Fine!" the beta werewolf replied. "Howlers . . . we are leaving this area. It's time to support our leader!"

CHAPTER 32

THE ALPHA TRAP

Back in Slough, the heart rate monitor in one of the hospital's private rooms started to pick up speed. According to the doctors, the patient would wake up in due time. His vitals were strong and once he fully healed he would be back to normal. However, even the doctors would be surprised by the rate at which Kai was getting better.

After the introduction of Altered, doctors and other medical staff learned how to take care of them. In essence, they were like superhumans with fast recovery times, but Kai was not an Altered. His body, after receiving the energy he needed, had begun healing itself, starting with his vital wounds.

The heart rate machine started to beep faster; his heart rate was rising, and eventually he opened his eyes. Immediately Kai sat upright, gasping for air, sweat on his forehead.

What . . . what was that? Kai wondered as he touched his chest, followed by his chin. Although his brain wasn't awake enough to process what had happened to him, he could still remember the sense of danger in the final moments before his unconsciousness.

"Did you have a bad dream or something?"

Turning his head, Kai saw someone sitting next to his bed, but it wasn't the person he had expected to see.

"Aunt—Miss Degrace," Kai said as he recognized Marie's mother.

"It's okay, feel free to call me Aunt Kiki or Aunty; it's just the two of us, after all."

"What happened to me? How did I get here? Where are the others?" Kai asked in a barrage of questions.

At that moment, as if someone had opened a floodgate, the memories started to come crashing into his head. It felt like his brain was splitting in two. Once the pain was over, Kai finally remembered who he had faced, and how badly it had ended.

"The others . . ." Miss Degrace replied slowly, seemingly trying to fish for the right words. She had been asked to look over Kai in their absence. She was prepared to look after him for a few days, so seeing him awake already left her no time to come up with an excuse.

"I can already guess from your reaction," Kai said as he placed his hand on his head. "Just tell me how long ago they left. I need to get out of here."

Kai started to pull off the needles, tags, and other things connected to his body as he prepared to rush toward Notsburg to help the others.

"They left hours ago, and you just woke up, Kai. It's a wonder you're already awake, but your body clearly needs more rest," Miss Degrace argued, her arms crossed. "You won't make it in time to help them, so let's just trust them. Don't you trust that Gary can do this without you?"

Kai's eyebrows were furrowed, as he was in deep thought. He had shared a lot of the information that he had gathered for their counterattack, so the Howlers wouldn't attack them without a plan, at least. Nevertheless, there was one variable that Kai hadn't accounted for in his plans.

I predicted that they might go for me, even to take me out of the fight, but I never expected there to be another werewolf . . . and the words he spoke . . . This whole thing, it's all a big trap to get Gary to fight him! Kai thought.

"Aunt Kiki, I get that you're worried . . . but I still need to go. It's because of me that this war started. I was the one who decided to help the Cardenez family, and I was the one who was overconfident. I trust Gary, but there's something he doesn't know!" Kai said as he got up.

The casino was a large building that actually had multiple floors. All casino operations were on the first floor, but the second floor housed the office of Slith, the leader of the Scatterbugs. He sat in his large chair, in a room full of jewels in their wall-to-wall display cabinets, but he wasn't alone. Ten of the strongest Scatterbug members were also present.

All of them stood in one place, waiting to eliminate anyone who pushed open the doors, not that they expected anyone to enter.

"They're doing a lot better than I thought," Slith noted as he stared at a large screen on his desk: the CCTV from the casino. Several video feeds showed how everyone was doing.

"I'm losing a lot of men!" Slith shouted, slamming the desk. "Oh well, I guess that just means less wages to pay." He started to laugh.

Meanwhile, standing by his side as usual was Midwak, and he too was intensely staring at the screen, looking at each of the Altered forms carefully.

"What's wrong?" Slith asked, as he could feel anger coming from Midwak. They had stayed in the room because of his warning that the attacking force was strong, so they should wear them down.

"Nothing . . . it's just that they are a lot weaker than I expected," Midwak admitted, which came as a surprise to Slith.

What would one expect from a Tier 3 gang in the first place?

Midwak was looking for those like him, those who belonged to the alpha group.

I can't believe it . . . the alpha is here, but there is only one other beta wolf! Midwak found it hard to contain his frustration. *I could smell the fresh scent on that guy, but I thought I was unlucky. Are you telling me that this alpha wolf is really so new that his entire pack consists of three members?*

What has he been doing this whole time? This damned alpha, he deserves to get his pack stolen from him! Midwak thought, but his plan was soon coming into action, because Gary had finally arrived.

CHAPTER 33

WITH ALL MY POWER

Standing on the other side of the doors, Gary hadn't pushed them open immediately. He had been running around the casino for a while, searching for the leader of the Scatterbugs. However, during his search, he had only found insignificant people. Staff managers had attempted to stop him, but the werewolf had dealt with them quickly, and they had barely slowed him down.

All of this had made him aware that the absence of the higher-ups wasn't a coincidence. Then, when he found the elaborate door, he heard the breath of many people inside.

I can smell him, and I can sense him as well. There's another werewolf on the other side, Gary thought. *The person who did that to Kai, who placed him up like that on display for everyone to see. Slough was meant to be a safe place for us Howlers, but while I was away, this damned werewolf came in and did that. To a member of the Howlers, to a member of my pack!*

With the anger and rage building inside him, and the image of Kai in his head, Gary pushed the doors open. There was no helping it, he had to face whoever was on the other side.

It was just as Gary had expected: five men on either side of the room, all in fancy suits, all looking down on him. Their ages ranged wildly, but what stood out the most was the fact that none of them had weapons.

Then again, it wasn't too surprising, because every single one of them was an Altered. They were confident in their skills, and in the fact that their own bodies were far deadlier than any weapon.

"Will you look at this?" Slith spoke with a large smile on his face, his hands out on his desk, displaying the large rings on his fingers. "A member of that damned Howlers gang has come all the way here, and what the hell is with that damned wolf mask?"

At the other end of the room were the two people that Gary had come here to see. From his clothes and his presence, Gary understood that the seated man had to be the leader of the Scatterbugs, and then there was the one next to him, Midwak, the one whose scent he had picked up from the outside.

New Quest received
Against all odds, you have entered the Scatterbugs base
An enemy that never thought of you as one is now forced into a tough situation
Quest: Defeat the Scatterbugs gang
Condition: The Scatterbugs gang will be considered defeated when all 11 Altered surrender or have been defeated

The quest that popped up just reminded Gary about how hard this task would be and confirmed the worst-case scenario. Fighting against one werewolf was already suicidal enough, but now he would have to face nearly a dozen Altered on top of that . . . This situation was nothing like the time he had barged into Olivia's office.

Why eleven? What about the one who is responsible for it all? Gary wondered as his gaze stayed on Midwak.

However, his system wasn't done with the messages just yet; an additional quest appeared.

New Quest received
You are in the presence of an omega werewolf
The omega outranks you
Should you lose a fight against him, the fate of you and your pack will be in the hands of his pack

Hang on, other werewolves also have ranks? I thought that was something exclusive to me and my pack because of the system . . . I'm at Bishop grade, so that means he has to be at least a Rook. No wonder he ended up beating Kai . . . No, now's not the time to think about that stuff. I knew he was strong all along, and yet I've come here to take revenge anyway. He might be a natural werewolf, but I bet I'm still stronger because of the system!

Gary Dem
Grade: Bishop [2/15]
Class: Warrior
Level 24
Health 250
Energy 300
Exp 2345/15564
Strength 36
Dexterity 28
Endurance 34
2 Pawn points
2 stat points unallocated

Skills:
Claw Drain (Level 1)
Once activated, half of the damage inflicted by the user will be used to recover Health.
The skill will take 15 points of Energy to use.
Skill duration: 2 secs.

Last Stand
When activated, the user's Health cannot fall below 1 HP.
The skill will take 0 points of Energy to use.
Warning: While Last Stand is active, you'll still continue to take damage as normal!
Skill duration: 60 secs.
Skill reset time: This skill can only be used once a day

Howling Force (Alpha skill—Level 1)
When activated, the alpha lets out a howl to energize nearby members of his pack.

Level 1: 10% overall stat boost.
The skill will take 0 points of Energy to use.
Skill duration: 15 minutes.
Skill reset time: 1 hour.

Alpha Bite (Alpha skill)
When activated, the alpha uses a special bite to attempt to turn a target.
An alpha's bite has a higher chance of turning a person into a werewolf.
The higher the alpha's grade, the higher the chance of creating a higher-grade werewolf.
The skill will take 0 points of Energy to use.
Skill reset time: 1 week

Magnetic Howl
When activated, the user can't help but let out a howl, activating the instinct of the person inside.
The skill will take 0 points of Energy to use but can only be used once every hour. The skill's effectiveness is dependent on the lust of the person around them.
All those that hear the howl are affected and have a sudden urge to throw their attacks toward the user.

Lethal Pounce
This skill can only be used within a certain range of the enemy. The skill will light up when it can be used on an enemy. The user pounces on its enemy, giving it a fifty percent speed boost. The skill can be used in succession, and there is no cooldown.
Energy cost: –50

With everything I have, I need to beat everyone in this room, including him, Gary thought.

"You are certainly skilled to have gotten this far. You know, that mask reminds me a lot of Midwak," Slith continued. "It was the same for him, he came barging into this room one day, but look at him now.

Now he is by my side as one of my strongest allies, which is why I'm willing to make you the same offer.

"Join us. You and the rest of the Howlers can join us. Submit, and the fighting will stop here and now. There will be no bad blood between us, and we can share the riches that we earn together. I think this isn't a bad deal, right?"

Gary was a bit surprised hearing that Midwak had also tried to attack the place, yet even more so to learn that he had failed. A bout of hesitation was starting to creep in, because in the end he wanted to keep everyone safe. Part of him knew that it was too early for him and the others to take on the Scatterbugs. They were still young, and they could always take their revenge after growing stronger in the future . . .

No . . . think about it. Like Kai said, all these people are the same. Who's to say he keeps his word? Even if I work with him, he might change his mind. I heard what he did to Numba's family just because they refused. I can't join with someone like that. I didn't break free from the Underdogs to join a gang like this. Gary shook his head.

"So . . . what will it be? If you refuse, you will never be able to reach me," Slith said.

Midwak walked forward until the two of them were side by side. "There's no need for him to reach you. He's here for me. This whole thing has always been something between the two of us."

The next moment, Midwak's entire hand transformed into that of a werewolf, and with a single swipe, his long, thick claws slashed Slith's throat. The others stared in shock as the gang leader bled out on top of his desk, a look of confusion ingrained in his dimming eyes.

1/11 Altered have been defeated

CHAPTER 34

KILL AND EAT

Any second now, Gary was ready to charge in, but he didn't know the best way to do it. Was Slith going to let the Altered attack him first? If so, during the fight Gary would be able to eat from them for Energy as he took them down one by one.

The problem was, the other werewolf would most likely know what he was planning on doing. If so, maybe he should just use his Full Transformation to take out Slith with a pounce attack to shock all the others, then head for the other werewolf.

In the end, all of his planning was for nothing, because he had never expected what happened next. Midwak, who seemed to be Slith's right-hand man, had killed him right in front of everyone.

"Why are you all so surprised?" Midwak asked, as he placed one foot on the desk and held up Slith by his head. Everyone could see that there was no life left in those eyes.

"You all knew that I was stronger than him, that I'm stronger than any one of you. Do you really think I followed the orders of such a scumbag because I liked him?"

One thing seemed clear to Gary: this wasn't an act, nor did it seem like it was planned. The other gang members who were Altered were clearly confused. They were shocked at this sudden turn of events and didn't know what to do.

"What, do you guys want to turn on me and attack me?" Midwak asked as he looked at them. "Go ahead, you headless chickens, but you won't only be going against me but him as well, and with that I say you have no chance! So I'll give you an offer: join me and accept me as leader of the Scatterbugs, or fight me and die."

Gary wondered whether he should fight or not, but while the Altered were making up their minds, he saw an opportunity to fight with some of his allies. As the saying went, the enemy of my enemy is my friend, and it certainly was the case in this situation.

"Are you just going to stand there?" Midwak asked Gary. "You must know there was another reason for me to kill him."

As Midwak was in the middle of explaining, his mouth transformed into that of a large wolf, and then he opened wide and bit right into Slith's shoulder, taking a large chunk out of it.

Blood dripped from his mouth as he swallowed. "You must know that we get stronger from eating those that we kill. We are more like beasts than like them!" Midwak said, as he continued to consume Slith's body in front of everyone.

It was a horrific sight, but Midwak didn't care at all; it was as if no one was watching as he indulged in his feast.

This is bad. He was already strong, and depending on how strong Slith was, Midwak could get even stronger, Gary thought. *I have to act now.*

Gary started transforming his legs as he charged straight ahead, but one of the gang members jumped in front of him. Gary didn't hold back as he transformed his arm.

One hit, I have to take all of these guys down with one hit! Gary thought, as he threw out his fist using all of his strength.

The gang member in front of him started to change; his body became blacker and his skin turned dark, almost like rusted iron. Gary landed a solid punch, but the gang member was still standing and hadn't moved from his spot.

"You must have fought some pretty weak Altered up till now, to be stupid enough to come in here, but there's a big difference between a Tier 2 gang and a Tier 3," the man said.

Some of the other gang members had started to creep toward Gary, but not all of them.

"You killed him! You killed Slith! I knew you were a dirty rat from the beginning!" one of the men shouted as he leapt up, aiming to stop Midwak in the middle of his meal on top of the desk.

The man started to transform in midair, growing a pair of rounded wings, and his nose turned into a snout like that of an elephant, only brown. It stretched out toward Midwak.

But Midwak grabbed the snout and pulled the Altered straight toward him with such strength that the Altered's body was yanked through the air.

With his other hand already transformed, he stabbed the Altered right through the stomach.

"This is great, another one to eat!" Midwak exclaimed, as he opened his mouth and bit right through the Altered's neck, ripping out parts of its body and swallowing them whole.

"I am the new leader of the Scatterbugs gang—Midwak!" he cried out, with a howl. "With this gang and the blood of an alpha, I will use you all to get my revenge!"

CHAPTER 35

I'M THE ATTACKER

Gary struggled to consider his next move. The alpha werewolf hadn't really come prepared with a plan in mind, aside from defeating Slith and Midwak, but with the sudden betrayal everything had turned even more chaotic. Still, the teenager thought that it might actually turn out to be a good thing; at least now he wouldn't have to defeat nearly a dozen Altered by himself.

At the back of the room, Midwak was dealing with the Altered who had wanted to avenge Slith. As valiant as his ideal might have been, he only ended up sharing in the gang leader's demise. What's more, the omega werewolf took a giant bite out of the Altered who was barely hanging on to life.

Is this what a real werewolf is like? He's far worse than those mindless beasts in the special class! Gary thought in disgust as he watched Midwak take another chunk out of the Altered. He wasn't even chewing, but greedily swallowing it down.

At least the behavior of beasts could be excused as animals acting on instinct, but a werewolf was still of sane mind. Midwak was just being himself, and that made the gruesome sight even more grim for Gary.

2/11 Altered have been defeated

Another system message popped up, confirming the death of the Altered who must have experienced the agony of being eaten alive. Surprisingly, that didn't deter most of the other Altered as they continued their combined attack on Midwak.

"What are you looking at?" one of the Altered closest to Gary shouted at him. Rather than join the others, who were eager to gang up on the strongest fighter among them, this gang member had decided to engage Gary before choosing a side. He moved to strike the alpha werewolf with his hands.

Gary reacted quickly and grabbed them, but the Altered was in the middle of transforming. Several long, thin limbs had emerged from his ribs: at least thirty sharp insectlike limbs with pointed ends. All of them went straight for Gary, penetrating his arms, shoulders, and ribs.

–38 HP
212/250 HP

"Freaking hell, that's a lot of damage!"

Even though Gary had increased his Endurance, in hopes of turning more into a tanklike character, he had hardly suffered attacks that took out chunks of his HP. Suffering such an attack, which had nearly managed to cut through him, made him realize that his Endurance still had a long way to go.

If Gary let go of the attack, he was afraid that the strange arms would go in deeper, so instead he pushed his opponent off him, using his Strength and causing the Altered to fall, but as he did, Gary saw another large object swinging right for his face. Ducking down, Gary rolled to the side and then pushed off his feet, ending up near the entrance door.

All of these Altered here are strong; this is nothing like the guys at the academy, Gary thought.

On top of that, they had now all finished transforming, and six of them had their eyes on fighting him rather than Midwak. They didn't look too happy about it, but they would have gone after Gary anyway.

I should be thankful Midwak chose now of all times for his betrayal. Fighting six Altered will be hard, but with a bit of luck, perhaps the others can injure him while I deal with my half.

Strangely, rather than assassination or a duel, Gary ended up in a sort of competition with Midwak, with both werewolves having to take out the Altered on their side before their fight would begin. One of the Altered had giant stingers on top of his forearms, which he pointed at Gary like they were guns and began to fire away.

Gary did not want to find out how much damage they could inflict, so he ran to the side, avoiding them as best he could, and saw that the first Altered who had attacked him appeared to have some type of iron skin on his body.

So far, he had just stayed still, because his defense was one of the strongest in the entire group.

If your defense is the strongest, then I will just have to make a stronger attack! Gary thought.

As he dodged, another large limb came at him from another Altered. Then another gang member stood in his way. Gary stopped and darted to the right.

One more Altered joined in on the attack, but Gary spun his body, heading straight for his target. If someone had been watching from the outside, they might have thought they were watching an Altered sports match. Gary was using the skills that he had learned as a rugby player to avoid the others coming toward him.

"He's really fast for an Altered," one of the gang members complained.

Now the iron-skinned Altered saw Gary coming toward him, but he welcomed the challenge with a smile.

"You think doing the same thing will make a difference?" the Altered taunted him. "You've already given it your best shot; face it, you're not getting past my defense."

"If my best isn't good enough, then I just have to be better than that," Gary shouted as he told his system to allocate the stat points he had kept in reserve for just such an occasion.

2 points have been allocated into Strength
Your base Strength is now at 38

This is not enough, I need to get stronger! He was aware that now wasn't the time to be stingy, so he converted his Pawn points to be able to enjoy an even bigger boost.

Would you like to convert 2 Pawn points into stat points?
Yes

5 stat points have been obtained
3 points have been allocated into Strength
Your base Strength is now at 41
2 points have been allocated into Dexterity
Your base Dexterity is now at 30

I focused too much on becoming a tank. I thought as long as I didn't die, as long as I took all the hits for the others, that they would survive, but in this situation, I have to think differently. I was the one who decided to attack the Scatterbugs, so now I need to have the Strength to attack!

Skill activated: Claw Drain
–15 Energy

Gary's nails extended slightly, and with his boost in speed, he lifted his arms and swung them down in a large X. His claws went deep into the iron skin, and the Altered who had been confident in his defense remained standing for a few seconds . . . until he fell to the floor.

+15 HP
212/250 HP
3/11 Altered have been defeated

CHAPTER 36

SYSTEM OVERLOAD

The Scatterbugs' Altered could tell that Gary was strong. From the moment they had seen him fight, they understood where the masked intruder got the confidence to attack their base.

Nevertheless, when he entered the room, none of them had been too worried about him. They also were strong Altered—strong enough that perhaps one of them could take over, or at least defeat a gang from a Tier 3 town.

This was how confident they were, but something strange happened. Gary suddenly became faster, and his strikes seemed to contain even more power in the span of a few seconds.

Seconds before the iron-skinned Altered was hit by those strikes, he knew he was in trouble. He had no time to prepare, no time to stop the attack; he could only trust in his own defense. Alas, the strong claws dug deep inside him, tearing into his body, and the long fingernail clipped part of his heart, killing him on the spot.

You have successfully slain an Altered
10,000 Exp has been rewarded
Congratulations, you have now reached: Level 25
A stat point has been granted

Multiple messages appeared in front of Gary, but they were more of a distraction than anything else. He had just defeated one of the strongest Altered in the room in terms of defensive abilities, but that still didn't faze the others as they all came toward him.

Shit, can you guys just give me a second to read my messages! Gary thought as he jumped from his position and dug his claws into the side of the wall. He was now stuck to it, but some of the Altered could fly; he was hoping that they would hesitate a little before coming toward him after seeing what he could do now.

Optional Quest received
Waste not want not
Consume the Altered
Quest reward: Additional stat points

Does it LOOK like I'm in any position to do so? Gary was more than annoyed that this Quest showed up at this moment. He hardly ever got a chance to kill an Altered, but from the handful of times he had done so, he had learned that it appeared to be the fastest way for him to grow. He was sure that it was the same for Midwak, though he didn't really know whether the Werewolf System enhanced this ability in any way, be it in the boost he gained or the time it took for the bonus to take effect.

The alpha werewolf could only hope so, because otherwise Midwak would become even stronger once he finished eating the Altered he had defeated. Unfortunately, even after his boost, Gary wasn't overwhelmingly stronger than the Altered in the room that he could eat at his pleasure.

Still, there were a few messages that Gary had to go through.

Main Quest completed
Who would have thought you would survive long enough to reach this milestone?
Since you've proven to be well suited for your current role, you've earned yourself your first Class Promotion!
Please select from one of the following Classes!

I don't remember this being a Main Quest, but whatever, I completed it at the perfect time. Becoming a Werewolf Warrior was a major upgrade to my power, but it took some time for the changes to take place, and it wasn't exactly pleasant.

Gary recalled that his body had gone through some extreme changes, so if this class promotion was the same thing, it meant he would be unable to fight for a while. Selecting something now might very well be the last thing he ever did.

Now he had an even bigger problem; just as Gary was about to check out his options, the Needle Altered started to fire more stuff at him, and the werewolf was forced to leap from the wall back down onto the floor.

"You can keep running, but eventually you're going to tire out! Spare us the nuisance and just accept your fate!" one of the Altered shouted.

Just then, a thick loglike arm grew out from one of the Altered and whacked Gary right in the stomach, sending him crashing into the glass cabinets against the wall.

–20 HP
192/250 HP

There goes the HP I just got back, Gary thought as he got back up. *I need to fight at full strength, I need to get rid of them all, but then I won't have any Energy . . . and I also need to find a way to eat their bodies to be ready for Midwak.*

Another large loglike arm was coming toward him, and, still hurt from the attack before, Gary had no choice but to use another skill.

Skill activated: Lethal Pounce
–50 Energy

Gary suddenly sped up and jumped toward one of the Altered, but it turned out to be the one with multiple sharp limbs, all pointed toward him. Gary braced himself as his body was embedded with dozens of the sharp limbs; only his head and stomach were saved, as he had curled himself into a ball.

Kicking off from the Altered, Gary got away, but he was bleeding heavily and had suffered a lot more damage than before.

–48 HP
144/250 HP

I have no choice, I have to fully transform and try to get rid of these guys as soon as possible. Then, hopefully, while Midwak is still distracted, I can take a chance and choose that class promotion. Hopefully it's something powerful, since it might be my only way to win this fight!

4/11 Altered have been defeated
5/11 Altered have been defeated
6/11 Altered have been defeated

There was notification after notification of the other Altered being defeated, and Gary gasped for a second as he realized something terrible. Six of them had decided to go after him, and he had only dealt with one of them . . . in other words, Midwak had successfully dealt with all of the Altered who had gone against him.

Glancing at the back of the room, Gary saw Midwak indulging in a feast of Altered bodies. He was growing stronger in this fight, eating them one by one, and once he was done, he would fight the alpha.

CHAPTER 37

A HOTHEADED MISTAKE

The longer the situation lasted, the harder it was for Gary to make a decision, because now he was running out of time. Midwak was getting stronger, and Gary needed to get even stronger still, but he couldn't even defeat the Altered who were in front of him that Midwak had managed to defeat so easily.

I hate to say it, but right now I could really do with some help. I'm an idiot; just because it worked out last time, I thought it would work out this time, Gary thought, as he looked at the Altered who had started to form a barrier so that Gary was unable to escape.

One of the Altered could fly and shoot stingers from its forearms, Gary hadn't been hit by them yet, but he could only assume that they were poisonous. Then there was the Altered with multiple sharp limbs protruding from its body.

That one was more difficult for Gary to deal with, since his tough hide wasn't thick enough to block the hits. Other than those two, there were three more. One was able to change his body into something that was as thick as a tree trunk.

It had hit him once already, sending him into the wall. This Altered looked like a regular human, which meant he had good control over changing his body quickly.

On top of that, there was one Altered whose skin was glowing yellow. A thick, gooey substance covered his body and hands. So far, Gary had avoided conflict with that Altered, as he was worried about what the goo could do.

Then there was the last of the lot, whose hands were gigantic, although *hands* was the wrong term to use, as they looked more like the giant pincers of a crab. They were red and looked like they would be able to crush anything.

I guess it makes sense that most of these guys would be similar to bug-type Altered. If I remember from my lessons correctly, most of the beasts out there are similar to the bugs we have today. I guess I just have to be thankful for one thing, and that's the fact that I don't have to go against Slith, whatever he was, Gary thought.

The first one to act was the Altered who was mostly human in form. When he raised his hand, it grew to the size of a tree trunk; the Altered extended it out then swung it toward Gary at full force.

Gary usually used his speed to avoid a hit, but one of the Altered fired his stingers toward Gary's right, while the Altered who was covered in strange yellow goo threw something out of his body toward the other side.

It hit the door behind him and solidified, and Gary was glad that he didn't try to test what it did. He knew exactly what they were doing; they had trapped him, and he had no choice but to take the hit.

If I transform into my full form, I will be at full strength. It will use a lot of energy, but after beating these guys and eating them up, I'll be able to take on Midwak. It's the only way to beat them and win this fight!

As the Altered attacked, Gary was bracing himself and preparing to use his skill, when a strange scent entered his nose.

"Let me deal with this!" a voice said, and suddenly a large man was looming over him. He grabbed the large tree trunk, bending his knees slightly. As the man breathed, steam came out of his large rounded nostrils.

"Austin?" Gary asked.

"Get your hands off our boss!" Austin shouted, as he lifted the person by the trunk and slammed him into the wall. The Altered's arm started to shrink, and as it did Austin lost his grip.

But the rest had entered the room—Olivia, Innu, and Marie—all of them wearing their masks and their black-and-gold uniforms.

"The rest of the gang has shown up?" the red-handed Altered said. "This isn't going to be an easy fight."

Just then a shirtless man approached them from behind, blood dripping from his mouth onto his chest. He no longer had shoes on either, because of his transformation, and only part of his trousers remained.

Midwak had finished eating the other Altered, and now he was ready to join the fight.

There's only one way to win this, Gary thought. He gritted his teeth, because he didn't want to say it. There was a high chance of one of his friends dying, but it was either one of them or all of them.

"Everyone!" Gary shouted. "Focus on the shirtless man, the werewolf. I don't expect you to win, but just hold him back for as long as you can, and I have one more order for you. Don't die!"

This was the only way Gary could see them winning, Gary needed to defeat the Altered to level up, consume their bodies, and evolve, and unfortunately his friends would have to be his shield, but just how long would they be able to hold that monster back?

Transformation has begun

"AWOOOO!"

Alpha's Howl has been used
A 10 percent boost has been given to those in your pack!

CHAPTER 38

CRAZY TO FIGHT CRAZY

Midwak was still standing on the other side, behind the groups of people. The desk had been destroyed and the entire area was covered in blood. Parts of bodies had been strewn about, and there were a lot of bones.

"Oh that sweet sound!" Midwak said. "It has certainly been a long time since I heard it!"

The Alpha's Howl had just been used, giving a 10 percent boost to Gary's power; it was only a temporary boost, so Gary wanted to save it for his fight with Midwak, but he wanted to give Olivia as much strength as possible before her fight.

Seeing the seriousness of the situation, none of the Howlers asked what Gary meant; right now they were just going to do as he asked, and even Olivia was taking the situation seriously. She stared at Midwak and his yellow glowing eyes.

It looks like I'm about to face someone who is even crazier than me! But for some reason my blood is pumping, Olivia thought, as her body transformed from head to toe. Because of the special design of the uniforms, they stretched instead of ripping.

Olivia (Beta Werewolf) has marked a target

Now a tracking mark had been put on Midwak so they could find him wherever he went. As a Hunter Class werewolf, Olivia had slightly longer arms and legs, and she was using them to her full advantage as she ran across the room.

The goo-covered Altered jumped in front of her and swung his arm, aiming the strange yellow substance right for her, but with a single leap she avoided the goo and along with it, the rest of the Altered.

With her sharp claws out, she was ready to rip Midwak's head off. Midwak grabbed Olivia's hands while he was still untransformed.

"You are *weak*!" His hands started to transform, and Olivia was unable to pull away. Before she knew it, he had lifted her into the air and kicked her right in the stomach, sending her crashing into the wall.

The only thing Midwak had transformed was his arms, and he was still able to overpower her. He looked at his hands, clenching them in and out.

"Yes, yes, yes! This is what I needed," Midwak exclaimed.

The other Howlers rushed in to back her up, and they saw that Olivia was far from being down for the count, as she had gotten up baring her teeth and letting out a growl.

"We have to help her!" Marie shouted; they all ran forward with Austin leading the way, but once again, another Altered stood in their path, blocking them from joining the fight.

It was the man with the huge red claws; he snapped them and the entire room rang. It showed what force was behind such claws. Still, Austin was ready to rumble, to match his power against the others.

That was until a large figure landed right in front of him.

"I'll get rid of them!" Gary awkwardly said. He was in his full transformation but was able to speak a lot more clearly since he'd had a lot of practice. "You focus on holding him off!"

When Gary was close to the red-clawed Altered, who looked ready to intercept any attack, he used his Lethal Pounce skill. His speed almost doubled as he shot from his position.

The claw hit nothing but the air, and Gary was directly up against his chest, biting the man's neck. Then he shoved his claws deep into the man's chest.

Gary lifted him in the air and pulled his claws out as he swung his arms, one after the other, cutting his body. He was using his full strength and his full speed now, and other than his claws the man's body wasn't as hard as the rest of him.

Thanks to the system notification, Gary could tell when the Altered was out of the fight because of his injuries.

7/11 Altered have been defeated

He stopped attacking, and as the man fell down, Gary took another large bite, this time from his shoulder.

Your Energy is being restored

Kill and eat, that's what I need to do to keep fighting, and then I can stop him; then I will be on equal grounds with him.

Gary's eyes were glowing red; his natural instincts were kicking in, and like Midwak, madness showed on his face, causing the other Altered to second-guess their next step.

Because of Gary, the others were all able to safely pass, and now they were focused on Midwak. At the back of the group Marie turned her head and saw a large werewolf with dark fur standing behind them.

For a second there, I was scared. But that's still Gary, right? The Gary who saved us, the Gary who is our friend. No, of course it is. Right now, Gary is doing all of this for all of us in the Howlers, and for Kai, Marie thought.

The Howlers were on one side of the room, fighting Midwak, and Gary was fighting the rest of the Altered on the other. Taking a step forward, Gary looked for his next target as he scanned the room.

I need to keep fighting, I need to level up, I need to eat them, so I can be on the same level as that omega werewolf!

"Only four more to go." Gary said, running straight in.

CHAPTER 39

THE STRONG OMEGA

Stubborn was one word that could be used to describe Olivia, and in this situation it was questionable whether it was a good trait to have. The moment she recovered from the initial clash with Midwak, she ran across the floor to reach him.

Midwak tilted his head to the side. "You're as much a pup as the grayling, and yet he was stronger than this. Tell me what makes you think you could beat me?"

When Olivia was finally close, she took one large leap and swung her hand toward Midwak's chest. He leaned back and she missed, then swung her other hand, trying to pierce his body.

"NOW!" Innu shouted. Three bolts flew into the air, hitting Midwak in the back and piercing his skin ever so slightly. The thick bolts had a small container inside that looked like a see-through battery.

Inside the container, blue sparks were moving about, and the bolts were activated, shocking the omega werewolf all over. His skin was becoming slightly transparent as the current ran through his body.

Innu hadn't joined in the fight; he was staying close to Marie, axes in hand, just in case they chose to target her. So far, Midwak and Olivia had been too fast for Marie to be of any help.

She was a good aim and a good shot, but she hadn't been in enough fights to get the timing right, which was why Innu was watching the fight carefully for the perfect time.

The bolts, while not lethal, served as a good distraction as Olivia left a large scratch across Midwak's chest. Blood dripped onto his abs, but it was hard to tell since his body was already covered in blood.

But nearly as quickly as the wound had been made, it was already starting to heal.

"That's some nice shock treatment," Midwak said, as he ducked under Olivia's strikes, and then with his werewolf hand, he reached out and grabbed her around the mouth. With his great strength, he needed only the power of his fingers to keep it shut.

Then Midwak punched her hard in the face with his other hand. Olivia wanted to scream, to howl, as the blow had felt like it had broken multiple bones, but Midwak continued to punch her while holding on to her mouth.

"Ha-ha, I can't wait until you are under my control," Midwak said. "Depending on how long you last, I might let you become my Luna!"

By now, even though Olivia was in her full werewolf form, part of her jaw and the side of her orbital bone all felt like they were broken. She recoiled from him, but with the constant punching, there was no point.

Swinging his arm back even farther, Midwak was going for even harder punches. As he swung straight toward her face once more, a large hand, even bigger than his own in its partially transformed state, grabbed his fist and stopped it in its tracks.

"How about you pick on someone your own size, asshole!" Austin pulled Midwak forward and threw a fist, hitting him right in the head. It flung backward and blood spattered out of his mouth.

Midwak looked at Austin with a smile; it looked like he wanted to say something, but before he could, another hand lifted him by his legs. With all of his force, Austin lifted him up high and slammed him to the floor, leaving behind a large crater.

The marble was broken into pieces. Austin lifted the werewolf and slammed him down again and again. Bones cracked and Midwak's arms and legs were in positions that weren't natural at all.

Austin was huffing and panting, and a lot of steam was coming out of his nostrils. Although the mask hid most of his face, part of it could be seen transformed. Right now, Austin was in his full form.

The beast that created his Altered form was a rare one, one that had a humanoid body, which was why it was hard to tell whether Austin had fully transformed.

"Man, every time I see him fight in that form, it just makes me . . . more jealous. If only I had won, that would have been me," Innu couldn't help but say.

Moments later, though, when the dust started to settle, Midwak stood up, his body clicking and cracking.

"Now, you certainly are a strong one, but it's truly a shame that you are an Altered!" Midwak said, as he strode toward Austin, who was ready for another round.

"Believe it or not, but I wasn't planning to kill any of you Howlers, because you all would make great additions to my pack!" Midwak continued. "There's a reason I didn't care about the Scatterbugs . . . and that's because they were already Altered.

"A werewolf can't turn an Altered, which means to me . . ."

In front of their eyes, Midwak started to transform; his fur was dark black, and he grew nearly double in size, muscles and width included. Now he was only a little smaller than Austin.

"You're only useful as a meal!" Midwak growled as he threw a punch at such great speed, it looked like the wind was being carried with it.

The fist hit Austin right in the stomach, lifting his body off the ground and sending him flying into the wall far away.

"I hope for your own sake that he's the only Altered!" Midwak declared with a smile, showing all of his sharp teeth.

CHAPTER 40

PERFECT LINEUP

If Gary wanted to help his teammates, the best thing he could do was to take out all of the Altered in the room as soon as possible. He would have to trust that they were capable enough to hold Midwak back.

Out of these four guys left, I need to get rid of the one that's the most troublesome.

Gary studied the man with the stingers on his forearms; although Gary hadn't been hit yet, the stingers always were distracting him from getting to the others, and he had the farthest range when it came to attacks.

When Gary had decided who would be his next target, he ran toward him in his werewolf form. He was leaning forward at an incredibly low angle. The muscles in his legs and toes were strong enough to lift his body just enough so his face wouldn't hit the floor, and once in a while he used his hands to dig into the floor, giving him a further leap of power.

Seeing this, the Altered leapt into action. The goo-covered Altered saw Gary and swung his arm, releasing a large amount of the substance toward him. The werewolf's hands dug deep into the ground, cracking it. The veins on his forearms bulged as he quickly pushed his whole body to the side, so the goo would hit the floor and harden in a matter of seconds.

Getting hit by that will slow down my movements, but it's covering his whole body; that's going to be a hard one to take care of.

The Altered who could change his limbs into tree trunks jumped in front of Gary, swinging his arm and transforming it midswing.

They're working together better than they were before! I need to avoid this, Gary thought.

Instinctively, Gary went with the flow as he leaned backward, and slid across the floor. He had built up so much speed that on the hard marble floor he was pretty much gliding across it.

As the tree trunk passed going over his head, Gary had his claws ready and tensed his fingers hard as they scratched right across it.

His claws broke through the Altered's skin, and black blood dripped from the wound.

In a smooth motion, Gary pulled his body up off the ground and continued running forward. Now there was only one Altered between him and the strange stinger man.

"Fine, fucking stab me then!" Gary lifted his forearms, and in his full werewolf form he was much larger than he was before. When the Altered's sharp limbs pierced Gary, they only pierced his forearms this time.

–12 HP

In my werewolf form, my hide is thicker so I take less damage, but that wasn't my goal.

Because of Gary's speed, the sharp limbs pierced his arms quite deeply; he had purposely relaxed them as much as he could, but now that the limbs were inside him, he tensed up.

His clenched muscles gripped the limbs tightly, and the Altered was unable to pull them out.

"Thanks for being my shield!" Gary said, as he saw the stingers coming toward him. Gary moved his forearms and the stingers hit the multiple-limbed man instead.

"Arghh!" the Altered shouted.

Peeking behind him, Gary saw that the other Altered was in the air. He then leapt up with his strong powerful legs, still taking his shield with him.

Then, when the two had matched height, Gary relaxed the muscles in his forearms and kicked the Altered off him. The sharp limbs detached from Gary's arms, and the Altered's entire body crashed into the other one.

While in midair, Gary flipped backward, landing on his feet, then darted toward the other two Altered once again.

The stinger Altered was still recovering, and with a swipe of his hand, Gary sliced a claw across his neck.

8/11 Altered have been defeated
Congratulations, you have now reached: Level 26

Gary had gained a large amount of Exp from killing the two Altered. He still hadn't had time to look at his system properly or use the stat points gained. At the same time, the bodies of the Altered he had killed were still intact.

If I can do this . . . if I can use everything, then I will be strong enough.

The other Altered were left confused and a little disheartened at the sight of another of their allies falling; Gary saw this as an opportunity. With the main distraction gone, he could perhaps pull this off.

One of the Altered had gotten up from the ground, along with another and now he could see it, they were almost forming a direct line.

Gary approached the Altered closest, and when he was in range . . .

Lethal Pounce
−30 Energy

His speed doubled in the short distance, and with his claws he stabbed right through the Altered's chest.

9/11 Altered have been defeated
Lethal Pounce activated
−30 Energy

The most dangerous thing about the Lethal Pounce skill was the fact that as long as someone was in range, Gary could use it consecutively, one after the other. The only downside was that it took a lot of energy, but there was plenty of food for him here.

The treelike Altered had no time to react as Gary landed on top of him and bit down on his neck, pulling out tendons and more, ending his life on the spot.

10/11 Altered have been defeated
Skill: Lethal Pounce has been used

Reaching the final Altered, Gary could feel the goo hardening, but it did little to slow him down as his claws penetrated the stomach of the Altered. As they sliced through, the Altered's organs spilled onto the ground, and Gary slammed his other hand down onto the Altered's head, smashing it onto the ground.

11/11 Altered have been defeated
Quest completed
Congratulations, you have now reached: Level 27
Quest update: A new threat has taken over the Scatterbugs head-quarters. Defeat the threat to get rid of the Scatterbugs.

It was quite clear to Gary that the new threat was Midwak, but with his energy down to almost nothing, and his strength still far less than his opponent, he looked at the Altered on the ground and had another thought.

It's feeding time.

CHAPTER 41

RED AXE

Without a doubt, ever since Austin had received his new Altered form, he had been considered the strongest compared to the others. As a human, his strength was already unnatural, and as an Altered it was even greater.

He was able to lift things that even Gary or Olivia would have struggled with, which was why it had been such a shock to see the Altered version of Austin whacked to the side of the room.

"Shit . . . Shit . . . Shit!" Innu mumbled to himself, as he left Marie's side and joined in the fight.

He had thought maybe Austin and Olivia would be enough; surely since they were an Altered and a werewolf, they could do more than he could in this situation, but now it felt like they would need everyone's help if they didn't want anyone to die.

"What are you idiots doing?" Innu shouted. "We knew this werewolf was strong, which is why we don't need to beat him. We only have two orders! To keep him here, and not die, so don't die!"

The situation reminded Innu of the kids at the orphanage. He had lost them all, and now he had a new family, the Howlers, and he didn't want to lose them too.

He activated the power in his weapons, and they started to glow slightly red. Fueled by his emotions, Innu drew out the power from the special Anti-Altered weapons and charged toward Midwak.

"Have I ever told you I hate werewolves?" Innu shouted.

Midwak swung the back of his hand, but Innu managed to dodge the blow. It was as if his senses were heightened and he could guess what Midwak's next move would be. Otherwise, even with the boost of the weapons, Innu would never be able to dodge such an attack.

The next moment, Innu swung one of his axes, aiming for the werewolf's stomach.

It cut through the skin, to both Innu's and Midwak's surprise, and rather than trying to take another swipe at the young gang member, Midwak jumped back and looked down at the wound to his stomach; it was healing, but at a slightly slower rate than usual.

That's not a normal weapon, Midwak thought. *Who would have thought that a gang like this would have such a weapon?*

Innu wasn't charging and striking like before, and his attack had given Austin and Olivia time to recover from the damage they had received earlier. Just like Midwak, their forms had good healing capabilities as well.

"I never thought that your group would be more of a challenge than those Altered I fought earlier. No, 'challenge' isn't the right word. You aren't stronger than them, you're just more annoying and persistent!" Midwak said, and when he looked to his left, he saw one of the Howlers standing alone.

"No . . . no!" Innu shouted, as he knew exactly what Midwak was planning to do.

Midwak was already sprinting toward Marie; she was far away, but even if she ran away now, he would surely catch up with her. Instead, she took out her crossbow, which was loaded with three bolts, and fired.

One of the bolts missed, hitting the floor. Midwak was running super fast, and her hands were shaking nonstop. Taking a deep breath, she fired two more bolts. One hit Midwak in the chest, and the other hit him in the shoulder.

The sparks started to light up, and blue electricity sparked all over his body, but it didn't slow him down at all. Not like it did before, when he was in his humanlike form. In his full werewolf form, he just took the hit directly.

Innu was desperately running after Midwak but was unable to catch up.

*It's my fault; I left Marie when I was supposed to be by her side pro-
tecting her. If she gets bitten or hurt now, it will be because of me. How
can I face Kai and Gary after that?*

Knowing he wasn't able to reach Marie, he felt his energy and
power draining out of him and into his axe. Innu didn't know what
was happening or why, but desperation caused him to throw the axe
through the air.

It spun multiple times, speeding up as it continued to glow red, and
struck like a bullet. Midwak was close to Marie but still out of reach
when the axe landed right in the back of his calf.

"AWOO!" Midwak let out a little howl of pain. Unlike the last blow,
the axe was lodged in pretty deep. It nearly caused him to stumble, but
he had caught himself with his arms.

Innu was trying to catch his breath; using the axe like that had
taken a lot of energy out of him. He was covered in sweat even though
all he did was hurl the thing.

"That won't stop me!" Midwak said as he got up and continued
toward Marie. She attempted to stab Midwak with her spear, but he
grabbed it and threw it off to the side.

"I didn't want to kill you, but there are plenty of talented humans
that I can turn." Midwak swung his hand right at Marie's face. She saw
the claws coming at her and attempted to move her head, but she was
too slow.

As the clawed hand came closer, the fingernails skimmed her
cheek, leaving a small cut, and suddenly Midwak lay on the ground.

Did he slip? Marie thought, realizing that her life had just been
saved.

Midwak looked down and saw something wrapped around his leg.
It was black like a rope, but it wasn't a rope, it was a whip, and Olivia
held the other end.

Olivia was in her full werewolf form, pulling on the whip. However, her strength alone was not enough to pull Midwak; Austin was
doing most of the pulling.

After wrapping the whip around Midwak's leg, Olivia quickly gave
the handle to Austin and wrapped it around his hand for stability. Olivia
then grasped the whip farther up and both of them pulled, just in time.

"You were right," Olivia said to the tired Innu. "We were trying to beat him before, when we should have just been buying time like you said. We understand our job now."

From the corner of her eye, Olivia saw Gary chowing down on the Altered.

CHAPTER 42

CLASS UPGRADE

After defeating all of the Altered, Gary didn't even choose to take a quick peek at the fight that was going on. The fact that Midwak wasn't attacking him right now meant that things were going well.

He looked at the Altered in front of him; with a swipe of his hand, flesh was coming off the bodies with ease. He would take a few bites before swallowing most of it whole.

I can't think of my actions, I can't think about what I'm doing right now. I can't waste a second. All I can do is focus on what I need to do.

The system message would appear when he had eaten enough of one Altered, and then Gary would move on to the next, repeating the process.

His energy had been replenished long ago, but he continued to eat to gain the stat points he needed. He remained in his werewolf form so he could eat as quickly as possible.

How strong was he right now, and what stats had he gained? He didn't know . . . all he knew was that he needed everything to be able to beat Midwak.

He heard a ding and looked around the room. His fur was covered in blood; some of it had dried, and parts of it were wet still. That was when he realized there were no Altered left for him to eat.

He raised his head to bring up the system screen.

Congratulations, you have now reached: Level 27

You can now select a new class based on your current class type (Warrior)

This was the message Gary had received at Level 25, although he had jumped two more levels since then. Now he had time to choose his options.

Paladin Warrior
This warrior excels in all aspects of fighting. They are a great defender, a great striker, and a great healer as well. The user's power will stem from righteousness. When they believe they are doing the right thing, they will gain strength like no other.
A special trait of the class allows the user to have a different set of skills, depending on what form the user takes (werewolf/human).

Any class upgrade would mean an increase in strength, that was for sure, but initially reading the message, he wasn't sure if it was right for him.

Although Gary had chosen the life of a gang member, there were times when he didn't think his actions were righteous at all. In a way, they were very selfish, and even looking around he saw the dead bodies on the ground, and was reminded of those he had killed in the past.

Still, it would depend on what the system meant; was it what Gary considered righteous, or was there a type of higher being making the decision for him? Perhaps the system itself? There was another aspect that interested him greatly, and that was the separate skills in his human and werewolf forms.

He had already seen how useful skills were, and if he didn't have to transform, the element of surprise as well as the versatility would be great, but he needed to look at his options.

Dark Warrior
This warrior excels in strength and healing, giving up nearly all forms of defense. Their skills are focused on doing the most damage they can to the one in front of them before they can be taken out.
Under the night sky, the Dark Warrior gets a boost in energy, allowing them to use their deadly skills on their opponents for longer.

Since both of the classes were deviations of the Warrior Class, Gary assumed they would be similar, but their descriptions seemed quite different. On top of that, they both had their pluses and downsides.

The Dark Warrior grew in strength when it was dark, just like the Paladin when it believed it was doing something right. Right now it was dark, so Gary would get a boost, but in the future would all his fights take place at night?

In the academy there were times when he had to fight at night, which seemed to go against how he had been building his werewolf body as a character so far.

Gary had been making his werewolf self a tank, with large amounts of HP, which allowed him to take a number of hits while also increasing his endurance so when he did get hit he would lose low amounts of HP, but he realized that when he was going against an opponent at this level, it hardly had any effect at all.

Crap, what do I do? Which one do I choose? Gary thought.

He would have loved to go through all of the options, take time to think, ask his friend Tom, or even Kai. They were the smart ones, not him, but the longer he would take, the greater chance that the others would be seriously hurt or killed.

I have no choice, I have to pick one, the one that's best for the situation I'm currently in; I don't have time to think! Gary thought as his option was selected, and suddenly he felt a great pain and a tingle all over his body.

Gary dropped to his knees, and then to the floor as all of his muscles felt like they were breaking down and he was reverting back from werewolf form to human.

Guys, just wait a bit longer, I'm going to kill that bastard! Gary thought, reaching his hand out toward Midwak.

CHAPTER 43

HOLD HIM BACK!

The Howlers were doing their best to hold Midwak back, and they couldn't break their attention away from him for even a second. Innu had already exhausted himself by throwing the axe. He was so tired that he had to prop himself up on his thigh.

"You guys are doing a great job . . . so I can't fall behind! I refuse to become a burden to you!" Innu yelled in an attempt to hype himself and his friends up. He dug really deep inside and rushed over to the Anti-Altered spear that had been chucked to the side. He grabbed it and made his way back to Marie, determined not to leave her this time.

With the combined strength of Austin and Olivia, they had not only managed to pull Midwak down, saving Marie from getting her neck clawed out, but they had also dragged him across the room. But he slammed his hands down, digging his fingertips into the marble floor.

"Annoying! You should understand by now that you stand no chance against me, yet you pests keep bugging me!" Midwak shouted. "Your futile resistance is utterly annoying!"

With his other hand free, the werewolf grabbed the whip and pulled on it. As he yanked it forward, though, Austin pulled back with equal force.

"If it's a battle of pure power, I won't lose!" Austin stated confidently. The Minotaur Altered let out another puff of steam. Olivia by his side wasn't sure if she was imagining it, but Austin's muscles seemed to be bulging even bigger.

Midwak knew that it would be tricky to break the whip, but then he noticed the weapon that was still stuck inside his body.

Midwak easily pulled the red axe out of his leg. Blood poured onto the floor, but now his body started to heal. He swung the axe and let it go flying straight toward the two in front of him.

Given that they were in line, it threatened to pierce them both. Austin immediately let go of the whip's handle; Olivia felt the rest of the whip slip from her hands as Midwak broke free.

Before she could brace herself for the impact, a large person jumped in front of her and she heard a strange thudding sound.

"You big ape, what are you doing!" Olivia shouted as she saw that the axe had hit Austin right in the chest; it was a deep wound, and his body began to shrink as he reverted to human form.

Olivia caught Austin just before he hit the floor and held him in her arms.

"Why did you do that? Do you really think I'm so weak that I need protection from a child like you?"

Olivia decided against pulling out the weapon. Just because Midwak had been able to heal from it didn't mean Austin could do the same. Altered might have a good healing factor, but the axes were special, not to mention that in Austin's current state it might be too much for him.

"I'm a big guy, I can take a hit like this," Austin replied, but his weak voice didn't give his argument much credit.

"Who cares, why would you try to protect me? I'm older than you, and not even properly part of your gang!" Olivia argued back.

"Who says you're not part of the gang?" Austin replied, letting out a cough. "How many times have you risked your life for us? Also, you're not that old, and you're really beautiful."

Were it not for his currently deteriorating condition, Olivia might have slapped him for that comment.

"Don't forget what your leader said! You're not allowed to die here!" Olivia shouted as she gently laid him on the floor.

"Our leader," Austin managed to say. "Protect . . . them."

Turning her head, she realized that she had been so occupied with worrying about Austin that she had forgotten about Midwak, who had untangled himself from the whip; his leg was in full working order and he was running toward Innu and Marie.

Innu, seeing this, charged toward Midwak with the axe lifted above his head. Midwak shot all his nails out like bullets, and they pierced Innu's skin, causing him a jolt of pain, with one of the nails embedding itself deep in his stomach.

He instinctively dropped to the floor and Midwak leapt toward Marie to finish her off.

While he was in the air, Marie prepared to stab him with her spear, until she felt something around her leg. Suddenly she was on the ground being pulled to safety as Midwak flew past her straight into a wall.

"Are you okay?" A hand reached down to help her up, and Marie saw that the AFA students had saved her. Izzy released Marie from her hair's grasp, and Numba took a position in front of the two girls.

"It's a good thing we came here after all," he said.

Midwak looked annoyed as he climbed out of the hole he had left in the wall.

"This is a surprise. The Scatterbugs aren't that weak, and there were plenty of them. What are you guys doing here? If Slith weren't dead already, he would die of shame from how weak his Scatterbugs have proven to be." Midwak shook his head.

Izzy, Ian, and Numba stared at Midwak, wondering what they could do; they had lost to him before, and he seemed stronger than the last time they had met. On top of that, although they were trying to hide it, they were exhausted from fighting just moments ago.

"Well, it's a good thing you're here now; it will save me the trouble of locating you later! Now die!" Midwak ran toward them, but the three were ready to do whatever they could to take him out.

"NO!" a loud voice shouted.

A brown-furred figure appeared in front of the students and grabbed Midwak's wrists. "The one to die will be you!"

The figure kicked Midwak in the stomach with both legs, sending him back through the hole in the wall, into the next room.

Class Promotion complete

CHAPTER 44

CHOOSING A PATH

A few moments prior, Numba, Izzy, and Ian had still been in the main gambling hall. The Scatterbugs staff and gang members were proving to be more than a handful; not only did they outnumber the three students by the dozens, but they were resilient as well.

"Guys, we seem to have a problem. I'm starting to recognize a few of the ones I hit in the very beginning. They're getting back up and rejoining the fight. Hey, assholes, just stay down, will you? Don't make us kill you for real!" Ian shouted.

The three of them weren't part of a gang, and while their strength as Altered made it easy for them to take out fully grown adults, they couldn't bring themselves to kill them. They knew it would be easy enough given the strength disparity between Altered and human, but the psychological trauma of taking a human life wasn't easy to ignore.

Ian's body was no longer covered in bristles; instead, only one large one stuck out of his forearm. He swung it against a gang member's blade, knocking it out of his hand, then stabbed him in the thigh as he kicked him in the stomach.

"Stay down unless you want a spike through your head! Surely the amount your boss is paying you can't be worth it to go through this!" Ian pleaded, but the gang members weren't giving up, unaware that the boss that they were so loyal to had already died.

"Do you hear that?" Izzy asked.

There was a loud constant sound, like small bangs one after the other; the whole building was shaking, and the machines were vibrating a little. Soon it became apparent what the noise was.

"I think it's a helicopter," Numba said. "It seems our little bridge trick only lasted so long, and now the reinforcements have come after all."

The sound of the helicopter soon stopped, and although no one wanted to say it, they were tired. Without the help of the rest of the Howlers, they would have to draw energy from somewhere.

It didn't take long for the doors to burst open.

"Arghh!" several gang members groaned.

"We're being attacked from behind!"

"Those aren't our guys! Who the hell are they?"

The Scatterbugs were shouting in confusion, and the three AFA students were also confused. That was until they saw who was attacking the gang members: a man in a clown suit, of all things.

"The Cardenez group can't just sit by while the Howlers attempt to attack the Scatterbugs!" Harry explained.

The chairman of the Cardenez group held a chain with a rounded end and slammed it onto the floor.

"If the Howlers fail today, the Cardenez group will follow! To prevent that, we'll support them with all our strength!" Harry shouted, as the Freaks, the personal security team that he had built, rushed to take care of the Scatterbugs' personnel.

"Father . . ." Numba whispered as he avoided a punch from one gang member, delivering his own to the face of another, sending him stumbling back.

"Go, son, I'm sure they need your help," Harry said to Numba.

The three of them saw that the Freaks seemed to have everything under control, so they nodded in confirmation before they ran off after Gary and the others.

That was how the three were able to arrive and back up Gary and his friends in their fight, and how they had managed to save Marie in the nick of time, but now they saw a person who they assumed was Gary in front of them.

"Everyone, you have done enough! None of you will die here today. Just stand aside and don't get in the way!" Gary shouted.

Just then Midwak sprinted toward Gary. He lifted both of his claws, and ten nails shot out from them, aiming right toward Gary.

Since the others were behind him, Gary couldn't avoid them; he slashed at them with his claws. He knocked three of the nails away, but the others hit him. They pierced his skin but did little damage.

"GRAHH!" Gary opened his mouth wide, saliva going everywhere as he sprinted forward. He and Midwak leapt toward each other, and Gary slashed his claws against Midwak's chest, slicing it open.

But Midwak grabbed Gary's wrist and pulled him forward, punching him in the head. Gary was startled by his strength, and he was pulled forward again as the omega tried to punch him a second time, but this time Gary grabbed his hand, stopping him.

"I'm glad you're a lot stronger than the betas you made!" Midwak said. "I see that you managed to use the time to get yourself a snack. No wonder you feel invincible right now! But there is still a large difference between me and you!

"I thought you had been doing nothing, but now I realize you are just a young alpha with next to no skills. I have no idea who made you like this, but it's clear that you know nothing about being a werewolf. A simple alpha like you can never take me down!"

Midwak's claws grew to twice their size and turned metallic; he lunged toward Gary, who stepped back but was struck in the forearm, receiving a large wound.

"You're right," Gary admitted. "I'm an idiot! If Kai had the same strength as me, if he had been the one to evolve, he would have already found the perfect way to take care of you, but for me it takes time.

"I'm just an idiot who will have to take you down with everything I have!"

Once the class promotion had ended, Gary had quickly checked his stats, hoping that they would give him a boost to defeat Midwak.

Gary Dem
Grade: Bishop [2/15]
Level 27

Health 250 >>> 300
Exp 2345/38,000
Strength 41 >>> 62
Dexterity 30 >>> 45
Endurance 34 >>> 48

Gary had gained quite a few stat points from eating the Altered as well, but glancing at the notification screen, he noticed that the more Altered he ate, the fewer stat points they gave him, though it was still far better compared to eating beasts. Nevertheless, the most impressive thing was what had come with his evolution.

Class: Dark Warrior
Under the night sky, your werewolf self will receive a large boost in your Energy
Your Energy is now doubled
Energy: 300 >>> 500 (+ 500)

CHAPTER 45

A DARK STRENGTH

286/300 HP
968/1,000 Energy

Gary had already been wounded by Midwak a couple of times, but thanks to his new Endurance, which had increased after his feast of Altered, as well as the class promotion, this attack hurt him far less than the ones before. On top of that, he had been able to heal the wounds, so the bleeding wouldn't cause more damage to him on the spot.

His new class allowed his healing abilities to work faster, and now they were no slower than Midwak's.

It was a tough choice to make, but it seems to have been the right one, Gary thought.

He had chosen what he considered to be best for the current situation. From the little information the Werewolf System had decided to share, he would receive a boost depending on how righteous his actions were. Having just killed a few Altered, he hadn't been feeling very righteous, not to mention his head was filled with the desire to get revenge for Kai by killing Midwak.

Meanwhile, the system claimed that as a Dark Warrior, he would get a particular boost during nighttime. Although it wasn't too late, the sky was already dark. It also stated that it would grant him strength, which was something he was lacking against Midwak. The class promotion had increased his Energy from 300 to 500, and Gary had been more than happy to see that the current time was considered to be nighttime, so that his current Energy reserve had actually doubled to 1,000!

Midwak leapt into the air with his hardened, elongated claws. They looked like blades sticking out of his hand, and he tried to swipe them right through Gary's head. But the alpha werewolf rolled to the side and the claws sliced right through the marble flooring with ease.

Before Gary could get up, Midwak shot out the nails from his other hand toward him again. Gary swiped at them with both hands, faring better this time and blocking most of them. But then Midwak leapt in front of the teenager and threw a punch right across his face, swinging Gary's head to the side.

−16 HP
270/300 HP

Gary swung back and made a light scratch on Midwak's chest, but the omega kicked him in the stomach. To his shock, Gary saw that even Midwak's toenails could elongate, piercing his body.

−20 HP
250/300 HP

"This is fantastic!" Midwak called out. "You're a living anomaly. Never in the history of werewolves has there been an alpha this weak! Someone above must be watching out for me, granting me this golden opportunity!"

Gary pulled Midwak's foot out of his stomach, then kicked him in the jaw with his heel. Gary was sure that the blow would injure the omega, since he had put all his speed and strength into it.

"That's it, Gary! Use your fighting skills to beat him!" Innu shouted from the side.

Even though Gary was incredibly strong, even after his evolution, Midwak was still faster, and his attacks were more powerful. On top of that, his werewolf body seemed to have a few more tricks up its sleeve, allowing him to do more things.

Startled, Midwak stumbled slightly onto his back foot; Gary didn't waste this chance and went in for the strike.

Skill activated: Claw Drain (Level 2)
–30 Energy
910/1,000 Energy

Gary's fingernails grew longer, not as much as Midwak's, but certainly an improvement. They struck the werewolf from the shoulder down, digging deep into his body, making him growl. Gary felt the flesh parting under his claws. But Midwak grabbed Gary's hand and used all his might to push it away.

"You bastard!" Midwak shouted as he kicked Gary in the thigh, and again in the stomach, creating distance between the two of them.

Gary slid across the floor; he was injured but noticed that his nails were still elongated, yet the next moment they disappeared.

+15 HP
265/300 HP

After healing, his body was feeling better, but it wasn't enough to make up for the damage he had sustained.

The Claw Drain gave me more Health than it should have, and my nails were even longer, and they lasted longer. And what is this?

Claw Drain (Level 2)
Once activated, half of the damage inflicted by the user will be used to recover Health.
The skill will take 30 points of Energy to use.
Skill duration: 5 secs.

Gary briefly went over the skill, noticing that it took more Energy, but also that the duration had increased. It would have been a problem before, but not with his current pool of Energy.

Under the night sky, the Dark Warrior gets a boost in their skills.

The system said skills, not skill, which means . . .

Midwak was charging toward Gary once more with his hardened nails; they were stronger than his, but Gary was willing to risk it as he ran forward.

Skill activated: Lethal Pounce (Level 2)
–50 Energy
860/1,000 Energy

There was a sudden shift in his speed as Gary leapt to the side, away from Midwak, which confused the werewolf for a second, but as he pushed off the floor, the alpha's body slammed right into the omega.

The two large werewolves skidded across the floor, and Gary was now firmly on top of Midwak. He lifted his hands and started to throw punches. Gary wanted to inflict as much damage as he could, and he didn't use his Claw Drain skill. Unfortunately, his opponent's thick muscles made it hard for him to get through with the claws, so it was better for him to deal more damage with his fists.

Gary pounded Midwak from above, one hit after the other, and the marble floor beneath was breaking bit by bit. The entire room was shaking.

"That fucking hurts!" Midwak shouted, and he stabbed his hardened claws right into Gary's side.

–135 HP
A major wound has been inflicted
130/300 HP

The pain was so great that Gary was unable to continue his beating.

"You're so focused on getting rid of me; do you think I pose no threat?" Midwak shouted as he twisted his hand, producing more pain.

–20 HP
110/300 HP

Kicking off the floor, Gary managed to roll away while holding on to his side, but it wasn't healing as quickly as the others were, and he was sure Midwak would soon be on him again.

"Maybe in your next life, you can try and beat me," Midwak exclaimed.

Is it not enough, eating all those Altered and earning a class promotion? Just what else do I need to do to beat a real werewolf? Gary wondered.

CHAPTER 46

HOW TO FIGHT AS A DARK WOLF (PART 1)

145/300 HP

793/1,000 Energy

Gary's Health was now below half, and although he had inflicted a few wounds on Midwak, he showed no signs of slowing down or weakening. He had used a bit of Energy, healing his vital wounds as well as staying in his full werewolf form, but he still had plenty left.

What's the point of having all of this Energy, if there is no use for it? Gary angrily thought. *I thought I had chosen the best class for the current situation, but maybe the Paladin was the better choice after all.*

The one thing about the Dark Warrior Class was that it didn't focus on defense at all; it mainly focused on attack skills. With the Paladin Class he felt like he could have lasted longer, but maybe that would have given him a chance to figure things out.

What can I do with all this energy? Gary thought.

Midwak charged with his long silver claws. Gary knew he wasn't fast enough to dodge the attack, not with his side injured, but there was a way for him to force his movement.

Skill activated: Lethal Pounce (Level 2)

–50 Energy

743/1,000 Energy

His body suddenly leapt to the side, avoiding the blow. With his skill temporarily raised to the next level, Lethal Pounce consisted of two jumps, one that moved in a random direction and the next one which would actually strike. However, he would have to strike no matter what. As soon as Gary's feet touched the floor, the muscles in his body reacted and leapt toward Midwak. He crashed into his side and saw Midwak's claws at the ready.

If I'm going to hit him anyway, I might as well get some of my Health back!

Skill activated: Claw Drain (Level 2)
−30 Energy

Gary's claws dug into Midwak's side. Thanks to the speed boost, his claws managed to pierce the thick hide, yet the strike paled in comparison to the omega's previous one.

+12 HP

"Nice dodging there, but you're now within my attack range!" Midwak shouted as he grabbed both of Gary's forearms and then lifted him over his shoulders and slammed him into the ground.

−20 HP

This is what I was worried about. I avoided one hit, just to get hit with an even bigger hit. The amount I heal isn't enough to make up the difference, so I'll just lose in a direct clash!

Midwak pointed his sharp nails at Gary's throat, attempting to pierce it. Gary used both hands to stop the attack, leaving Midwak's other hand free. He tried to punch Gary's face, but Olivia's whip pulled his hand back.

With his opponent slightly distracted, Gary kicked him in the chest, freeing himself from Midwak's grasp.

That's the second time Olivia's saved me. There's no saying there will be a third. I need some way to deal with him, Gary thought as he charged in and dug his knee into Midwak's ribs. With both hands, he grabbed the black-furred werewolf's head and pulled it down, while delivering another knee into his stomach this time.

"ARGHH!" Midwak let out a pained howl and pulled back the hand that wrapped in Olivia's whip. Without Austin to help her, Olivia wasn't able to overpower the werewolf. Left with no other choice, she let go of the whip, but the momentum caused her face to hit the floor.

"You want to drag this out? It will just end in your painful death!" Midwak exclaimed as he made a fist and punched Gary in the ribs on one side and then the other.

I can feel it . . . even in my werewolf form, my ribs are breaking. If I were a human, he would have smashed all my bones by now. Shit, I don't know what to do, but I need to hold on! Gary thought as he kneed Midwak in the stomach once more.

But Midwak threw out his fist again, delivering blows into Gary's side over and over, and this time the bones were breaking with a loud crack.

"LET GO!" Midwak shouted.

43/300 HP

Gary was seriously injured, but he needed to continue, to keep doing as much damage as he could. He gritted his sharp teeth, piercing part of his bottom lip, but pulled Midwak's head down again and kneed him in the stomach.

Midwak felt his legs give a little, but ultimately he stood strong.

"Fine, if that's what you want, I'll give you a warrior's death!"

Unlike Gary's, Midwak's claws were long, and he stabbed deep into Gary's side, then pulled his claws out and stabbed him again.

14/300 HP

Because of how Gary was forcing his head down, Midwak was unable to finish him, but it didn't matter, because there were other ways to take down the werewolf in front of him.

He shoved his clawed hands forward, ready to pierce Gary, and he could tell by the alpha's eyes that there wasn't much more life in him. This would be it, one final strike that should finish him off.

Those watching by the side ran forward; they had held back so far, on Gary's orders, but watching him fight so desperately, they had to do something.

"You're too late!" Midwak smiled as his claws landed deep in Gary's stomach.

Midwak could feel with each strike that Gary's grip around his head was weakening; the brown-furred werewolf had to be running on fumes. When Midwak tried to move his head, though, Gary still had a tight grip around it.

What . . . how is he still alive? Midwak thought.

Suddenly his head was pulled down more, and once again a knee was delivered right into his stomach, just as powerfully as before, and this time Gary let go of him, allowing him to tumble down on one knee.

The others stopped, seeing that Gary was now standing and Midwak lay on the ground.

"I figured out the best way to use my new powers." Gary smiled.

Skill activated: Last Stand (Level 2)
1/300 HP

CHAPTER 47

HOW TO FIGHT AS A DARK WOLF (PART 2)

Blood dripped down Gary's sides and midsection, and his arm was still bleeding, albeit slowly healing. Comparing the two werewolves' bodies, no one would think Gary was winning this fight. In fact, ever since it began, there hadn't been a moment where it seemed as if the alpha had been winning.

Nevertheless, right now Gary was the one standing, while Midwak was down on one knee.

"I have seen many resilient werewolves, but you . . . you're like a freaking zombie!" Midwak shouted in annoyance as he jumped up and tried to strike Gary in the head. But Gary lifted both of his arms to parry the blow, defending his head, while kicking Midwak in the stomach again.

With Last Stand at Level 2, I have 1 minute 30 seconds to turn the tide; I'll have to make the most of it! Gary thought.

Gary charged in, ignoring Midwak's counterattack as the omega swung his arm toward Gary's bad side once more. The alpha swung his fist in an uppercut. Although Midwak's blow landed, barely any more blood gushed out, not because it was a weak strike, but because Gary's body seemed to have already lost most of it.

Unfortunately, Last Stand didn't grant him invincibility, meaning Gary could and did feel all the pain he was suffering. Still, he trusted in the skill, so he focused everything into delivering a large blow to his opponent's stomach, lifting him in the air.

"How? How are you still standing?" Midwak appeared to be losing his cool, swiping at Gary again and again. Gary turtled up, focusing on blocking the strikes to his head, pinning his elbows close to his chest. He wasn't keen on testing the limits of his temporary immortality. System or not, he couldn't imagine he would survive if his heart or brain got injured, so he would protect them for now.

Then, there was a break, a slight gap, when Midwak needed to catch his breath. Moving in again, this time swinging his hand out from the side like a hook, Gary slammed the omega in the stomach once more.

However, his side was badly hurt, and Gary was unable to deliver another blow.

"What is he doing?" Ian asked. "How is Gary still alive, and why is he just hitting the stomach all the time?"

Everyone watching thought it was strange as well. There were few chances for Gary to attack in this fight. Midwak was able to hit Gary almost four times as much, so when Gary did get a hit, why wouldn't he go for a vital strike?

"He's slowing him down," Innu said. "Strikes to the stomach eat at your stamina, mess up your breathing, and slow you down. Gary noticed that Midwak in general is faster than him, but . . . I don't know what his plan is. If he continues like this, then he's going to die!"

The others thought the same; what crazy plan was Gary trying to come up with? Right now, the teenager was suffering from the fact that Last Stand did nothing to stop his accumulated damage; he still felt all the pain, and his injuries still needed more time to heal, something he sorely lacked.

He was struggling just to stand from the blows on his body, but he bore through it, throwing another punch, aiming at the same spot again. It was as powerful as the others, causing Midwak to spit out blood.

This damn alpha, he is resilient, and each of his strikes have the same amount of power!

"You can't win like this! Spare yourself the trouble, since we both know it's only a matter of time!" Midwak growled, not looking too good now after the repeated hits in the stomach, but Gary looked ten times worse.

30 seconds remaining

This is it, it's now or never! Gary thought, jumping back, but only slightly, as he kept focus on Midwak.

"This is payback . . . for Kai. You should have never touched one of my people," Gary shouted, his hands nearly dangling on the floor. Midwak took a step forward, but the next second Gary was gone from his sight.

Skill activated: Lethal Pounce (Level 2)
–50 Energy
Skill activated: Claw Drain (Level 2)
–30 Energy

Jumping out from the side, Gary slashed Midwak's shoulders, cutting deep, then landed in front of him. Midwak tried to rise and attack Gary from above, but he disappeared again.

Skill activated: Lethal Pounce (Level 2)
–50 Energy

Gary reappeared at Midwak's side and slashed at his back four more times. Midwak desperately swung his arm behind him but hit nothing but air.

Skill activated: Lethal Pounce (Level 2)
–50 Energy
Skill activated: Claw Drain (Level 2)
–30 Energy

Two claws stabbed Midwak in the stomach; Gary pulled them out and stabbed him twice more. Midwak tried to bite him but missed. From the right, a claw snatched his face; the nails caught the inside of Midwak's mouth and split it apart. Gary was using the Lethal Pounce skill to avoid and strike, and each time the Claw Drain skill ran out, he renewed it.

The others saw Gary moving at a crazy speed, leaping from one place to the other, attacking Midwak, inflicting large cuts all over his body, while Midwak looked like a lost werewolf hitting nothing but air.

A fist coming in from the left hit Midwak in the side of the face, sending him crashing to the floor.

Gary finally stopped moving and stood in front of him. Looking up from the ground, Midwak was confused, because Gary looked better than he had before.

182/300 HP
243/1,000 Energy
Last Stand has come to an end

"You told me I would need multiple lives to beat you, didn't you?" Gary walked up to Midwak, who was now badly injured from the repeated wounds. He got up off the floor, but his stomach was in incredible pain.

His only answer came in the form of a fist, which wasn't even a claw anymore, but Gary knocked it away, punching Midwak in the nose. The alpha then threw out another fist, hitting him again in the face.

Before Midwak could fall down, Gary grabbed his head, using his hands to close his mouth, and pulled it forward.

"Don't mess with my fucking gang!" Gary shouted as he threw his fist as hard as he could, hitting Midwak clean on the side of the mouth, shattering his teeth, and his whole body collapsed to the floor.

With that hit, his body was now shrinking, turning back into its human form. Midwak was spent; he was out of energy and he knew his body could no longer put up a fight, but he finally realized something.

"Now I see . . . your sudden boost in strength, being able to fight like that. In my former pack they called ones like you Dark Warriors or Night Warriors, though there was an even better name . . . Red-Eyed Hunters."

CHAPTER 48

WHAT TO DO?

The others blinked, letting out several deep breaths, because they could tell that the fight was over, but it was hard to believe. Every step of the way, every second during the fight, they felt like their leader could have come to an end.

"Gary really won the fight against that monster," Ian said out loud.

"Honestly, Gary is pretty amazing, I . . . don't even understand what happened. How was his body able to heal at that speed? It was like he got a second wind," Numba said.

The Howlers, although surprised, didn't have too many questions, because they knew that Gary wasn't an Altered but this mystical thing called a werewolf and they understood very little when it came to the subject.

"That's just how our boss is," Innu said, watching Gary's body start to shrink. Gary was reverting to his human form as well, conserving his energy, but he still had enough to turn back into a werewolf if need be. "He seems to always get the job done somehow."

With the fight seemingly over, they wondered what was Gary going to do to Midwak. The AFA students, no longer needing to fight, were looking around and taking in the scene in front of them.

They felt sick as they saw the dead bodies, ripped apart and ruined. They had realized during the fight that Gary's Altered form was similar to Midwak's, and there was no question that this was all Midwak's doing.

Is Gary going to kill him? Izzy thought. *He has to, right? It's not like the police can just lock someone like that up, and leaving him alive means risking that he might come back for revenge.*

While everyone worried about what Gary was going to do next, Olivia ran over to the boy who lay on the floor. The axe that had been in Austin's chest had fallen out at some point, and she could see there was no wound there.

"Hey, are you asleep?" Olivia asked in an annoyed voice. "Answer me."

Austin opened his eyes. "I'm awake . . . I saw Gary kick that guy's ass, so I thought I deserved a little rest."

If a regular Altered's chest had been pierced by that axe, they would have been done for, but Austin's Mystical Altered self was far more resilient than the others had given him credit for.

"Midwak, is it?" Gary said as he walked over to the werewolf on the ground. "You wanted to kill me and take over my pack."

Gary knelt down and placed his hand around the other's throat, gripping tightly.

"You hurt one of my gang members, you put him on display to get my attention, to bring me here, right? Well, you did a great job. I'm here now, and I'm going to make you pay for everything you put me and my group through."

While holding Midwak's head up by the neck with one hand, Gary transformed his other hand, the nails elongated. With one thrust, he would end Midwak's life, and put an end to this entire mess involving the Scatterbugs.

"Gary, wait!" a voice shouted from the doorway, echoing in the room, and as everyone turned around their eyes lit up.

"Kai!" Marie called out. "What are you doing here? Shouldn't you be in the hospital?"

"I'm fine," Kai replied, as he hurried to Gary's side. Gary waited, until the three werewolves were looking at each other.

"Gary, you exceeded my expectations," Kai said, praising their leader. "I trusted that you would do a good job, but I was sure you would need extra help. I even asked Harry Cardenez to lend me a chopper, all in an attempt to make it in time to assist you.

"Well, so much for arriving like a hero and have you owe me one. What's more, since you did all of this on my behalf, I guess I'm the one who owes you one."

Gary loosened his grip around Midwak's neck as he saw that Kai was up and moving and even joking around. Still, the green-haired teenager noticed that Kai seemed to have some difficulty speaking; his jaw just wasn't the same as it was before. He wasn't even wearing a mask because he had been in such a rush, making the large scar on the bottom of his entire mouth visible for all to see.

"Gary," Kai said, placing his hand on his shoulder. "As the one who suffered the most from what that piece of shit did, I know more than anyone that he shouldn't be forgiven . . . but I think it's in our best interest to keep him alive."

Listening to this, the others were left with their mouths wide open. How could they let Midwak live? He was more dangerous than the rest of the Scatterbugs combined, and based on his personality he would surely come back and attempt revenge.

"The Scatterbugs are a large gang, and with nobody else around, he's the only one who can take over," Kai explained. "If we send our people, it will just end up as a large-scale war. There will be those who won't be willing to listen to us, and even if we subdue the Scatterbugs, there'll be countless infighting.

"But if Midwak joins us and is part of the Howlers controlling the Scatterbugs for us, just like Olivia has done with the Pincers, there will be less pushback, and if anything, Midwak is strong enough to deal with any problems that might arise by himself."

Kai did have a solid point, but Gary had never considered the possibility of taking over the gang. Admittedly, his plan had only involved getting there and dealing with the werewolf somehow. Still, now that Kai had mentioned it, the omega was the only one left from the Scatterbugs' higher-ups. He was the only one who knew the establishments and the relationships with the people and more.

Taking over a Tier 2 city was impossible for a Tier 3 gang for more reasons than just a general lack of strength.

"As if I would comply!" Midwak laughed.

Gary was surprised at his reaction. Not that he was particularly interested in sparing him, but with Kai, his primary victim, being the one to vouch for him, to still resist the opportunity to save his own hide . . .

"Aside from the gang aspect, there is another reason to keep him alive. He is like us, but unlike us he knows far more about what it means to live like this. We have no idea when we might stumble upon someone like him in the future, but that information might be crucial in learning how to deal with others. Next time, we might not be as lucky."

Gary had also considered that, and it was the major reason why he hadn't killed the werewolf outright. His Werewolf System, as useful as it was, unfortunately kept most things secret from him, but Midwak had admitted to knowing things about his evolution and more. The chance to question a real werewolf was invaluable for them, especially since they had no idea how many were out there.

"As an omega, he doesn't belong to any pack, so why not invite him to ours? With the rules, we can ensure he won't do anything stupid," Kai further coaxed Gary.

Hearing this, Midwak broke out in laughter, sounding like a madman. The action was clearly hurting his throat, but he showed no signs of stopping.

"You pups really are cute, but let me be the bearer of bad news!" Midwak crowed amid his laugh. "Your alpha here may have defeated me, but he's not strong enough to force me to join your pack!"

CHAPTER 49

A QUEST COMPLETE

Kai knew quite a bit about werewolves from his own research and from what Gary had told him, but he didn't know that werewolves themselves were a lot more complicated than what could be read in books.

A lot of what the system had informed Gary about, with the chesslike ranking system and the pack rules that could be changed, was hard to explain. There were times when Gary thought these things were unique to him, but judging by Midwak's reaction, that wasn't the case at all.

The rules of Werewolves seemed to be more widespread than he believed, because it was clear that Midwak knew why Gary was unable to invite him into his pack.

"I'm a Bishop, while Midwak is classified as a Rook. According to the system, an alpha is unable to force those who are a higher grade than them into the pack. If that's the case, even if I changed the pack rules to make it so Midwak would be uncontrollable, it would be impossible."

The pack rules, and the fact that the others listened to the alpha in the first place, and even the change into an alpha, all seemed quite magical, but that was not important now.

Gary raised his hand, transforming it into its werewolf form.

"Is this really the only way?" Kai asked. He was upset because Midwak was a huge asset to them. There was so much information, and not only that, but so much they could do with the Tier 2 city. Without Midwak, they would have to give up on Notsburg for now, and it would perhaps be taken over by another city. They just didn't have the strength or personnel to control a Tier 2 city at the moment, not at the level they needed.

Gary had made his choice. His clawed hand turned into a fist, and tensing his feet, he launched a blow right at Midwak's head, hitting him square in the temple.

It was a strong blow that would have cracked most people's skulls, and in this case they weren't so sure he hadn't. Midwak's eyes rolled into the back of his head as he collapsed on the floor.

"Is he dead?" Kai asked.

"No . . . there is one more thing we can try," Gary said.

With that hit, just as expected, there was a ding sound coming from his system.

You have defeated the leader of the Scatterbugs. (The new temporary leader, at least)
It seems you are growing, and your werewolf pack needs to grow with you!
20 Pawn points have been awarded

"Twenty Pawn points!" Gary couldn't quite believe the number, but in the past whenever he did things that required him to act the ugliest in the whole gang, or at least everyone in the pack, he had received a large number of points.

Originally he used the Pawn points in exchange for stat points, making himself stronger, which had been the goal so far, but now he was in a situation where his rank mattered, and it was what he was banking on.

Now he had enough points to evolve to the next rank, and possibly change it so the others were higher as well.

Additional Quest reward!
You have defeated a werewolf of a higher rank
Your grade will now evolve from Bishop >>> Rook

Gary felt a slight tingling sensation all over his body for a second; it felt like ants were rushing up his blood vessels on the inside, but it quickly disappeared.

Wait a second, did I just go up a grade as well? Without having to use any of my Pawn points?

When he looked at the system, this seemed to be the case, as he still had 20 Pawn points available.

2/50 Pawn points needed to go up to the next Grade
20 Pawn points available

The leap in Pawn points I need to go to the next grade is high, but there should only be two more grades, Queen and then King. Although this type of situation, where there are high-ranking omegas, would hardly occur again.

Gary walked over to the fallen Midwak, who was starting to get up, still in a slight daze, and the screen popped up in front of Gary.

Because you have defeated the omega wolf, you may now decide its fate:
1: Kill the stray omega wolf.
2: Invite the omega wolf into your pack.

"Do you think I have no will?" Midwak said as he rubbed the side of his head. "You think you can control me?"

You have chosen to invite the omega wolf into your pack.

At that moment, Gary's eyes were glowing red, a bright red that stared deep into the omega's eyes, and although Midwak was trying his best to put up a fight, he was unable to look away; his muscles were tensed up in his neck, but he could do nothing as his eyes changed from yellow to blue color.

The werewolf Midwak has joined your pack.

"Change the pack rules!" Gary said out loud, so the other werewolves around could hear.

"The werewolf Midwak is unable to attack members of the Howlers Gang and those who are under our umbrella.

"The werewolf Midwak must follow the orders of all core members of the Howlers when asked.

"The werewolf Midwak is unable to kill unless he feels that his life is threatened.

"The werewolf Midwak is unable to bite and turn others!

"The werewolf Midwak cannot leave the city of Notsburg without the permission of the core members of the Howlers!"

With that, all of the original rules that had been created for the werewolves had been removed, and all of the new rules were used to restrain Midwak in every way possible. The rules had originally been put in place to restrain Olivia.

Gary trusted Kai, but Olivia had been more loyal than perhaps even she realized. She had started to care for those around them and had saved members of the Howlers multiple times. Even now, she was by Austin's side.

At the same time, not once had she tried to fight for the alpha position.

"These rules, you're trying to keep me as a prisoner!" Midwak screamed at the top of his lungs, showing his displeasure. "You think you're smart by doing this; well, you're a fool! You think I don't know what you are?

"The second I've recovered, and it's daylight, I'll challenge you for the alpha position and take it right from under your nose. You've just made my job a lot easier by trying to keep me by your side!"

It was true; Gary would have to fight Midwak all over again, and Midwak was the type of person who would fight him every month without fail.

Gary had been worried about this, but with his twenty Pawn points, he was sure that he could make himself quite a bit stronger. But part of the reason Gary had been able to beat Midwak was everyone else fighting him beforehand, and the night sky not only gave him more energy but allowed his skills to reach a new level.

"Do you think you can?" Kai asked. "We won't just let you attack our leader like that. You might be able to beat us individually, but all of us can stop you."

"Yeah!" Izzy shouted. "And do you think you can just waltz in to challenge Gary while he's in the AFA? You're strong, you stupid wolf, but I would like to see you try to take on everyone at the academy."

Izzy, listening in on everything, was getting a grasp on the situation and, frustrated by the taunts, she had to say something.

"But it doesn't have to be that way," Kai said. "There is a reason why you did all of this, right? A reason why you tried to take over the Scatterbugs. You didn't care about the Cardenez company, that was all your old boss's doing.

"Maybe we can scratch each other's backs in this situation," Kai suggested.

CHAPTER 50

A WHOLE NEW WORLD

A lot of work needed to be done in the casino, and the first call of action was to make everyone aware that the leader of the Scatterbugs was no more. It was fairly easy to do, especially since the Cardenez group, along with the Freaks, had already dealt with most of those inside the casino.

Some Howlers went downstairs and made the announcement, showing as proof the rings that Slith had worn on his hands.

This had disheartened the people, but even more so, the news would spread out to the entire city. It would take a while, though, as there was no easy way for the customers or the gang members to leave the casino.

There were a few emergency boats that could be used to transfer the customers back to the mainland, and for now, the Cardenez group were helping with that, as ordered by the Howlers.

Kai knew there was a lot of work to be done, and it needed to be done quickly. There were multiple problems with what was going to happen. How would the remaining Scatterbug members react if any of the enemies they had made took action? The longer everything took, the greater the chance of disturbances.

While Kai was busy searching the entire casino, Gary and Innu were looking Midwak over. They had brought him to a VIP gambling room away from the main area that had a poker table in the middle.

Midwak wasn't tied up or anything, but they had made sure not to give him any food. Having been beaten so badly, he was out of energy, and a werewolf needed to eat.

Keeping him in this state was the safest thing to do, and it would be dark for quite a bit more. The AFA students were helping Harry Cardenez's group, but Harry himself was with Kai, as they both had raided the offices along with Olivia, finding all of the paperwork they needed.

"Really, what is the point of keeping this stuff in a safe? Any Altered could slash through these things anyway," Gary said to himself as he pulled out the paperwork while his hand started to transform back into human form.

They were searching for all the deeds, the company files, and more. All of it was in Slith's name, which was problematic. In Olivia's situation they had forced her to sign everything over, but in this case, Slith was dead.

"I can take care of it," Harry commented. "I have some talented people. There will be quite a big price to pay, but I will take care of it all. After all, you and your gang have done more than enough. You have protected my family members and my entire business. I never dreamed that this would be the outcome."

For a moment, Kai breathed a sigh of relief, because he had someone he could rely on. So far in the journey of the Howlers he had been doing most of the work. He had Olivia, who was well versed in business, and his own knowledge from when he worked under his father.

For the first time, he had someone he could fully trust to do things.

"It was a good decision going fifty/fifty on that deal. It looks like we have a great partner for now and in the future."

Now they only had one big problem left, and the outcome would determine how easy it would be for them to take control over Notsburg.

Eventually, all of the Howlers had entered the private gambling room where Midwak was being kept. Harry and the others were still busy dealing with the gang members and finding someone who could sort out the documents for them.

When they entered the room, they still felt a heavy presence as Midwak sat in the chair. They couldn't believe that he had been beaten; he had no shirt on and was clearly out of energy, but his eyes remained defiant. They always looked like he was ready for a fight.

"You must be getting pretty hungry, right?" Kai asked as he sat down. "We know more than anyone that a werewolf's hunger is an unbearable pain, and I'm sure as soon as you get your energy back, you no doubt will try to take us all on."

Midwak chuckled hearing this.

"Do you think I'm an idiot? If I tried to fight him now, while it's dark outside, he would have the advantage. You really know nothing about werewolves, do you? I can't believe I was beaten by such an amateurish pack!"

Gary hadn't told the others about his evolution, so it was safe to say they were confused; he was surprised as this wasn't the first time Midwak had made such comments, and now it was clear that he knew what Gary was.

"You're right," Gary said. "We know nothing about werewolves, but right now, you are in my pack. We are in this together, and it's quite clear that without information from you, we might all end up dead.

"You want to live, don't you? There is a reason you want to live, a reason why you fought so hard and wanted to take the alpha position. Now that you're in my pack, I want you to answer some questions for us.

"For the sake of your survival and your own goals . . . who are you? Why are you an omega wolf, how many werewolves are out there, and what do we need to look out for?" Gary asked.

He didn't realize it, but this set of events would open up a whole new world that Gary never even knew existed.

CHAPTER 51

A DIFFERENT WORLD

The Howlers were all waiting for Midwak to answer, as they were quite interested in Gary's past. Why was he a werewolf? Where did they even come from? Although the teenager had confided in them, he too lacked the answers to many questions about his new being. He knew he wasn't fully human anymore, but neither was he truly an Altered or a beast.

They weren't even sure if Midwak would answer their questions. He had no reason to help Gary, so Kai had offered him something to eat, sure that this was something the omega werewolf would desperately crave.

They had chopped up the body of one of those who had died during the initial ambush. They weren't about to risk him regaining too much Energy, so they used a human, rather than one of the Altered. None of them wanted to disrespect the dead further, but Kai justified these actions by choosing to believe that it was more important to care about his living friends.

"Do you think food would really tempt me?" Midwak asked with saliva dribbling from his lower lip.

If Midwak wasn't going to talk, then Gary might have to change the rules, but the first rule stated that Midwak would have to follow the orders of the Howlers, and something was compelling him to speak.

"First, you are all idiots!" Midwak declared, his eyes darting toward the bag with the meat. "If you really knew anything about the world and what really goes on behind the scenes, then you would have continued to stay low, but now your gang has taken over a Tier 2 city.

"It's not every day something like this happens, and take a wild guess how often a Tier 3 gang manages to pull off such a stunt. All eyes will be on you soon enough; you'll be investigated because everyone will want to stay cautious around the Howlers."

Although this was all true, Gary didn't regret his decision for even a second. The elated look on Numba's face and the satisfied look on Kai's when they had seen Midwak defeated seemed well worth it.

"What's done is done," Gary said. "We'll have to move forward and deal with things as they come up."

Midwak let out a big sigh. It was unbelievable to him that he had lost to the people surrounding him. The fact that they were utterly clueless about how deep in trouble they were only infuriated him further. In a way, giving them a little bit of information would make him look less bad.

"Argh, it's so frustrating dealing with idiots who don't even under-stand how fucked they are." Midwak cursed. "First off, what happened to me is none of your business, and it won't help you in any way, so the short version of my story is that I'm a werewolf who used to run with a different pack.

"I've never cared too much about our history, so while I can't tell you exactly how old it is, it's been around for ages, might have even been around since the first werewolves. I don't know about today, but while I was a member, it was *much* larger than your sorry excuse for a pack. One day I was kic—I left the pack, because of some disagree-ments, and eventually ended up meeting Slith, who gave me a spot with his Scatterbugs. I stayed by his side because he had a knack for making money, as well as for gathering strong people.

"Even though at any point I could have taken him out and taken over the gang, I didn't because I'm not a fool. He was the perfect smoke-screen, helping me avoid any unnecessary attention to myself. I know that the moment I turn up on their radar, they will send someone to take me out. Well, things changed with your leader's existence.

"It's been . . . heck, I don't even know how long it's been since there were two alphas. I've only heard about such a thing from some old sto-ries. I guess I should have known that you would amount to nothing more than an anomaly. After all, who would be dumb enough to turn you into an alpha, of all people?"

Gary was trying to hold in his anger, because every time Midwak talked, he did so in such a way as to continuously insult them.

"To sum it up, you got kicked out of your pack, which is much bigger than ours, and now we have a problem in that the other alpha will not like Gary's existence?" Kai repeated, earning himself a nasty glare from Midwak by using the phrase *kicked out*. "Where are they, what are they doing, and roughly how many werewolves are there? Do you have any idea how and why Gary became an alpha in the first place?"

Midwak shrugged. "How am I supposed to know? I just told you that I did all I could to avoid their attention, so I sure as hell didn't do any investigations into them. From what I know, alphas are either created when they take over the position or naturally selected, but there is a tale that is told to all werewolves: 'There can never be two alphas that coexist.'

"There's a reason why I only heard about two Alphas from old stories; whenever there have been two packs, they would all eventually clash with each other one way or another. If I became an alpha, the first thing I would do is turn as many people as possible. A werewolf grows in strength from turning others, and having a large pack is a big plus for any alpha. It's really a travesty, him having this wondrous power, and what did he do with it? There's a grand total of three of you little whelps!" Midwak laughed as he finished.

Gary could guess why an alpha would get stronger. He remembered from the system that he received a Pawn point for every werewolf that he turned. And for all of those that they beat, who were killed while he was around them, he would get additional Exp as well.

"Does this mean that the werewolves will come after us, the second they're sure of our existence?" Innu asked.

"After you? Please, how egocentric can you be?" Midwak waved his hand. "You're neither a werewolf nor an Altered. Even if you have beaten a Tier 2 gang, at best you've evolved from maggots into flies in their eyes. The only reason to pay any attention to you in particular would be because of your axes, so congratulations, you've moved up from fly to rodent."

"Is that because they are one of the Kings?" Kai asked, as he had somewhat figured it out already.

"Thank the heavens there is at least one smart person among you." Midwak smiled. "See, I knew it was a good thing keeping you alive, I really liked you. I nearly feel a smidgen of guilt now for what I did to you back there. Are you sure you don't want to work with me and betray your green-haired friend to become the boss?"

There was a stern look from everyone in the room when he posed his suggestions. If Midwak was sure about one thing, it was that these "idiots" were as dumb as they were loyal to Gary.

"You're right, the werewolves are one of the untouchable Kings, meaning neither the gangs, the government, the AFA, NIRV, nor the Altered Hunters can do anything to them. The Kings are above all of these, and none of those organizations can touch you.

"And let me tell you something else: you would be an idiot to think that they don't already know about you. Trust me, the only reason why they have yet to pay you a visit must be because they have their own troubles keeping them occupied."

Gary was confused. Midwak had just stated that the werewolves were above all of those organizations he had mentioned. Only another King could really compete with them in terms of power and influence, so what troubles would they have?

"You just told us how scary these werewolves are, so what troubles would they have?" Olivia asked the question Gary was thinking.

It looked like Midwak wanted to bang his head on the table, but he restrained himself as he looked straight at Gary dead in the eye.

"You're a Dark Warrior, correct?"

The others were now losing track of the conversation, but Gary knew the name well, as he had recently learned about it.

"You are quite the lucky one," Midwak continued. "Given what you are, they probably won't outright kill you; you might prove far more useful to them alive. Think about it; werewolves who have lived for a long time essentially have no equal. You might be a pup, but I bet you've felt it already, given our speed of growth; not even the top Altered stand a chance compared to our elites.

"So what would give them troubles in this world, and why would you, a Dark Warrior, be given the nickname of the Red-Eyed Hunter?"

Red eyes? Gary thought. "Omega wolves have yellow eyes, beta wolves blue, and red eyes are the alphas . . . so am I an alpha hunter?"

In that room, only one person had somewhat figured it out, but the mere possibility of his answer being true sent shivers down his spine.

CHAPTER 52

RED-EYED HUNTER

After Gary had turned Kai into a werewolf, the blond teenager had spent his limited free time doing extensive research on the type of creature he had become. Unfortunately, given that barely any people believed in their existence, his main source of information had been old myths and legends.

He had to admit that most of them were unreliable about the truth of the matter. For example, he had felt nothing upon touching silver. After exhausting the sources he could find, Kai had started to read the only other type of media that discussed werewolves . . . fantasy novels.

With those Kai had the opposite problem; there were far more than he could read in his lifetime, though he had encountered some useful pieces of information. He wasn't sure if any of the authors had ever met a werewolf, or if those cases had just been lucky coincidences.

In any case, one of the similarities most of those fantasy novels shared was that one type of creature was often described as a sort of natural enemy of the werewolf: the vampire. Even more fitting, one of their characteristics were their red eyes.

"Are you telling us that vampires are real?" Kai asked Midwak, who merely smiled at the correct conclusion. While the others had trouble coming to terms with this, the trio of werewolves had only various levels of shock. Given their own existence that defied common sense, was it so hard to believe that there were other things out there?

"The Dark Warrior is a type of werewolf that is stronger under the night sky," Midwak explained. "One of the biggest advantages we have over those bloodsuckers is the fact that we have no problem with broad daylight. Well, there might be some exceptions, but that doesn't matter right now.

"There are too many theories about how it all started, but suffice it to say that we and they have a blood feud going on that won't end until one side is exterminated. Since most of the fights happen at night because of their condition, you're a werewolf that is greatly sought after."

From Midwak's explanation, Kai understood how important Dark Warriors were for the werewolves. Although packs were separated from each other almost like different families, they had a common enemy, and for now they were leaving Gary, not because they knew what he was, but because they had bigger problems.

"I can't believe it . . . are they really out there? Is it true what they say about them sucking blood and that they can turn you into one of them if they do?" Marie asked, feeling her skin crawl as she imagined a large set of teeth sinking into her neck, but the face of a pale-skinned beauty also entered her mind.

"Maybe it's not too bad to be bitten," Marie mumbled to herself, and shook her head as she snapped out of it. "How's it possible for them to exist with nobody knowing it?"

Midwak looked toward Marie first and licked his lips as if she were a delicious snack, but under the table Gary kicked his shin hard. The omega reacted by trying to bare his teeth and transform, but it didn't work, as he didn't have any energy to keep up the transformation.

"What are you so surprised about? You didn't know about Werewolves for most of your life, but now you do. Just because you have never seen them before doesn't mean they don't exist." Midwak snorted.

"Are they one of the Kings?" Kai asked.

Midwak answered by shaking his head. "Unlike us, they can't pass as Altered, so it would be hard for them to fit among the Kings. Besides, from what I know about them, they seem to be a secretive bunch. That being said, they still have managed to infiltrate most parts of society with none of you even suspecting anything.

"Gang members, police, politicians, CEOs, there's no way to know for sure. The vampires . . . are idiots. Despite their ability to easily take over everything, for some reason they choose to do nothing. It's hard to understand them."

The group had already learned a lot from Midwak, and they continued their questioning, including which of the Kings was the leader that they needed to look out for.

After that, it was time to discuss what would happen with Notsburg and Midwak. The Scatterbugs would officially become part of the Howlers, and the one who would lead this separate division would naturally be the omega.

If anyone opposed that decision or if any disputes happened in the meantime, he would deal with them. Kai's prediction was that after Midwak defeated those who defied the new order a couple of times, things would calm down.

After all, unlike Olivia's business, the gambling establishments would remain open as they were. The gang members would continue to get paid, so for them the biggest change would be the person on the other end of the checkbook.

"There, you've learned more than enough, now let me eat!" Midwak demanded as he sniffed the air.

"Not yet." Gary stood up. "I want you to challenge me right now. I already know that those in the pack can only challenge the alpha once a month."

"If you know, then why would I challenge you now?" Midwak asked, his eyes asking the teenager if he was stupid.

"You're free not to, but then forget about the food. As you said, we've learned more than enough, and I don't particularly care whether you die or not. You tried killing all my friends," Gary answered, staring at him with red eyes. "I understand that you could be a powerful asset, but if you don't want to cooperate, then we'll find a way to survive even without you.

"The way I see it, you need us far more than we need you. After all, we're your best chance to actually get revenge on the alpha who did this to you, right? You can't do that dead, so there's one good reason for you to agree to fight me now.

"I'll let you challenge me once a month whenever you want. You only need to beat me once for the position to be yours, then you'll be free to do whatever you want with the pack and the gang."

The others looked at each other in shock. They couldn't imagine a gang without Gary. They thought he must have had a ploy to stop the monthly challenges, but hearing him now, he didn't.

"Don't get me wrong, I'm not just going to let you beat me. I plan to beat you every month, proving to you why I deserve this position. From what you said before, the other alpha will eventually come for us, so if I can't even beat the likes of you, then the pack would be better in your hands anyway.

"Think about it," Kai chimed in. "You have nothing to gain by refusing Gary, but if you stay in our pack, you'll eventually have the opportunity to fight against your former pack."

Midwak started to contemplate. The young alpha had barely defeated him, and they all knew that the omega's downfall was a team effort. The real question was how quickly would Gary be able to grow in the span of one month. Would it be enough to beat him again? Even if it was, as long as they continued to fight, Midwak was sure he would be able to beat him eventually.

I've worked under Slith for years, what's a few more months under this twerp, Midwak eventually concluded.

"Fine!" he shouted as the pain in his stomach was becoming unbearable. "I challenge the leader for the position of alpha!"

A ding was heard from Gary's system, but just as quickly the message disappeared.

"I admit defeat." Midwak ground his teeth, as those words were a little hard for him to say.

Kai looked at the two werewolves, thoughts swirling around in his head.

I know what we're doing is dangerous, having someone trying to stab us in the back at all times, but Midwak essentially wants to take over the pack, so he has a shared interest in helping us get stronger.

The only thing is, Gary needs to make sure he keeps getting stronger, so he keeps on top of Midwak, but maybe this is a good thing and will skyrocket his growth. You have already grown at an incredible pace,

Gary, but now I have to ask you to continue to do so. I wonder just how much stronger you'll get, Kai thought.

With the "fight" over, Midwak finally received his food.

It didn't take long for others to learn about the amazing feat the Howlers had accomplished.

CHAPTER 53

REACTION TO THE HOWLERS

A change in leadership of such magnitude was naturally impossible to keep under wraps. Information was being passed around among the local gangs, who continued to spread the tale far and wide.

Over the span of a couple of days, everyone in the underworld was aware that the Howlers had taken over the Scatterbugs. A Tier 3 gang from practically a no-name town had managed to expand into a Tier 2 city in under a day. Such a thing was thought to be impossible, and were it not for all sources reporting the same, it would be even more unbelievable given that the Scatterbugs' strength and influence had been rumored to be on par with some of the Tier 1 gangs.

Given that it was impossible to hide the truth for long, Kai had expected some faction to challenge them, yet not a single one, not even from a Tier 1 city, had come forward. Rather, from what Kai had gathered through his information channels, the price for any type of information about the Howlers had become a hot commodity.

The news had spread out into all corners of the world, with each person reacting to it slightly differently. In the town of Slough itself, some people were beyond surprised at what happened.

"How is this possible?" Ben Clove tensed his fist and lifted it up in the air. Moments before he slammed it down on his desk, he managed to stop himself. The mayor had been forced to replace his desk far too often in recent times.

"When the hell did they manage to grow so strong? It feels like yesterday they barely had the power to manage to take a piece of Slough, and now they're expanding into Tier 2 cities. This has to be some sort of sick joke. Their group isn't even that large to begin with."

The more Ben thought about it, the more he was kicking himself. He started to really miss the days when his only worries had been the Underdogs and the Gray Elephants.

"With the income from Notsburg's casinos, they will have no problem funding a campaign for a candidate of their own choosing. If they do so, it won't be too hard to replace me with one of their own. I'm not even sure if Jayden can do anything to stop them now."

Nevertheless, Ben Clove didn't want to admit defeat, not yet at least. He felt like Slough had practically been in his grasp, and he was unwilling to give it up. Fortunately, there was still some time before the next election, so until then, he just had to bide his time. After their expansion, he was sure that soon enough someone would appear to take care of the Howlers. They might be able to defend themselves, but as long as they were busy, it meant they wouldn't focus on him . . .

Similarly, another Clove had learned about what had occurred in Notsburg.

"Holy crap!" Jayden exclaimed as he was resting in a dressing room, checking on the latest news involving the Howlers. He was in the middle of a photoshoot for a new skincare product; his white skin that was almost illuminated was always perfect for advertising products, as well as his fame.

I always knew you were crazy, Gary, but I appear to have severely underestimated you. Next time I see you, I'll have to ask what made you pull such a stunt? Just what could have happened to make you choose this path? When I told you to come and reach me, I expected you to do so through the AFA ranks, not by going down such a dangerous road that might turn you into the enemy of all the Kings.

Still, I'm sure you have your reasons for doing so. Perhaps our lives will intertwine more, sooner than I thought.

Others were keeping an eye on Gary, and he wasn't even aware of it.

At the AFA, Professor Humfree sat at his desk, stroking his beard.

It can't be a mere coincidence that this has occurred during his leave of absence. We've all acknowledged his potential, but his growth keeps exceeding our expectations. I wonder what he will choose to do next. Given his power, it's only a matter of time until he graduates, and he might very well change the lives of those he is close with in the academy itself.

In the academy, it wasn't only the professors who were keeping an eye on Gary. Apollo was sitting with his two close friends Snow and Wu.

"Has your father told you to do anything?" Snow asked.

"Ha!" Apollo laughed. "You've met my dad. Did he strike you as the type who would tell me to make friends with him? I've always known there was something special about him, and now he's proven me right once more.

"Based on how Sty and his father were, something like this was bound to happen sooner or later. The only surprising thing is that it was the Howlers who acted, whereas we were the bait that would be taken by another King. After finding someone as great as him, I should have guessed that there would be others just as great.

"Anyway, all this means is, if me and him don't end up clashing in the academy or in the AFC, then we will do so outside it."

Apollo was without a doubt looking forward to Gary's return.

In a city where the sun shone the brightest by the seaside, Sin the well-known King was standing on his balcony looking out from his villa. His enjoyment of the scenery was interrupted when a couple of men wearing dark red clothing entered the room.

It was the uniform of the Phoenix gang.

"Sir, we have brought in the two people that you have asked us to deliver."

Two more people entered the room; one looked to be in his midtwenties, while the other was clearly a teenager. They immediately got down on their knees and placed their heads down.

"Excellent," Sin said as he turned around and walked toward the two of them. Neither of them looked special, but he had called them here for a specific reason.

"The two of you haven't been in our group for too long, but from what I hear, you have proven yourselves useful to us, so I would like to thank you for that," Sin stated with a smile.

The two people on their knees weren't so sure, but it felt like the floor was getting a little hotter, and it felt like it was coming from Sin himself.

"As long as you keep up the good work and show your loyalty to the gang, your treatment will reflect your standing. All right, enough of that, I have called you for a different reason. The two of you come from the town of Slough, and I happen to have an interest in it. What can you tell me about the Howlers?" Sin asked the kneeling Raven and Gil.

CHAPTER 54

FINISHING WHAT I STARTED

All of the Howlers were extremely busy. Those from the Scatterbugs were getting used to the new rules and how their new leader intended to run things. Of course, if there were any disagreements, Midwak had permission to use violence.

However, that violence was limited because of the pack rules that were currently in place. On top of that, there was also the Cardenez group. No longer under any threat, they could continue with their development plan.

Two new factories were being built, one in Slough to help with jobs and generally to level up the town, and one in Notsburg. The progression was beyond what Harry had thought he would be able to do with one factory, and this was all because Kai was giving more funding to the Cardenez group than they would have ever gotten out of either deal; the money came from the Scatterbugs.

All of this was important to Kai, because unlike other groups who might have moved to the larger city and developed from there, they were staying in Slough. The biggest city would usually be the base, and from there they would claim lower cities so other places didn't attack them.

However, the Howlers were staying in Slough, while looking after the areas around them. This was all on Gary's orders, as he wanted to grow Slough out of poverty and make it a place that could compete with others.

With everything working like clockwork, Gary decided that it was time for him to head back to the academy. Numba, Izzy, and Ian were all on the bus with him heading back.

They had overstayed a few days, as they had wanted to return with Gary, for more reasons than one, and during that time they had also decided to visit their families as they wished to discuss something with them.

"Wow, it's all starting to make sense now!" Ian said as he pulled his hair back. "When you told us to get you blood that time, I thought it was because you were a crazed Altered, but this is huge!"

Since the others had found out a lot about Gary, it was too much for him to cover up. They had seen multiple people transform into beings like himself, and words were thrown out left, right, and center.

It was too complicated to come up with a lie that made sense, and besides, Gary didn't want to. These were his friends who had helped him and his other friends through a tough situation. They had risked their lives, and they deserved to know the truth.

"I think what is even more amazing is that these, um, creatures I guess I should say, have lived among us for so long without us knowing about them," Izzy said. "Think about it. They would have existed in a time before there were even Altered."

While Ian and Izzy were talking in excitement, Numba had kept somewhat quiet as he listened to Gary's story. It made him wonder if this was the difference between the two of them.

Was it why Gary was improving so fast, and would they ever catch up to him?

"Remember, a lot of this stuff is new to me as well," Gary answered. "And there are still those who are stronger than me, and I'm not just talking about people like me, but others like Jayden."

Hearing Gary speak about himself in a humble way had caused Numba to snap out of it. Gary was right; there were still plenty of Altered out there who were incredibly strong, who could beat Gary even the way he was now.

If that was the case, then stating that Gary was different from them and that was why he was stronger was the wrong way to think.

"I meant to ask you something," Gary said. "I see that you still have a bandage on the wound you received; is it not healing?"

There was a nervous look on Izzy's face when he asked this question, because the bite mark really was still there. It was the longest wound she'd ever had, and it was especially significant since she was an Altered; there were other things as well, but Izzy had yet to mention them to the others.

"It's okay. The doctor said there is nothing to worry about. It's just taking longer to heal," Izzy replied.

The answer didn't give Gary confidence. At the time, Gary had thought the wound would just go away, and Midwak had said something that had lessened his worries: that werewolves were unable to turn Altered into werewolves.

Since this was the case, Gary hadn't even asked Midwak about it, and only now had it become a concern for him.

The only Altered I know who was bitten by a werewolf was the one who worked for White Rose. The quickest way to get an answer is to contact Kai to contact Midwak. I don't really want to talk to that guy directly if I don't have to.

"Anyway, what are you planning to do, Gary?" Izzy asked. "I mean, it's great that you're coming back to the AFA with us and all, but I can't help but feel that maybe your gang will run into more problems in the future. The more I think about it, since you're the leader . . . you can't just stay in the academy."

Of course Gary had thought about this a lot, and he'd had quite a few discussions with Kai about what he needed to do. The original plan was for Gary to become an AFC star who was sponsored by the Howlers. This would give the group recognition and a chance to get sponsors from big companies using Gary's AFC name. However, there was no longer a need for that. The Howlers name was well known now, and with the Scatterbugs funds, as well as their casinos, the gang was no longer strapped for cash.

On top of that, Gary's name was being used to invest in all sorts of different areas in Slough, including the new factory.

"You're right," Gary sighed. "I need to return to the Howlers, for more reasons than one, but there is still unfinished business in the AFA. I plan to stay here, pass the assessment, and join the AFC.

"I will have my debut match with them, so I am registered in the AFC. After that, I guess it will be time for me to head back."

There were saddened faces, because they knew that the first assessment was only two weeks away. They knew that Gary would pass, which meant their time with him was limited. Unlike Gary, they didn't run a gang.

Their dreams were just to support their families and join the AFC.

"Hey, we can't be sad," Ian said to the others. "We knew this was going to happen, and we talked about it before. If Gary said he was going to stay, then we were going to convince him to leave, but the green-haired idiot has figured it out himself.

"Gary . . . our alliance is always ongoing, and even more so than before. We all went back to our families after that, and we . . . want to be a part of you, a part of the Howlers, and we have made our alliance official with our families."

"What do you even mean by that?" Gary asked.

"It was Kai," Izzy said. "We knew you would never accept, but something about that guy of yours, he seems to take a good deal no matter who it's with. The Howlers already own a percentage of our family's business in other cities."

"Which means that the alliance is official. Although my family's company was the first," Numba added.

Gary didn't know what to say. How could a bunch of students he had only known for a short while do so much for him? Why did they trust him so much? It was because of this that Gary felt like he needed to get stronger.

Stronger, so he couldn't lose those around him, because it had already been a dangerous call. The bus finally stopped and they had returned to the AFA. Meanwhile, Gary wasn't the only one who had the same feeling.

In the Howlers, two members had learned a lot after that fight of theirs, and they were willing to go to any lengths to get stronger.

Both Marie and Innu thought, *This is what I need to do*, as they took two separate paths in their search for strength.

CHAPTER 55

INNU'S PATH

For the Howlers, things were as busy as ever. However, thanks to Kai and his systems, there was a lot less burden on the other members. He didn't trust most of the core members with dealing with delicate matters, which was why he was having a hand in everything instead.

This left many of the core members to their own devices. Although they could now travel out of Slough without much trouble, and Kai even suggested they take a trip to Notsburg once in a while, most of them rejected the offer.

Since Midwak was still there, there was a sense of uneasiness. Even if he was supposed to listen to them because of the special pack rules, it just felt strange to rely on some magical power.

One of the members in question, Innu, stood outside an apartment building. He was carrying a large cardboard box, and he was sweating from going in and out.

"I can't believe we're moving!" Kevin said, as he carried out a much smaller box. "Man, my brother is really the best."

Innu smiled as he heard this and puffed out his chest slightly.

"It's true, I never thought this would happen," Suzan said, grunting as she tried to lift a heavy box, but Innu quickly grabbed the box before it fell over. "I mean, you even managed to convince that stubborn Kai to give us funding toward the new orphanage."

Suzan had officially adopted Kevin, the only survivor of the Black Rock orphanage. After what had happened, Suzan wasn't sure if she could ever do the same type of work again, and Innu wasn't going to force her if she didn't want to.

He would continue to support the two of them as much as possible. Eventually, though, Suzan realized it was in her nature to look after young ones. She kept paying out of her own pocket for kids she found on the street, and she had decided to open the orphanage again.

There was still no official funding for it, which meant it would have to be privately owned, which also meant that Innu was putting all of his money toward Suzan's dream.

Before the Howlers were doing well, Innu still wasn't living a lavish life, and many arguments ensued between Innu and Kai because of this, stating that more money needed to be put toward the orphanage.

Now, though, with the Scatterbugs' funds, they were able to upgrade the orphanage, and Innu was able to move Suzan and Kevin to the same apartment building that Gary's sister lived in.

"This is all because the Howlers actually managed to take out the Scatterbugs!" Kevin was excited, and of course after the last incident they were involved in, they had come to learn Innu's position in the gang.

"You must've kicked some serious butt when you were there!" Kevin excitedly said, as he threw out some punches and kicks in the air, but he stopped as he looked at Innu, who wasn't smiling.

Kicked some butt? Innu thought. *No, that isn't what happened. I was barely helpful at all.*

Flashbacks to the fight were playing in Innu's head. How strong Midwak was, how weak he felt, and how Marie had almost been killed multiple times, even though it was his role to protect her.

After helping the others move, Innu had found out that one of the rooms in the apartment building belonged to him. According to Suzan and Kevin, they had always wished for Innu to stay with them; they just never had a big enough place for it.

Of course, Innu was overjoyed at this fact, since he had been living on his own for a while. He was so excited that he had decided to move out that day and move in with the others.

When he was unpacking things in his room, his hands fell onto the red axes, and once again he was left thinking about the fight. Actually, it was more accurate to say that it had never left his mind since they had left Notsburg.

These red axes, they're powerful, but I still can't use them properly, and it makes me wonder, with just these alone, how far can I go? If the Howlers start to get involved with bigger gangs, other Tier 2s and Tier 1s, even other werewolves . . . I don't think I can keep up.

It was obvious that Innu wanted to get stronger; he didn't want to get left behind, and he still wanted to help the Howlers. As a core member, he felt like it was only right that he be as strong as the others.

Innu felt that his skills were some of the best. There was always room for improvement, but compared to an Altered, that wasn't the type of strength that he needed. The axes gave him a boost in power, and although he could wield them, he had no idea how to use them to their full potential.

Which was why he was also thinking of alternative solutions. Now that the Howlers had taken over Notsburg, their funds were more than capable of buying an Altered solution. Whether that was by making contact with NIRV, or one of the other groups, or even the auction house . . . they could buy a solution.

The auction wasn't for a while, and honestly Innu wasn't so sure about becoming an Altered. It meant getting attention from a lot of people, and there was always the chance that his Altered form wouldn't suit him. Innu also liked fighting with weapons and his own hands and fists, and he felt like he would never use the transformed state; it just felt like a waste.

This led to the other solution he was thinking of: asking Gary to turn him, just like Kai had been turned. Gary seemed reluctant to do something like that, and for the same reasons as becoming an Altered, Innu was against the idea.

Think, then . . . is there a way for me to get stronger . . . to have the power to compete with Altered, by just staying as I am? Innu thought.

That whole night after moving in, Innu was stuck in his room racking his brain. The other two were concerned that he hadn't even come out for dinner, but they left him on his own, as they were sure it was something important.

Damn it! Why did everyone have to get so strong and so fast? I have to compete with that damn bull man; how is that even fair?

Eventually Innu had fallen asleep after thinking about it all night, and the sun was starting to rise. He looked out the window and heard kids talking.

"When did I fall asleep?" Innu said to himself, rubbing his eyes. When he took a second look out the window, it hit him. There was a way for him to get stronger the way he wished.

Innu leaned up against the wall as he tapped his foot on the ground. Eventually, the bell rang and a rush of students left the school.

"Hey . . . isn't that Innu? What is he doing here? Didn't he drop out of school?"

"Who?" another student asked.

"Ah, he wasn't here for long, he transferred and then dropped out."

Ignoring the words of the others, Innu continued to wait, until he had finally found the person he was looking for; he almost leapt from the wall as he stood in front of one of the students.

"Oh, what are you doing here?" Blake asked.

"I need to talk to you about something."

They headed to a nearby park and were now sitting on a bench next to each other; Blake had heard everything that Innu wanted to say.

"So you want me to train you?" Blake replied.

"Yeah, I mean it makes sense, right? You're an Altered Hunter and you guys learn to take out Altered even though you aren't an Altered yourself. There has to be a way the top guys take out those things without turning into them," Innu explained.

"There are maybe some things I can show you, but you have to know that I'm basically a beginner Altered Hunter myself. I don't know all the tricks that my dad knows or that those above him do. Although I could teach you what I do know, there is a bit of a problem."

"Problem . . . what's that?" Innu asked.

"If you really want to get stronger, and you want to learn our techniques, then you would have to join us. You would have to become an Altered Hunter."

CHAPTER 56

AN ALTERED HUNTER'S LIFE

"Become an Altered Hunter?" Innu repeated. He stood up from the bench and began walking away. It was such a crazy thing to suggest.

Altered Hunters were seen as something akin to terrorists. Being an Altered was not illegal according to the law. The fact that Altered Hunters killed Altered for next to no reason, just because they were Altered, was never something that Innu wanted to align himself with.

"Is it that big a deal?" Blake asked, as if he could read Innu's mind, and he grabbed his arm to stop him from walking away. "If you truly believe that Altered Hunters are so scary, then why did you approach me in the first place?" Blake asked. "And you have to think about your own situation as well. Aren't you in a gang? Haven't you already killed for your own survival?"

When Blake put it like that, Innu started to have second thoughts. He had approached Blake not only because he believed he was skilled but because he was a nice person.

At the same time, just like Innu never believed he would become an Altered Hunter, he had never seen himself working in a large gang either. It was just a way to make money for a short while until he found something else.

"But . . . I don't want to join the Altered Hunters," Innu replied. "I just want you to teach me a few things . . . a way to beat the others."

Blake sighed as he went on to explain.

"As I said before, I can't just teach you what I know. If they found out about it, I would be in serious trouble. Also, if you want to grow, you will need more guidance than just from me.

"For one, a lot of the Altered Hunters' strength comes from their equipment: the armor they use, the weapons they are allowed to carry. Then you have the high-star rankers. Those are the ones that you will need guidance from for real strength, not just me, and to do that you would have to join the Altered Hunters."

Everything Blake was saying was convincing, and since Innu didn't have any intention of becoming an Altered, it wasn't a bad path to take. However, what about the gang?

"How can I become an Altered Hunter? The whole reason that I want to become stronger is so I can help them. As the gang grows, there will be more Altered in the gang, and won't I get swept away with Altered Hunter stuff?" Innu argued.

Blake finally stood up and looked Innu in the eye.

"You don't have to leave the gang," Blake stated. "The low-star Altered Hunters blend in with society. It's part of their job and their role. Being a gang member is no problem, and we have more freedom than you think.

"Take me, for example. I have helped out the Howlers because I consider Gary . . . a partner." Blake had stopped himself for a moment from saying another word. "I know that there are Altered in the Howlers, but I don't act on it. I admit that from time to time, you may have to be called, but based on your position, you could inform the others."

The more Blake talked, the more Innu was convinced, but he needed time to think about it.

I can see he's on the edge, but if I'm honest, if he does join the Altered Hunters this will be good for me as well, Blake thought.

There was an ongoing problem that Blake had yet to resolve, and that was the fact that the Altered Hunter Association wanted to send a partner to his city. Originally he had worked side by side with his father, but his father had been reassigned to another location.

Blake had achieved his first star, and with recent events he was close to getting his second one. Since he was an official Hunter he needed to have a partner, but there was something else that could be done as well.

Just like how Blake had worked under his father, he could take on an apprentice. If he took Innu under his wing, they wouldn't send a partner. If Innu decided against the idea, then Slough would have another Altered Hunter to deal with, and they most likely wouldn't be as kind to the Howlers as Blake had been so far.

"You want strength, right?" Blake asked. "I understand, believe me; you will get the strength you are looking for, and if we need to continue to help Gary, we can do so together."

As he said those last words, Blake held out his hand, trying to seal the deal. Innu looked him up and down, and something about Blake was drawing him in.

Is it his handsome face? I mean, I don't even swing that way, but I think it's making me attracted to him. No, maybe he just has a way with words.

Innu shook his head, as he had finally made a decision.

"I'll do it. I'll become an Altered Hunter," Innu said, shaking Blake's hand. "But it will be in name only. I want to make that clear, especially if Gary ever finds out."

"Gary?" Blake smiled. "You don't have to worry about him. He's not even an Altered."

The two of them chuckled for a little bit, and Innu was ready to get into action straightaway.

"All right, so what are you going to teach me first, or where are you going to take me? Is there like a secret shop where you store all your armor, or a cool car or something?" Innu said excitedly.

"Sorry to burst your bubble, but it's nothing like that, and technically you're still not an Altered Hunter yet," Blake answered.

Innu was almost deflated to the ground at that point; all of the excitement was draining out of his body. He already had resolved to join the Altered Hunters, and he thought he would have gotten something out of it.

"Do you really think someone like me has the authority to do something like that?" Blake asked. "There are a few things that need to be done for you to become an apprentice Altered Hunter.

"First, I will need to contact the base and inform them that someone is interested. After that, two star-ranked Altered Hunters will need to evaluate your skills. If the two Altered Hunters agree that you have potential, then it will be reported back. After that, you are an official Altered Hunter!"

It seemed like quite a long process, but now Innu understood why the Altered Hunters were all quite skilled. Not just anyone could join.

"I'm guessing you can count as one of the Altered Hunters; who's the other one? Will it be your father?" Innu asked.

Blake shook his head.

"He is busy at the moment; they will most likely just send someone who is close by. When they do come, it would be best to make sure no incidents happen when they arrive. Otherwise, it might cause more problems than we realize."

That was the last thing that Innu wanted to do. The true strength and the numbers of the Altered Hunter Association were unknown, but it certainly wasn't something that the Howlers wanted to deal with.

"What about the test? Is there anything I need to do to prepare for it?" Innu asked.

"I don't think so. Usually the Altered Hunters decide between themselves on how to test you. Most likely you and I can just spar in my father's dojo; with your skills, I'm pretty sure they would accept you in a heartbeat."

When they were done talking, Blake pulled out a strange phone-like device that looked more like a radio and started to type away on it. Meanwhile Innu was a bit nervous.

He had no idea what this meant, or what the outcome would be, but it did bring him a little excitement for what he would learn.

I can't wait. If I get strong enough, then I can start fighting that damn minotaur again. The look on his face will be worth all of this in the end, Innu thought, as his rivalry with Austin was strong.

"Well, that was fast," Blake said. "It looks like there is a Hunter nearby; he will be here in the evening."

CHAPTER 57

THE HUNTER SYSTEM

Since Blake had already been informed that the Altered Hunter was on his way, he had decided to wait at his father's dojo. It was the first time Innu had been in such a place, and he couldn't help but stare at the front garden and the whole place in awe.

"I know you said Altered Hunters have different jobs, but I guess your dad must be a pretty high-ranked Altered Hunter to afford all of this," Innu said.

"Haha, not quite," Blake replied. "My father only recently got promoted to a four-star Altered Hunter. The organization is quite wealthy, since they have a lot of Anti-Altered equipment that they can sell. Don't ask me how they get their hands on this stuff. Anyway, you have to remember that Slough is only a Tier 3 town."

What Blake said was true, but with all the recent developments, shopping malls and more were being put in place as the people started to have more expendable money and higher wages; it was slowly starting to look quite impressive.

When they got inside the dojo, Innu sat down and so did Blake. The two of them talked for a while, but they didn't have much to say to each other, so after that they played on their phones as they waited, waited, and waited.

In the end Innu had to fill the silence, as his phone's battery was starting to die.

"Okay, tell me, you were talking about ranks before, and I know that you have the stars on your shoulder, but how many Altered does one have to kill to get a star, and what's the highest rank?"

"That's a good question. Essentially, a five-star Altered Hunter is the highest in the association; after that, there are no more stars to be gained, but there are higher positions. The Altered Hunter Association has branches all around the world.

"Each country has a head, and captains underneath to support him. There is no limit on captains, but there is only one head. As for the stars themselves, one has to kill five Altered in total to gain their first star.

"However, if an Altered kill is assisted by teammates, depending on the situation and how much one contributed, it would count as well. We Altered Hunters are quite prideful, so if we believe we didn't play a big part in taking one down, we wouldn't claim credit for it."

Five Altered sounded like an incredible number, and since Blake had a star it meant he had already faced a number of Altered.

No wonder he's so strong, Innu thought.

"And what about the other stars, then? How many Altered would one have to kill for that?" Innu asked.

They spoke about it like it was no big deal. Unless one was an Altered themself, no one in their lifetime would believe they could take one on.

"For a second star, one would have to take out fifteen Altered altogether; after that, for the third star the number is fifty; then for the fourth star it's one hundred and for a fifth star over two hundred fifty. Of course, some are way above that number, but there is no way for us to tell, as they don't track their kills after that."

Innu started rapidly coughing, he had nearly choked on nothing he was so surprised. After his coughing fit was over he went over the numbers again.

"Wait, I didn't even know that was possible! You're saying that your dad has killed over a hundred Altered, and some have killed even more. But I thought Altered were rare; how can that even happen?" Innu asked.

"You have to remember a couple of things. First, although the stars indicate how many Altered you have killed, that does not indicate your strength; rather it shows how dedicated you are to the goal of elimi-nating all Altered. However, the more stars, the more high-level equip-ment you are allowed access to, so the two things do go somewhat hand in hand.

"The second point is that Altered are becoming more common. More companies are coming out with easier ways for one to become an Altered, and more DNA is coming out on the market. Still, let's say that one percent of the population are Altered. One percent of sixty million is still six hundred thousand people."

Innu had never looked at it that way before, and judging by the fact that becoming an Altered was usually associated with the rich, in the higher-tier cities, there were bound to be more Altered than here.

With Innu's curiosity satisfied, the two decided to wait some more, but after a while Innu couldn't help but open his mouth again.

"Where is this guy . . . has something happened?" Innu asked.

"He is later than the time stated . . . I hope nothing has happened," Blake replied.

The towns and cities of the world were never a quiet place. Crime was rampant even with larger gangs in control. In most cases, the larger gangs didn't even care about the smaller groups in their cities, as long as they didn't interfere with their own business.

At the same time, the police were corrupt and understaffed and unable to do anything. The only ones that were worth mentioning were White Rose, but because of the Crazed Altered as well as the Altered Hunters, they were busy too.

In Slough, this was no exception, as students left the university feeling like there was no future. With fewer activities to do, and gangs seen as an easy way to make money, there was still plenty of trouble.

However, unlike the other cities and gangs, Slough was trying to clamp down on gang-related activities. The Howlers often patrolled hot-spot areas for delinquent activity.

If they saw potential in someone, they would invite them to join their gang, giving them a sense of responsibility. Because of the current rules, when things were too difficult for regular Howler members, they would inform their leader, and if they needed more help they would inform their core member.

Riding on his motorbike, with his hair blowing in the wind, Austin had received one of these calls and was heading to the area to deal with the situation.

I thought these types of calls would start to die down once we took care of the Scatterbugs, but I guess there will always be people foolish enough to push someone's buttons. Still, we really need to start training these guys, so we get called less.

Eventually Austin arrived at the location, a large open park with several pathways that led to large platforms. The students often used it as a drinking or dancing area.

After he had parked, Austin let out a sigh as he walked down one of the pathways and noticed something strange.

If there was a fight going on, I would hear people shouting at the top of their lungs or cursing at each other, Austin thought.

As he went deeper into the park, he reached one of the open squares, and he couldn't hear shouting but instead he heard lots and lots of groans. When he got closer, Austin saw several members of what looked like an orange color gang on the ground holding on to their arms, legs, and stomachs, moaning in pain.

I got called all this way for a color gang? Really? But if they're the ones on the ground, then . . .

Austin's question was answered when he saw Howlers on the ground as well. Only one person was standing.

"Did you do all this?" Austin asked.

The man was facing the other way, with a few bloodstains on his shirt. As he turned around, his long plaited hair swung slightly.

"This?" the man replied. "This is not what it looks like. My phone is dead and I was asking for directions. The two groups were fighting and started to attack me out of nowhere, and I had to defend myself."

Since the man was uninjured, he had to be a skillful fighter. Austin's old instincts kicked in.

"Some of those people belong to my group, and you seem like a strong fighter," Austin said, punching his fist into his other hand.

"Hey, trust me, kid. If you're thinking about doing what I think you're going to do, it's not a good idea," the man replied.

CHAPTER 58

A HUNTER'S STRUGGLE

Ever since Austin had become an Altered, it was hard for him to find opponents that he could brawl against. Completely overpowering a person might be good for one's ego, but it wasn't good for sharpening one's skills.

At the same time, even though he could fight against Kai and Olivia, it didn't give him a variety of opponents and skills to go up against. A person also fought differently when they knew their opponent and what they could do.

However, there was also the likes of Midwak, who was too strong for him, so he needed someone just right, and considering how a single person was able to take out around fifteen people on his own, Austin guessed this person was quite skilled.

"I won't transform, otherwise this fight might be a little too easy!" Austin said as he threw a heavy punch from the get-go. He didn't hold back in terms of speed, and Austin was already strong before becoming an Altered.

However, the punch hit nothing but air, and his opponent had already moved to the side.

"Look, judging from your clothes you're in some type of gang, right? I don't want to get involved in this mess, and as I said, it's best if you don't fight me," the stranger said.

To illustrate his point, the stranger moved to kick Austin from behind. When his foot landed and he pushed forward, though, Austin didn't even move.

It feels like I'm pushing against a giant boulder or something, how much muscle and balance does this guy have?

Austin swung his arm behind him, aiming to hit the man, who quickly moved his feet out of the way. Instead of punching him, though, Austin tried to grab him and only managed to grasp the sleeve of his shirt.

As the stranger pulled away, the entire sleeve was ripped off completely.

"That's not good, that's the only change of clothes I had." The man shook his head.

Austin looked at the man's bare arm and saw the markings on his shoulders: little stars.

Aren't those stars the mark of an Altered Hunter? Austin thought. "One . . . two . . . three . . . four . . . five stars?"

Although many knew about Altered Hunters, not many knew about the stars or what they meant, but Austin did know that in front of him was an Altered Hunter.

If he's an Altered Hunter in this city, then he could be related to Blake. Gary told us to let them be and not get involved with them.

Meanwhile, the Altered Hunter was sighing to himself.

This kid has a lot of strength . . . Could it be? I left my equipment at one of the safe houses since this was supposed to just be a small task. I'm not here to look for Altered. I should turn off my brain once in a while.

Surprisingly, his attacker was no longer clenching his fists and had dropped them down to his side.

"I guess I was a bit rash since I don't recognize you, but I'll warn you," Austin said. "If you see the black-and-gold uniform, don't get in the way of what they are doing. It's us that run this area." Having issued the warning, Austin started to walk away.

"Wait!" the man shouted. "Do you mind giving me a few directions?"

As expected, the man had asked where a particular dojo was, and it was of course where Blake lived. Since he had become a full-time gang member and the Howlers had taken over Slough, Austin knew of all the areas and gave him directions to where he needed to go. The man thanked him and was off, but he turned around, wanting to say one last thing.

"I just wanted to let you know, it was a good thing we stopped that fight." The man smiled and lifted his foot. "Because I would have won."

He slammed his foot into the ground. It didn't shake, nor did it feel overly strong; it was just a simple stomp. Then the man ran in the other direction, as he knew he was late.

Out of curiosity, Austin went over to where the man had stomped the ground.

"What is this?" Austin's eyes weren't fooling him. There was a two-inch-deep footprint. But that wasn't the only strange thing about it; there were no cracks around it.

"This is just not something that's possible for a human," Austin said. "But I'm certain he was an Altered Hunter; there's no chance that he was an Altered, but then how is something like this even possible?"

Then Austin realized that if the two of them had gone face-to-face with all of their strength, it wouldn't have been an easy fight like he thought, and there was a chance he might have lost.

Following the directions, the Altered Hunter had finally arrived at the required location. He could see it just up ahead.

I really should have kept my equipment with me. I never expected to run into trouble in a Tier 3 town.

After a gentle knock on the door, Blake answered, and when he saw who it was, he bowed his head in greeting. Innu, standing at his side, did the same.

"I welcome you, my fellow Hunter," Blake said.

Innu noticed that his sleeve was ripped, and he saw the stars that were marked on his arm.

Freaking five stars! Five stars! Of all the Hunters they could have sent to Slough, they sent a five-star Hunter! After learning what a five-star Hunter was capable of, it was only right for Innu to panic.

"I'm sorry I'm late. My phone died, and I had to ask some people for directions," the man said politely. "You're Blake, correct? My name is Ashen, it's nice to meet you both. Sorry, but do you mind if I use your toilet?"

Blake pointed toward the dojo, and Ashen ran past them both.

"I have to ask, do all five-star Altered Hunters go around showing off their markings?" Innu asked.

"I'm not too sure myself. This is the first time I've met a five-star Altered Hunter. At least face-to-face like this." Blake was concerned; it was easy to tell from his body language. "We should get this test done as soon as possible, so he can leave. If he stays for a while, who knows what will happen if he finds out what's happening."

Innu couldn't agree more; if anything did happen, he would feel guilty, because the whole reason Ashen was here was to see him.

"All right, let's get this assessment started," Ashen said, having returned from the dojo with a big smile on his face.

If anything, the one saving grace was that Ashen seemed to be a happy person.

As they entered the training hall, Ashen and Blake were talking back and forth. The two of them had to come up with a test of some sort.

Blake was trying to suggest a sparring match between himself and Innu, but since they knew each other, Ashen was against the idea. However, Ashen noticed that Innu had brought something in a large black bag, almost as large as one that a person would use to carry skis.

"Do you mind if I take a look in here?" Ashen asked.

Innu gestured that it was okay, and when Ashen opened the bag, his eyes lit up as he picked up the pair of red axes.

"These are nice, really nice. I'm guessing they're yours?"

Still too scared to speak, Innu just nodded.

"Do you know how to use them properly?"

Innu wasn't so sure what he meant by the question, but he answered, "I think so."

"All right, well, if that's the case, just show me how to use them, if you can. I think that will be sufficient to pass," Ashen said.

Blake was left confused; he didn't know what Ashen meant, but perhaps both he and this five-star hunter could learn something that would boost their strength.

CHAPTER 59

USE YOUR WEAPON!

The dojo was dead silent, which was only making Innu more nervous as he stood in the center holding on to the two red axes. What didn't help were the two people standing to his side who were intensely staring at him.

"Just try to breathe, relax, and ignore that we are here," Ashen said.

I was doing that, until you started talking to me, Innu thought, annoyed, but he needed to show what he had.

Closing his eyes allowed him to focus more. He was trying to go into a deep state.

I'm not too sure what that Hunter meant when he said, do I know how to use the axes properly, but I can guess. There were those times . . .

Innu started to think back to when he was fighting against the gang members; power from the axes would be drawn out and into his body, giving him more strength, allowing him to move faster, and more. But there was also something else.

When he was fighting Midwak, it felt like rather than the weapons giving him energy, his energy was being drawn into the weapons. In the end, it had worked out as it allowed him to injure Midwak, but after that, Innu himself was unable to move.

Which way is the right way to use the weapon? Is that what he's asking? Innu was conflicted, but when fighting Midwak, he had acted out of desperation; it wasn't something he could turn on and off.

But Innu had gotten the hang of the other method. Energy from the weapons filled his body, and, opening his eyes, Innu swung the axe again and again, cutting through the air cleanly.

Since it was a demonstration, though, Innu didn't just use the axes. He also used his legs, ducking down, rolling across the floor, then pushing himself off the ground and kneeing the air, swinging both axes at the same time.

While Innu was showing off his skills, Blake took a look at Ashen by his side to see his reaction, and there was an incredibly large smile on his face.

"I wonder who is the opponent in his head, for him to be fighting that hard," Ashen said to himself.

Blake took a second look at Innu after hearing those words, and that was when he realized something. Although Innu was showing impressive skills and fighting with great strength, he wasn't slowing down.

It was as if he was in a panic while fighting, and soon he would be worn out. A few seconds later, Innu dropped down to the ground, taking quick, deep breaths.

"And . . . I'm dead," Innu said, as if he was disappointed, and the phantom image of Midwak that he had created in his mind started to disappear.

During his little demonstration, Innu thought it would be best if he used his skills on an imaginary opponent. Because he wanted to bring out the best of his skills, he wanted the strongest opponent in his head, which was Midwak.

In hindsight, having lasted only about a minute against the phantom before tiring, he was regretting it, until he heard someone clapping. Turning his head, he saw that it was Ashen clapping, with a big smile.

"You are an impressive person," Ashen said. "In a place like this, in a town like this, I never thought I would meet someone like you. When I saw the weapons I thought they might have been wasted on you, but that doesn't seem to be the case.

"Blake, you certainly have an eye for talent. How do you know someone like him?"

Blake froze for a second before answering, but Innu answered instead.

"At an underground fighting tournament," Innu said. "I didn't go to school, and to make money I fought in different underground fighting venues, but was I really that impressive? I felt like . . . I couldn't use them properly."

Ashen walked over to Innu and held out his hand, asking for the axes, and Innu gladly handed them over.

"The fact that you know that means that you are thinking in the right direction," Ashen explained. "When I asked you if you knew how to use the weapons, I was talking about the special properties of the weapons.

"You see, with certain Anti-Altered weapons like these, energy can be drawn out of them to improve one's strength. You are quite clearly capable of doing that, but let me ask you, have you ever experienced energy leaving your body and going into the weapon?"

Innu's eyes lit up; he knew that joining the Altered Hunters was the right thing to do, and he nodded.

"Well, you see, that's because you were putting your own internal energy into the weapon." As Ashen held on to the axe, it started to vibrate slightly, and something similar to heat radiated from it.

Ashen lifted the axe and swung it down. There was a sharp sound, and for a second there appeared to be an actual cut in the air before it disappeared.

"This energy that we have inside us is known as qi. If you want to use the weapons to their full potential, you will need to learn how to use this energy. Then the weapons will power you with their energy, and you will power the weapon with your own, but you always have to be careful.

"Qi is an energy like none other. If you give too much of it, you will be out of the fight, and in some cases if you push it too much you will deplete your own life energy. So keep that in mind when you're using weapons like this."

Blake was listening intently because it was the first time he had heard of such energy himself. His father had never taught him something like this, and as far as he knew, this wasn't something that the Altered Hunters taught each other.

"I've never heard of this before," Blake mumbled.

"It's not something that's shared, really." Ashen smiled and scratched the back of his head. "Honestly, some Altered Hunters use it without even knowing. Not many know about it like I do.

"It's only because of my position outside of being an Altered Hunter that I came to learn this, but that's too much for you guys to know about."

Blake knew what Ashen meant; he was talking about his regular day-to-day role, his cover. Just as Blake was a high school student, or Innu was part of the Howlers, while being an Altered Hunter.

It made Blake think about what role Ashen had, to be able to learn about this power in such detail.

"Think of this as a reward for both of you. For showing me such a talented person. Knowing about qi will allow you to search for it a bit more. Anyway, it's safe to say that you have passed. Congratulations on becoming an Altered Hunter."

After learning all of that information, Innu had nearly forgotten what this whole assessment was about, but it was clear that he had taken the first step onto his path of getting stronger.

"If you ever see me around the Altered Hunter Association, feel free to show me how much you have improved. I look forward to it," Ashen said as he stretched his arms and let out a big yawn.

Blake bowed.

"Thank you for taking the time to come here, and thank you again for passing on your knowledge."

"No problem, I will inform the Association, and then whenever you have time, pop down to get your equipment and register." With that, Ashen walked toward the exit from the dojo.

It had been an eventful day and Ashen still couldn't believe it. He had met two interesting people and he hadn't been in Slough for long. It certainly was an interesting place.

"Wait!" Innu called out.

Ashen stopped in his tracks.

"I . . . don't have time to wait, or figure this out on my own, and I'm not the brightest person, I just go based on my instincts, but that won't work this time. Which is why I want to ask you . . . can you be my teacher? Can you stay and teach me?"

Blake turned his head, as this wasn't part of the plan. The whole point of him getting Innu to join him was so another Altered Hunter wouldn't join, and they wanted Ashen to leave as soon as possible.

"Please . . . even if it's just for a day or two. I know you're very busy, but I promise, whatever you tell me to do, whatever it is you need . . . I have someone I need to protect."

Ashen turned around, still grinning.

"It's just like I thought. You are really impressive. All right, Let's do this. I can't show you how to use qi in just a couple of days, but I think there is something else you can learn."

CHAPTER 60

LEARNING A NEW POWER

There were a lot of talented people in the Altered Hunter Association, and Ashen could have taken a few of them under his wing. The problem was, nearly everyone who was brought into the Altered Hunters was introduced by someone else.

Even Blake himself had been brought in by his father. This meant that all the talent was pretty much accounted for. Meanwhile, Ashen was too busy doing his duty to try to find someone to train on his own.

It wasn't that Ashen never wanted a pupil; he was just far too busy. He wanted a talented student while also training them in the Altered Hunter Association from the ground up, and right now was the perfect opportunity, so he said yes without hesitation.

There is also something interesting about this town. If I have a pupil here, then I can use it as an excuse to visit more often, Ashen thought.

"Thank you, thank you so much!" Innu said, bowing his head to the floor.

"As I said, I don't have much time that I can spend here. I already wasted most of it getting lost. So it will be best if we start now," Ashen said.

It was already late in the evening but Innu stood up as straight as a bamboo shoot, ready to take on anything.

"All right, follow me, let's head out to the streets," Ashen said.

Innu and Blake followed him out of the dojo, but Ashen turned his head and cleared his throat.

"I'm sorry, Blake, but what I'm about to show is between a master and pupil only. I hope you understand."

With that, Innu and Ashen walked off, leaving Blake at the dojo, dumbfounded and staring into space.

What just happened? Blake thought. *Is a five-star Altered Hunter just roaming around the streets of Slough? No, I shouldn't even be worried about that. What is he going to teach Innu that I'm not allowed to see? Is Innu going to become a better Altered Hunter than me?*

After seeing Ashen's skills, Blake knew that he had a long way to go, and he understood that it might not be right for him to be taught by another. However, his father was away most of the time, and even when they were together his father's teaching methods were mostly self-teaching methods, and there wasn't really any teaching involved at all.

Now I feel restless, Blake thought.

As he followed Ashen out of the housing estate and into the city, Innu started to worry as he realized something.

Wait a second, where is he even taking me? Why am I following him? Didn't he say he's never been here before? Innu thought.

"This should do," Ashen said as he walked down a large alleyway between two restaurants. The alleyway was wide because the restaurants threw their garbage behind the shops, and the area absolutely stunk to the point where Innu was finding it hard to keep his food in his stomach.

Why is he taking me here? Is there some sort of secret technique to train your stomach so you can learn to use qi better? Innu thought, because Ashen seemed to be completely fine with the smell.

Turning his head left and right, he saw that there was no one else present, so he picked up a small stone and threw it into the air a couple of times.

"Do you remember what I said before?" Ashen asked. "I won't be teaching you qi; that would take far too long, and with what I have told you already, you should be able to figure it out on your own. If that's the case, then I am not really going against the rules.

"But what I am about to show you is something completely different, and it might seem a bit out of this world."

If Innu hadn't met Ashen before, he would have thought he was simply overhyping his capabilities, but after seeing what he could do, he was expecting something big.

Ashen then took the stone and threw it down the alleyway; it went quite some distance but eventually dropped onto the ground.

"Am I missing something?" Innu asked.

Ashen smiled and picked up another small stone.

"Watch carefully, watch it till the very end."

Ashen threw the stone down the alleyway once more, and Innu tried to not blink. The stone continued and just like last time fell down onto the ground again.

"I didn't see anything different," Innu said. He wondered if this was all a big prank.

"All right . . . I'll try to make it a little more obvious for you," Ashen said, holding out his hand, and this time there was nothing in it, with his fingers stretched open.

Innu watched carefully, and suddenly a small stone appeared. Ashen clutched it at that moment and started to throw it up and down again.

Innu looked left, then right, and rubbed his eyes.

"That stone . . . where did it come from? Did it just fly into your hand? What is this, is it a magic trick?"

Ashen chuckled.

"It's not magic, although I'm not quite sure what it is myself. You see, one day, I was just able to do things like this. Control where objects moved. When I was throwing the stone earlier, if you had paid attention you would have seen it swerving to the left or right.

"But as long as the object isn't too heavy, I can bring it back into my hand like so."

The stone was now levitating in the air in front of him. Innu was sure that there were no strings, so he had to just believe what Ashen said.

"When I saw your axes, it made me think of this. Imagine if you had this power? If you learned how to transfer your qi into the axe and threw it toward your enemy, if you could control its path, it would hit your enemy without fail, and then with the power, the axe could come back right to the palm of your hand."

As Ashen explained, Innu imagined it: how useful something like this would be when going up against Midwak.

"You see, this isn't something the Altered Hunters teach you, nor is it related to my current position. This is something that one day I could just do. It allowed me to hunt for Altered easier, and I haven't shown any others this skill or ability, if you want to call it that."

Now Innu understood why Blake wasn't allowed to tag along. After hearing Ashen's explanation, he had a thought.

"Wait, you said that you just knew how to do this one day, and no one taught you it before, right? So does that mean you're not even sure if it's something that can be taught to others?" Innu asked.

Ashen nodded.

"That's right; I have been wanting a student for a while now, to see if it's possible to teach others how to do this. Oh, and of course, if this all does work out. I would tell you to only use it in emergencies. If people found out about this, they might hunt you down and take your body apart."

Innu didn't like the sound of that, and he was a bit disheartened that he might not be able to learn this ability. If so, then wouldn't a lot more people have such powers? Or maybe they were just hiding themselves like Ashen.

In the end, Innu couldn't help but think how much of a plus it would be if he could do something like this in a fight.

"Let's do it, let's try to learn this power!" Innu said excitedly.

"I knew you were the right person for this." Ashen smiled.

Innu quickly grabbed some stones off the ground, as he was ready to begin his training. He would work day and night for this, and time was short.

Meanwhile, Ashen looked at him, thinking that if this worked out, maybe it would change the world, or even the future, but one thing was for sure, Innu would become a five-star hunter in no time.

"Ashen, are you okay?" Innu asked. "Your nose is bleeding."

Ashen quickly wiped the side of his face.

"Oh . . . this . . . it's all right, let's start your training."

CHAPTER 61

A DIFFERENT PATH

Marie sat in the Wolf's Pool Club, her head down on the bar table. While the teenage girl was feeling down, business continued as usual around her; White was happily serving guests like any other day. At this point, the profit from the Wolf's Pool Club wasn't really relevant for the Howlers, but Marie's mother was more than happy to continue working there.

The core members all appreciated her effort, due to the fact that it was running as normal on a day-to-day basis, and with the club not standing out so much, it made for the perfect hideout.

"What's wrong, Marie?" Kiki Degrace eventually asked. It was obvious to anyone that something was bothering her daughter, judging by the ever-increasing number of sighs she was letting out.

"It's hard to explain. Do you think I did the right thing by dropping out of school? Do you think I should go back?" Marie said, sharing some of her burdens.

Letting out a sigh of her own, Miss Degrace stopped cleaning the bar, went to her daughter, and started to massage her scalp. "Sweetie, nothing is stopping you from going back to school, but is that really what you want?"

"It's hard, you know," Marie continued to complain while enjoying the head massage. "Back when we all left school, I was so determined to help Kai and Gary out of trouble, and I would like to believe that I really did help them. I was doing my best to get stronger, I was really putting in the work to get better with . . . the dagger and weapons."

For a second, Marie's mother stopped massaging her head, looking around shiftily to ensure that nobody had heard her. As thankful as she was to the Howlers for everything they had done to help the two of them, as her mother, Kiki despised the fact that Marie was involved in gang business. She knew what she possibly had been doing and tried her best to disregard it, but rather than worry about her own feelings, she needed to look out for her daughter.

"Now, though . . . I can't help but feel that I'm useless . . . that I just get in the way," Marie continued. "I thought I was needed, but when I really think about it, am I any different compared to anyone else with the same weapons?

"The people we met in Notsburg were nearly strong enough to hurt Gary . . . and from what we learned, our enemies in the future are likely to be even stronger. I'm just a normal girl, nowhere near as special as his new friends."

Marie started to think about the AFA students she had seen, like Izzy, who had saved her life. Although they were the same age, one was a dropout while the other was a student at the most prestigious Altered academy. Given her abilities, she could help Gary far better than Marie ever could.

"I understand how you feel, sweetie . . . There were many times when I felt weak and helpless, and there will always be times when you can't do anything but rely on the people around you. You may not be at the point where you wanted to be, but let me ask you this: Do you think people like me and White aren't helping out the Howlers?"

Marie turned around and saw White, as popular as ever with the boys, as she gave them their drinks. As soon as she turned away, they couldn't stop whispering about her. It was an open secret that many of their regulars only visited to see her; it was clear that she was building up her own little fan base.

"I'm not sure what to say," Marie replied.

"While it is certainly true that the Howlers are a gang, a gang doesn't function simply by having many strong fighters. Besides, at this point, I see it more like a corporation. The whole thing cannot exist without everyone doing their part. No matter how small that task, it all allows the Howlers to be as successful as they have been. So let me ask you, while you may not grow strong overnight, is there really nothing you can do to support the Howlers right now, even if it's something small?"

Marie thought about it; maybe there were other ways that she could help, but the thing was, if she were to do the same as White right now, just working at the bar, or helping out at meetings and such, then she didn't think that she deserved to stand side by side with the others.

While nobody could deny that she was one of the Howlers' core members, she knew that it was mostly because she had been a member since the beginning. When she looked at the others and compared herself to everyone else, there was a big difference between them and her, and that was strength.

As a core member, to continue standing with the others, she needed strength. The talk with her mother had helped, but not in the way that she thought. It allowed her to realize she didn't want to be just a little help to the Howlers; she wanted more.

"I have to go somewhere!" Marie said as she quickly left her seat. "If Kai asks where I am, just tell him I've gone home for the day to rest up."

Marie hadn't informed any of the other members where she was going. It was quite late, but after what she had been through, the streets just didn't seem as scary anymore.

On the bus she had taken, she noticed something. Three teenage boys were being incredibly loud, blasting out their music and hitting each other. It was bothersome, but Marie wasn't going to get involved, and just like everyone else she was ignoring them.

However, one thing was concerning. Two boys were sitting in one seat and were constantly hitting their third friend behind them. The bus was full, and a woman who was seated next to them seemed to flinch each time one of the boys went in for a hit.

"Damn you, Yami, hold up your hand properly. I need to show you how I pounded that guy's face earlier!" the boy said.

Yami, the one sitting next to the woman, held up his hand like a boxing pad, ready to take the strike. As the other boy threw out his fist, the bus went over a small bump, spoiling the boy's aim, and he hit the woman in the face.

"Did you jump in front of my fist? What the hell is wrong with you?" the boy shouted.

The others clearly saw what had happened, including Marie, yet the boy was blaming the woman.

"But . . . you hit me," the woman said, holding her face.

"What the fuck are you saying, are you trying to blame me?" the boy asked.

"Hey, small dick!" Marie shouted, standing up; she couldn't take it anymore.

"What, small dick? Are you talking to me?" the boy said, pointing at himself.

"Well, seeing as you're the one who replied, then I guess I was on the mark." Marie smiled to herself, and the other boys laughed at their friend.

"You're the one who hit her, so if anyone should be apologizing it should be you. Why are you getting involved in other people's lives?" Marie asked him.

Rage was building up in the embarrassed boy, and as Marie approached the woman and helped her up, he kicked Marie in the shoulder, sending her falling to the floor.

"I see you act tough, but you fall over just as easily as all the others." The boy smiled.

This was the feeling that Marie hated: feeling weak. These were just some teenage boys, they weren't Altered or gang members, and they were able to humiliate her. What should she do next?

Gritting her teeth, she leapt up and tackled the boy. He didn't fall down, but she punched him on the chin and caught him by surprise.

"That hurt!" the boy yelled, yet before he knew it, his whole body was being electrocuted by a strange object. It was an Anti-Altered weapon, a baton that Marie carried at all times along with a bunch of other weapons.

When the sparks finally ended, the boy fell to the ground, passed out. His friends, after seeing this, didn't want to get involved, and as the bus came to a stop, they quickly picked up their friend and dragged him off.

Marie put away her weapon and saw that it was her stop as well, and rather than checking if the woman was okay, she walked away.

"Thanks for the lift. If you need any reimbursements of any kind, just contact this number," Marie said as she pulled out a business card and handed it to the bus driver. It was a card that Kai had made in case circumstances like these popped up.

The driver and the people on the bus were stunned. They didn't know what to make of the strange occurrence.

Either way, it seemed like the incident just confirmed all of Marie's fears, which was why she was here, on Burnham Street.

CHAPTER 62

MARIE'S PATH

Burnham Street always looked impressive, especially at night, but gone were the days when it transformed from a street full of restaurants to a seedy red-light district. Now it was full of classy bars and fine-dining restaurants.

It was quite impressive how they had managed to transform the clientele and keep it just as busy as before. A lot of this had to do with investments and pushing from Kai, but the real person behind it was the one who had run the red-light district, and that was Olivia Pearl.

Marie looked up at the large octopus above the restaurant; various purple and pink lights glowed inside, with people cheering and more.

"Remember why you're here," Marie said to herself as she pushed the door open. Immediately, she was met by two large bouncers dressed in black suits.

"Whoa there, missy, aren't you a bit too young to be heading inside?" one of the men said, while the other laughed.

"I'm not here to party, I'm here to see Olivia Pearl," Marie said.

"The owner?" one of them replied. "We weren't told that there would be any appointments today."

Marie had run into something like this more than once. If she wasn't wearing her gang colors and mask, they treated her just like everyone else, but this was meant to be a secret meeting.

"Can you just tell her Marie is here to see her? I promise you she'll l understand." Marie was getting frustrated; she had already had a bad day.

"A lot of people try that one. Unless you can show some ID that says you're over eighteen, or book an appointment in advance, then I can't let you in," the man said.

Out of frustration, Marie decided to walk away, or at least she made it look that way, as she bolted and attempted to run right past the two bouncers, but they quickly blocked her path.

As she crashed into them, she fell on the floor, landing on her backside. Looking up, it was only then that she realized the sheer size of the two people.

I'm not sure if even an electrified baton would take these two out, Marie gulped.

"Look, if you don't leave, then we might seriously have to hurt you!" one of the men said as he pulled back his fist, ready to hit Marie, but someone grabbed it.

"What are you doing? Were you really going to hurt a little girl?"

When the bouncers turned around, they saw Olivia, with her bright red lipstick and a fur wrapped around her neck. They immediately bowed.

"I hired you guys to follow the rules, not to cause trouble, and you two remember her face. If she comes here again, you are to let her in immediately," Olivia said as she offered a hand to Marie.

Rather than taking Olivia's hand, though, Marie got up herself. The gesture had brought a smile to her face. The two went inside and Marie followed Olivia to the second floor. A lot had changed compared to the last time she was here. There were a lot fewer rooms and more open space.

They entered a small room that appeared to be for entertaining guests, as there were only two sofas, a table, and a well-stocked bar on the back wall.

I don't feel great about coming here on my own . . . I almost forgot how scary Olivia is, Marie thought.

They were alone in the room, and Olivia's confidence was overwhelming, making it hard for Marie to even speak.

"I was surprised when I heard your voice calling my name," Olivia said. "That's why I went to the door. Since I didn't receive a call, I can only assume you have decided to come here and see me by yourself.

"It's rare that just us two girls hang out with each other, so tell me, why are you here?"

Making a fist as she scrunched up the skirt she was wearing, Marie took a deep breath.

"I'm too weak the way I am now," Marie said. "The others . . . I really don't think they understand how I feel. If I brought it up to them, they would say it's okay, that there's no need for me to do anything, but I don't want that. I want to get stronger.

"And you . . . you're strong, in so many different ways!"

Olivia raised her hand, as she very well understood how Marie was feeling.

"I'm not going to say what the others would say to you, that you are young, or you have time, or that there is no need.

"Which is why I want you to get to the point. What do you want from me? Do you want me to train you? Teach you how to fight? Because that won't work. Our bodies are naturally different, which is why I used weapons in the past, before I was changed."

This was it, this was the question Marie had been reviewing through her head, what she had planned to do.

"You're right, everything you said is right. Which is why I have come here, because I want you to turn me. I want you to turn me into the same as you!"

It was clear as day what Marie meant. The group had learned that Olivia had been turned by Gary, and that Kai had been turned as well. Which meant that she too could be turned.

"I know what you're thinking, but if I went to Gary or Kai, neither of them would ever agree to turn me. They would say there's too much risk! They wouldn't listen to me. How am I supposed to do nothing while they take all of the risks?" Marie argued, even though Olivia hadn't said anything.

She was thinking about it. In the past, the pack rules didn't allow her to hurt the other Howlers, but since they had all been changed recently to keep Midwak in check, that was no longer a problem, but there were other issues.

"There are a few problems here. First, I don't even know if I can turn you, as I have never turned anyone before. We don't even know if that's possible. On top of that, don't you think that me turning you would put me in their bad books?" Olivia replied.

"I'll explain it to them, I'll tell them I forced you, that I gave you no choice, whatever the case I'll make sure you won't get in trouble . . . but please, you're the only one who can help me. Even if we're not sure it will work . . . we have to try."

In Marie's head, it was simple: Olivia would bite her, on her arm or such, and in the worst case she would have a mark there for the rest of her life, but in a best-case scenario she would become like the others and she could stay by their side.

"I've always quite liked you, Marie; that is the only reason why I am willing to listen to your madness and give it a shot."

A giant smile appeared on Marie's face, but Olivia wasn't done.

"But I need to ask you again, are you sure? There is no reversing this process. Your normal life will disappear; there will be a hunger inside you and a desire to kill, as well as dealing with the full moon. It is not something that everyone can handle."

Marie didn't hesitate as she nodded; she had already been thinking about it for a while.

"Very well." Olivia stood up from the sofa, and started to take off her clothes. Since she wasn't wearing her gang uniform, transforming would ruin her clothes, and she quite liked what she had on at the moment.

At first Marie covered her eyes out of embarrassment, but she couldn't help but peek through her fingers at Olivia's beautiful, perfect hourglass figure. She was getting a little red in the face looking at her.

That was until she started to transform: fur growing from her body, her limbs elongating, sharp large teeth protruding.

Although Marie had seen this transformation a few times, she never could get used to it, and her heart started to thump.

However, rather than looking away, she reached out her arm, and Olivia's large teeth sank into her skin.

CHAPTER 63

A NEW BETA

Marie kept her eyes closed, getting ready for what she had asked for. The moment Olivia's fangs pierced her skin, a sharp pain radiated throughout her body, and she screamed out, starting to regret her decision.

What if Olivia doesn't stop there? What if she was only waiting for a chance to get back at us and decides to keep on eating me? The teenager's delusions only lasted so long before her body started to pump out adrenaline, and her arm started to feel cold.

"Are you just going to stand there with your eyes closed the whole time or what?" Olivia asked. Opening her eyes, Marie saw the bloody wound on her arm; it was dripping blood but it wasn't as bad as she had imagined. Meanwhile Olivia was reverting to her human form and changing back into her normal clothes.

"Since I've never done something like this before, I thought it was best if I transformed. Sorry for scaring you a little," Olivia apologized. "I highly doubt biting you in this form would accomplish anything other than making your face turn redder."

That comment alone was enough for Marie's face to flush a little more as the accompanying image went through her head. She quickly shook it away as Olivia approached her again now that she was fully dressed.

"So do you feel any different, other than the pain on your arm?" Olivia's question was filled with curiosity.

"Not really; if anything I feel strangely fine. Not sure what it will be like once the adrenaline is gone, though. What was it like for you, after Gary bit you?" Marie asked.

Olivia had to think back. Honestly speaking, she didn't remember a lot of it, other than cursing Gary for barging in on her base and outright challenging him for the alpha seat.

She hadn't done so ever since. Part of her knew that if they were ever to battle again, her loss was a foregone conclusion. The fact that Gary had managed to beat Midwak proved as much. Besides, there really was not much reason for her to rebel. She had the same power if not more than she did as the leader of the Pincers; as long as everything continued this way, she would be satisfied.

"Oh, wait." Olivia finally remembered something. "I forgot to warn you, get ready for some serious pa—"

"Ahhh!" A scream echoed in the room, followed by a thud.

Marie was rolling around on the floor helplessly, digging her nails into the carpet, trying to tear at it as if it would help her in any way. The veins all over her body were bulging, as the blood shifted and flowed up and down.

It hurts so much, my heart feels like it's going to explode . . . am I going to die? Marie started to fear for her life.

The pain continued and she wanted to scream to let it out, but only silence came out of her mouth, as if her body was denying her even this after the first bloodcurdling scream.

Every time she attempted to scream, pain started to emerge from a different area, even worse than before. Olivia was left with nothing to do but watch the poor girl on the floor for over five minutes. She knelt down by her side with a worried look.

I don't remember the pain going on for this long; has something happened? Could there be a problem since I was the one to bite her?

Olivia grabbed Marie's hand, and Marie's grip was far stronger than usual, stronger than human, that was for sure. Were it not for her being a werewolf, she felt like her entire hand would have been crushed.

"Don't you dare die on me now, girl! You said you would explain to the others that this whole thing was your idea! How can you do that if you're dead?"

It was Olivia's unique way of encouragement, but it was better than nothing. The pain continued on for another hellish five minutes; Marie's heart had no time to rest, beating fast during the whole ordeal.

And for what could have been the first time for Olivia, she felt somewhat bad for what she had done, because it was her bite that was causing all of this pain.

"Don't die! You wanted to show the others what you have, right? Well, this is the price you have to pay. You were too scared to leave, because you thought they worried too much about you; well, prove them wrong and get through this!" Olivia screamed.

The pressure from Marie's grip on her hand was starting to fade, and her heartbeat was starting to slow.

"No, no!" Olivia shouted. "Are you even listening to me? If you die, I'll kill you myself!"

Marie's grip had completely relaxed, and it was over. All of it was over.

"Thank you . . . thank you . . . I . . . I could hear . . . you loud and clear," Marie answered weakly.

Having arrived at the academy, Gary was resting in his room. Without any warning a message popped up.

A new beta werewolf has joined the pack
1 Pawn point has been awarded

At first he thought it was a mistake, but the message was clear as day.
What is going on? Did one of the others bite someone?
Gary remembered something from the system, claiming that those he turned could turn others as well.

However, he never thought the others would do such a thing, because even with his Alpha Bite there was no guarantee, merely a lower chance of failure, which he could only assume to be synonymous with death.

If the alpha already had a low chance of a bite succeeding, then what were the chances of a beta succeeding and turning someone?

Who was it? There are only three other werewolves in the Howlers pack, and I doubt Midwak would try to pull something so soon. Was Kai testing something without informing me? Maybe . . . or could it have been Olivia? Why would any one of them try anything so dangerous?

Getting on his phone, he sent each one of them a message to call him ASAP, but unfortunately all of them seemed to be busy. Remembering he had another way to check, he opened the Pack menu via his system.

Howlers Pack

Alpha Werewolf—Gary Dem
Grade: Rook (1/50)

Beta Werewolf—Olivia Pearl
Grade: Knight (0/5)

Beta Werewolf—Kyle Hamper
Grade: Knight (0/5)

Beta Werewolf—Midwak Convel
Grade: Rook (0/50)

Beta Werewolf—Mai Degrace
Grade: Pawn (0/1)

That was when he saw Marie's name written there.

"What is going on?" Gary picked up the phone again; he needed to find out some answers.

Before doing anything, Olivia waited for Marie to regain some energy. They both waited a few minutes to see if there were any more signs of pain, but everything was okay with the both of them. Marie clenched her hands a few times, and she could feel a difference in strength from that little act alone.

Her nose was also sharper, able to pick up many smells in the air, stronger scents she couldn't even describe, and her ears were also capable of picking up on the conversations happening on the floor below.

"I really have changed." A wave of emotions came over Marie, and tears were falling down her face.

"Most people would be frightened, or hate the fact that they've become a werewolf, and yet here you are crying tears of joy," Olivia said sarcastically, with a slight smirk on her lips.

Marie quickly tried the ultimate test as she tried to transform. She gritted her teeth, imagining her body changing, yet nothing happened.

"Yeah, I tried that as well, but I'm afraid it's not as easy as it looks. After your first full moon it might be different, but just changing is only the beginning. It's going to be tough from here on out. Did you think just becoming a werewolf would change you? Well, it did, but I imagine that just like becoming an Altered, you'll still need to put in the hard work, though you're lucky that I can share my own experiences with you."

"No, that's okay, I can do it my—"

"What, you don't have a problem letting me turn you, but now you're about to reject my kind offer?" Olivia asked as she leaned in closer.

Marie felt like she was unable to refuse; if she did, then maybe worse things would happen, and through this experience she had learned that maybe Olivia was a nicer person than she seemed.

"You are a good person; I can't believe you did all that stuff before. Is there a reason for it?" Marie asked the question that was on her mind but quickly realized that she could be overstepping.

"A reason?" Olivia replied as she thought back, but she was interrupted by her phone vibrating on the sofa.

She picked it up and saw that Kai was calling.

She didn't think anything of it, but as soon as she answered the call she wasn't even able to get a word in.

"What did you do?" The growl from the phone sent shivers down her spine as well as Marie's.

CHAPTER 64

KAI'S ANGER

Gary's initial reaction was twofold when he found out about Marie. The first was worry, wondering if she was okay.

To his mind, for Marie to have turned was only plausible if she was forced into it. Someone must have bitten her trying to take control of her.

However, the fact that she was now part of the pack made Gary wonder what the other person's intentions were by turning Marie.

Because according to his system, if Marie were to die now, she would disappear from the list, notifying him immediately.

Which was when the second emotion took over: anger. For whatever reason, someone had deliberately risked his friend's life.

He picked up the phone and called the person most likely to have turned her. However, Kai told him that he was not the one, and he knew Midwak was still in Notsburg, leaving only one possible suspect.

"All right, at least the good news is that Marie was successfully turn—"

Before he could finish, Kai had already hung up, sharing Gary's anger. Unlike their leader, he was close enough to demand some answers in person.

I can't say I'm not a little worried for Olivia, seeing as Kai treats Marie like his little sister. Well, whatever happens, she only has herself to blame. If it were Amy in this situation, I don't know what I would do. Still... perhaps I should give her a heads-up that Kai might be on his way.

Calming down, Gary felt like what was done was done. She was already turned, and there was nothing they could do about that but help her.

Looking at his system, Gary saw the number of Pawn points as disposable, and he felt that maybe it was safe to upgrade Marie. If it was like the others, she would get a class upgrade as well.

Kai's call to Olivia ended abruptly. She was unable to get a word in; Kai kept howling at her.

"How could you be so stupid? I was just starting to trust you. Do you know who she is?"

Marie could hear everything, and she shook her head. Neither she nor Olivia had ever seen him act this way.

Kai was the cool, calm, and collected one; even in a tense situation he never acted like this. Marie couldn't lie, either; the fact that he was acting this way made her a little happy.

"That went about as well as expected," Olivia noted as she rubbed her ears after Kai hung up. They were hurting from all the shouting.

"It sounds like he's on his way here. You heard it as well, I didn't even have a chance to explain myself, and I doubt he will have cooled down by the time he arrives. Since this was all *your* idea, you've got a pretty big job ahead of you, missy."

There was an awkward smile from Marie, but a promise was a promise; she wouldn't let Olivia get in trouble for this.

Moments later a large limousine drove down Burnham Street. Usually late at night or early in the morning you could drive on the footpath, but during the day when there were so many pedestrians, the road was closed, so the sight of the car as well as the particular car that it was had caught a lot of attention.

It stopped just outside the restaurant with the giant octopus sign, and the door was opened aggressively.

Kai was the first to exit the vehicle; he wasn't wearing his gang uniform or his mask, revealing the scar he still had across his jaw thanks to Midwak.

Following behind him was a large figure, strangely wearing fluffy gray pajamas, but nonetheless there was a serious look on his face.

This is a bit embarrassing, Austin thought, as he felt the eyes on him. *I was just getting ready for sleep, but how could I ignore a call from Kai when he sounded so angry?*

Kai hadn't really explained much; he didn't have time, but since he was seeing Olivia and a fight could very well break out, he wanted to call someone, and Austin was the only one who answered, otherwise he would have brought Innu as well.

Regardless, they walked inside the venue, reaching the two large bouncers inside.

"What is with today and these kids trying to get in? Since when did this venue become so popular with the young ones?" the bouncer complained.

"Austin," Kai said, and he already knew what he needed to do.

Stepping forward in front of the bouncers, the two large men couldn't help but let out a laugh. Unlike Kai, who looked his age, Austin looked more like an adult, and no matter how big he was, his outfit led to a burst of laughter.

"I'm sorry but there is no sleeping allowed inside," one of the bouncers joked.

Austin grabbed their shoulders and with a simple push hurled them into the door, sending one of their heads right through it.

Hmm, I need to control my strength a bit more, Austin thought.

The music was so loud that no one was aware of what was happening inside. So when Austin and Kai entered, they didn't get too much attention at first as they walked through the crowds to head upstairs.

However, soon Austin was drawing a lot of attention.

"Oh, I like your style."

"Why did I never think of that? I think this could set a new trend. We should implement a pajama night!"

"Hey, this might sound strange, but can I rub your clothes?"

People were blocking Austin left, right, and center, and Kai was already by the stairs where there were even more guards.

"Hey you, you're not allowed up here!"

These were all technically members of the Howlers, so Kai didn't want to hurt them. As they tried to grab him, he quickly took a step forward and tripped one of them up.

The other guard was still running down the staircase, and Kai used his power to jump over the person before quickly rushing up the stairs.

"Olivia, come out here!" Kai shouted, knowing that she definitely would hear him from the second floor.

Just like that, a bunch of guards came out from their rooms hearing the shout, and Olivia emerged at the end of the hallway.

"Everyone get back in your rooms and stay there; this is a very important guest!" Olivia said.

The guards retreated behind their doors, as Kai's eyes started glowing blue.

"What is this? You want to fight me, without even hearing me out? That isn't like you." Olivia smiled.

"Hear you out?" Kai said as he walked forward, his arm transforming. "There is nothing to hear about the fact that you went behind not just my back but Gary's as well and turned her. You didn't even consult me. Do you think you can do something like that to someone I care about?" Kai rushed forward but as he did, Marie quickly stood between them, spreading her arms out.

"You can't hurt her, Kai!" Marie shouted. "If you do, I'll never forgive you."

"Mai, move," Kai instructed.

"No! Stop being so stubborn and just listen."

"She's right, you know," Olivia added. "Why don't you listen to what Marie wants for once, rather than doing everything for her. You are not in control of her life; she is in charge of her own. So listen to her."

Although Olivia's words seemed to only anger Kai more at first, hearing what she said and seeing the desperation in Marie's eyes calmed him down, and Marie saw it as her chance to explain.

"I was the one who approached Olivia; I was the one who asked her to turn me. Just take a look at your current behavior. This is why I knew I couldn't go to you or Gary.

"I know you guys care about me, so you would have simply said there was no need. That you two would protect me, but I want to be with you guys . . . side by side, not hiding in the back! Even if you say I don't have to do this, I can help in my own way. I want to help in my own way.

"Back then, when we fought Midwak, if it weren't for Innu, if it weren't for Izzy, I would have died. I know that.

"So I couldn't just stay by your side as I am now. I had to change. You can't blame Olivia; all of this was my own choice!"

Kai's arm started to revert back to normal, his eyes no longer glowing as he thought about Marie.

I thought I was doing a good job of protecting her, but she's right, I never considered how she felt. I just didn't want to lose another person that I cared about so much. I didn't want her involved in all of this to begin with, and now she's more involved than she needs to be.

I can't believe that she was so scared of me that she felt like she couldn't even ask me.

Just as Kai was about to speak, Marie's phone received a message from Gary.

Brace yourself.

CHAPTER 65

PICK ONE

Through a process of elimination, Gary determined that Olivia had to be the one who turned Marie into a werewolf. Kai's reaction indicated that he was not responsible, and Midwak was also ruled out. Given Olivia's past actions, including her use of the whip to save the group, Gary could not imagine her acting with harmful intentions.

In the end, Marie was safe, and Gary had to address the new reality he was facing.

Now that she is a werewolf, there's a good chance that she won't just be involved in gang matters, and that Midwak's old pack might go after her in the future. In that case, the best thing to do is to allow her to evolve, and assign her a class.

Having gone through the process himself, Gary knew that receiving a Class was quite painful. Remembering Kai's transformation and Olivia's complaint about no prior notice, he decided to warn Marie in advance by sending her a text.

Feeling confident in his decision, Gary smiled to himself and opened his Pack tab. He then allocated the necessary Pawn points toward Marie and watched as the system reacted as expected.

Congratulations, one of your Beta Werewolves (Mai Degrace) has been upgraded to Knight Grade
You may now select her class
Hunter Class

A Werewolf Hunter is fast, agile, and sneaky. They focus on killing their prey quickly, out of sight and from the shadows. They are able to track their targets from a great distance and have great focus.
Class perks include: more and better Marks, improved tracking

This was the same class he had assigned Olivia. It was handy to have her as a Hunter as Gary could mark targets, giving her a boost in power. While she could do it as well without a system of her own, she would only do so subconsciously, once her killing intent for a target exceeded some unknown value.

As for the tracking features, Gary's theory on that was that Hunter class werewolves had a larger detection range for marks. He himself had realized in the past that the ones he had marked, like Tom and his sister, had turned more and more faint the greater the distance. Because of that, though, he would know when one of his friends was in trouble; following them via scent was next to impossible.

Given that their pack already had a Hunter, Gary felt that another one wasn't really necessary, though part of his decision also stemmed from the fact that the system didn't recommend that option.

Warrior Class
Werewolf Warriors can be considered the vanguards of their pack. They lead their pack into battle with their great strength. They have exceptional fighting ability and courage, but it is because of this trait that they also have the highest fatality rate.
Class perks include: wide range of skills to select from, large Energy pool

This option was of course what Gary had chosen for himself. It was a strong class, and unlike the others, he already knew the advanced options that one would be able to select. Although he didn't think that the role of a Dark Warrior would suit her, it might not hurt to switch her to the Paladin class in the future.

However, I don't like the fact that the Warrior Class has the highest fatality rate. Although the classes beyond that level are good, I'm not sure if I have enough points to shoot her up to a grade where she can select her next class. I also have no idea what the class promotions for the other two classes are; for all I know, they might be just as good, if not better.

Protector Class
A Werewolf Protector boasts one of the sturdiest bodies of their race.
They use their own body to shield their fellow pack members from
any harm, making sure they will survive.
Class perks include: extra Endurance, faster healing

Unlike Kai, Marie only has access to the three base classes. Does that
mean that he only got that extra option because I used Alpha Bite to turn
him? Was it purely luck? Or could it have something to do with natural
aptitude? The system also didn't recommend any of them this time, so
does that mean Marie is simply an all-rounder? Gary wondered, but
then he recalled that when he had to make a choice for his class promotion, there also had been no recommendation.

Given the last option, Marie's small stature didn't fit the image
Gary had when he thought of a Protector class werewolf. He felt like
this was a role suited for someone with a large wall of muscle like Austin. He also had yet to experience what the Protector class could do, so
it was a bit of a risk.

Going by the class perks, the best advantage the Protector class
seems to have is that they should be very hard to kill. A hard body, and
fast healing. Although the name sounds like they would only be good as
defenders, that doesn't have to mean that they have no offensive capa-
bilities.

There's also no reason for Marie to completely change and give up
what she has been doing to fit such a role. Nothing is stopping her from
continuing to be a backline support, only with the added benefit of ex-
treme defense and great healing. This way, she should be able to survive
long enough for any of us to help her out in a bad situation. I also believe
Kai would support such a choice.

The more Gary thought about it, the more he talked himself into
this being the optimal choice for her.

You have selected the Protector class
The process will now begin.

CHAPTER 66

A NEW PERSON

While Marie went through her transformation, Gary looked at the remainder of his points, and going by the numbers, he had enough to evolve both Kai and Olivia to the next grade. Whether this would result in them advancing in their class, he wasn't so sure. After all, his own class promotion had been the result of reaching Level 25, but his pack members didn't have any levels.

I should probably stop here and do it the next time I see them in person. It's likely that I'll have to make a choice between two options for them as well, and it would be better to ask their opinion rather than deciding it now.

Sending out another text, Gary apologized to Marie for what she must be experiencing right now. He also sent another text to Kai telling him not to worry if she suddenly fell into extreme pain, because she was simply going through the same process as he had when becoming a Shapeshifter class. He also asked to be kept updated on any changes. Pretty pleased with himself, Gary finally decided to get some shut-eye for the night.

The next day, Gary attended his lessons at the Altered academy. During the morning break he talked with his friends as if nothing had happened the day before. They brought up their future lessons, and some said they were more confident compared to before based on the experience they had had.

Gary noticed that Izzy was quieter than normal, which seemed to be related to her wound that had yet to disappear. However, once lessons finished, it was time for Gary and Numba to go somewhere. The two had been lucky enough to make it exactly one day before their special lesson, so that's where they were headed.

The situation in Slough took longer to deal with than I thought. Which means I have two more special lessons to attend before I decide to take the Altered assessment and get out of here. I made my decision and told the others already, Gary thought.

The thing was, Gary had gotten a boost from the Altered that day, far more than he would have gotten from the beasts that had their crystal removed. So honestly, unlike before, he didn't feel like he would lose out too much if he stopped attending. Nevertheless, he would still have his debut match to become a proper AFC fighter.

The two had met up with Crowley and were walking through the halls. They returned to the training room and put on their red-and-blue uniforms, and that was when they saw someone they had completely forgotten about, someone who had been impacted by their visit to Notsburg personally.

Sty looked tired as he put on his uniform; he even stuck his leg through the arm sleeve, and then on the wrong side a few times. It was quite clear that he wasn't in the right place.

When Numba saw him, he hated to admit it but he felt bad for the guy. Although he was a Grade A scumbag, he was also a kid who had just lost his father, even if he had been the leader of the Scatterbugs. When they met back at the AFA, Numba had expected Sty to go crazy, to shout at them or attempt to attack them, but he hadn't said a word.

Losing a father, even if he is a dick, would be bad for anyone, Numba thought. Although he knew that he was merely adopted by Harry Cardenez, Harry was like his real father, and he knew he would be heartbroken if anything happened to him. Perhaps it was even worse to lose someone you actually were related to . . .

Just then, Apollo came over and stopped in front of Gary.

"You were away for a while; I was starting to get worried that you would leave the academy." Apollo smiled. "But then I heard that your gang took over the Scatterbugs; I can only guess that's the reason you went back."

Numba couldn't help but smirk inwardly. "If only you knew what role exactly he was playing in that."

"Your gang is impressive, just like you." Apollo continued to praise the green-haired teenager. "Just to let you know, my family has decided to take in Sty, so don't feel too bad. It's not like you had anything to do with the decision. It sucks, but things like this happen, and let's get on with this assessment."

Things were going smoothly, perhaps too smoothly for some strange reason, but Gary kept his mouth shut to not jinx himself. He preferred to stay uninvolved in any future academy matter, since he would be leaving soon anyway.

"I have an announcement about today's assessment," Crowley informed them. "Because of the performance both teams have shown during the inspection, the beast chosen for today is a particularly strong one. For your own sake, I can only highly advise you to work together. Today isn't a time to make this into a contest over who is stronger; your main focus should be on surviving this encounter!"

Gary was ready, and despite his teacher's warning he didn't feel afraid, not even a little bit. After his fight with Midwak, a beast seemed like a minor thing in comparison, but still a great stepping-stone on his journey to get stronger. After all, he had a powerful werewolf on his back who was going to try to take his spot each and every month now.

"Let's go!"

CHAPTER 67

A NEW GARY

Crowley had said before that if they ever did a special lesson together, the beast that they went up against would be a strong one. So it was safe to say that they were all a little nervous as they entered the room.

Gary looked up at the observing room. Since it was a one-way mirror, he was unable to see through it, but he could sense the people behind it, most likely from NIRV again, watching everything that was going on.

No mark . . . it looks like Tom wasn't able to come this time, Gary lamented. *Before, I was a little shy in hiding my powers, worried about what they would do, but the academy has done a good job in protecting me so far, and outside, they would have to go through the Howlers to get to me.*

Everyone except Sty looked ready for what was to come out of the door in front of them. He was still absent-minded, and it was clear to his fellow students that they should not rely on him today. He seemed to lack motivation and was just going through the motions.

On the other hand, Gary's behavior was different this time. Rather than step back, he inched forward until he was side by side with Apollo.

"Oh . . . have you decided to show us something interesting this time?" Apollo asked. "You're not the only one. While none of us were able to do much against Jayden last time, it's different now. There's a reason why I'm always at the top."

Gary wasn't sure if he was imagining it or not, but he felt something strange coming from between Apollo's hands: particles of frost around his fingers.

Did he learn how to use a skill with his Altered form? Gary wondered.

It seemed different from Xin's yellow bolts of electricity; his was more blue. Still, Gary didn't have time to worry about that, or about how strong the others were getting.

The sound of the door opening made them stop their chatter and look toward the beast that was slowly coming into view. It had a set of hooves and large muscular legs, like the bottom half of a horse.

This came as a big surprise after hearing that this enemy would be a tough one for them to battle. This creature was small and compact, rather than large and bulky as they had all imagined it to be. As the door slowly lifted more, they saw its chest, which was almost exactly like that of a human.

It had a stunning muscular body with human hands. So far it looked like a mythical beast, the centaur of legend, but there was something different about this one. It had no head, or at least the head was not where one would expect.

On top of the human body was a neck, but it led to nothing, as if somebody had cut it off. Rather, on its chest they could make out a face that stuck out a little from between its pecs. It was smiling, with fully white eyes.

"That doesn't look like any beast I've ever seen," Wu exclaimed in shock.

"Yeah, it looks like something straight from my nightmares," Numba added.

James, the head of the NIRV team at the AFA, was inwardly smiling, or rather outwardly, though he was doing a good job covering it with his palm.

These kids have no idea what they are facing, but seeing as the study of beasts isn't part of the curriculum, this doesn't surprise me. Even if we told them that they're looking at a bona fide humanoid beast, they wouldn't understand the implications.

NIRV had done a lot of research into beasts, especially after re-creating them from fossils. Different beasts emitted different amounts of energy, and the only way to measure the level of energy emitted was from the crystals after their death.

However, the more data they collected, the more proficient they became in estimating the strength of a beast based on the fossil used to create it. Regardless, there was one thing that would turn their knowledge on its head, and that was beasts in humanoid form.

Sometimes the crystals gathered after their death emitted a low amount of energy, yet for some reason they were far stronger in battle. They had learned this the hard way, concluding that humanoid beasts were at the top of their class.

This was not going to be an easy task.

When the door was fully open, the beast started to scrape its legs across the floor. Moments later, it charged directly at all of them.

"We should wait and see what it can do first, and then attack it, right?" Numba asked Gary, who had yet to do anything.

Instead, the others acted. Wu went forward, as he wished to match the centaur beast in strength. Antennas protruded from his head, and his form slightly bulged. Since the beast seemed to have no deadly weapons on its body, Wu felt like this was the perfect opponent for him.

At that moment, the two of them collided, yet Wu was easily pushed back.

It's so strong! Despite its smaller size, it's even stronger than the centipede monster!

Wu was suddenly lifted off the ground by the centaur. Seeing this, Snow came in to help, jumping with his powerful legs toward the beast, but the centaur threw Wu right into Snow, causing the two of them to tumble.

"Hee hee hee!" The face on its chest emitted a horrible shriek that could only be interpreted as wicked laughter. Suddenly a large heavy fist came down from above. Apollo was in the air, grasping his hands together in a type of hammer strike.

As he swung, a blizzard of cold air followed his hands, and they smashed into the floor, missing their target but destroying the tiles underneath. The centaur stood smiling a distance away.

That thing is so fast, and it's almost like it's teasing us, Numba noted, wondering if his explosive speed would be enough to contend with it, or if his fate would be the same as Wu's.

It looks like Apollo did learn a skill, but I'm not the same either.
As Gary started to join the battle, the clock hit six p.m.

Under the night sky, your Werewolf self will receive a large boost in
Energy
Your Energy is now doubled
All skills have temporarily increased in level

When Gary was close enough, he could see the centaur still not moving; it had the human trait of arrogance and this would be its downfall.

Gary transformed his arms and legs.

Skill activated: Lethal Pounce (Level 2)

He jumped away from the centaur, which turned its body, but before it could do anything, Gary had jumped a second time. This was part of the Lethal Pounce Level 2 skill.

Hitting his target, Gary plowed his transformed arm right through the beast's chest, holding its head in the air.

CHAPTER 68

CLASSIFIED INFORMATION

One moment, everyone was ready to fight with everything they had. After seeing Apollo, Wu, and Snow struggle against the beast, they knew this was going to be a difficult task, and a thought crept in at the back of their minds: what if this time they weren't strong enough?

These types of situations would enable them to grow, yet all of their built-up feelings vanished in a moment. They looked at Gary, who had pulled his arm back out of the beast and planted his feet on the floor.

The beast fell to the ground with a loud thud, unmoving, clearly having been killed. It had happened so soon, so fast, and with no sign of struggle.

"You . . ." Apollo said, looking at Gary, and for the first time he was speechless. Throughout their meetings and journeys in the academy, Apollo had always felt superior to Gary, even though he was interested in his strength. Yet now, after seeing what had happened, he was finding it hard to believe.

Shaking his head, he smiled.

"Not only did I think I was already far ahead of you, I thought I was continuing to put distance between the two of us. I saw most of your skills when you fought against Jayden, and now you're on this level . . . how quickly are you growing, and when will you hit your peak?"

It was only for a moment, but Apollo was feeling shocked. He wondered if this was how others felt when they saw his power, but he soon realized that all of this was a good thing.

There was someone his age who could be competition. It just meant he needed to work harder if he wanted to lead his own gang in the future and take them to new heights.

I was unsure before, but if your gang is as special as you are, I believe that the world will soon learn that there is a new king. The question is, which one will fall so you can rise? Apollo thought.

When a beast was defeated, a team of NIRV workers would come out and dissect the beast to find the crystal. This time, they were a bit slower, perhaps because the beast had been killed so quickly.

"*I can tell that those guys are stunned by Gary,* Numba thought. "Look, Wu and Snow can't even look at them. I can't believe it myself, but Gary hasn't even shown them everything he has, because he can't."

Numba was feeling lucky that he had met someone like Gary, and that his family was now deeply connected with him. As long as Numba was with him, he thought they could achieve great things.

The workers arrived and got to work as usual, and Gary's request was granted. He was allowed to have the body of the beast before it went away.

It feels like there is more energy lingering in the body than usual. It's a shame, I thought maybe I could get the crystal and see if it would help me even more, but it wasn't where I was expecting it to be.

After consuming the beast, Gary saw an increase in his stats.

Dexterity 45 >>> 47
Endurance 48 >>> 49

It was more stat points than he usually would have received, but now since his stats were so high, the increase looked minimal, and in a way it felt minimal as well.

I guess it makes sense to not feel as much of an improvement. If I had 1,000 stat points and gained 1 point, then the difference between 1,000 and 1,001 wouldn't be great, but the difference between 1 and 2 is double. Still, a small margin in a fight could be the difference.

While Gary was busy in the special room feasting on the beast, someone else was also surprised by the results of the day's special lesson.

I wasn't expecting that at all, James thought. The NIRV employee looked at the computer screen again. He saw the transformation and the defeat of the beast.

The humanoid beast was meant to be a real test for them. To be honest, I wouldn't have been surprised if one of them died today. Yet, because of him, that didn't happen.

Lifting his head, he looked at the others.

"Did you gather information on the students' Altered forms like I asked?" James said.

Another employee stood up.

"We did check, and even bought information from the other companies to see if they had any records on Altered forms that were like that of a wolf. We found nothing. However, when I dug into the NIRV files a bit more, I did find something related to it."

After the strange request, James was looking into Gary more and more, and he was only getting more curious.

"Unfortunately sir, I was unable to access the files," the employee replied.

"You couldn't access the files? Did you use my access code?" James asked.

"Yes sir, since it was a request from you, I even requested to have access to the files, thinking that it was some mistake. After all, it's just information on some Wolf-type Altered, but the request was denied."

So there was information in NIRV that not even an employee at James's level could get access to. Now he was really intrigued.

If I can't get access, then I will just have to do some research myself. Let's see, if you can defeat a humanoid beast so easily, then it's only fair to up the level of the next special lesson. James inwardly smiled.

CHAPTER 69

A DEAL WITH THE PHOENIX

The Phoenix gang was one of the most well-known Tier 1 gangs in the country. The main reason for this was their leader, Sin, who wasn't one to shy away from showing off his powers. Unlike most of the Kings, who seemed content with secretly ruling from behind the scenes, Sin was very public in displaying his face and fighting on the front lines, especially if there was a group that annoyed him.

Even though his face was so public, the other Kings didn't attempt to go after him or increase their influence, which, in a lot of ways, showed the power the Phoenix gang had. This was precisely why two people from a small Tier 3 town had decided to join them: Raven and Gil.

The two of them had nothing left behind at Slough. Gil's parents had long since abandoned him; his consistent streak of getting into trouble had caused them to eventually give up on their son.

As for Raven, his parents had died, leaving him and his brother on their own. Trying to make a better life for themselves, he had joined hands with his two friends Brandon and Yovan and had founded the Gray Elephants, who had managed to become one of the two overlords of Slough. Alas, his friends, as well as his brother, had all messed with the wrong people and had ended up killed.

As if fate had brought them together, Raven and Gil had nowhere else to go, but they shared a clear goal, and that was to punish the person they held responsible for all of their recent troubles: Gary Dem.

Unfortunately, there was nothing they could do on their own. They both knew his strength; he had proven himself by taking out the Underdogs. Being in the de facto strongest gang made them as untouchable as a world-renowned celebrity; they needed help, and so Raven had decided to leave town and join the Phoenix gang.

Coming from a Tier 3 town, despite being the vice leader of a prominent gang, Raven had no choice but to start from the bottom, same as Gil. Nevertheless, this didn't bother him. The two of them were always quick to volunteer for any and all jobs, be it to clean up one of the gang hideouts or to get rid of dead bodies or evidence of crimes committed. Doing the dirty work that no one liked to do had quickly earned them a favorable impression from the others.

Neither one was a stranger to gruesome sights; some of the scenes they had witnessed would make any normal person faint, but eventually they had grown numb to such things. When they were given their first proper task, it allowed them to commit to what they needed to do, which was easier than they thought.

The gang was impressed, and slowly they were being recognized for their talents. They were given more important jobs that required them to get stronger.

Raven had always been a skilled fighter, and Gil had natural strength and agility from his rugby days. They often trained against each other and continued to improve their fighting skills, but it wasn't enough to stand out. In a Tier 1 gang, there were many like them who were just as skilled or just as strong.

At some point they hit a wall. Without rising to a higher position they would have no influence, but those who were able to rise up were at least Altered, something that they could never be unless a miracle occurred.

Unbeknownst to them, their wishes would soon be granted. It was next to impossible for either one of them to meet with Sin, the leader of the Phoenix gang, not only because their standing was far too low but also because he was often out and about doing his own thing. Nevertheless, for some reason they couldn't even begin to fathom, one day they were called out in front of him, since Sin seemed to have some interest in Slough. Because they were natives, he asked for all the information they had on the place.

They shared everything they knew, with Raven giving more of the detailed information about the underworld: how the Underdogs worked, what members the Howlers had, and more.

A few days later, as they continued their normal duties in the gang, they were called once more, only this time they were to head to the large villa in the mountains overlooking the sea.

Both Gil and Raven sat down nervously as they looked at the surrounding guards and Sin in a dark red jacket, looking out at the view from his balcony.

"I called you two back because I wanted to thank you for the information you provided before," Sin explained, still not turning around. "I am a fair boss who rewards those who are helpful, and you have been very helpful in this situation."

One of the men who was standing by the side wearing sunglasses came over with a metal briefcase. He slammed it on the table in front of them and opened it, revealing two syringes.

Is this what I think it is? Gil thought with excitement. *I've only heard the others talk about it, the new method to become an Altered. It's Altered solution . . . he's really allowing us to become Altered!*

Although Gil was over the moon, the same couldn't be said for Raven, because he noticed something about the syringes. The liquid inside was black, and it was moving around as if it were alive.

This seems awfully like the same liquid he wanted us to disseminate among the Gray Elephants . . . and it turned them all into those mindless monsters.

Sin turned around and immediately noticed the look on Raven's face. "From the looks of it, you have seen this before."

Raven was quite surprised, because in their last meeting Sin had seemingly forgotten all about him.

"I can already guess what your main concern is, so let me calm you down. This solution has been vastly improved. Think about it, what would I have to gain from turning two of my own men into Crazed Altered? If I wanted to get rid of you, would I really have to use such methods?

"I am offering you this chance because I have big plans for you two. Whatever reasons you have for leaving Slough, you will be able to return with no problem at all if you take this.

"And, to go one step further, this is your choice, your reward for being loyal; I will not force you to take it."

Raven looked at the syringes again; they were slightly different from the one he had given them. The black liquid was sitting on top of the other color inside the tube rather than mixing with it. Also, last time only part of the solution had been used which could have caused the bad side effects.

Gary is growing stronger, and according to my information, his whole group is also improving at a frightening speed. If I wish to have any chance of catching up, to get revenge for Hawk, I need to take risks. Raven had convinced himself, and he grabbed the syringe and stabbed it into his shoulder.

CHAPTER 70

TAKING IT SERIOUSLY

The sound of the familiar alarm went off, and almost immediately Gary reached out his hand, stopping it. Instead of just hitting the snooze button or staying snuggled in his sheets for a few minutes like he used to do, he got up straightaway, rubbing his eyes.

After that, he stood up and started to stretch. Raising his arms as high as possible toward the ceiling, he did a few more stretches and then reached toward his toes.

It was still dark outside, and his lessons wouldn't start for a while, but he still put on his AFA uniform and headed outside. On the way out of his room, he passed a few of his notebooks that contained several drawn images and written words. They were his notes from the videos he had been watching last night.

Outside, Gary headed to the large track and field area. The track was a standard 400-meter oval, while in the middle of the field was some training equipment. After a brief warm-up, Gary began sprinting around the track.

This was Gary's new routine. Late at night he would study Altered matches from the AFC. Although he knew that Altered were stronger outside the AFC, because of their skills that were banned inside the ring, they were still talented at hand-to-hand combat.

When Gary fought in his werewolf form it was very physical, so getting better at hand-to-hand combat was important. During his time as a werewolf Gary had been doing a lot, and he had been training as well, but not the way he would have been training at the AFA.

Instead he was getting stronger through his system and his were-wolf self. He didn't regret it, because it was the fastest way for him to improve, and it possibly was what saved his life.

Now, though, eating beasts would raise his stats by one or two points, which wasn't much of a difference, so he needed to improve in a different way.

That's why I've decided to go back to the basics. Analyze the skills, replicate how they fight. I remember Eddy and Xin. Both of them were strong and skilled at controlling their powers. The debut students train by increasing their strength without transforming, in order to make their Altered forms stronger and deadlier.

I'm not an Altered, but I feel the same can apply to me.

All of these things had led to Gary making his own routine, to do everything he could to improve and get stronger.

After a few laps around the track, Gary stopped for a moment and thought back to some of the skills that he saw on the video. He was attempting to replicate some of the kicks, but they were very difficult.

Unless I film myself or have a mirror, it's hard to check my form to see if I'm doing it right, and even if I learn the skills, it's harder to find a use for them in actual combat unless I have a sparring partner.

For a second, Gary thought about asking Numba or one of the others, but asking them to wake up this early was just unfair. Regardless, Gary continued to go through the motions as he imagined the opponents on the screen in front of him.

While he practiced, multiple thoughts were going through his head. One of them was how far he had come: from being a transporter for a gang to being the leader of a gang and taking over Slough.

From there, he were now in charge of a Tier 2 city and was bringing in more wealth than he could spend. Unless it had to do with Altered solutions and Anti-Altered weapons.

Kai's plan is working as well. The investments in Slough are being made in my name, and people are starting to learn about me. It's scary sometimes how far ahead that guy thinks, Gary thought, but his mood soon went sour.

It's crazy . . . me a successful business tycoon. I still remember when we were struggling with our bills and were unable to even buy meat. Now our family never has to worry about money again . . . and yet my mother isn't able to experience any of this. She hasn't been able to enjoy a stress-free life. When will you wake up?

"Gary?" a voice called out from behind.

Judging by the sky around them, Gary thought it was around six a.m.; the sun still hadn't risen, so who would be out here at this time who knew his name?

When he turned his head, he saw another AFA student in her uniform.

"Xin, what are you doing here?" Gary asked; he couldn't help but stare at her smooth face and glowing eyes.

"What do you mean? I come here every day, it's you who's here for the first time," Xin replied.

The truth was, Xin was quite happy to see Gary and surprised to find him here of all places. After their last meeting was cut short, she had checked to see if Gary was okay, only to find that he had left the academy on some urgent business.

"Right . . . I just thought that I should train a bit harder, and take the academy a little more seriously," Gary answered.

The comment annoyed Xin a bit, because during her whole time in the academy she *had* been taking it seriously, and she wondered how he could be so relaxed. Which caused a few unexpected words to come out of her mouth.

"Fight me."

CHAPTER 71

FIGHT ME

Taking a step back, Gary was a little startled at the sudden request. In the first place he never expected to see Xin, and when he did see her, he often fumbled his words or found it hard to speak.

So, when he heard this, he was really fumbling now.

"I . . . fight . . . me . . . me . . . fight . . . you," Gary said, struggling to get his words out.

"Yes," Xin replied. "Gary, I've seen how strong you are. How strong you have become and how you beat the others. At the moment, everyone says that I'm rank 1 in this place, but is that really the case? How can I say I'm rank 1, when I haven't gone against you?"

Rankings were never something Gary cared about since coming into the AFA. In his head, his dreams were too small in the first place. Just getting into the AFA was a dream, along with getting this far and being a part of the AFC.

He didn't have any goals when it came to the AFC or the AFA, but it wasn't the same for Xin.

Is facing Xin a good idea? Gary thought. *I have to admit, I'm interested to see how strong she is, but if she loses . . . what would it mean to her?*

Gary knew he had improved by leaps and bounds since fighting the Scatterbugs. Even if the two had fought before, Gary might have lost but only by a little; now, though, he felt like it was almost unfair.

On top of that, because the night sky was still dark, he had the advantage of his class. Although he could limit himself while fighting

Xin, she was skillful enough to know that he was holding back. For Gary to put up a fight, he would be unable to hold back.

For all of these reasons, he eventually came up with an answer.

"I'm sorry, Xin . . . but I don't think I can."

It was clear that this wasn't the answer she was expecting, and from the look in her eyes and her tensed-up body, it was almost as if she was angry.

"Why? Is it because you like me?" Xin replied. "Do you really think that I'm going to be thankful to you for being a gentleman and not fighting me? You know I'm not that type of person."

"It's not that," Gary replied; he was trying to think of a way to explain himself without revealing his secret. He looked at the ground, unable to look Xin in the eye, and she realized that maybe she had jumped the gun.

"I'm sorry . . . I was a little annoyed at you and let my anger come out," Xin explained. "You see, Gary, you're amazing; I still remember you when I met you at school. You're so strong and you keep growing stronger.

"You know, I have a big reason for being here, for joining the AFC: for you. I felt like you were only here because of me. At first I thought it was sweet, but then it started to make me feel strange.

"You managed to get here just on those feelings alone. Is that how you are so strong? Then does that mean that my own resolve is weaker, or is it just the fact that you're so much more talented than me?

"I'm sure this might even be something that you can't answer yourself, so I wanted to learn through fighting against you. I thought I might get my answer that way. You should know that before the assessment of the academy students, the debut students will have their first match.

"After that, we will be shipped to clubs or professional teams to work on climbing the AFC, which also means I won't be here anymore. That's why I wanted to fight you, before I left," Xin explained.

There was a lot in what Xin said, and although some of it was partly true, not all of it was. Gary did come to the academy because of Xin, but there were other reasons, and as for why he got stronger, it was because he was carrying a lot of weight: the weight of the Howlers gang, the weight of his friends, and the weight of his family. There was a lot riding on Gary's strength, and even now it was why he needed to continue to grow stronger.

"Xin, I'm not good at explaining things, so I want you to do something." Gary held up his hand, as if he were going for a high five. "I want you to transform and use all your strength and do whatever you can to move my hand from its position."

Xin didn't understand the point of this, but she decided to go along with it anyway. She placed her hand against his, and the two of them were now touching. She first tried to push using her arm strength, but there was no movement at all from Gary.

Then she used her whole body weight to push, but again there was nothing.

What is this? I'm not weak . . . so why can't I move his arm? Xin thought.

Holding it in place, she decided to take things a bit more seriously. There was a little spark in her eye before she shifted her feet, twisted her hip, and pushed in one go as hard as she could against Gary's hand.

It was with such force that it would have sent a normal person flying across the field, but with Gary nothing happened, and his hand remained in place.

"I know this is nothing compared to a real fight, and you're more skillful than me. I have no idea what your Altered form is, and there's never a sure win in any fight, but right now I don't even know how to control my strength properly."

Hearing Gary, Xin started to think about the fight she had seen him in, how out of control he was at the time.

"The last person I would want to hurt is you," Gary explained.

Xin couldn't help but smile as she heard this.

"Well, I guess that just means I have to get so strong that you don't have to worry about that." Xin smiled.

The two of them continued to talk, about school life, their troubles, and a little about their families, but they left the matter of fighting each other behind.

It was nice for them to enjoy just casually chatting. Over the next few days, Gary continued his lessons, but he wasn't as chatty with the others as usual; he was quite diligent at studying, and it was the first time the others had seen him like this.

At the end of one day, as Gary was getting ready to head back to his dorm room, Izzy stopped him in the hallway, twiddling her fingers while looking at the floor.

"Is something wrong? Is it the bite mark?" Gary asked worriedly.

"No, no it's not that," Izzy replied, even though the bite mark was bothering her, but that wasn't why she was here. "I'm sorry, but I wanted to ask you this all day, but I couldn't find the right time and I have to ask now.

"It's my parents, they want to meet you."

CHAPTER 72

GARY, NOT THE LEADER

Meetings with adults hadn't exactly gone well for Gary so far, and that would include the one he had with Harry, Numba's father. Although Gary was now supposedly a great figure, it was hard for him to get over the age hurdle, so when he was speaking to others, unless it was aggressively, he tended to shy away.

"Wait." Gary held out one hand while pinching the bridge of his nose with the other. "Why do your parents want to meet me? What did I do? What have I done, is this a good thing or a bad thing?"

It was only natural for him to have a lot of questions, and Izzy had expected this reaction.

"I'm so sorry," Izzy shyly replied. "I really didn't want to do this, and I tried to explain, but unlike Numba and Ian, my parents can just be a bit difficult at times."

Letting out a big sigh, she began to explain.

"You see, after everything happened, Ian and I decided to talk about the official alliance between our families. Honestly, I didn't think it would take much convincing. After all, the Howlers have been in the limelight for a while. Everyone knows that they now own Notsburg.

"Us being from a Tier 3 joining up with a power that can rival a Tier 2, along with my recommendation, seems like a no-brainer, but . . ." Izzy paused for a second as she touched the wound on her shoulder.

"It seems that my parents don't like the fact that I was hurt helping out the Howlers. I tried to convince them on the phone, but I couldn't. So they said they want me to bring the boy that got me so obsessed with this idea."

It was clear that Izzy had told her parents some of what happened, but not everything, because there was an important detail in what she said. Her parents wanted to meet Gary, not the leader of the Howlers.

If they had asked to meet up with the Howlers to discuss the alliance, Gary would just send Kai in his place, or ask Kai to do all the talking about the finer details, as he had been doing so far.

The problem was, her parents wanted to meet *him*.

"Wait . . . so why do they want to meet me?" Gary asked.

"Well, I told them that we had made an alliance beforehand, and the reason we got involved was because we were chasing after you and trying to help Numba. I didn't tell them anything about you being the leader of the Howlers; I thought you wanted to keep that a secret.

"You really don't have to see them, they just insist a little."

Gary really didn't know what to do. What were Izzy's parents even expecting of him? What did they want to see? But when he looked at Izzy and heard the tone of her voice, it seemed that if he didn't go on this journey, she would be put in a difficult situation.

She did end up saving Marie, and she did help when the academy wanted a blood sample. Compared to that, what she's asking now is very small.

"I'll meet with your parents." Gary smiled. "It's only right after everything you did, and you are even hurt because of me, so I should at least go see them, right?"

Izzy smiled, and she bowed a couple of times to thank him.

"I can't promise that it won't be awkward, but I'll try to make it as easy as possible," Izzy said. "And don't worry, we won't have to take many days out of the academy, maybe just one; I know we've already taken a lot.

"Anyway, I'll go right to my parents and they will arrange a meeting. I'll tell you the details as soon as I know something."

With that the two parted ways and went to their rooms, but Gary felt a little strange.

I know I'm not going into battle, but why does it feel that way? he thought.

Izzy's mother had just received news from her dear daughter, and almost immediately she had called for a group of people to enter her office. They were all lined up in front of her.

She looked down at her notepad that was filled with notes, and then looked up at all those she had assembled.

"My daughter fails to realize her own feelings. I know her well, and based on her words and her tone of voice, it seems like she has fallen for this Gary Dem." Her fist slammed against the desk when she said the name.

"Izzy is bright and strong, and in most situations I would trust her in a lot of things, but when it comes to love she has no experience. I mean, the girl doesn't even know she has feelings herself.

"Which is why, tomorrow, I want you to do whatever you can to find out the true nature of this Gary Dem. Find out everything about him from head to toe, and find out whether he is good enough for my daughter."

The response was quick, extremely quick. The next day Gary was putting on his AFA uniform and in the middle of doing so he received a text saying that the meeting would be that day.

I have a bad feeling about this, Gary thought.

CHAPTER 73

A STRONG FAMILY

It was fairly easy for students to get a day off at the academy, and because of Gary's position it was even easier for him. It wasn't as if he were a failing student. When the time came, he followed the instructions Izzy had given him.

He headed outside to the driveway of the academy, there she was waiting; unlike him, she wasn't in her AFC uniform. She appeared to be dressed up a bit, the most dressed up he had ever seen her.

She was wearing black shorts with fishnet stockings and a black crop top that showed her chiseled midriff in a different light that Gary had never seen before.

"Now I feel a bit underdressed." Gary said.

"It's okay." Izzy smiled. "It's just when I see my parents, I always feel a bit more comfortable in something like this. They will understand."

It was finally hitting Gary that he was going to see Izzy's parents; it was a strange development because he wasn't going as someone from the Howlers, but as someone from the AFA who knew their daughter but happened to be in the Howlers.

They waited for a bit, and it felt weird. Usually they chatted freely if they were on their own, but it was always about stuff in the AFA; now, without Ian, it felt awkward to say anything.

Just as Gary was about to open his mouth to try to say something, he heard tires screeching. He looked up and saw a van drive around the corner and stop right in front of them.

"Oh, no," Izzy mumbled to herself as she saw the van. It wasn't just a regular van; on the side was a large picture of someone cooking with a wok and tossing food in the air. It was one of the many food vans that her family owned.

The problem wasn't the van itself, though; it was who was in it. The passenger's and driver's doors both slid open.

"So . . . I'm here to pick up a Gary . . . is that correct?" The voice came from the driver, a muscular man wearing a sleeveless shirt and a bandana, who was smiling broadly.

It wasn't just him, though; a row of people came out of the van, standing tall, all staring at Gary. They all wore bandanas and sleeveless shirts, like they were part of some gang, but they were just cooks.

There were a total of five including the driver, four men and one woman, who looked less like a cook than a fighter, based on her toned muscles.

"Gary . . . these are all of my cousins; everyone, meet Gary . . . and please don't embarrass me," Izzy said.

After introductions were done, with a nice firm handshake and a look up and down from everyone, they entered the van and were on their way. Gary and Izzy sat in the back of the van, and Izzy couldn't stop shaking her head.

She couldn't believe her parents, because they hadn't sent just one of her cousins, but all of them, and it was quite obvious what they were trying to do.

"So, Gary, it's a big day, meeting one of your classmates' parents; don't you think you should have dressed up a bit? What's wrong, don't you own a nice suit?" one of the men asked.

"That isn't his fault, you guys suddenly wanted to meet as soon as possible, and besides I told him to look casual," Izzy replied before Gary could answer.

Another cousin of Izzy's, named Shanesea, was seated just in front of him. She turned her head, looking Gary up and down, and reached out to grab his biceps, stroking his arm almost.

"I kind of like what you're wearing; it shows off your body," Shanesea said with a wink. "Tell me something, Gary, how experienced are you?"

"Experienced?" Gary replied, gulping, and his heart rate rising a bit.

"Come on, you know what I'm talking about, are you still a virgin?"

"Shanesea!" Izzy screamed, red-faced, growing even more embarrassed by her family's antics.

"Oh, come on, you guys are practically adults, is it really so strange?" Shanesea said. "I mean, isn't he a member of a gang? Surely he has done worse things than that."

When Shanesea put it like that, it did make Gary think. He had killed people, but he had yet to do the deed. As a young adult, his priorities were certainly in the wrong place.

"Speaking of your gang, I've heard a lot of things about the Howlers!" The man named Maz shouted, as he was busy driving the car. "Although your gang has done a lot of impressive things, what about yourself? How can you promise to protect Izzy? Are you even in a position to promise that, and does your gang even pay you well for your current position? What if you have a family? It's expensive to have a family, what will you do to fund that?"

Gary kept silent, because the truth was, he was the leader of the gang they were talking about, although they didn't know that. Because of this, he had more money than he could handle for the rest of his life, but it was hard to explain his position to these guys, and Izzy knew that as well.

"The Howlers support Gary a lot, that's why he's in the AFA to begin with," Izzy answered for him once again.

The interrogating questions continued while they were on their journey, but it came to an end when Maz slammed on the brakes.

"What's going on?" Shanesa asked.

"It looks like we've got trouble," Maz grunted. Through the windshield they saw a barrier made of cars and cones on the road heading into the city, and a number of unfriendly-looking people stood in front of it.

CHAPTER 74

BECAUSE OF YOU

"All of you inside the vehicle step out now!" a voice shouted.

Looking through the window, Gary saw a man slapping a baseball bat into the palm of his hand, and behind him about ten people stood at the barrier.

If it's just ten people, then I can deal with them, but why are they even here in the first place? Gary thought.

"Everyone, let's just listen to what they have to say; this isn't our territory. We didn't expect this to happen," Maz said, pushing a button to open the side door of the van and let the others out.

Izzy had told Gary some of the details. In order to set up the appointment quickly and not cause too much trouble for Gary, Izzy and her parents were to meet him in a nearby town. The town was a nearby Tier 3 town, chosen for safety reasons.

If someone caught wind that a member of the Howlers was entering a Tier 2 city that they didn't own, she feared it would ruffle a few feathers.

Since Maz was the oldest of the group, he strode forward to confront the man who stood in their way.

"I'm sorry, it's been a while since we were last in this town. Has something happened?" Maz asked.

The man with the baseball bat looked behind them before answering.

"The town is now under the care of the Rhino Horns!" The man pointed to himself. "To enter the town safely, we require an entrance fee, for five of you . . . that would be one thousand dollars."

It appeared that the man had made the number up on the spot. Not many people would just carry a thousand dollars around on them, even if there were five of them, but the van that they were traveling in wasn't exactly run down.

Izzy's family invested a lot in their food business and upgraded their vans whenever they could. On top of that, there was a till inside that contained quite a bit of cash.

"This wasn't the case before, sis, what happened?" one of the men asked. They were too far away to be heard by the others up front, and whispered just in case.

"This is somewhat of a guess, but an educated guess," Shanesea said, looking at Gary. "This town wasn't owned by a gang in the past. They were kept in check by the Scatterbugs and were on their payroll.

"I heard that there were actually a lot of Tier 3 town gangs that worked for the Scatterbugs. Since they're no longer a thing, the gangs have gone back to their more traditional way of making money."

Gary understood what Shanesea was saying, that somehow this was indirectly his fault. The Howlers were the ones who had taken out the Scatterbugs, and although they kept most of the businesses running in Notsburg, they didn't continue on with the small or dark parts of their business.

That wasn't Gary's way, but he was unaware of the ripple effect it had.

"I remember Kai saying that the Scatterbugs had also asked us to do some of their dirty work. Since Slough has been less impacted by the local troublemakers these days, I forgot that most cities and towns were actually like this."

"One thousand . . . that seems a bit exorbitant," Maz said with a nervous smile. "I'm happy to pay you an entrance fee, but can't you come up with something more reasonable?"

Out of nowhere, the man swung his fist and hit Maz right across the face. It was a clean hit, and Maz's legs buckled a bit, but he didn't fall to the ground. The attacker was clearly startled, as a strong surprise attack would normally knock someone over, but Maz, although a cook, was a wall of muscle.

"The price is the price, and that's final," the man said. "Either you give it to us, or we will forcefully take it from you," the man with the baseball bat said, and the others were advancing to back him up.

Maz was a little worried, because Izzy's parents should be in the city by now, and he wondered if they were dealing with the same thing. He didn't know what to do.

"Why are you so slow at answering? That's it, check the van and see what cash they have on board!" the man ordered, and the others started to move.

"Hey, you touch that van and you're dead!" Shanesea shouted.

"Yeah, what do you think you're doing? Do you want to mess with our family?" one of the younger men shouted.

"Your family?" The baseball bat man laughed back. "A bunch of cooks! What are you going to do, stink our city out?"

The man with the baseball bat moved past Maz to join the others to search the van. Maz couldn't help himself as he grabbed the man by the shoulder to stop him.

Once again, though, he shrugged Maz off and kicked him straight in the stomach.

Crap . . . do I get involved? Izzy thought. *Although Maz looks scary and works out a lot, he's a friendly giant. He's never been in a fight in his life.*

Fueled by adrenaline, the man lifted the baseball bat and swung it down. Izzy was too late to act and wouldn't get there in time.

But Maz saw a figure standing in the way, the bat held in his hand.

"I didn't want to get involved." Gary sighed.

CHAPTER 75

THE BEST CHOICE

Gary had easily blocked the baseball bat; the attacker was trying to pull away but could not. The situation had changed in a matter of seconds as those approaching the van turned back to see what was happening.

Gary . . . you're getting involved because of my family, Izzy thought. *I'm so sorry for this happening, it should have been me, I should have been the one to protect my family . . . but . . .*

"What are you trying to do?" the man asked, still acting tough. Even if the boy was strong, he had numbers on his side and the person in front of him looked like a kid. "Do you really want to get involved? You know what will happen, right? We won't just stop with you; we will track down who this van belongs to and go after everyone you care about for messing with us. So it's better to just take a beating and get out of here!" the man shouted.

Gary reached into his pocket with his other hand and pulled something out, while pushing on the bat to move the man away.

"Here, this should be enough, right? This is what you asked for, so will you let us go?" Gary asked.

The man almost fell over but caught himself; when he regained his balance, he saw a stack of bills in Gary's hand, and not just a few either.

He snatched the money out of Gary's hand and started to count it, and soon he was smiling.

"You should have just done this from the beginning. Of course you can go through! Men, clear the path!" he shouted.

The others were shocked. Because Gary was part of the AFA, they thought he was going to fight, especially as a gang member, but he had done what they least expected and complied with their request.

Maz got up off the ground, and they all got in the van and drove off without saying anything. They continued along the road for a while, until Shanesea spoke up.

"I can't believe you just did that. You complied with their request and handed them a load of money. How much did you even give them? Two thousand?" she complained. "I thought you were some gang member, I thought you were going to kick their ass . . . man, you're much more of a loser than I thought."

Honestly, Izzy was a bit surprised as well. The situation was getting to be too much for her; even she would have fought back, and she had seen Gary fight before.

"Gary, why did you give them the money?" she eventually asked, still curious.

"He must be some rich snob!" one of her cousins interrupted.

A stare from Izzy that could kill silenced him right away.

"Trust me, I care about money more than anyone. I know how much it can change a situation, and my heart hurts inside knowing I gave away that much," Gary said.

Gary wasn't lying either; he would have done crazy things in the past for that amount of money. It was hard for him to remember every time he thought about it, but he had his reasons.

"I believe if we can get out of a situation with nobody getting hurt, that is the best solution," he continued.

"Do you really think so?" Shanesea asked. "They do things like that to extort people. Now that you have given them money, they know those methods work, so they will try and try again.

"It's because of people like you who give in to gang members' demands that the general public just accepts the fact that all these gangs run the towns and cities. You might have saved us, but the next set of people that come along, they won't be so fortunate."

The van was filled with silence once more as it continued to its destination. Things in the town didn't seem so bad; there were a few gang members around, but they didn't bother the van and it eventually reached their destination, a hot pot–type restaurant.

It was an authentic place with a wooden sign on the outside. It didn't look like a chain, and it had that feeling of being family run.

"We will head inside first; just wait until we call you in," Maz said.

This left Gary and Izzy waiting outside the restaurant.

"Are you nervous?" Izzy asked.

Gary didn't answer straight away; it was almost as if he had something on his mind, but he did eventually answer.

"I was at first, when we were back at the academy, but now that we've arrived in this town, I seem to have calmed down a little," Gary answered. "I don't know what it is, but this town reminds me a lot of my place, where I was from before all of the changes."

Izzy was happy to hear that Gary wasn't nervous anymore, but she wondered what he was thinking; ever since they met those gangsters at the outskirts of the city, he seemed to be deep in thought.

"Well, my parents can be stubborn at times, but they are nice people. Don't worry so much. You have done enough by just coming here; I will do all the convincing!" Izzy pumped her fist.

Just then, the door opened and Maz came back outside.

"They are ready to see you now."

CHAPTER 76

CAN YOU PROTECT?

The two of them followed Maz into the restaurant, and, as somewhat expected, it was completely empty. According to Izzy, the restaurant wasn't owned by her family, so the most likely case was that they had booked the whole thing out.

There was no staff, no other customers, only tables, but two people sat at one of the tables. Gary instantly recognized them as Izzy's parents. Maz led them to the table.

"Gary, please introduce yourself; this is Mrs. and Mr. Shamone, from the Shamone Group," Maz said.

Gary bowed to both of them; he never really cared for respecting elders and such. He thought it was quite a silly rule. Was he supposed to respect someone like Damion just because he was older? It was often the older generation that had allowed a situation to deteriorate. Which was why he didn't usually just bow to those who were older than him.

However, in this situation, he was just a young person from a gang, while Izzy's parents were in charge of an entire restaurant group.

"It's a pleasure to meet both of you; my name is Gary Dem, from the Howlers of Slough."

Izzy sat down and tugged on Gary's shirt, indicating that he could sit down as well. The strange thing was, not even for a second did Izzy's parents glance at Izzy; instead, they were staring at Gary.

This is a bit awkward, Gary thought. *The others probably went in before me to tell them what they thought of me. I can tell that Izzy's cou-*

*sins don't have a good opinion of me . . . still, either way it's a good thing
I listened to Kai.*

Remembering the boy he was growing up, Gary never would have
carried that amount of money in his pocket. Kai had suggested it to
him, saying that he never knew when he would be in a situation where
he might need cash.

Sure, he had his trusty card on him, but it wasn't as if criminals
went around carrying a card reader, and in the end, having cash on
him had helped.

"I will start first," Mrs. Shamone said. "First, thank you for coming
to see us on such short notice. I am aware that both of you will be busy
with things in the AFA, and from what Izzy has told us you are quite
the talented student."

Izzy was fidgeting next to Gary, and when she heard those words,
she tilted her head away from him.

"However, Izzy is our only daughter. We didn't give her an Altered
solution because we wanted her to become a fighter, but for her to better her own life, and to run the business for a very long time without
getting harmed.

"But now she tells us that she has formed an alliance, with a gang
at that, and not just any gang. You Howlers have been wild, taking over
a Tier 2 city, and have been growing quickly.

"I am worried, you see, worried that your gang will continue to get
attention from others. You will become involved in more things, and
in the end it will put my daughter in harm's way even more. She has
already been injured on your last expedition, which is why I wish to
break the alliance that my daughter has formed with you."

Turning her head, Izzy slammed her hand on the table.

"That was my own choice, I already told you that!" Izzy com-
plained. "Gary didn't ask me to come. I decided to help Numba and
Gary. It's only because of him that I have been able to get so far in the
AFA."

"An agreement isn't made lightly," Izzy's father said. "Which is why
we have decided to do the right thing, and have asked for you to break
the agreement on your end. Our daughter is young and doesn't know
what she is agreeing to."

"Are you listening to me?" Izzy shouted; she felt like she was being completely ignored, like she was invisible.

Gary thought about what the two were saying. It was true Izzy had gotten hurt, but he tried to imagine how she felt in this situation rather than her parents; after all, he could relate more to her than to them.

He remembered the times when his friends had come together to help him; it was a good feeling to have.

"Do you have the power to protect Izzy?" Gary asked.

The two were a bit taken back by the question.

"We are not a gang," Mrs. Shamone answered. "But we do have influence in our city."

"A Tier 3 city, where your only influence is money?" Gary replied. "Then I would say you have no influence at all. If the Howlers gang wanted to, we could come in and take over your city by force, and then wouldn't you have to comply with us?"

The two were getting annoyed at Gary's words. Although he was speaking about his gang, the way he was speaking about the situation was too light.

"I'm not saying the Howlers would do such a thing, but my point is, that could happen at any time. An internal fight, a war, one of the Kings, one of the other gangs, even Altered Hunters.

"We live in a world where this could happen anytime, and it makes me wonder how far your good relations with the current gang of your city would take you.

"My alliance is with Izzy; I will do everything in my power to help her if she needs it. If she wishes for me to extend that to her family, then I will do so, but the decision is up to her. I think she knows that I would never do or ask for something that would intentionally put her in harm's way.

"The fact is, this alliance is between us two, two people who have their own lives, and you can't break it. What? You want to stop me from protecting your daughter? Go ahead and try."

The room was stunned into silence; all of Izzy's cousins were on the side, watching. How could such a simple student say such powerful words? What gave him the confidence to talk to them like that?

Where was this Gary at the border? Shanesea thought.

"I guess there is nothing left for us to talk about," Mrs. Shamone said.

Gary stood up and bowed toward the two of them.

"Wait, Gary, where are you going?" Izzy asked.

"You should spend the rest of the day with your family. I'm sure you miss them and they miss you. You never know what might happen, so treasure this time." Gary smiled, thinking about his own mother, and started to leave the restaurant.

"What do you think?" Izzy's mother asked.

"I think our daughter certainly has her eye on an impressive boy," her father said.

Izzy was now the one left confused; she had thought her father and mother would be angry, but instead they were smiling. But she was left wondering why Gary left just like that? Why did he sound as if he was in pain with that last sentence?

After leaving the restaurant, Gary felt that there was something he needed to see; he didn't waste any time and soon he was back at the barrier. The thugs were detaining a group of four people who looked like a family trying to make their way back into their town.

"Do you think we were joking?" the man shouted, as he swung his baseball bat and started to hit their car over and over, making large dents on it.

"But we have lived here all our life and have never had to pay a fee. If we pay you, we won't have enough money to pay our bills!" The man pleaded on his knees, grabbing the attacker.

His wife and two young children were watching.

"Get off me!" the man shouted, lifting the baseball bat in the air.

When he swung it down, the baseball bat snapped in half, and a fist came out of nowhere and hit him solidly in the face, sending him flying into the air and then landing on the cold, hard ground.

The other gang members saw only a young man standing there.

"I want you to take me to your leader, and tell them the Howlers are going to take over this town," Gary said, strong and proud. "Oh, and where the hell is my money?"

CHAPTER 77

A GROWING LEADER

Late that night, Izzy had returned to the academy, but on her own. In the middle of the conversation with her parents, Gary had wandered off. She had done as he asked and spent time with her family.

They didn't do a lot of exploring, though, since it wasn't a safe town nor was it one where they had much influence. Instead, they talked about what had happened, and her parents had a lot of questions about Gary, including some personal questions.

When she eventually left her family, she sent a message to Gary asking if he was still in town or if he had left, but there was no reply. In the end, she decided that the best thing for her to do was just to return to the academy.

It was hard for her to sleep that night, because she kept thinking about one of the questions her parents had asked her.

"Izzy, it seems you might be more interested in this person than just as a friend," her mother said. "If it's him . . . I guess he would be acceptable."

Izzy tried to reply, but her lack of an answer made her parents see right through her.

She was so embarrassed by the thought that she grabbed her pillow and shoved her face into it as she let out a large scream. Soon she took the pillow off and started to think.

I mean, it's not like I don't like Gary, but I can tell he doesn't see me that way, Izzy thought, and images of others started to appear in her head. Xin for one, and there was another person who was already part of the Howlers: Marie.

There are so many people around him, and the way they look at him . . . I can tell they feel a certain way. Honestly, I'm not sure I want to throw myself in the middle of all of that. For now, I just want to be a part of what he creates.

The next day had arrived. Izzy had eventually fallen asleep, and now she quickly looked at her phone, but there was still no message from Gary. It was now starting to worry her a little. What if he had gotten lost? Maybe his parents actually didn't agree and had attempted to kidnap him.

Her thoughts were going wild, but she soon remembered what type of person Gary was. It was highly unlikely that he had been kidnapped. Either way, she would have to focus on herself and continue going to her AFA lessons as she had been doing.

Her family said they would update her on the status of the relationship between them and the Howlers. When she got to class, she made her way over to Ian and Numba, who couldn't help but notice that she and Gary weren't at the academy yesterday.

"So what did you do, did you finally confess to him?" Ian asked.

"Not you, too." Izzy sulked. "No, I just needed to talk with him and my parents about the relationship between our families. Numba is already a big part of the Howlers, and because your family works in a similar field it was quite easy to convince them, but mine . . . they were worried about me."

Just as they sat down for the lesson, they saw that Gary had arrived. He walked up to sit with the others as if nothing had happened.

"Gary . . . you're here, when did you get here, when did you arrive, why didn't you reply to my messages?" Izzy asked.

"Look at this." Ian nudged Numba's arm. "They're having a lovers' quarrel the first thing in the morning."

Izzy and Gary ignored the comments, even though they could hear them loud and clear.

"I saw your messages this morning, but I had already arrived at the academy, so I thought it would be nicer to see you in person," Gary answered.

It was a good enough answer, but Izzy was still worried.

"What . . . what did you do, after the conversation with my parents, I mean. You just left, did you stay in the city?"

"Nothing much," Gary answered, opening up his notebook. "I just explored the place a little."

Izzy's parents and cousins had also arrived back at the city. In the morning they had decided to get to work, and were ready to contact the Howlers and try to form a stronger relationship with them.

According to Izzy, through Gary they had already expressed their interest in helping them out, but they weren't sure they could trust Gary's word. After all, he was just a teenager, even if he was an Altered. He could simply be trying to say he had a lot of influence in the gang to impress her.

"Maz, if you could please set up a meeting with the Howlers when you can, that would be great; if they are too busy we can simply set up a call," Izzy's mother ordered.

Maz nodded.

"Yes, ma'am, about the Howlers group . . . We have been keeping an eye on them since we might soon go into business with them, and it seems an interesting development has occurred.

"Remember the town of Mikton Green that we were in yesterday?"

Izzy's mother took off her glasses, paying close attention to Maz's words.

"Well, you see, it seems that as of today, Mikton Green is under control of the Howlers. The gang that was there has agreed to comply."

Mrs. Shamone blinked a few times while she digested what she had just heard.

"Why would the Howlers bother with a town that isn't even close to their current territories? There is nothing special there, and there's no advantage for them to control such a town."

"I agree," Maz said.

They could think of only one reason. Gary, who was part of the Howlers, had been in the same town, and they knew what had occurred there, but even so . . .

Just because a member of the Howlers was there, why would they do such a thing? Even more so, how did the whole town get taken in a single day? It seemed impossible that this would be related to Gary Dem, but at the same time, they had no inkling of another reason.

Sitting at his desk, Kai was looking through several pieces of paper.

"Gary, do you just love to give me more paperwork?" Kai complained, but soon he leaned back in his chair and smiled. "Still, I can't believe it. All on his own, he took down a Tier 3 town gang and their leader. Day by day, he's acting more like a gang leader. It's good for us, especially with where we want to go: all the way to the top."

Back in class, the lesson had finally ended, and Gary remembered something as he approached Izzy. He took out his wallet and handed her a wad of money. Numba's and Ian's eyeballs nearly popped out of their heads.

"Gary, what is this for? Why are you giving me money?" Izzy asked.

"I almost forgot," Gary replied. "Your parents, it seems they paid that stupid fee to get into the city as well. I met up with and spoke to them. They decided to give the money back in the end, so that belongs to them."

The money was already in Izzy's hand, but she was finding Gary's explanation hard to believe.

He just spoke to them? I don't think they were the type of people just to give money back just from speaking to them.

It seemed like a kind gesture, so Izzy couldn't really say much, and the rest of the day just continued like normal. The week at the academy went by relatively fast, with Gary focusing on lessons and enjoying his time with the others, while the Howlers continued doing what they were doing.

Innu and Marie hadn't been seen around the Wolf's Pool Club a lot, and Kai wasn't there much either. He was paying a visit to each of the families that wished to make an alliance.

There was more to the alliance than just helping watch each other's backs; Kai wanted to do something with the money to help them by investing in their cities. He was spending money that would help them out in the future, and doing it with people he could trust.

Then came the day of Gary's last special lesson at the academy, before he would take his assessment to become a debut student. It was the last chance for him to fight a beast and gain stat points, and he wondered what NIRV had in store for him this time.

CHAPTER 78

SOME ENTERTAINMENT

The Howlers had been nonstop busy after taking over Notsburg. Or more accurately, Kai had been busy working alongside Harry mostly, because of the investments they were running.

To put it simply, Notsburg was an incredibly large money maker, and because they had a leader who didn't care about extravagant yachts, bribing other gangs, or buying expensive cars or jewels, they had a lot of money on their hands.

At the same time, Kai didn't want to just waste this money. He didn't want to spend it on things that wouldn't give them a good return. After all, although their wealth was extensive, when it got to this point, it was more about power and influence.

Who cared how much money one had, if one of the Kings at any point in time could just forcefully take it away from you? At one point, Kai was considering using all the money they could to buy Altered solutions.

There were a few problems with that: there were only a number of Altered solutions out there, and they would be competing against others, and who would he use it on? It was a good reward to have for creating loyal Howler members.

However, he needed to be careful; making their own gang stronger in this way, if they were betrayed, could fall pretty harshly on them.

In some ways it was one of the reasons why they were able to take over Notsburg more easily, due to Midwak's betrayal.

While Kai was in the middle of thinking about what to do with a large amount of the cash, a call came through to his phone.

"Speak of the devil," Kai said. "What do you want, Midwak?"

Midwak had made the Scatterbugs' main casino his own home. There weren't many changes, apart from selling off a lot of the tacky shiny jewelry.

After all, Midwak had lived with the gang for a while and he had gotten used to it, so he wanted to keep it this way. At the moment, though, one of the private rooms was a bloody mess: broken noses here and there, blood all over the cards and chips in the room and on the table. Meanwhile, Midwak was holding up a long-haired man by his head, his front teeth shattered.

"I just thought I should let you know something," Midwak said on the phone. "A gang called Ashes just came in. They were making quite a big fuss."

If Kai had done his research correctly, Ashes was a gang from another Tier 2 city. They didn't have a high profile like the Scatterbugs, but a Tier 2 was a Tier 2 at the end of the day.

I thought something like this might happen. The surrounding cities will want to test out the new owners. It's a good thing we have Midwak to deal with it all, and he should be strong enough to scare most away, Kai thought.

"Since they came here, I'm guessing they might be coming to Slough as well. I can't kill these guys without your permission, so what do you want me to do?" Midwak asked.

"Just send them back; if they sent some people to test us, it might not necessarily be a bad thing," Kai ordered. "What I'm more surprised about is, why did you call me? Do you care about our gang?"

Midwak was laughing so loud that Kai had to pull the phone away from his ear.

"Are you an idiot? This is my gang! I can't have it crumble to pieces! Otherwise there will be nothing for me to use!" The phone call ended there before Kai could say anything else.

A few days passed, and the Ashes gang had contacted Harry of the Cardenez group for a meeting. They had no clue how to get to the Howlers, but the Cardenez group was quite public; the request was passed on, and eventually a meeting was set up in one of Harry's factories.

In the corner of the factory, Harry had an office where he overlooked things, and now Kai and Austin were in attendance with their masks on, and Harry was also present.

Kai would have brought more people with him, in case this was all a trap, but they were in friendly territory, and the others seemed quite busy these days, so he decided not to bother them.

"Hi to you all, my name is Ash and I am the leader of the Ashes. I think you can guess how our group was named." The young man chuckled.

The gang leader wore a striped suit and had two guards by his side. He appeared to be in his early twenties. His hair was neatly done up and swept to the side, and he had the face of a model.

"I first want to explain that I have no intention of fighting you," Ash explained. "We didn't get involved with the Scatterbugs, and we certainly don't want to get involved with you who defeated them.

"But you need to understand, empires fall because they are spread out too thin. I needed to test your capabilities and see if you still had a hand in Notsburg, strong enough to protect it, and that was certainly the case."

This was one of the guesses Kai had for Notsburg being attacked.

"You see, I wish to have a partnership with you. Our gang runs a large entertainment company called AJ Entertainment. We are scouting talented actors, singers, and more all across the entertainment sector.

"Our business is doing well, but two things are troubling us. First, the matter of funding for rapid growth. As our stars get bigger, other companies wish to poach them with better deals; this also links with our other problem.

"If our stars have contracts, these poachers tend to resort to other ways to deal with them. Because of this, and your great strength, I have come to you to make a deal. Of course, I know that this is a big ask in many regards, which is why we are willing to offer part of the company to make it worth your while."

It was an unexpected proposal; Kai thought that maybe the gang would face a war with another Tier 2 before something like this came along, but perhaps he had underestimated the Scatterbugs' reputation.

The other gangs were too afraid to go to war with them.

"I will have Harry check the financial situation of the company and come up with an offer that he thinks is suitable and fair, only if he thinks it is a good investment for us," Kai explained. "But we do have a problem.

"If the Howlers are known to have invested in a large chunk of your company, it could cause problems. Some will think we are teaming up, trying to grow stronger to take out those above us.

"If the Kings got word of this, they could very well start a war. Maybe that's one of the things that you're worried about, and is one of the reasons why you want to make this deal, but I have a solution that won't cause us problems.

"We have a person we use for situations like this; on paper the person who will own part of your company will be Gary Dem." Kai smiled.

Of course, Gary had no idea that his name was being spread throughout the cities, that he was becoming an influential figure, a tycoon with practically an unlimited amount of money to spend.

Soon companies would be coming to him just to ask him to get his name on their product, because they would believe he had golden fingers, and everything he touched would make money.

Meanwhile, the real Gary was in a different situation altogether. He had gathered with all the others who were getting ready for the special lesson. The two teams put on their red-and-blue outfits, but Gary noticed that one outfit was missing.

"Did you forget to clean my suit or something?" Gary asked.

Crowley looked a bit nervous.

"That's not it, young one; they have suggested that you take this special lesson alone this time, while the red-and-blue team will fight together."

"Alone?" Gary said.

CHAPTER 79

DANGER, DANGER!

When the special lessons were first introduced to everyone in the room, the teachers explained that they were put into teams of three for their own safety. That if they wished to defeat some of the beasts, they would need to work together, and that at times all six of them would be put in the same room together, if the beast they were going up against was a strong one.

Which was why it was safe to say that Gary and the others were deeply confused.

Are they telling me to go on my own because the beast I will go up against is weak? Gary thought, but he quickly shook his head at that silly thought. *After what I did last time, that wouldn't make any sense. I practically took out the beast on my own last time. So why would they make me fight alone . . . unless they have discovered something, or they want to find out something . . . is this a trap?*

NIRV didn't exactly seem to care for the students' lives as much as the teachers, so Gary wouldn't put it past them to set up a trap.

At the same time, one student who was part of the special lessons was disappointed to hear this.

They're letting him fight on his own? Apollo thought. *It has to be because of his strong performance from last time. They let him fight a beast on his own, and they have asked me to team up not just with my regular partners but the others as well.*

Apollo was having mixed emotions: determination that he needed to work harder, but also anger. He knew there was a gap between them now, but he thought that NIRV was treating him lightly; it was as if they thought there was a huge gap between them.

"There must be a lot of confusing thoughts going through your head," Crowley said. His eyes looked slightly watery, as if he was worried, which didn't give Gary any confidence. "I have to admit, this is a first for the special lessons."

Whenever Crowley stopped rhyming, it usually meant what he was saying was important.

"NIRV has been monitoring you from day one, and as they witness you growing and defeating beasts more and more, they become confident in predicting what level of beasts you can beat.

"After all, this is a plus for NIRV as much as it is for you. So I warn you all, this time the five of you will be fighting a strong beast, and you won't have Gary by your side. As for you, Gary . . ." Crowley paused for a second.

"I usually wouldn't give you my opinion as a teacher, but I believe they want to push you as far as they can. Usually we wouldn't allow a single student to take a test on their own. These special lessons are dangerous as it is, but the principal has agreed, even with the professors' and my rejection.

"However, it's up to you. You don't have to do this, but if you do, NIRV has promised you another reward, bigger than the one that you asked for before. I also want to inform you that if you do decide to go ahead with the lesson, I will be very close and will try to protect you if anything goes wrong."

It was quite a bit to think about. In the first place, Gary felt like the man called James, who was behind this whole project, didn't like him from day one. Asking for the remains of the beasts' bodies had already put him on the suspicious list.

If he really went up against a strong beast, there was a chance he would have to transform, and then NIRV might get closer to the truth.

This was going to be my last time, though, Gary thought. *My last time taking the special lessons. The others will continue while they are here, but I don't know if I'll ever get a chance to fight against a beast again.*

And as for the reward, if they really are saying I can request what I want, what if I request a beast crystal? If I eat that along with the beast body, won't I gain a lot of stat points? And I plan to leave the academy after having my debut fight anyway.

Turning back wasn't something Gary did often, and since he was already here, and already had convinced himself beforehand that this would be the last lesson, he had to accept.

"I will take the lesson on my own, but only if they accept my request of allowing me to take the beast crystal," Gary said.

Judging by Crowley's expression, it wasn't the answer he wanted, but he understood and smiled.

"I will inform them of this."

Crowley went over through a side door while the students waited in silence; all of them seemed to be thinking about their own things. Sty was still separate from the group, but his eyes were a little less dark.

"NIRV has agreed to your request." Crowley answered when he returned. "You are to remain here, though, while the others take their assessment first."

With that said and done, the other five entered the room when the doors opened, and Gary remained on the other side. He was waiting patiently, and with his enhanced hearing he could somewhat hear what was happening on the other side.

There was a lot of shouting from all of them as they asked for each other's help with their various skills. There were screams of pain as well, some from Numba, which caused Gary to worry a little.

When he heard Numba speaking again, though, he was relieved, and after what seemed to be a long fight, the lesson seemed to be over, at least for the other five.

Inside the room itself, most of them had broken bones and were so exhausted that they couldn't even keep up their Altered transformation anymore.

"That was a tough one . . . and Sty," Numba said as he watched him being taken away by the medical staff. "He nearly died."

In the assessment, the student who had been hurt most by the beast was Sty, and Numba, for some reason, felt bad for him even after everything that had happened. Either way, it looked like Sty and the rest of them would live, but they all realized that without Gary they had struggled tremendously.

James had come down with the rest of the staff and clapped his hands as he congratulated the students.

"You all did splendidly. If you wish to go and rest up, then please feel free to do so," James said with a smile.

"I want to stay," Apollo replied. "I want to stay and watch Gary fight; is that allowed?"

"I want to stay as well," Numba added, even though his arm was completely bent the wrong way.

"Of course, of course; we should all watch from the viewing room. I'm sure today we might all witness something special." James smiled.

After the room had been cleaned up, the door finally opened, allowing Gary to enter. He could smell the blood from the others, even though it had been cleaned.

Since the last special lesson took longer than I thought it would, it's already nighttime, so I get the skill and energy boost from my class type, Gary thought. *It should be enough for me to defeat any beast that comes through there without having to fully transform.*

Up above, James was making sure all the systems were ready.

"Okay, proceed to start the lesson!" James shouted. "Let's go ahead, and see what is so special about your Altered self, and why someone like me can't even get my hands on your file."

The door slowly opened, and the first thing that hit Gary was the scent of the beast. It was strong and pungent. Through his new nose he had smelled a number of different things before that he had never experienced as a human, but this . . . the smell was reacting to a thought in his head.

This beast smelled violent. It didn't make sense, but all sorts of words were coming through Gary's head as he smelled the beast, and when the doors finally opened his system reacted as well.

Danger! Danger!
A Quest has been received!
A dangerous beast has appeared
New Quest received—Survive

Gary had seen this before, and he had nearly died. What was in store for him this time?

CHAPTER 80

A TRICKY BEAST
(PART 1)

Originally Gary had gone into what he deemed was his final special lesson confidently. He knew it would be a little bit tough, but he never imagined something on this scale, that would trigger a warning from the system.

A beast that will really give me as much trouble as when I faced off against Midwak . . . is that even possible? Gary thought.

The barrier had been lifted, allowing Gary to see the beast at last, but at a glance it was hard to tell if it was fierce or not, and he had no idea about something that NIRV knew: that this beast was classified as humanoid.

It was standing on its two muscular legs that looked like tree trunks. They were thick and solid, and it was hard to see where the toes were. The muscular body continued upward on its humanlike shape, but the beast appeared to have an exoskeleton around its chest—almost like an external rib cage.

The exoskeleton continued as parts of white bone around the darkened purple skin going out toward its forearms and reaching up toward its head, to where one could only see its eyes peeking through.

I can't tell how strong it is, but this thing is definitely something that will give me nightmares for the next few days, Gary thought. *The question is, should I be careful, or just try to take it out in one blow?*

If Gary hadn't received the message from the system, he would have gone in immediately. With his hesitation, the beast was the first to make a move. It lifted its large hand, which had a white skeleton structure over it, making it four times bigger than a regular hand, and proceeded to cut part of the flesh from his body.

It was a strange act; why would the beast hurt itself? When the blood hit the floor, though, it started to spread; it didn't look like blood at all, just a pool of darkness. Soon figures started to rise from it.

They were forming a shape similar to the beast in front of him, and their bodies started to take shape. Now there were five more beasts identical to the one in front of him.

In fact, if Gary hadn't been watching closely, he would have no clue which one was the real one because the wound had already healed.

Okay . . . so the right thing to do would have been to attack first, because now I have to face five of these things, Gary thought. *I better go in now, before the situation gets worse.*

Watching from the viewing deck, Numba and Apollo were paying close attention, and they couldn't believe what they were seeing.

"There is a beast that can do something like that? It's now six against one!" Numba exclaimed.

"Yes, it is," James answered. "But let's not all throw a hissy fit and panic until he is in trouble. Who knows, your friend might surprise you."

Crowley was giving him quite the side-eye, as he was ready to jump in and help Gary at any moment. A beast with this type of power was something he had never seen before in all his time supervising the special lesson. If he had been worried before, he was extremely worried now, as his foot was tapping against the floor.

Back in the room, Gary ran forward as fast as he could; knowing that his opponent was tough, he had fully transformed his legs to give him speed, and both of his hands were transformed as well, giving him the deadly claws and the werewolflike strength that he needed.

I don't get a complete boost in power unless I go into my full werewolf form, and being a Dark Warrior, the boost is only in energy and skills and not my own strength, but if I can't learn to take down a beast like this, then when those werewolves that are even stronger than Mid-wak show up, how am I supposed to protect my friends?

When Gary was within range of one of them, he decided to use his Lethal Pounce skill. The beast ran forward and struck, but it hit nothing but the air. Gary was thankful that he'd used Lethal Pounce, because the strike looked as fast as he was.

Jumping off to the side, he ended up right in front of one of the other beasts, but since he was in his Dark Warrior form, Lethal Pounce was a Level 2 skill that made him jump again, but this time it was an attack.

His claws hit the beast in the chest and dug in, and the impact of his power and weight caused the beast to fall over. Gary used his legs to make sure he was stuck to the beast as he continued to hit it over and over again on its chest, until eventually it just popped.

The beast's body exploded into black liquid, and there was no longer anything left for him to hit. In his confusion, another beast swung its skeleton hand toward Gary, who was quick enough to react with a swing of his own.

When his claws hit the hard skull, his hand stopped in midair and there was a power struggle between the two.

These guys have great strength, and I've lost track of which one is the real one and which one is the clone, Gary thought. *On top of that, my sharp claws would usually tear through anything, but they can't get through the hard white parts of their bodies.*

There was one more problem, but Gary was dealing with it in real time; as the other beast swung toward his other side, he couldn't hit it away, as he was in an awkward position while trying to push the first beast back. The skeleton-like giant arm stabbed right through his forearm.

−18 HP

The third one was on him, swinging its claws toward him. It stabbed right through his stomach, and the white part protruded on the other side.

Critical injury
−65

Shit, Gary thought, as he tasted blood in his mouth.

CHAPTER 81

A TRICKY BEAST (PART 2)

Gary had suffered a serious injury; the attack had pierced through his body but he could feel his muscles hardening around the claw, keeping it in place. The beast was strange for a number of reasons, mainly because Gary was still trying to figure out why it was so dangerous.

He thought it must be its power to create copies of itself with its blood. While he was fighting against the others, the beast had managed to make another clone of itself.

Thankfully, it seemed the max number of copies it could create was six; otherwise he would really be in trouble. Yet what was actually the most troublesome for him was the sharpness of the claws.

They were going through his thick werewolf hide like it was nothing, at least in his current state.

There's no point using Magnetic Howl in this situation, because they're all coming for me anyway! Gary thought as he saw two more clones coming his way. *Screw you!*

Using a surge of strength, Gary quickly grabbed onto the clones' large white skeleton hands and pulled them in closer, while adjusting his grip for a better hold.

The veins across his hands and neck were showing even though he had thick fur. He lifted the clones up in the air for a second, then chucked them against the one in the center, crashing them into it.

Using his legs, he then pushed off the ground and pulled out the skull hand from his body as his blood dripped onto the floor, and he retreated to a safe area away from the six of them.

Emergency healing is in progress; your wounds will now be healed

Suddenly Gary was feeling a bit better, but close to one third of his health was already gone with just that small confrontation.

"Gary has good strength," Apollo said. "You can tell from the footsteps they make that those beasts are heavy and full of muscle. That wasn't an easy thing to do."

Numba didn't say anything; he was just worried about Gary. He was a bit stronger since fighting Midwak, but this was an entirely different situation because of the ability of the monster to duplicate itself.

This Altered form is more impressive than it looks at a glance, James thought. *It's more versatile, has an extreme increase in speed and superior strength, and its healing capabilities are the best that I have seen so far. On top of that, it allows the user to be incredibly resilient. Usually, an Altered would be lucky to have one of these traits, and then its skill would prop up its strength to be extraordinary.*

The beasts seemed to be well coordinated, as they stuck together in formation. This allowed Gary some time to step back and think but also made it hard to find an opening. When he went up against Midwak, he could use the same skills over and over, especially the Lethal Pounce skill, but there was a problem in this case when fighting multiple enemies.

Gary couldn't fully control his Lethal Pounce skill; he couldn't just go to whoever he wished, so to use it in succession, he could only injure them slightly before going to the next one. He'd learned from his first attempt that just one attack with the Lethal Pounce skill wasn't enough to take them out.

But do I have anything else that I can try?

Since it was his best and only option, he decided to try it as he rushed in. When he got close again, he used Lethal Pounce; he avoided the first hit, and it looked like a repeat of last time as he hit one of them right in the chest.

Lethal Pounce

Using the skill while his claws were stuck in the beast, his strong legs pushed the beast back, sending it stumbling as he went toward the next one. He touched the ground and jumped up.

But two claws were coming right toward him, helping the other beast. Gary crashed into the two white claws with his own, flinging them back.

However, this move had stopped the Lethal Pounce attack, and now the beast he had originally attacked was ready with a fist. It slammed into the top of Gary's head and sent him to the ground.

–34 HP

I feel like I got hit by a hammer! Gary thought. The plan had failed just like he thought it would because there were just too many of them. When Gary came in with the first pounce, they all moved around, creating a circle and not giving him much space to maneuver out of the way.

The beasts couldn't match his speed when he was using the Lethal Pounce skill, but they were able to track him, and if they knew he was aiming toward one of them, they were able to react.

At least my head didn't crack open, otherwise the fight would have been over, but I'm sure I've lost some brain cells.

But he didn't have time to complain about the pain, because when he looked up, the beasts were still surrounding him.

"We need to get him out of there!" Crowley shouted. "Cancel the special test or he's going to die."

Crowley started to move, but James got in his way.

"You can't do that, not yet!" James shouted back. "Not when he hasn't shown what it is he's hiding!"

CHAPTER 82

THINKING AHEAD

Crowley looked the NIRV employee right in the eyes. There was a slight hint of obsession. He didn't care about the student at all; it was obvious from the words that he had just used, but he was hesitating.

NIRV funds the academy a lot. It's because of them that the academy can continue staying on top. It also officially sponsors the AFC. If I put my hands on him, there will be trouble, Crowley thought.

"It seems that you have come around," James said. "You should know that the future is most important, and the future is Altered and NIRV."

James calmly walked past the teacher and continued to watch the lesson, until he felt a hand land on his shoulder.

"End this lesson now, or I'll chuck you in there with the beasts myself!" Crowley threatened.

James smiled smugly. He held a relatively high position in NIRV, of course nowhere near the top, but if Crowley touched him, he could make sure he lost his job and could never be hired as a teacher in any academy ever again.

James opened his mouth. "What are you going to do about i—"

Crowley raised his fist and punched him in the face. His whole body spun around as he was thrown against the glass. The students and the rest of the NIRV employees stopped what they were doing.

This was a first; nothing like this had happened before, and they didn't know what to do next.

With a reddened and swollen face, James was about to shout back, but his eyes were suddenly glued to what was happening down below.

"I told you! I told you everything would be okay!" James smiled.

Gary had just been hit on the top of his head, and it was a heavy blow, just as strong as Midwak's, and because he was not in his full werewolf form, it seemed to affect him more than usual.

By the time Gary was able to react, the other clones of the beast had surrounded him. He was trapped, with their claws coming right toward him.

If I use Claw Drain, if I use Lethal Pounce, none of that is going to help me out. When I hit one of them, the others just attack me . . . and my health, it's down to around half! Gary thought.

Shit, I have no choice. What's the point in trying to keep a secret, if I end up dying in the process?

There was nothing else he could do, so he unleashed his full power.

Full Transformation will now begin

Gary's whole body started to change. One of the biggest differences between full transformation and partial transformation was his sheer size. Because of all the muscle mass, his body grew as well, and on top of that, his face no longer looked human.

Immediately, the first thing Gary did was use another skill.

Lethal Pounce

Moving from the side, he then punched one of the clones. He was much heavier in this form, and even though the beast seemed ready for what was going to happen and had blocked the attack by lifting its hands, Gary still knocked it over on its back.

His claws didn't carry on swiping like the last time, because if he did he would have gotten hit, and there was no point risking hurting himself more unless it was the real beast. Immediately he jumped up, and the claws avoided him as Gary moved away.

Now that he was no longer surrounded by the beasts, the others watching could see his full werewolf body.

"Is that what his full transformation looks like?" Apollo asked. Apollo could feel the strength emanating from its body. In many Altered forms, the mixed transformation was the strongest form.

A fully transformed Altered form was often worse. But Apollo sensed that this was different, and James, who had seen thousands of different Altered forms during his work, felt that there was something different about this.

Just because Gary had fully transformed didn't mean he was going to win this fight. He would still be in the same situation in the end. Even if he was a little faster, a little stronger, and more resilient, it wouldn't help when he was fighting against this many strong opponents.

Worst case, I could convert my Pawn points to stat points, but I wanted to save that for the others. If they are attacked again, it's better for them to be as strong as possible. Besides, I can't just rely on increasing my stats every time there's a fight, Gary thought.

If only I knew which one was the real one . . . then I could end this.

Then Gary had a lightbulb moment. There was a way he could find out which one was the real one. Rushing forward, Gary prepared to attack, but this time he wouldn't use Lethal Pounce, because that would just chuck him in the middle of the beasts, into the heart of the mess.

Instead he went to the beast that was most outward and swung his claw. The beast swung its skeleton arm in return. When the two clashed, this time rather than meeting in a draw, Gary knocked the beast's arm away, and with the other claw, he stabbed it right through its neck.

"Crap, that wasn't enough to kill you? You're pretty resilient, just turn into goop!" Gary shouted as he swung his other hand.

Two of the other beasts swung their bonelike claws, stabbing him again. The wounds weren't as deep as before, but Gary was still quite badly damaged.

–24 HP
–18 HP

Still, Gary was able to land an attack on the beast in front of him, and just like the last time, it turned into black liquid that pooled on the floor. Pulling out both of his claws, Gary retreated, keeping track of what was happening.

I have to pay attention . . . which one is it?

He then spotted one making a wound on its arm to replace another clone that had just been defeated.

You have marked a target

Even if he saw which one was the real one, eventually he would lose sight of the real beast, but now that he had marked it, there was a clear trail that would allow him to pinpoint the real one.

Without wasting time, Gary decided to use the strongest skill he had.

Lethal Pounce has been activated

He jumped on one of the beasts, but it wasn't the one he was going for.

Lethal Pounce

Moving immediately from that target, he went on to the next, but once again he failed to land on the right one, until finally:

Lethal Pounce

Gary had hit his target.

Claw Drain
Last Stand activated

Using all the skills he had, Gary continued to strike at the real beast with his claws. The other beasts were attempting to strike at him, to get him off the real one, but it was pointless.

Even though Gary wasn't as close to death as during his fight with Midwak, he needed to focus on beating the real beast, and eventually all five of the other beasts had popped into black liquid, and the beast had been defeated. Gary stood over its dead body, covered in blood and large wounds.

This is shit, Gary thought. *If it weren't nighttime, and if there had been more than one enemy, I would have died. Last Stand isn't a skill I can use repeatedly, so if I had to fight again I would be dead . . . I can't just keep relying on that skill.*

Looking upward as he transformed back to his normal self, Gary was a bit annoyed at those who had watched from above. This was far more dangerous than he ever imagined, and the beast certainly was a strong one; it was likely that they would give him another crystal and not one from this beast.

Gary looked at the body in front of him.

I have to make sure I get what is mine. Gary shoved his clawed hand through the beast's body, searching for something, and he eventually found it, pulling out the crystal.

Once again he looked up at the glass, before opening his mouth and taking a bite out of the bloody beast crystal.

CHAPTER 83

EATING A CRYSTAL

Everything that Gary was doing right now was based on a theory of his own. Altered gave him more stat points than the beasts that he killed and ate. The beasts had the crystals removed from their bodies, and the flesh only had a hint of power in them when consumed.

But Altered were created using the crystals that came from beasts, which led Gary to his sudden and rash decision to bite into the crystal. Ideally he would have attempted to eat the body with the crystal in it, but that would have been a strange action to take, not that biting into the crystal wasn't.

In Gary's head, since he ate things to gain power, he thought it was the next best thing. His hard jaw crushed the crystal, and as the pieces went down his throat and into his stomach, he felt a bubble of energy building up.

He was too far in at this point, so all he could do was continue eating the crystal until it was completely gone.

"WHAT IS HE DOING?" James shouted, and banged his fists against the glass. "He just ate a precious crystal from a highly powerful beast. That crystal could have sold for millions and he's having it as a snack."

There were more shocks heading James's way, as he started to remember the tests that were first conducted with the crystal. What benefit would a person derive from eating a crystal? If they were a regular person, consuming raw energy in that form would be enough to kill them.

At least that was what happened in their tests. If an Altered did such a thing, there was one of three outcomes. Some Altered could use the energy to boost their power, although it was temporary, so it was deemed unhelpful, as there were better uses for the crystal.

Others suffered the same fate as a human; the energy of the crystal was just too much for the Altered form to handle. This usually happened if the Altered was created using a weaker crystal than the one consumed.

Finally, when other Altered consumed a crystal, nothing happened. Their bodies could not absorb the energy released by the crystal, so they gained no temporary boost but also did not have any negative side effects.

To put it simply, the benefits for eating a crystal were next to none.

I thought he was some type of researcher, maybe working for another corporation undercover. I thought that was why he was asking for the beast's body, and for the crystal . . . but this person is just a fool! James thought.

But after Gary consumed the crystal he didn't feel like a fool, as his system screen had responded as he had hoped.

First, there was a message for completing the quest and having managed to defeat the beast.

Quest completed
Congratulations, you have now reached: Level 28

Because it was the first time he had killed such a beast, there were quite a few Exp bonuses that allowed him to level up and gain a free stat point, but there was also the quest reward on top of that.

Skill upgrade!
You are free to permanently increase one skill to the next level!

This is good, Gary thought. *The Dark Warrior Class allows all my skills to go to the next stage as long as it's nighttime, but during the day the skills reset back to what they were before. Upgrading one of the skills will make me stronger during the day, and if the Dark Warrior Class still takes effect, then the skill might go to an even higher level.*

Gary was pleased, but it wasn't the right time to pick which skill to upgrade, and before the NIRV employees came out and gave him hell, he wanted to check how many stat points he had gained from eating the crystal.

Strength: 62 >>> 65
Dexterity: 47 >>> 50
Endurance: 49 >>> 54

The stat increase is a lot larger from eating the crystal and my points have improved quite a bit, but that was most likely because of the beast itself.

Gary imagined that not always eating a crystal, Altered, or beast would give him points. After all, there were differences in the strength of beasts. He guessed that at some point the weaker beasts or even Altered, if he were to eat them, wouldn't give him any stat points at all.

The stronger I get, the harder it's going to be to grow, but is there even a cap on this thing? After fighting Midwak, it feels like a werewolf's growth is almost endless; after all, Midwak said there were some above him.

While Gary was thinking about all of this, the door opened; as usual there were the NIRV employees in their special suits with their special equipment, although Gary wondered what they would try to get from the beast this time, now that its crystal was no longer inside its body.

Then he noticed someone else among the NIRV staff: James, the NIRV researcher.

"What do you think you are doing?" James shouted. "Do you have a death wish or something? You ate a high-tier crystal! One that had yet to hit the market. I'm going to rip that crystal straight out of your body!"

Gary had expected this reaction. He had acted so rashly because he was leaving the academy soon, and it was his last lesson anyway. On top of that, although NIRV was big, James himself was unable to do anything.

"Stop it!" Crowley shouted as he stepped between them. "You have already done enough, and you said that he was allowed the crystal; he can do with it as he wishes."

"Yes, a crystal, but not that crystal! Now get out of my way. I will take him back to NIRV myself and we will see what they have to say!" James said as he tried to push past Crowley, but the teacher grabbed James's shoulder and pulled him back.

"You will do no such thing; I have had enough!" Raising his fist again, he punched James in the face, sending him flying across the room.

CHAPTER 84

NIRV BLOCK

Crowley had delivered a solid hit, and it looked like he might have forgotten to hold back a little. After all, he was an Altered and James was just a regular human. It came as no surprise when James was unable to get back up; he had passed out, and the other NIRV employees stood there like deer in the headlights.

"Gary, you did nothing wrong, that crystal was your reward so don't worry, I will make sure nothing happens to you. The lesson is over, so head back to your dormitory and get some rest," Crowley ordered.

Gary did as told and started to leave the special lesson area; they would need Crowley to take them through the maze of tunnels anyway, so they could only really exit from this room.

While leaving, Gary couldn't help but think that Crowley was pretty cool back there.

He's a good person and a good teacher, Gary thought. *Without him, I wonder how NIRV would have reacted?*

A little while later, as Crowley took them back as normal, there was no speaking and all of the students were afraid to talk. Just before he left them, he had a final message to give them.

"There will be no special lesson next week," Crowley said. "All students are to participate in the assessment. I wish you all good luck, and I'm sure you already know that if you manage to impress and become a debut student, then you will no longer take part in the special lessons, which I think is the best for all of you."

Heading back to their dormitory, Gary and Numba couldn't help but talk about what happened.

"I wonder if something had happened to Crowley. I mean, he hit a NIRV employee who sponsors the AFA and the whole special lesson thing in the first place. It's quite possible that he could get fired," Numba said.

Gary hadn't thought of this, and if Crowley was to get fired because of his actions, he would feel extremely bad about it.

"Think about it: with NIRV's connections they could probably make sure he never gets a teaching job again," Numba continued.

His words were just making Gary worry more and more.

"Anyway, what made you eat that crystal in the first place?" Numba asked. "Is that something . . ." He looked left and right before placing his hand to cover his mouth and whispering, ". . . a werewolf does?"

"I think so, it was a bit of instinct," Gary said. It was already enough that Numba knew he was a werewolf; there was no need to tell him about the system stuff.

When Gary was alone in his room, he thought his last lesson was quite the experience, but he also couldn't help thinking about what Numba said.

Will Crowley really lose his job? They can't kick him out for just doing the right thing, can they?

Gary decided to send a text to a certain someone, as he had come up with an idea, just in case.

Unfortunately, things moved far quicker than anyone could imagine, and Numba's guess was right on the mark. It was only about an hour or so later that evening after the special lesson.

Crowley had been called into a meeting with the professors. The professors had high positions in the academy and ran most of what went on day to day, but they were not the principal nor were they the ones behind the academy in the first place.

As soon as Crowley entered the office, the looks on their faces said it all.

"Please do not have that pained look on your face," Crowley said, with his hands held behind his back, his head held high. "All I have to say is everything that I did, it was without regret. As for you three, I know you would have fought for my position as hard as you could."

The speech had caused a lump to appear in all three of the old men's throats.

"You have always cared for the students, and as a teacher it is nothing less than what we could have asked for," Humfree said. "Unfortunately, the ones that you angered this time are too far above us.

"One note, though, we did manage to stop them from taking any action against the student, Gary. However, because you laid hands . . ."

Crowley raised his hand, as he had expected this would happen, just not this fast.

"I will be okay."

The next day arrived and Crowley left; he went to the nearby Tier 3 city where his home was, wondering just what he was going to do now.

Of course, he got on his laptop and started to apply to other academies. There were plenty of Altered academies in the country, maybe some abroad where he could teach if need be.

Sure, they weren't as prestigious as the AFA, but with his résumé, he should easily get offers. They would be coming to him.

Soon though, emails started to come back, and each of them said the same thing. After reading one after another, Crowley's positive attitude was starting to fade away.

Is this NIRV's power? All of them are rejections, not even a telephone interview, Crowley thought. *I guess it makes sense; no one would be crazy enough to hire me and go against NIRV. Does that mean I have to give up being a teacher?*

In the end, Crowley bit the bullet and decided to apply to become a regular combat instructor, and there was some level of success, as he was given a face-to-face interview.

A few hours later, he received a call stating that his interview was canceled and they would no longer be processing his application.

Will I even be able to get a job at this rate? What, did that damned James tell every corporation not to hire me? What a petty bastard. I bet even if I did get hired, he would find out where I worked and tell them to fire me.

What am I supposed to do?, How am I supposed to live?

The weariness of being an adult was starting to set in; he dragged his hands down his face, but just then he saw a call coming to his number.

I put my résumé online; maybe that's someone contacting me! Crowley thought as he immediately answered the phone.

"Hello there, am I speaking to Crowley Corvus?" the speaker asked.

"Yes, I am free to talk."

"Excellent. Mr. Corvus, my name is Kai, and I'm speaking to you from the Howlers Corporation. I have a very interesting offer for you."

CHAPTER 85

A FRESH START

Crowley found himself in a taxi staring out of the window. Life felt a little crazy for him at the moment. He was an adult, thirty-five years old, and had his career path quite set out.

He enjoyed his job, loved what he did, and didn't mind if he had to do it for the rest of his life. Which was why he found the current situation frustrating and strange. The car was filled with his belongings, all taken from his apartment, and he was leaving the city he had lived in for a long time in order to head to a new place.

I can't say I've heard much about Slough, but when I did some research it seems they have been in the news relatively frequently, Crowley thought. He wasn't the type to focus on what was happening in the outside world, because he had dedicated himself to his job, and now he had lost that.

Honestly, I don't know much about the Howlers either, but it was too good an offer, and I couldn't refuse.

Crowley was thinking back to the phone call he had received. He was in a desperate situation; an adult needed money to live and get by. There were no benefits from the local government apart from housing in the lower-tier cities, which was a life that was hard to rise up from.

The Howlers were offering a generous wage, one that matched what he had earned at the AFA, which was hard to believe. A Tier 3 town that was able to do such a thing seemed almost too good to be true.

What tipped him into accepting the offer in the end was the fact that it was better than what the AFA offered. The job included free accommodation and meals, and the job role was quite similar as well.

If there was anything he needed, the man on the phone had said that they would try their best to get it for him. Every bone in Crowley's body was telling him that it was a scam, but while he was on the phone he had received another rejection email and decided to give it a go.

When the taxi finally arrived in town, Crowley was awestruck. The roads didn't have potholes, the sidewalks were wide with decorative trees planted every so often, and the buildings were well maintained.

This doesn't look like any Tier 3 town I have been to . . . this looks almost like a Tier 2 city.

Because Crowley wasn't involved in gang business, he only read the news that was available to the public, so he knew nothing about the fact that the Howlers controlled Notsburg as well as having partnerships with many of the other Tier 3 towns.

A lot of wealth had been invested in upgrading Slough, and when the annual GDP was calculated, it would soon be recognized as a Tier 2 city.

Maybe I didn't make a bad decision after all, Crowley thought.

Near the center of town, the taxi stopped in front of a modern high-rise apartment building. Crowley didn't even have to open the doors himself, as two men opened it for him.

"Mr. Corvus, may we take your bag for you, sir?" one of the men asked.

Crowley was fine taking his own bag, but he still thanked the person for offering. His strength made the bag fairly light anyway, but he did notice that the two men who greeted him by name weren't building staff; they wore a different uniform, one that was black and gold.

"This is a key to your apartment; inside is your schedule for this week. If you need anything, a work phone has been provided with several contact numbers stored in it," one of the men explained. "We hope you enjoy your stay here, and we look forward to working with you, teacher."

The last word caught Crowley off guard; how did these people know he was a teacher? He didn't really have fame outside the AFA;

he could only assume that whoever he spoke to on the phone had informed everyone.

Regardless, as he entered the apartment building, he noted that the floor was made of marble and there was plenty of staff to help and ask about things. The more things Crowley observed, the more he thought he had made the right choice.

He was starting to feel a little better about what had occurred now.

Change is good at times; maybe it pays to do some crimes. He chuckled to himself, thinking back to when he hit James. The fact that he was rhyming was proof of his good mood.

When he made his way to the elevator, he saw that the door was in the middle of closing, and someone was inside.

"Wait!" Crowley shouted; he ran to catch the elevator, but not so fast as to give himself away. Altered were rare beings after all, and if the public knew of this they would be quite surprised.

Still, there was no need for him to reach the elevator door, as the young girl inside had pressed a button in time.

"Thank you," Crowley said. He stared at her for a few moments, as there was something a little strange about her.

"I haven't seen you before; have you just moved in?" she asked.

"Yeah, it looks like we're on the same floor. I guess we're neighbors. It's my first time in this town as well," Crowley said. He found it a bit strange talking to a girl, but for some reason he couldn't help looking at her from the corner of his eye.

When the elevator reached their floor, they exited into the hallway and went their separate ways to their apartments. The girl quickly unlocked her door and then closed it behind her.

Why did I keep looking at her? Have I seen her before? But I've never been to this town. That's impossible; maybe she was an AFA student? Crowley thought, then shook his head as he went to his door.

When the girl was inside her apartment, she started to rub her shoulders, as she felt chills all over her body.

"What's wrong, Amy?" White asked, as she was busy watching TV.

"I think there's some pervert on our floor; he wouldn't stop staring at me," Amy replied.

"A pervert in this building? I doubt it, but you never know these days," White replied. "Speaking of which, if he is a pervert, we should go to that class that Kai sent us. He told us to be there, that self-defense class."

"Oh, it starts tomorrow, right?" Amy said. "Yeah, maybe it will be good, you never know what could happen. What are you watching anyway?"

It looked like an Altered match was going on. She never thought White would be into those things, but she was a strange girl.

"Introducing from the town of Slough, our sparky fighter from the AFA in her debut match, XIN CLOVE!!!!" the TV announcer shouted.

CHAPTER 86

TEACHER CROWLEY

Crowley woke up refreshed as if all of his worries had vanished with a good night's sleep. The bed was more comfortable than anything he'd had before, and he still couldn't believe the apartment he was in.

Marble floors, underfloor heating, top-of-the-line cooking appliances with an island, and a balcony he could go out on and see the sights of the city, where there seemed to be quite a bit of construction going on.

It wasn't that the AFA paid him badly; far from it. They needed to pay the teachers who were Altered a good wage, because Altered had so many opportunities they could take.

The treatment he had received so far was next level, but he had to be cautious. The fact that everything was overly nice in some ways made him worry that this whole thing could be a scam. It was a common technique to sucker one in.

According to Crowley's schedule he would give two different types of lessons in the afternoon. There was a general self-defense class, and then there was also a special class . . . but there was no information on what that special class would be.

Crowley thought about contacting one of the people on the phone he had been given, but decided against it. If it was really important, they could always contact him; besides, it was his first day and he hadn't decided whether he would be staying.

He turned on the TV, and a sports announcer was speaking.

"The students this year coming out of the AFA have been incredibly impressive, with all of them achieving their first win in the ring. The question is where will they go from here. Many promotional teams, as well as professional groups and corporations, will be looking to sponsor these incredibly talented fighters.

"From there, will any of them be able to make a dent in the top fifty, whose foundation has remained unshakable in the AFC for a long period of time now?"

While the announcer was asking these questions, clips from previous fights were playing in the background. In the AFC, Altered weren't allowed to use their special skills, if they had the power of lightning, fire, and so on.

However, they were allowed to partially or fully transform into their Altered forms, and if they could do something different with their new body, such as use their long tongue, they could do so.

However, what had come off as impressive was that of the Altered students who had fought in their debut matches, none of them transformed yet they still won their fights.

This had happened in individual cases before, but not the entire group, and it showed just how far ahead the AFA was compared to all the other academies.

Last night, Crowley had watched the matches, supporting the students and cheering them on, even though he was no longer part of the academy. It was nice to see them all doing well, and he hoped that those he had taught in the special lessons would go on to do well.

I will be watching you all and supporting you even if I never see any of you again, and as for the green-haired one, I hope he doesn't feel guilty for what happened to me, Crowley thought.

After he had unpacked his things and set up his room the way he liked it, the time for his evening lesson came more quickly than he had thought. He needed to arrive early to see what exactly he was dealing with.

He followed the directions he had been given and arrived at a large development that looked like it had been built very recently. It was a shopping mall that had a modern, twisty design on the front, with a large screen showing advertisements that changed regularly.

Seriously, where did this town get this type of money? It looks like it's expanding as well. I thought Tier 3 towns didn't have these nice things because they would just get destroyed by the locals. Maybe the gang that runs this place has a tight grip on everyone here . . . speaking of which, I didn't really look into them.

But with my strength, even if I do run into trouble, it shouldn't be harmful, but I should still make sure not to offend the wrong people.

Heading inside the shopping mall, he went to the fifth floor. It had a glass panel that went across nearly the whole floor, and mats were laid out inside along with different types of equipment.

It was close to being top quality; it wasn't quite what the AFA would have, but it was pretty close. He put his bag of tools down; it contained some equipment he had brought himself, but now he realized that he wouldn't need it.

You could fit about a thousand people in here; just how popular do they expect this class to be? Crowley thought.

While he was getting things ready and wondering what to teach for his first lesson, people began to enter the training room; they gave friendly waves as they arrived in groups of two or three.

The thing that stood out was the uniform they wore; it was black and gold, the same as the people he had first met. The students kept coming in, and there were already about fifty in the room.

That's when he recognized one face, and she recognized him as well.

"It's . . . the perv!" Amy said loudly, pointing.

Not many things would cause Crowley to be embarrassed, but in a room full of people he hadn't met before, being called a perv would do it.

"I'm not a perv!" Crowley said. "I'm a teacher. I used to be in the AFA, and now I am teaching classes here."

"The AFA!" one of the boys shouted, and soon nearly all of those in the room were asking Crowley questions. They couldn't believe that they really were going to be taught by someone from the AFA.

They also had nonstop questions for him about those in the AFA.

"I guess this was Kai's big surprise," White said. "No wonder he lives on the same floor as us. Kai must have decided to pay him quite a bit."

Amy got nearly all of her information about the gang from White. She knew who was in the gang and what they did, but she was still unaware that her brother was the leader, only that he was in the gang itself.

It was why she was happy that he was in the AFA, rather than focusing on this gang business.

Eventually two more people that White recognized came through the door; they came to the Wolf's Pool Club from time to time.

"Come on!" Kevin shouted. "Innu told us this is important, we have to be here on time."

Kevin was practically dragging Suzan into the room, and they stood at the back, waiting for the class to begin. Eventually there were two hundred people in the room, mostly dressed in the black-and-gold uniform, with a few people that wore their own clothes.

Eventually a man wearing a mask entered the room; his blond hair was visible creeping out the sides, and when the others noticed him they all bowed.

"We greet you, sir!" they shouted in unison as Kai joined Crowley at the front of the room.

"There are going to be a lot of classes with a lot of students from now on; if you need anything, please don't hesitate to ask," Kai said.

Crowley was in disbelief at the reaction of the others; this didn't seem like a corporation or a company but more like . . .

Have I joined a gang without knowing it? No, that can't be, Crowley thought. He was trying to dismiss it in his head; even if he had joined a gang, he was just a simple teacher. He wasn't in the gang itself, and that was *if* it was the case.

"I do have a question, actually," Crowley asked. "The special lesson, what's that for? There wasn't any information."

"That?" Kai smiled. "Well, there is a reason why we wanted a teacher from the AFA. Because we need you to train our Altered, of course."

CHAPTER 87

A GROWING GANG

Although Gary had originally requested the favor, Kai felt like this was a huge plus to the Howlers. Even if Crowley wasn't directly involved in the gang, having him teach the regular members on top of the Altered on their team would help them grow in strength.

It was why Kai was treating him so nicely; on top of everything he had heard that this teacher had done for Gary, he had also made a good first impression.

"Remember that you need to go to the Altered training sessions in the evening with Marie from now on," Kai said, as he sorted through and signed several documents on his table.

"Yes, you've told me quite a few times, but is it really okay?" Olivia replied. "If Marie and I show our forms, won't he notice that we are all the same type of Altered and get suspicious?"

"What do you think is more likely, for him to think we all have just taken a serum from the same type of beast, or that we are all hungry bloodthirsty werewolves that kill during the full moon?" Kai replied.

Olivia had to admit that he had a point.

"Speaking of which, we need to speak to Midwak and see if there is a way to better control this. We have about two weeks until the next full moon, and it will be Marie's first. This is a problem that I didn't predict; because more of us are werewolves, the fewer there are of us who know our secret and can help keep us in place. Innu also has been away more and more lately.

"Everyone survived by the skin of their teeth the last time, and there will be one less person to help them."

There was another problem, though, and that was whether to trust what came out of Midwak's mouth. It was best to meet Midwak with Gary; that way he could change the pack rules to get him to tell the truth.

Shifting through the papers, Kai came across a contract and quickly read the details.

"Will you look at this; I didn't think they would accept our terms, but it looks like they have." Kai smiled.

"Go on, what are you so happy about?" Olivia asked, a little interested.

"Do you remember that Tier 2 entertainment company that wanted to team up with us? AJ Entertainment? It looks like they have accepted our demands. As of today, the Howlers will own ten percent, while the business tycoon Gary Dem will own fifty percent. Which gives us majority control of AJ Entertainment."

"I didn't know you wanted to own an entertainment company so badly. Are you obsessed with one of the celebrities they have?" Olivia asked.

For the first time Kai's face went red. Olivia was joking, but it reminded her that although he had a mature head on his shoulders, he was a teenage boy after all.

"That's not the reason." Kai cleared his throat. "Accepting this deal is them agreeing to work with us, and that we will be the head. However, to all the other gangs this just looks like a simple business deal.

"Besides, with this business deal I'm sure they can do quite a few things, but you can see that this deal has put Gary on the map as well. I've already had multiple requests from people who wish to meet Gary Dem for a chance to invest.

"In the gang world, the business world, government, and so on, connections are an important thing. All we need now is for Gary to debut and leave the academy. When he does, I'll have set up everything for his return."

"And when will that be?" Olivia asked.

Kai shrugged; he didn't have a firm date in his head.

That day, though, Gary and the rest of the students would take their quarterly assessments. The teachers would look at their results and decide whether they were ready to debut in the AFC.

Of course, Gary didn't have much to worry about, as he had already been offered this opportunity, but he wanted to prove to himself and everyone else that he wasn't skipping any steps and would take the assessment along with everyone else.

Xin already had her debut match, and she was amazing. I also heard she had received multiple offers from professional teams that day. Just as she said, she's no longer a part of the academy anymore.

I don't know when I will see her again, but with everything going on with me, it might be for the best that we don't see each other for a while. Otherwise, she could just be in more danger, Gary thought.

The assessment began, and it wasn't a game, but a few different exercises that the debut students had done during their training. Everyone was trying to achieve the highest score they could, without using their Altered forms.

Gary had gotten the top score on every single activity; Apollo was in second place. There were some surprises, though; Numba, Izzy, and Ian performed far better than anyone had expected. They had placed in the top ten in most activities, and this was thanks to them experiencing things that the others hadn't. It had pushed them to their limit, giving them another reason to get stronger.

Finally the assessments were over, and Eddy, the teacher for the debut students, announced who the debut students would be.

"First, I want to congratulate you all for improving so much, and I would like to say that today's results just mean that you aren't ready yet. It's not that we think you aren't strong enough to enter the AFC, it's that we believe that you should enter the AFC when you are at your very best.

"Which is why, with regret, we announce that only one student will be debuting this time: Gary Dem."

CHAPTER 88

THE ONLY DEBUT STUDENT

The result was surprising, to say the least, and that was for all of them including Gary. Occasionally no students would be selected for a debut match, but the students had been keeping an eye on each other during the assessment stage, and they thought there were a lot more than just Gary who were ready.

In the end, none of them could say anything, as the result was final. At the same time, they were unaware that Gary had broken quite a few records at the academy, including being the quickest to go from entering the academy to becoming a debut student.

All the students dispersed from the room, vowing to do better next time, while Gary had been given a set of instructions. He would no longer be living at the normal dormitory and instead would stay in a separate building altogether where he would learn with a personal teacher.

"Don't you think this sucks?" Ian said, as he shoved a bunch of clothes into a box without even folding them. A visible vein pulsed on Izzy's forehead as she took everything out and folded the clothes before putting them back in.

"Why are you even helping Gary pack if you're just going to make things take ten times longer?" Izzy mumbled.

"I agree, we won't be training with you anymore and probably will hardly see you around the academy," Numba added. "On top of that, don't you think you'll be lonely? I mean, you're the only debut student so it will just be you and Eddy most of the time."

"It will be okay," Gary replied. "I never planned to stay in the academy for long. Usually, even the debut students go through some training before they have their first match, but I have a feeling I won't be waiting long."

Although it might have sounded as if Gary was being cocky, the others knew he was right. They had already asked Gary to become a debut student, and he had grown far stronger than he was back then.

They saw it during the assessment. What more could the academy teach Gary? He was quite possibly stronger than even the teachers.

"This won't be goodbye," Izzy said. "So let's not act like it is. We will be right behind you. Remember we are in an alliance, so you can come to us whenever you want and we'll help you."

Gary smiled as he replied.

"Same to you."

The building was detached from the main academy, off in the corner. Gary had been here a few times before; he hadn't realized that the debut students' rooms were above the training room on the second floor. After unpacking in his new room, Gary headed downstairs, where Eddy was patiently waiting for him.

"It looks like you kept your promise; you said you would wait till the assessment, and here you are." Eddy smiled. "Are you excited?"

Gary had imagined that if he had never joined the gang, he would have been over the moon at what was about to happen. So then why did he feel so hollow?

Is it because there's no one with me? Is it because I would rather be with my friends or in my hometown with the other Howlers? Gary wasn't sure, and he felt a bit lost.

However, one thing still spurred him on, and that was thinking about the other debut students before him, in particular Xin. He had watched her match along with all of the others, and they had practically become superstars overnight because of it.

This was in a lot of ways the only connection he still had in common with Xin, so he wanted to hang on to it.

"I wanted to ask, why was I the only debut student selected? Surely there were others who would do well, like Snow, Wu, or Apollo," Gary said.

"So that's what was eating you up?" Eddy replied. "Just as you said, some that could have debuted, and don't get me wrong, Apollo is stronger than most of the students we have ever debuted. I have no doubt that if he were to fight now, he would win his match.

"But if you listened to my words carefully, you would remember that we select debut students when we think they are ready. The others still have a lot to learn from the academy."

Although this answer was true, there was another reason for it: Crowley's request before leaving. They were to protect Gary. While he was still in the main academy, it was hard to keep him under watch.

Who knew what NIRV would attempt to do? It was the same if they had put other students with Gary. In a way, Eddy was now Gary's personal bodyguard, and they would get him to have his match and leave the academy as soon as he could, for his own safety.

"Regardless, today is a day of celebration, and it should be about you, and I think there is something that might surprise you," Eddy said. "I'm sure you know already that the media can't stop talking about the recent crop of debut students. They are the next big thing, and many companies have reached out for interviews, commercials, and more.

"Well, because of this, tomorrow we have some guests coming over who want to interview you!"

"Interview me?" Gary repeated, not really sure this was a good idea. Then again, no one knew the face of the Howlers leader, and if he became an AFC fighter, his face would be shown to all anyway.

"Yes, they want to get the latest scoop. They want to talk to the next star in the making. I think you will do well, and you could make quite a bit of money from this."

Gary's ears perked up at this; old habits didn't go away.

"Anyway, they are with a fairly big company called AJ Entertainment, so be on your very best behavior."

CHAPTER 89

AJ ENTERTAINMENT

When he woke up, Gary wondered where he was for a second. The room was larger than the one he had been sleeping in, and he was exhausted, but he soon remembered that he had changed rooms yesterday.

Man, I hate when that happens; it must be because I was so tired yesterday. What time did I even go to sleep?

Gary was starting to remember what had occurred, after Eddy had told him that AJ Entertainment would be coming to interview him, and the two of them went through a series of questions together: what his responses should be, how he should act, and just overall what he should do on that day. There was a good chance that the interviews would be broadcasted, and Eddy would get the blame if the AFA was seen in a negative light.

I think he told me so much stuff that I can't remember any of it. Gary placed his hand on his chest; it was beating faster than normal, and his system made it clear that this was the case.

Without realizing it, Eddy had actually made Gary more nervous, and there was a lot of pressure on him.

All right, I'll take a quick cold shower, get dressed, and ask Eddy a few things before they arrive.

Gary put on the standard AFA uniform that he always wore. It was tight on him but gave maximum flexibility, and the material allowed it to stretch even if he changed into his werewolf form.

It also showed off his muscular physique, and he could even see the outline of his abs through the shirt. Of course, it wasn't just Gary who looked amazing in the AFA uniform; all of the students had spectacular athletic builds, but Gary's was more lean than muscular, and he could thank his werewolf self for that.

He headed down the stairs into the debut student training room, still drying his green hair with a towel.

"Hey, Eddy, when are the others supposed to get here?" Gary asked, but he stopped as he sniffed the air.

The towel was blocking Gary's view; he detected Eddy's familiar scent, but quite a few other smells were mixed in that he didn't recognize. He put the towel down and looked up, and saw that he was right.

"Ah, Gary, it looks like they decided to arrive early and get to know you better." Eddy smiled nervously, and he looked like he was sweating.

A woman wearing a black-and-white suit and glasses walked over. She had a small birthmark above her lip that made her stand out, and she immediately put her hand out.

"Nice to meet you, Gary Dem," she said.

Gary tried his best to give a firm handshake, as Eddy had told him to do.

"My name is Elanor Evans. I am a manager and a scout from AJ Entertainment. Your teacher has already told us a few things about you, and we are interested to see what it takes for a student to become an AFA student.

"We are also planning to run a broadcast with you and one of our new presenters, so we're hoping you can show us a few things," Elanor explained.

Elanor had a confidence surrounding her, and eagle-like eyes that were looking all around at once. Gary could tell that she was trying to analyze him, and the fact that she was a scout meant that she was looking at Gary for reasons other than his AFA status.

Eddy had also said that perhaps AJ Entertainment might ask Gary to do a few advertisements and such. The academy had no policy against this; it was just unusual for students to get offers before they had joined the AFA.

It was only being considered because of what had happened with the last debut students.

"Clem, come over and introduce yourself!" Elanor called out.

As the young presenter ran lightly across the floor, Gary felt like he was looking at a shooting star. She was a little older than him, yet she sparkled; her skin, her clothes, and everything about her attracted his gaze to her.

"It's nice to meet you, Gary." Clem bowed. "This will be my first broadcast, so I hope we can work together to make this a good show."

BPM is rising
There are no enemies around you!
Your heart is already taken by another, please don't confuse the system

"Shut up," Gary said.

Eleanor, Clem, and Eddy were taken aback by this, and he realized what had happened.

"Sorry, I didn't mean you. My hearing is sensitive, you see, because of my Altered form. Some loud birds outside were annoying me. I promise I didn't mean you!" Gary apologized.

Clem seemed to accept this and continued on, but a furious heat was coming from Eddy. If he made a mistake, it looked like Eddy was the one he had to worry about.

Gary and Clem went over the program details: what they would talk about, what demonstrations Gary would give, and more. They wanted everything to be natural, so there was no script; there were no questions for Gary to read and come up with an answer beforehand, but they gave him a general idea of what would happen today.

The guards who had come with AJ Entertainment would also be helping out. They were all dressed in suits, but based on their demeanor, Gary recognized that they were most likely members of a gang.

After that, it was finally time for the broadcast; the camera was set up and Gary stood next to Clem onscreen.

Kai was doing the usual in his office when he suddenly got a string of texts. If it had been just one he wouldn't have looked, but since they were constant he had to take a peek.

Marie? She hasn't written to me in a while. I wonder what's up.

You have to turn to channel 55 now!
Tell me when you see it
Do you see it?
Have you turned on the TV?

Kai wondered what could be so important to distract him from his business. With a sigh he reluctantly turned on the TV and turned to channel 55, where he saw a watermark in the corner: *AJ Entertainment.* That wasn't the shocking thing, though; it was the dumbfounded, red-faced kid on the screen.

What is going on? Why is Gary on TV?

CHAPTER 90

GREEN HAIR ON TV (PART 1)

The news of the Altered fighter's debut had spread throughout the country, but the segment wasn't expected to draw much attention. After all, the newcomer hadn't even fought yet, and it was his first public appearance.

Any viewers were likely to be students from the AFA or other academies, or aspiring to join the AFA. AJ Entertainment aimed to get ahead of the competition with this broadcast.

However, in a certain classroom, the students were using their break to tune in. When they saw a familiar-looking green-haired student on the screen, a heated debate ensued.

"Hey, isn't that Gary from our class? What's he doing in the AFA?"

"Can't you read? It says it's an interview about an Altered about to debut in the AFC."

"That's crazy! How the heck did he of all people become an Altered? I could understand Blake, but him? If some company scouted him, then even I have a chance to become one!"

"Yeah, yeah, dream on, buddy."

At the same time, Marie's message had reached the rest of the Howlers core members. They decided to take a break from what they were doing to turn on the TV and check out the interview of their leader.

"Amy, come here, you have to see this! Your brother is on TV!" White shouted from the living room.

Bursting out of her bedroom, Amy vaulted over the back of the sofa, landing on the cushion to stare up at the TV on the wall.

"He really is! But why does he look so stupid?" Amy wondered aloud.

Even those who had already entered the AFC were tuning in to watch the broadcast. Xin murmured Gary's name as she watched the red-faced teenager fidget uncomfortably on the screen.

It was clear to everyone that today's guest was anything but comfortable with the camera on him; his eyes were darting around, at times looking dead into the camera, and he nervously scratched his head from time to time, unsure as to what else to do with them.

The hostess tried to ease Gary in, having started with a few simple questions: what it felt like to be part of the AFA, whether this had always been his dream, and so on, yet so far all his answers had come out quite awkward.

"Moving on, Gary, one of our trusted sources informs us that this time you are the only student debuting. Is this because the AFA is lacking in skilled students, or is there something about you that clearly sets you above your peers?" Clem asked.

"Um, I can safely say that there are a lot of talented students at the AFA," Gary answered as he thought about his friends and everyone who had been part of the special class. "As far as I know, the academy doesn't just pick those who are strong, but those who they think are ready, and it just happened that I'm the only one who passed that evaluation.

"I used to be just a regular guy myself, so I don't consider myself superior to anyone else. Actually, I believe I'm living proof that in the Altered world, you can transform yourself and achieve your goals through hard work and dedication." Gary spoke the words he had rehearsed with Eddy, confident that they conveyed his message effectively.

It was a good answer that was meant to make him more sympathetic in viewers' eyes, but his presentation was robotic; yet Eddy still gave him a thumbs-up from the side.

"It's good to stay humble, and your body speaks volumes as to how much hard work you must have put into becoming stronger," Clem noted in a sexy voice, as she touched Gary's biceps and then went on to reveal his abs as the camera panned toward them.

When the camera panned back up, Gary's face had taken on a new shade of beet red.

"Oh shit, it looks like he's getting a stiffy on live TV," one of his classmates said, unsure how Gary would ever live that down.

"In those tight shorts . . . no wonder the camera didn't pan down below the waist."

"I don't blame him, just take a look at the hostess and tell me you wouldn't react if she touched you?"

Back to the broadcast, Gary's face looked like a tomato, and Clem chuckled. This was a good opportunity to get Clem some fans as well as Gary.

"Gary, you mentioned earlier that you work out every day to improve your abilities as an Altered. I'm sure that the AFA providing you with access to top-of-the-line equipment must have played a significant role in your progress. As someone who also values physical fitness, I would love it if you could give our viewers a glimpse into what kind of workout regimen you follow as an Altered," Clem said, her eyes shining with interest.

The surrounding equipment wasn't too fancy; most of it could be found in any gym: weights, a rowing machine, a gym ball, a skipping rope, and the like. But there was also equipment more geared toward Altered.

Since they wanted to show the difference between an Altered and a regular human, Gary decided that the bag launcher would be the ideal machine for that, especially since it had been one of the first ones he had seen the other AFA students use. He explained to Clem, and in extension the viewers, how to use it.

It was the training that Altered did in their regular form anyway.

The student would stand on the platform and hit the heavy bag with as much power as possible, and it would then move across the room. The harder the bag was hit, the farther it would move out.

It would then return to the student, marking how far they had hit the bag; the goal was to hit the bag in the same spot with one's full strength over and over.

"Tell us, Gary, how long could you hit the bag for?" Clem asked.

"I haven't actually tested my limit," Gary replied, putting his right hand on his chin. "If I were to make a careful estimate . . . maybe a day . . . a day and a half. Maybe longer if someone brought me some food every few hours."

The guards couldn't help but chuckle, which was picked up by the camera, and it panned around to show some of them not hiding their laughter.

"Dear viewers, allow me to introduce some of our other guests. These are the guards who work for AJ Entertainment, and they are some of the best in the industry. Although you might not see it with their uniforms on, underneath their clothes they have bodies that are just as impressive as Gary's.

"Now let me ask you the question that all our viewers must want to know the answer to: Why did you laugh?" Clem asked.

CHAPTER 91

GREEN HAIR ON TV (PART 2)

The men who had laughed, after seeing that they were on camera, stood up straight and broadened their chests.

"If you are giving us permission to answer honestly, then I will do so, ma'am," the man in the middle said. "All of us have used this machine as part of our training to stay in shape. It certainly seems easy from the outside looking in, but hitting at the same point each time, with the same strength, is an incredibly tiring task.

"I have also seen many Altered from AJ Entertainment perform this same exercise before, so in my professional opinion, no matter how talented an Altered may be, to be able to do this for an entire day without rest is an absurd answer. Knowing that, we couldn't help but laugh.

"I don't blame him, though; he admitted he has never tested his limit, so he might just be overestimating himself . . . or trying to impress the beautiful young lady."

Elanor had a large grin on her face. This was a perfect response; a confrontation like this always stirred up viewers. Even if there were a lot of viewers, saucy clips that stirred up drama could be shared and, in turn, bring in more viewers to the actual airing.

Did I really overestimate myself? Gary wondered, looking down at his fist. *Here I was actually downplaying it, since I thought it would sound too unrealistic if I told them that I feel like I could keep it up for days.*

Gary was basing this on his past calculations, yet he had actually improved a lot since that time. On top of that, thanks to his class, he would actually benefit from a large increase in his energy during night-time, which would further add to the time he could keep it up.

"As I said, I never tested myself, but I still believe I could keep this up for at least half a day," Gary said, not refuting the guards' opinion. Rather, he proceeded to show Clem how to throw a punch properly before hitting the bag, making it fly back some distance, but it was clear the hit was used just to demonstrate the action, and he put no force behind it.

A lot of the viewers were inclined to believe the guards, based on their own experience or what they had heard from others. There were even records of some Altered doing this exercise before.

So far, the green-haired student had only left the impression of a somewhat naive and nervous youth on the viewers, making them doubt his claim. His indirectly admitting that he might have been wrong, rather than keeping a cocky attitude, helped his image, though.

After Gary had shown her how to do it, it was finally time for Clem to punch the bag, and so she did, hitting it dead in the center. It went along on the ratchet around twenty inches, proving that the bag was heavier than it looked.

When the bag came back, she was ready to hit it again, and she managed to strike it in the same spot. It came back a third time, and she succeeded again, but finally, on the fourth punch, she had made it go back only around fifteen inches, thus ending the exercise.

"I'm telling you all now, that is a lot harder than it looks," Clem said into the camera. "It's not about it being tiring, but producing the same amount of power. I'm a fit person, but that's really not something I'm used to doing."

"I have an idea," Elanor shouted from the side. "Why don't we get one of the guards from AJ Entertainment to give it a go? I think that would be a fairer comparison for the viewers. There is no need to hit it until you tire. Just hit it as far as you can four times, like Clem did."

Elanor was trying to stir up trouble, and of course, the guard captain who had spoken up looked happy to go along with the idea. He walked forward and took off his suit jacket, revealing a white undershirt that showed off his muscular chest and tattooed arms. They were far larger than Gary's and looked just as muscular.

"This training is usually designed for Altered in their normal human form, which is why even in this exercise . . ." The man swung his fist into the bag, sending it back around ten yards; it was a powerful hit that was recorded on camera.

". . . some humans are able to get better scores than Altered out there."

The man smiled as he hit the bag again and again. For all four hits, he managed to get the same distance as the first time.

Stopping, the man looked toward the camera and flexed his biceps. This was the type of person viewers usually disliked, but because he could back up his cocky attitude, they were unable to say anything bad about him.

"That guy is a beast! Are we sure he's really not an Altered?"

"Did you hear the sound of the bag every time he hit it? He must be one of the strongest humans on the planet."

Eddy and Gary had come to the same conclusion: that the man wouldn't have been able to keep that up for long, maybe two minutes at most. Limiting the activity to only having to hit the bag four times worked in his favor, and they wondered what point he was trying to make by showing off like that.

Gary had never claimed he could hit it the farthest. That wasn't the true goal of the exercise. The comparison should be about who could hit it with their full strength for as long as possible, no matter how far; this was fair to all shapes and sizes.

"All right, everyone, so now Gary, the debut student from the AFA, will demonstrate how it's done, and show us the difference between a regular person and a debut student!" Clem exclaimed.

Before Gary approached the platform, Eddy walked in front of him.

"Gary, you are a person who represents the AFA," he said loud and clear, so that everyone could hear him. "So I don't want you to embarrass us; hit that bag with all your strength."

Gary smiled, because he had still been thinking of holding back, but with the teacher's permission and the smug look on the guard captain's face, he nodded as he walked up onto the platform.

One of the spectators said, "He's an Altered and a student at the AFA, so he should be able to beat him, but if it's only by a few feet, I would be embarrassed."

Another commented, "They're not allowed to transform into their Altered form during this exercise, so maybe he will get a lower score."

Gary readied his position, not using his Controlled Transformation. He threw a punch and hit the bag right in the center, bending it nearly in half. It traveled along the railing so fast that sparks started to fly.

When it reached the end, the bag flew off the machine, the chain detached itself, and the bag crashed into the wall, leaving a large dent.

The camera caught everything, and the look of disbelief on everyone's faces, even Eddy's, and then it finally returned to Gary.

"Maybe I should have held back a bit," Gary muttered as he saw the shocked gazes.

CHAPTER 92

A STAR IN THE MAKING

The cameraman was carefully showing the damage to the equipment, how the metal rail had snapped and the chain linked to the bag had snapped as well. On top of that, the wall had been smashed and the outside of the bag ripped, its insides pouring out.

If an Altered had done the same thing to a normal bag, it wouldn't be so much of a surprise, but this was the AFA. The equipment had been made with those who would be tested on it kept in mind.

It was strong, reliable stuff, and as the personal teacher for the debut students, Eddy had never seen anything like this.

His strength is off the charts; I'm sure he wasn't this strong before. Did he improve this much in such a short amount of time? If Gary had gone as wild now as he did back then, I don't think even I would have been able to stop him. I doubt that I would win if I went head to head in a battle with him.

Does Gary now have the ability to be in the top fifty of the AFC?

Eddy was already imagining it; depending on how many AFC wins in a row an Altered had, and how convincingly they won their matches, they would be placed against higher-level opponents more quickly.

Not everyone in the AFC was an automatic superstar, and it was really only those who had the potential to reach the top fifty. Just as Gary had managed to enter the AFA and cause a storm, Eddy was imagining the same thing happening in the AFC.

However, he had no idea that Gary had no interest in those things at all.

"I'm really sorry, I didn't expect that to happen." Gary apologized with his hand behind his head, embarrassed. "That isn't something I'm going to have to pay for, right? You guys have insurance for things like this . . . right?"

Out of all the things to worry about, of course, Gary would be worrying about money and cost, while he had unknowingly caused a stir.

"Everyone, did you see that?" Clem said, pumping her fist toward the camera. "This is the difference between a debut student and the rest. The AFA has been producing extremely skilled fighters, and it looks like this might be one of the most skilled yet."

Right after Clem said those words, Elanor told the cameraman to cut the recording there. Their air time had just about to come to an end, and she wanted to leave the viewers wanting more.

"They ended the program there! What about the green-haired kid? When is his debut match? What about his Altered form? Aren't they going to show us more?"

"That guy looked like a weakling, but he managed to break the bag off the rails."

"He even damaged the wall! Is that normal? Can every Altered do that?"

It was quite common for people to question the power of an Altered. After all, it wasn't something most people came across every day, apart from in the AFC. Other than documentaries like this one, they didn't have a way to compare Altered to each other in terms of strength.

"That had to be a setup; it's clearly a fake video so more people tune in to his debut match!"

"What, you think they got a fake wall as well? Idiot."

"FML, if you guys can't clearly see how fake this video is, then I feel sorry for you. Let me sell you this bridge I made."

There were quite a lot of accusations online, because some Altered who were watching from other academies were even calling the video fake. Since they used the equipment, they felt that it was impossible for a student to do something like this.

Elanor was going over the initial reaction and she knew it wasn't fake, which made her think that the publicity, whether good or bad, didn't matter either way, because eventually when Gary did have his first match, everyone would be changing their tune.

Elanor went over to talk to Eddy; Gary caught it for a few seconds, but soon Clem was in his face with a big smile and both hands behind her back.

"That was amazing . . . I really didn't think you had it in you!" Clem said. "You really are strong, and it was such a nice feeling to see that after that big ape showed off."

By "big ape," it was obvious she was referring to the guard, who immediately stood up tall and couldn't even look Gary in the eye. Since they had hit the same bag, he also knew that it wasn't a setup.

Some Altered were quite arrogant and held grudges easily, so he hoped that this Altered wouldn't take it out on him, but Gary wasn't like that either way, so he had nothing to worry about.

"Thank you, I train quite hard so I'm confident in my skills, I just felt a bit awkward when looking at the camera." Gary could also hear his phone pinging now that the program had ended.

"I think with your looks, your body, and your personality, you could become a one-of-a-kind star," Clem said.

"A star?"

"I agree," Elanor said, approaching Clem and Gary while a bright red-faced Eddy stood in a daze behind them. From the beginning, Gary could hear Eddy's heartbeat speeding up when he looked at or spoke with Elanor, so it was clear he was head over heels for her.

"Gary, it's up to you, but we can make your debut huge," Elanor said. "If possible, we would love to take you to AJ Entertainment and have you sign a contract. You will have to stay with us for a week or so, but in turn we will run a whole documentary of you, leading up to your big match.

"You will also be able to meet other stars and other Altered under the AJ Entertainment banner. Let me know what you think."

Gary really didn't know how to answer; if they made a program about him, then they would also be asking a lot of questions, but in the academy Gary had gotten used to being a good liar.

He also remembered that Kai wanted him to make his debut as big as possible, as people would wonder who was sponsoring Gary, and the group supporting him would be the Howlers.

In turn, others would want to join the Howlers, and they could build their own Altered force as those who idolized Gary signed up.

"Doesn't that mean I'll be out of the academy for a week? I would have to ask my teacher for permission," Gary replied.

"He already gave me his blessing," Elanor said, and Gary realized now what she must have been doing before. "Here is a sample contract for you; of course, the details can be changed."

Gary looked at the contract, and the first thing that caught his eye was the amount they were willing to pay him.

"Two hundred thousand dollars just for seven days of work? I would be stupid not to take it!" Gary said with a smile as he shook Elanor's hand.

Since Gary didn't run the finances, he was unaware that at this point in time two hundred thousand dollars was pocket change for the Howlers. If Gary needed it, they would have given it to him in a heartbeat.

Later that day, just so Kai was aware of what Gary was planning on doing, he sent him a text message with details.

"I can't believe it." Kai shoved his hand on his forehead. "This idiot is getting excited over two hundred thousand dollars and he doesn't even realize how much he owns of the company that's paying him! Well, he already signed the contract, so I guess the only way that he can break the contract is by getting permission from, well . . . himself."

CHAPTER 93

A NEW CITY

Nowadays, most of the Howlers' business decisions went through Harry and his team. Kai didn't mind their input; he was happy to admit that the Cardenez team had far more experience, and ultimately it was up to him to make an executive decision.

Nevertheless, Kai still liked to have Olivia by his side. While she was not as business savvy as the rest, in some decisions, especially those pertaining to their gang, she had better insight, a knack for knowing what was best for the development of a gang. A lot of the Howlers' current chain of command, with captains leading their own groups and such, had actually been proposed by her.

"So what do you plan to do? Do you want to inform Gary about the purchase of AJ Entertainment? Make him ask for more money from his own people?" Olivia asked with an amused smile on her face when she imagined his reaction. "He'll be traveling to a Tier 2 city, and if something does happen it could stir up quite a bit of trouble."

"At this point, I think it's best if we leave things as they are," Kai replied. "Judging by how excited he seems, we would spoil his fun if we informed him that he is basically working for pocket change. Besides, he's putting all his trust into us looking over the gang's finances, with very lax rules to go by."

"Still, this is a partnership with the Ashen gang. Although most of their business seems to stem from AJ Entertainment, who knows what goes on behind the scenes. There are plenty of entertainment companies that are involved in shady business," Olivia cautioned.

"Yeah, but this is Gary we're talking about. If AJ Entertainment turns out to be corrupt in some way that he doesn't agree with, then he will be the first to speak out against them and stop associating with them. That, or more than likely he'll do something to fix them. Right now, they believe that Gary Dem from the AFA and Gary Dem the business tycoon are two different people.

"It'll be good to have someone on the inside to check if they have any skeletons in their closet. Gary also has the protection of the AFA right now, so there should be someone to prevent any worst-case scenarios."

Olivia smiled. "You're right, but you do know that I was never worried about what *they* would do; if there are skeletons in their closet, they should be worry about what *he* will do."

The next day, Gary was getting dressed, putting on one of his nicest suits, a gift from Kai. At the time, the blond teenager had stressed that when doing business he needed to wear a nice suit, so he would be taken seriously, but so far Gary hadn't had many opportunities to put that lesson into action.

As someone from a family with barely any disposable income, he didn't have much stuff in the first place, and although his financial situation had taken a drastic turn, Gary had yet to go on a shopping spree, something he had intended to do if he ever became famous as an Altered fighter. As fate would have it, he was already rich and currently on his way to becoming an Altered fighter.

Eddy said I wouldn't be doing any fighting before my debut, so I should just focus on looking my best . . . but I just feel so uncomfortable in these clothes. It feels as if I'm pretending to be someone I'm not, Gary thought as he looked at himself in the mirror. Uneasiness aside, he had to admit his reflection looked sharp. Kai had done a great job in finding a suit that was a nice fit on his body; it just wasn't stretchy like his gang uniform or the AFA uniform.

He was dressing sharp because today was the day he would be heading to AJ Entertainment. Everything had been arranged for him to enjoy an experience that was rare among debut students.

Just think about the money, Gary told himself. *Imagine getting such a large payment just for a week's work of showing up and answering some questions! And now that I think about it, I'll even get to hang out with celebrities, singers, dancers, and other Altered as a bonus!*

It was a position that many would pay a hefty price to be in, so he told himself that he ought to enjoy himself. He received a message on his phone informing him that his ride was already there. The driver would take him to Mancull, the Tier 2 city in which AJ Entertainment was set up.

Eddy had apologized earlier about being unable to accompany him, and had told him that all the details would be shared with him upon his arrival.

Entering Mancull, Gary was quite impressed. Although it wasn't as flashy as Notsburg with all its large buildings and signs pointing to various casinos, Mancull had its own feeling. A large river flowed through the center, and there was plenty of greenery mixed in with the buildings, such as planted trees that had perfectly been put in place.

It was a city that had a lot of thought put into it, and the same could be said for AJ Entertainment's headquarters. It was a large towerlike building, and it wasn't just tall but wide as well, especially at the base, which was as big as a shopping mall.

There also appeared to be an addition being built on the right side. There was no sign or any clue as to what they were building, but one thing was sure, they had put a lot of money into it.

I wonder where they get the money to afford such a large building, and even add to it?

The building was on the river, with a private, secluded pathway in front of it. There were walls around the building, and plenty of guards on the outside.

I guess it makes sense to have the place heavily guarded and private, since it's a building with plenty of celebrities, after all.

Gary could already see trouble as his car went through the gate; hundreds of photographers waited with flashing lights.

The paparazzi are watching this place like hawks, even following some of the cars that come out, just to get a photo for their story. Gary gulped. *Well, this might not be as relaxing as I thought. I'll have to be careful while I'm here.*

CHAPTER 94

A NICE SUIT

After passing through the gate, getting into AJ Entertainment was no problem, as Gary's driver had given him a visitor's pass before dropping him off. He was told that he would need it on the first day before they gave him a real one.

As he walked up to the entrance of the building, Gary saw a number of people he recognized. They were actors he had seen from TV series and movies, and models, some of whom he had seen on the drive here on billboards advertising products.

Outside, in the gardenlike environment, they were talking amongst each other. Others seemed to be practicing dialogue for their next role, and some were just singing away out in the open, though with all the noise going on it was hard to make out specifics, even for Gary's ears.

This whole place has such a nice atmosphere. I feel like I've stumbled straight into a gossip magazine. So far I haven't spotted any top celebrities, so I guess they're the up-and-coming stars like me. The real successful ones must already be living in the Tier 1 cities. Still, I recognize a good fifty percent of them.

I wonder what it would be like to own a place like this? Gary wondered, stopping in front of the entrance and staring upward at the glass ceiling. *Right now, I'm just the leader of a simple gang, but I can still dream big. There are different ways for a person to build influence and wealth, and who knows, maybe it won't stay a dream. Then I could bring Amy along, so she can talk to all the people she watched on TV.*

The reception area was the total opposite of the serene scene outside. Inside, everything was hectic. A multitude of guards accompanied the stars, followed by what Gary could only assume to be their managers and assistants. They were all moving across the halls, running to head outside, trying to catch up on a far too tight schedule.

Now that he was in the middle of it all, Gary was unsure what to do next. He had only been given simple instructions, and he was hoping someone would meet with him and explain what to do.

Worst case, Gary had believed he could just ask someone for help, but now that he was here, people were too involved in their own world to pay any attention to him; they just walked right past. He raised his hand a few times, uttering a rather loud "Excuse me" awkwardly, but nobody stopped, not even a guard.

"You look a little lost." A man's voice suddenly sounded from behind him.

Turning around, Gary saw a young man in his midtwenties. He was dressed in a nice suit and flanked by two guards. The guards' clothing and demeanor were nearly exactly the same as the ones that had tried to show off during his interview.

"You would think with your green hair you would stand out, but as you can see colored hair is pretty normal around here." The man pointed with a friendly smile.

Gary noticed that this was indeed the case. In order to stand out more on camera, a majority of the stars had colored their hair, many of them using some very unnatural shades. Ironically, Gary's green hair used to be unnatural, but thanks to his system, it had somehow turned into his natural hair color, with no option to do anything about it.

"It's not the time to be handing out visitor passes, meaning you're meeting someone today," The man concluded.

"Yes, I was asked to come today, and I'm supposed to meet Elanor. All of it was a bit last minute, so I wasn't told much else," Gary admitted.

The man was looking Gary up and down, paying special attention to his suit. It was tailor-made, and the material was exquisitely sewn. Most wouldn't be able to tell with the naked eye, but as someone who had worked in this business for over a decade he had developed a knack for spotting such things.

The small emblem of the make of the suit revealed that it was made by the company that had exclusive rights to use that special material. The suit the green-haired person was wearing was specially made, from one of the top designers in the world, and would have cost a pretty penny.

Even the stars of AJ Entertainment would have to spend a good chunk of their income to afford something like this. It was what had attracted the man over in the first place. He thought he might have had a meeting he had forgotten about, and was surprised to see a teenager instead.

He must be the son of some important person from a Tier 1 city. I doubt just anyone would be walking around in a suit like that. If he's meeting up with Elanor, could he be a potential scout? He seems awfully young for that, though.

"Sir, we are running a bit behind schedule," One of the guards whispered into his ear.

"Sorry, I won't be able to direct you myself, but if you head down this hallway and to the right, there's a door with her name on it. Just give it a knock, and she should be there," the man politely instructed him. "Before I go, mind telling me your name?"

"Ah, my name is Gary, sir," he automatically answered, since the man looked a bit older than him and since the others were calling him "sir," it only felt right.

"Nice to meet you Gary, the name is Ash. We might see each other again some time," Ash said before he walked off with a smile on his face.

Gary . . . I have heard that name a few times recently. Has it become popular again? Ash thought as he continued to walk away.

Following Ash's instructions, Gary walked down the hallway and saw the door with *Manager Elanor* written on a plaque. He knocked a couple of times.

"Who is it?" a female voice asked.

"It's Gary, from the AFA," he answered.

Immediately the door swung open, but instead of Elanor, he was greeted by Clem.

"Gary, you're here!" she cheered, immediately grabbing his hand, making his heart rate go faster as she dragged him into the room. "Come, let me introduce you to everyone."

Elanor was in the midst of talking to three other people, all of whom stood out just as much as Clem. Turning her head, the manager noticed his arrival.

"Oh, Gary, you're already here? I'm sorry, I believed you would come later," Elanor apologized. "Please sit down, it's great that you're here. Allow me to introduce you to the people who will be with you for the next week."

CHAPTER 95

ROOKIE STARS

Gary was inside what he could only assume was a changing room. There were countless seats with mirrors and makeup set out, and a number of different costumes on clothes rods for them to choose from.

Originally Elanor was going to have Gary wear something nice for his first day, which would consist of photo shoots and interviews. She had learned that he was from a Tier 3 town, and his story truly seemed like an underdog's rise to the top, which the public ate up.

Which was why she was surprised that he had such a nice suit on. So she decided that there was no need for him to change and it was best that she introduced Gary to the rest.

"We have decided to create a program around the news stars of AJ Entertainment, although they have had a few appearances on the big screen already and have grown quite a following, so they are a bit more experienced than you," Elanor explained.

Three other stars were in the room, starting with Tyson Broner, a slick teenage boy with a light brown mullet. It was a look only a few people could pull off, and Tyson could.

He was an Altered, but not from any of the other academies. Instead he was picked up quite early on to be used in ads for various products and services, including how to become an Altered. He seemed to mainly do ads for a competitor of NIRV and showed off his skills from time to time on the screen, but it was hard to tell how strong he really was.

Based on the ads Gary had seen, the moves he displayed seemed more flashy than practical.

The other stars who would be traveling with Gary were female. They were both a little older than Gary, in their late teens or early twenties. One of them had golden curly hair that fell to her shoulders.

Her hair was something even Gary had to appreciate even though he didn't really have a hair fetish. Her name was Spring Rosewater; it didn't ring any bells for Gary, but her family name did.

"*Wasn't she that famous actress who was always the romantic interest in those drama shows?* Gary thought.

He was right, and Spring was about to shoot her own first drama, which was why they thought this would also be good publicity for her.

Both Tyson and Spring seemed unimpressed by Gary, just giving him a few glances and saying a few words here and there.

Those two are quite different, I can tell. If one is an Altered and not even in the AFA, he must have come from a wealthy family that was able to make him an Altered. And the fact that Spring is a Rosewater means she also had a wealthy upbringing as well. Unlike me, who struggled for so long, Gary thought.

The third star was a short black-haired girl named Rachel Ruth. She was an upcoming idol who was about to release her first album. She had released a few solo songs that had done well, and went viral on Poutube for some of her covers.

I know her as well; although Elanor says these are new stars and rookies, they are almost a bunch of super rookies who have already caught people's attention. He was unaware that he was also a super rookie after his broadcast.

Clem gave him a big smile; Rachel and Clem were more respectful with their greetings, and he felt he would get along with them more easily.

"So, the first order of the day is to get your makeup done. The makeup team will be here any second and then we will get a few of your face shots in the building before I talk about what we will be doing next!" Elanor clapped.

Just like that, the makeup team came in and started their work, Although as they did, Gary couldn't help but sneeze.

"Achoo!" Gary sneezed onto the mirror.

"What is wrong with him?" Spring leaned away in disgust. "Is he sick with some kind of disease?"

"Spring, are you saying that you've never sneezed before?" Clem asked.

"Sorry, I think I'm sensitive to the perfume and the makeup," Gary explained, as his nose was going a bit crazy.

"It's okay, I think you look good as is anyway," the makeup lady said, and because of that, Gary was the first one to be done.

While they were waiting around, Spring mentioned that her throat was a bit dry.

"Gary, do you mind fetching me some water, if you're not doing anything?" Spring asked.

"Um . . . sure."

"Could you get me some juice as well?" Tyson asked.

Gary went out to fetch what they needed; he wasn't doing anything anyway, but Clem and Rachel eyed each other with a concerned look.

When Gary returned, Spring and Tyson asked Gary to do a few more things; they were essentially making him their errand boy. This continued as they went to take photos in the building.

Afterward, Elanor told them to head outside, where a vehicle was waiting for them. Spring and Tyson asked Gary to grab their bags, which he did.

"Hey, Gary, you do know what they're doing, right?" Clem asked, pulling him to one side.

"It's okay," Gary answered. "Trust me, this is nothing, you know my first job was an errand boy." He was thinking about his transporter days, and besides if this was their level of bullying, then they would never survive in the AFA.

"Let me take your bags as well," Gary said. He easily carried Rachel's and Clem's bags, and he handled all five with a smile as he entered the vehicle.

"Gary, you don't need to do that; that's what the guards are for," Elanor said.

"It's okay, it's good exercise; I have to keep my muscles working. Remember, I will have information on my debut match soon," Gary answered.

They sat in a luxury minibus that was used to transport stars; it carried things that they might need in an emergency. Elanor stood in the center as she explained what was going to happen.

"We want you all to be a success countrywide, and to do that you need to be able to relate to your audience regardless of where they come from," Elanor said. "There is a TV crew in the van behind us that will be following all our movements. They will document our super rookies as they experience life, which is why we have decided to film in Gary's hometown, Slough."

CHAPTER 96

STRUGGLES OF A POOR BOY

Of all the places that AJ Entertainment could have taken them, it had to be Slough. It wasn't hard for Gary to guess the reason, as it would be strange to have a program in a town with no connection to any of them.

He would be surprised to learn that any of his co-stars came from a Tier 3 town. Judging by the way they behaved, they had to have grown up in at least a Tier 2 city, if not Tier 1.

If Kai knew anything about this, he should have informed me, so our visit will definitely be a surprise to him and the others. I wonder if that's a good or a bad thing, Gary thought. *Honestly, not many people know what I look like. Ideally, I just won't run into anyone I know, and Kai might make sure that I won't.*

While they were traveling in the bus, a single guard accompanied them, an older gentleman, and he stood up to lay down some ground rules for everyone.

"Now, I know a lot of you have never been to a Tier 3 town before, so there could be a lot of things that you aren't used to seeing," the guard said.

"Prepare to meet scum who roam about in the streets, like teenagers who will purposely try to cause trouble with you just to fight and prove something. Unless you're looking for a beating, it's in your own interest to *not* stray from the group, and stick with me."

Some of the others seemed to be in shock to hear this; the picture that the guard was painting wasn't a pretty one.

"I can't believe you managed to survive in such a dangerous place," Tyson said. "I don't think I could ever do such a thing."

Gary had no clue what Tyson was imagining, but more than likely he failed to understand just how bad it had really been. Gary's family had been in the lower bracket of a Tier 3 household. With a single mother supporting both her children, they had been only one rent increase away from having to move to Tier 4.

"Hey, think before you speak; this is Gary's hometown we are talking about!" Rachel said.

Gary was of a mind to defend Slough; after all, he was technically the one in charge of it, but right now he was here as Gary Dem, rookie from the AFA, not Gary Dem, boss of the Howlers. He also couldn't deny that there was a truth to what the guard had told them. Everything had been like that during the reign of the Underdogs.

Now, however, hardly anyone would dare to start trouble out on the streets. Yes, there were still gang members roaming around, but those were members of the Howlers making sure that any troublemakers who started anything were quickly subdued. There was a scuffle once in a while, but that was true for any city or town.

Gary was amazed by the luxury of the minibus; he was playing on the large touchscreen display where he could select any entertainment he liked. Once in a while he made audible noises showing that he was impressed. Elanor couldn't help but smile at his innocence.

"I'm guessing you've never traveled in style like this before."

Once again, Gary didn't know what to say. The limo Tyler drove them around in also had amazing features; the green-haired teenager just never had had the time to use them, because when he was traveling, he was concerned with other thoughts.

"That makes me wonder, why did you agree to join our program?" Elanor asked. "I saw something change in your eyes when you saw the contract."

Gary answered almost immediately.

"It was the money," Gary admitted, which shocked nearly all the others. "Where else would I be able to earn two hundred thousand dollars for a week's worth of work?"

"Two hundred thousand dollars!" Clem nearly jumped out of her seat. When she looked toward her manager, though, she saw an awkward look on her face.

"Gary . . . I'm sorry to correct you, but you seem to have misread the contract. The budget for this entire program is two hundred thousand dollars; in other words, that's how much we have to pay all of you. In your case, you might get twenty thousand at the end of it all," Elanor explained.

His heart sank. It wasn't that he thought it was a small amount; he had been expecting a certain payout, so he was shocked to realize that it was a fraction of that.

"Haha, this idiot!" Tyson laughed. "Did you really think someone who has next to no following at all would get two hundred thousand just for a TV appearance? Do you think AJ Entertainment has unlimited amounts of wealth to pay starter rookies like us that kind of money?"

"It's okay, twenty thousand is still a lot for just a week's worth of work, so I'm grateful for the opportunity," Gary retorted, a tinge of sadness in his voice. He didn't like Tyson's tone, but what he said made sense.

"This is a one-off," Spring said. "These types of programs don't come around a lot, and usually to lure you in there is a large up-front payment. They think of it as investment money. Based on your future jobs, the company takes a percentage to go toward paying back the debt, and once it's paid, then you start earning money.

"Did you not have your agent read the contract properly? Well, I guess you don't have one; it figures, this is what happens to people who are money hungry, they just end up poor. No wonder you were stuck in a Tier 3 town for most of your life."

"*Spring!*" Clem shouted. "You can't say that! You and I were lucky enough to be born into a household with a lot of money, but all of that is because of our parents' hard work! You should be grateful that we have never had to struggle, so how can you say something to him when you have no idea how hard it is to get out of that rut?"

"Haven't worked for this? Hmph, do you think I didn't work hard for this? Don't you know how many people try to become an actor, how many people go to university and compete against each other? I never used my mother's name and did everything through my own effort"

"That might be the case, but that's where you're wrong," Gary said. "Everything you just said is a privilege that most people like me will never have. You competed at a top university, while I never even got the chance to go to a university in the first place.

"And let me guess, you worked really hard in your acting lessons, right? Well, whose money did you use to pay for it all, huh? While you were working hard, do you know what me and my family were doing? Trying to do *everything* we could to put food on the table. I had no time to worry about how good my grades were because I was more worried about whether my mother would have to skip out on dinner *again* after coming home from her *MULTIPLE JOBS*, just so me and my sister wouldn't starve."

It was clear that the comment had rubbed Gary the wrong way, and everyone had gotten an insight to what his life had been like.

"And this is why I think it's best if we all experience what life is like for others, so we can connect and understand everyone's struggles," Elanor said with a smile, trying to change the atmosphere.

Fortunately, they were about to enter Slough.

CHAPTER 97

POPULAR MAN

When the group entered Slough, they all started to look out the windows of the minibus, even Elanor. Several of them had never been to a Tier 3 town before, but what they saw was beyond surprising for all of them.

"There seems to be a lot of scaffolding and building work going on," Rachel said. "The streets are quite clean as well."

"I don't see young teens roaming the streets with weapons in their hands either," Spring said.

Gary thought she sounded almost disappointed.

Elanor was disappointed as well. The roads were smooth and not covered in potholes. Plenty of the shops were open, rather than being boarded up with smashed windows.

"This is only a part of Slough," Elanor said. "I'm sure not the whole thing will look like this. For now why don't we just stop off at the hotel while the camera crew gets ready, and we can start our journey from there."

If the town was better than they expected, they would just have to roll with it, and Elanor would get as many reactions from the stars and the public as possible. After all, they had a whole week together, so if this wasn't what she was expecting, they could always go to other towns.

"Slough has improved a lot," Gary said, seeing Elanor deep in thought. "It might not be the place you were expecting, because a lot has changed recently."

Elanor smiled back, as if to tell Gary not to worry. He was certainly a caring boy and she could see that even in this situation, he cared about how it would affect her job.

Eventually the group reached the hotel in Cipen. It was a luxury hotel that Gary had been to before; he remembered it well because it was where he had met Jayden that one fateful night.

AJ Entertainment spared no expense in getting the best they could for their stars. The group got out of the minibus, waiting outside with their guard, Greg, for the van behind them with the TV crew to set up.

"Your hometown is quite nice," Clem said with a bright smile. "The hotel is better than I thought it would be as well."

"Are you serious?" Spring replied. "If this place was in a Tier 2 city it would be considered three-star, but it's a five-star here. You can be honest; Gary should know that his hometown is a dump."

When he considered the improvements in Slough, hotels were at the bottom of the list for Gary. This was because Slough never got much tourism in the first place, and they were mainly used by businesses setting up projects nearby.

Although Slough was growing, that was mainly because of the workforce for the new jobs and businesses, people who were moving in to live in Slough rather than coming for a short trip.

Those who moved to Slough were usually from a Tier 3 city or lower anyway, so they didn't care about the standards of the hotels.

"Well, I guess every place has its rich people. Look at that car," Tyson pointed out.

On the hood was a small statue of an angel; the car had large wheels and stretched out fairly long. It would have to be special-ordered, as every vehicle was made to the specs of the customer. On top of that, they didn't just make cars for anyone with money; one needed to have influence to get the company to make one of these. It was a sign of true wealth to have one of these vehicles.

"I bet you don't even know what that car is, based on what you told us before," Tyson said, pointing at the car.

"I don't." Gary answered honestly; he knew the normal brands, and he had seen this car a few times, but he didn't care what brand it was. Why would he care what brand the car was as long as it got him from A to B?

"You talk as if you could own a vehicle like that." Rachel smirked.

Tyson went a little red-faced because it was true. Even his family would have to think twice before buying a car that cost just as much as a nice house. Soon, though, the car that Tyson had pointed at started to move.

It drove around the circle where guests could be dropped off and picked up, which was where they were waiting. Then the car suddenly stopped right in front of them.

"Oh, is this something Elanor prepared for us?" Clem asked.

"Wait, we're actually going to ride inside that? Holy crap!" Tyson couldn't hold in his excitement.

When the door opened, Gary's eyes widened as well, as he saw a familiar face.

"Gary, what are you doing here? You didn't tell us you were coming back; if you had, I would have picked you up," Tyler said with a smile. "Oh, and check it out, Kai gave me permission to buy a new car. She's beautiful, right?"

The people standing behind Gary were stunned by the interaction.

"How does Gary know someone so rich?" Tyson asked.

"Can't you tell from their conversation, he's obviously just a driver for someone else," Spring said. "He's most likely just friends with the driver."

"Oh, I see, well, if you want I can give you all a lift to where you want to go," Tyler said.

"No, it's fine, we have our own van, so don't worry about that," Gary replied.

With that said, Tyler gave a wave and got in the car to drive off.

"Was he a friend?" Clem asked.

"Yeah, I never expected to see him here of all places, to be honest," Gary answered.

With that said, Elanor had returned with the camera crew, as it looked like they were ready to begin filming.

At the same time, Tyler was driving off with a smirk on his face.

I see, so Gary's filming again. Well, I'll just have to let everyone know that Gary's back and they should make sure to treat him and his guests the best they can while they're here.

CHAPTER 98

GARY THE TOWN HERO

The TV crew consisted of a team of three people who followed the stars around the prestigious part of Slough, Cipen. The stars were instructed to act natural as they strolled past buildings and chatted with each other. Elanor was determined to showcase the best of Cipen without exposing any negative aspects of the other stars.

Gary noticed that Spring suddenly changed her tune as soon as the cameras were rolling. Gary suspected that Spring and Tyson were aware that any negative comments could cost them their fans, so they decided to play it safe. Prior to filming, she had mentioned how her city had better stores and buildings, but now she was practically gushing over everything in Cipen.

As was expected of stars who wished to be in front of the camera for their whole life.

"All right, everyone," the producer said, addressing the stars and the TV crew. "As you know, this program is going to showcase the best of Slough, and since we're in Gary's hometown, I was hoping he could take us to some of the popular sites and maybe even show us where he grew up."

As usual, Gary didn't mind, so he nodded, and thought it would be best, since most of the Howlers wouldn't be around his old house anyway. Since he hadn't informed them, he didn't want to make a big fuss. Especially since he wouldn't be staying for long.

Getting back in the vehicles, they headed to their next destination, and soon they were able to see some of the roots of the place being a Tier 3 town. The buildings weren't as modern as they were before.

They were older-styled, and even the electric cabling system was a mess of tangled, disorganized black cables. On top of that, the people walking in the streets weren't as well-dressed; their clothing was often shabby and mismatched.

The others were stunned and felt bad for the people on the street.

"It looks a lot better than it did before," Gary said with a smile.

"Are you saying it was worse than this? That's impossible," Spring said. "You're just trying to say that so your story sells better."

Gary's words were genuine, and he wasn't lying about the state of the town. In such a large town, change would take time and money, and the recent acquisition of Notsburg had provided a significant injection of funds. Slough was gradually being improved, starting with emergency maintenance of essential services like food, water, electricity, and internet, which were previously unavailable to many residents of the area.

Thanks to the various schemes put in place, the residents of the poorer areas could now access these essential services on a daily basis. However, one of the biggest changes wasn't something that outsiders would notice unless they had lived in the town before.

The sense of community and togetherness had improved significantly. People were more willing to help each other out, and there was a renewed sense of hope for the future. Gary was proud of this, and he hoped that it would continue to improve over time.

"Hey, I notice something odd about this town. I keep seeing these people in black-and-gold clothing everywhere we go. They were in Cipen, and they are here as well; do they belong to some sort of club?" Tyson asked.

"No, they belong to the gang that runs this place," the guard answered. "Gang members typically show their allegiance by wearing clothes in the colors of their gang. It informs the locals who to not get involved with."

Nevertheless, Gary considered this a significant improvement compared to before, when color gangs and other troublesome groups had caused chaos on the streets. Thanks to the efforts of the Howlers, more people were now happy to walk the streets without fear. Most simply ignored the gang members, with some keeping their heads down, while a rare few would talk with them.

"Is that right, Gary? Are the ones dressed in black and gold really . . . gang members?" Clem gulped.

It had become more than apparent to Gary that people who were raised in higher-tier cities were naive about these sorts of things, making him wonder how they had grown up. Had the Tier 2 gangs been better at hiding their influence on the public, or had their parents been more successful in hiding it from the tweens? Surely, they would at least have heard of the Kings, at least.

He wondered why his gang frightened Clem, when the Kings didn't. Was it just because they came from a Tier 3 town? Were gangs from poorer areas just considered bad?

"That's right," Gary answered. "However, this gang isn't as bad as you seem to think. You mentioned earlier that the town is nicer than you had expected it to be; well, it's mostly thanks to them. They took over not too long ago, and ever since things have improved."

"Hmph, improvements with dirty money they probably just stole from the people in the first place. You are really naive if you think the gang is doing this all without a hidden agenda," Spring piped in.

Gary could only let out a sigh, since he felt there was no point arguing. She had clearly already made up her mind, so it would just be like talking to a brick wall.

When they reached the estate, everyone exited from the vehicles, and soon a crowd of people who lived in the apartments had started to gather. The cameras always seemed to attract attention, and they noticed something else as well.

"Isn't that Gary?" one of the residents called out.

"Yeah, he used to live here. I haven't seen him in a while; I guess he must be busy with his business."

"I saw him in the AFA interview recently as well. I was surprised to see someone from our town there. I guess they must be filming something."

"Maybe we should say hello and go thank him."

The residents weren't keeping quiet about the green-haired boy who had grown up there, but hearing all these comments, Gary was surprised himself. Most didn't bother to even learn his name, yet now all of a sudden they knew who he was.

There was a reason for that, which Gary was unaware of. Kai had started to spread Gary's name as the person behind the maintenance of the apartment buildings. He was the one who had allowed them to all make their apartments livable again, and they all wished to go over there and thank him for it.

"It looks like you're quite popular here," Elanor said.

"It's to be expected," Tyson commented. "How many Altered do you think this town has? He's probably one of the few famous people who have come from here."

Walking up to the old landlord, Gary smiled at him. "Is it okay to have the key?"

The old landlord, who wasn't really the landlord anymore, gave Gary the key straightaway.

"There is no need to ask, the whole thing belongs to you anyway," the man said.

The others didn't understand what the old man meant by this, and assumed he meant the apartment they were going to look at. They thought someone who was an Altered would have had enough money to move out of this place to somewhere like Cipen.

When the group were ready to head up the stairs to Gary's apartment, the other residents couldn't take it anymore; they got in Gary's way.

They crowded around him, and stepping forward first was a mother with two kids, each one holding one of her hands.

"Gary, we thought we would never get the chance to see you again, so we want to say sorry, and say thank you. Thank you for everything you have done for us . . . thank you for giving us a better life."

Elanor didn't understand what was happening, but she signaled her camera crew to capture every single bit of this sentimental moment.

CHAPTER 99

A BUYOUT (PART 1)

After the first woman had come over to thank Gary personally, it started a chain reaction, causing more and more of the residents to approach. All of them praised him for what he had done for them. They hadn't seen him in a while and felt like they might never get the chance to see him again.

"I won't have to be cold this winter because of you!"

"My toilet finally works; it flushes properly and I don't have to punch my crap down the toilet anymore!" another resident shouted, with some onlookers staring at him for sharing something a bit too personal.

"Without having to worry about any rent increases in the future, I can finally put that money I had saved up to splurge a little on myself. Thank you for letting me live my life a little more stress-free."

Gary Dem, the business tycoon of Slough, had bought up the entire building. He hadn't stopped there either, as the entire area was now under his name. Learning about the fact that someone had been buying up the buildings where the less fortunate citizens of Slough lived, the residents had naturally been wary, but old man Morten, Gary's previous landlord, managed to figure out who was responsible for all of this, since the deed had to be signed over and there was a condition in the sale that old man Morten was to be a caretaker of sorts.

After the buyout, many small changes took place, but they had a big impact on the residents. On top of that, many had seen Gary's program on TV, and learned that he had become an Altered.

Before that, they had wondered about the old landlord's theory that Gary was responsible for all of these improvements; after all, where would he have gotten that money? Now, however, seeing him introduced as a rookie from the AFA about to appear in the AFC, it started to make sense. They didn't really know how Altered made money, or how much they made, but among the locals it was common sense that Altered were rich, or at least the ones behind them were. Even though this wasn't true for every Altered, it wasn't common knowledge.

"What is happening? Why are all the people thanking him?" Spring asked.

"I don't know, I thought it was just because they thought he was a celebrity, you know being an Altered from the AFA and all, but that doesn't seem to be the case. They sound like he helped them out personally," Tyson said.

"Did he help them all out before he was part of the AFA?" Clem wondered.

After allowing them to all say their thanks, and capturing it on camera, Elanor was happy with the results so far. They were ready to move, but at that moment Gary noticed something. While the grownups had wanted to say their thanks, the children were playing with sticks, and some looked bored, not having anything to do.

At the same time, some of them even looked hungry. In the end, Gary had only solved a small part of the problem.

He remembered that there were many days when he had pretended to have eaten over at Tom's so that his sister could eat her fill.

"Elanor, the money I'll get paid at the end of the week, would it be okay to get it in advance?" Gary requested.

The woman could see what Gary was looking at, but she had to make sure what he meant; she wanted to get his words on camera.

"Well, it's not exactly the norm to pay any of you before your work is over, but we can always make an exception. Is there any particular reason you want it now?" Elanor asked, leading him to answer in the best possible way.

"I . . . want to feed everyone here. I've noticed that many of the children look hungry. These days I get to eat as much as I want thanks to the AFA, but I still remember the days when there was only so much my mother brought home. I want to treat everyone here to a free meal . . . and if I have some money left over, maybe get some gifts for the kids. I promise that I'll finish the seven-day program without fail," Gary answered.

The others had overheard this, and they couldn't believe it. To feed everyone here and buy the children gifts . . . this was guaranteed to use up his entire payment. In the best case, he might have a little cash left over, but more than likely he would be left with nothing.

"I would be a monster to deny your request if that's what you want to do with it, but I need to make sure. Are you certain that you want to spend your payment in such a fashion?" Elanor asked.

"Of course," Gary answered without hesitation.

With a few taps on her phone, she wired the money to Gary's account. The next moment he went over to old man Morten and asked him to contact all the residents and treat them to a meal. Should any money be left over, he was to purchase some gifts for the children.

"Gary . . . are you sure that man isn't just going to keep the money for himself? How can you just trust him with such a large amount?" Clem asked.

If people knew who Gary really was, not a single person would attempt to take his money. There was no need for that, though; Morten had helped out their family more than once, not to mention that the Howlers had paid more than the market value when buying the apartments from Morten, who thought it was all Gary's money in the first place.

"Let's hurry and go to my apartment and get out of here, before the others find out," Gary said.

CHAPTER 100

A BUYOUT (PART 2)

Elanor was truly touched by this action of Gary's. She could see that some of the others were thinking about following suit. She wouldn't mind, but with how much time had passed, even the stars should be aware that many of their fans might see through it as simply a stunt, a way to become even more popular with the people. The thing was, Gary was doing this, and he didn't even want credit for it, letting the old man deal with it all, and leaving before they would even get the gift that he had prepared for them.

She would certainly come back at some point and get the others' reactions after Gary had left.

Heading up the elevator that was now working and had the buttons intact, they reached the top floor. Quite a difference from the days when Gary had to climb the whole flight of stairs every day.

No amount of cleaning could get rid of the dirt that had literally become part of the walls, floors, and doors. One could tell that the others were a bit frightened to touch the walls. Using the key, Gary opened the door for the rest of them.

"Welcome to my crib," Gary said cheerfully. "Sorry, but I always wanted to say that once."

It was hard for them all to fit through; they had to walk through the hallway one after the other, and the camera crew struggled to move around to get good shots, but they were able to see how small everything was.

Walking through each room, Gary described his upbringing, where he ate meals with his family, where they would talk, and so on.

"Wait, there's only two bedrooms; didn't you say you had a sister as well?" Rachel asked.

"Yeah, I do. My sister and I had to share a room until last year," Gary replied, looking a bit embarrassed. All the girls looked at each other in that moment; the room was already small compared to what they had, and to share it with a boy of all things sounded like a nightmare, and in that moment they all felt bad for Gary's sister.

"Your life must have really changed after you became an Altered, then?" Clem asked.

"It did," Gary answered. "But other than the financial struggles my family went through, I don't think it was too bad before that either. The people here are nice, my family was well looked after. It was bad before, but now I really think Slough has become a nice place for people to live."

With the tour done, it was time for Gary to take them all to some local sites. Gary waved goodbye to the residents who had changed into nicer clothes, just as several food delivery drivers were arriving. It looked like they were getting out of the area just in time. With that, they got in the minibus and were on their way to the next destination.

"I have to say, Gary, I would have never been able to live in a place like that," Tyson said. "And to give away your money like that. You might be unaware of this, but the advance we are getting is more money than someone would usually get on their first program . . . the way you act so carelessly with money, one would think you grew up with tons of it, but then we saw where you lived."

"I think it's because I lived like that. Sometimes I find it crazy how money, which is nothing more than paper that we assign a special value to, is the reason why people go hungry and have to worry. As I said, I've reached a point where I won't have to go hungry anymore, so if I can make other people I know and care about happy by giving up on being richer than before, I won't hesitate for even a moment."

As they traveled, the conversation steered away from Gary's generosity, as Spring asked about a man named Ash.

"Elanor, are you able to get me a meeting with Ash? He missed the one last week; we were supposed to talk about another promotion," Spring said.

"Ah, I will try, but to be honest, Ash has been pretty busy these days," Elanor replied. "I suppose I can tell you all this, but the truth is, AJ Entertainment recently was bought out by another company. Ash is no longer the majority shareholder. I don't know the details of who yet, though."

News of a takeover was always worrying, and Elanor was quick to calm down their worries.

"Don't worry, Ash will continue working as the director at AJ Entertainment; this was actually his decision. It's why we are able to invest more in productions like this. On top of that, Ash told me that the new company has allowed AJ to continue working the way they have been. Although it's technically a takeover, effectively it's more of an investment, so none of us should be affected directly."

"I'm happy to hear that," Rachel said. "Still, I thought AJ Entertainment was already a big company. Who would have the means to buy out the company just like that?"

"Whomever it is, they must be a pretty big spender. We should find out; maybe they will have more connections for us," Tyson suggested.

"I guess that means we should be careful if we see any new visitors around the building as well. Who knows, they could be part of this new company, so the last thing we would want to do is offend them," Spring said.

CHAPTER 101

HELLO, BOSS

The minibus didn't travel too far away from where Gary used to live, as there was a little street that he wanted to visit to see how it was doing. He also felt that the next place they would visit would provide more information about Slough than just showing the well-developed areas.

It was a row of shops that were still in the same area that had opened not too long ago, and the place Gary wanted to visit was a bakery.

"So why have you decided to bring us here? Is there any special meaning to this place?" Eleanor asked.

"Ah, I just wanted you to have a taste of the local food, and besides if people ever visit Slough I want to let them know that this is where they should go if they want the very best." Gary smiled.

He was sure that some visitors would come to Slough because of the program, and in turn, why not help out the local businesses? He remembered that the last time he had come here, he had met a sweet young woman named Naomi, and he wanted to repay the favor for her niceness, and she really did make good food.

The whole group entered the shop, and when they did, they all immediately froze, and Spring took a big gulp. Inside the shop were four young adults, all dressed in black-and-gold clothing.

"Are they . . . they . . . gang members?" Spring whispered.

"I think it might be best if we all get out of here," the guard said, although his job was to protect them and he felt confident he could do that. He didn't want to get on a gang's bad side. On top of that, the guard was trying to size up just how large the gang was, but as they traveled in the minibus they saw countless people in black-and-gold clothing.

It was clear that this was the gang that ruled the streets of Slough, and it was best to not get involved.

Before they could make an exit, though, the men turned around with bags of pastries in their hands.

"Oh . . . isn't that Gary?" Park said with a wave.

Park was one of the subleaders who worked under the core members, and the last time Gary returned to Slough, he had dealt with some troublesome members of the Howlers who were using their name for no good.

Park however, had no idea this was happening, and he turned out to be a good person in the end. He was also one of the many members of the Howlers who had turned up when they were going to raid Notsburg. That day Gary had decided to remember the faces of everyone who had arrived, as he would return their loyalty to them.

"Boss, I promise we aren't here to cause any trouble," Park quickly said, as he remembered what happened the last time. "It's just after last time, well, we became regulars of this place."

Hearing the word *boss*, and not just Park but the ones behind him acting in a panic, had caused the others to be confused. Why was Gary on good terms with these people, and why were they calling him boss?

"Gary . . . we're okay, right, you know these people?" Clem barged her shoulder into him.

"Yeah," Gary replied.

"So they're not going to hurt us?" Rachel asked.

"Hurt you guys? If you are the boss's friend, then of course we would never hurt you, and besides how could we even lay a finger on someone like him," Park said.

With that said, the men waved their goodbyes and quickly left the bakery. They could tell that their presence was causing the others to feel a little scared, and they wouldn't want that.

"What was that all about? Why were they calling you boss?" Tyson asked.

"I'm not really sure," Gary answered.

It was true, Park and the others shouldn't have known he was the boss, because whenever he made public appearances he wore a mask.

"It was because of what happened last time, of course," Naomi said, as she came from behind the counter wearing an apron with flour all over it.

"Here, let me show you."

Naomi pulled out her phone, and it didn't take her long to find the semiviral clip that went around in Slough. It was a video of Gary dealing with the gang members, fighting them just outside the bakery.

"It's amazing, right? They call him boss because they respect him, of course, and they know that Gary would give them a beating if they ever tried something again," Naomi said, punching the air a couple of times.

Gary was embarrassed, to say the least, seeing himself fighting in his hometown.

"He fought those guys when they were messing with my bakery, and ever since, I've never had a problem again," Naomi continued.

"Wow, you went up against gang members just for a bakery?" Rachel said. "You're crazy even if you are an Altered. What if they went after your family?"

"I guess it isn't too much of a problem; if they knew Gary was an Altered, then the gang might not want to go up against him because of their losses. It's the same for me," Tyson said, seeing that everyone was talking about Gary so much that it was making him feel a little ill.

"I had plenty of offers from gangs. They know my strength after all."

"Gary, the more I learn about you, the more you are starting to become this town's little hero; this is great!" Elanor said with a big smile. "Let's head to the next area. When I was researching Slough, one of the destinations was Burnham Street, and it's getting close to dinnertime."

Hearing the next destination, Gary wanted to object, but he didn't really have a good reason to, because Burnham Street was one of the places he was most likely to run into others who knew him.

Meanwhile Clem was starting to wonder about the way everyone had treated him so far; it wasn't normal, and she was starting to think that there may be something bigger to this.

CHAPTER 102

A SPECIAL GUEST

With no protest from Gary, the group had ended up on Burnham Street, a row of mainly restaurants and bars that went on for about a mile. The street was compact and filled with people, being one of the more popular places for people to hang out in the evening. This was one of the nicer parts of Slough, because it was one of the areas that used to be run by Olivia, so it was already generating substantial wealth.

There had only been slight improvements, such as replacing the more seedy places and investing in new equipment for the more run-down restaurants.

"Wow, this place is busier than I thought it would be," Rachel said.

"Yeah, I agree," Gary replied.

What he didn't realize was that because of the new factory and other developments, there were a lot more people in Slough than usual, causing quite the rush on the street.

"Hey, it's those guys again," Tyson pointed out.

He was facing the people dressed in black and gold. It wasn't the same ones they had met at the bakery, but the street was filled with them. They were standing between the restaurants as if they were guarding the place.

"It's most likely that the gang is in control of this food street as well," the guard said. "But I guess we're in luck; the locals don't seem to be afraid, so as long as we're not trying to get involved in their business, we should be fine."

What surprised the guard more was how much a single gang dominated a Tier 3 town. He had been to a few himself, and seldom was there just a single big gang. There would be some that controlled the majority of the town, but Slough was being run similarly to Tier 1 cities, where the whole place was owned by a single King.

As they walked down the street, they had a lot of options to choose from. They struggled to decide, but as they got closer to the end, Gary was getting more nervous, because they were getting closer to where she would be.

"Why don't we just pick this restaurant . . . the Wild Boar," Gary said. "Otherwise we might not be able to get a table."

Elanor thought Gary was right; by the look of things, it was so busy that they might be waiting a while.

The Wild Boar restaurant was themed like a jungle, with leaves on the walls, tusks on the tables, and a large painting of wild boars in the main dining room.

It also had a stage featuring live music to top it off. It was clear why the place was popular.

The owners had obviously had quite a bit of fun decorating the place. However, as Gary had expected, it was relatively busy. In the reception area, four groups were already waiting to be seated, all of them around four or five people.

There was also a large group of about ten just in front of them who were asking if there were any seats. Since the AJ Entertainment group was rather large themselves, including the camera crew, they thought it would be a while until they sat down.

"I'm sorry, sir, but it looks like it's going to be at least a thirty-minute wait for a group your size," the hostess told the other large group. "As you can see, we are quite busy today."

The man at the front was wearing a fancy suit and had spiked blond hair.

"Come on, is that really the best you can do? I can pay double, or triple if you want. Heck I'll even pay for that table's meal if they will get up and help us get our seats."

The hostess pulled a wan smile; it was clear the man was being difficult.

"I'm sorry, sir, but we want everyone to have an enjoyable experience and come back to this establishment over and over again, so I'm afraid we can't make exceptions."

Gary and his group stood behind the blond man's group so they could overhear everything, and expected it would be quite a wait, but since it was their fault, and it looked like everywhere on Burnham Street would be the same, they didn't mind.

In the end, the blond man sighed in defeat and sat down in the waiting area, where they served a few snacks for those waiting to nibble on and even had some board games.

"Hi there." Elanor smiled. "Unfortunately we didn't make a booking and we have quite a large group with us. We don't mind if you have to split us up into different tables."

The hostess looked at the tablet in front of her before pulling a face that didn't say she had good news.

"Unfortunately, the best we can do is put you on two tables that will be free in around forty-five minutes, is that okay?" she asked.

Since there was no choice and there were at least snacks they could eat in the meantime, Elanor gave a smile and said it was fine.

The group was ready to sit in the reception area and wait with the others, but then something strange occurred. One of the people in black-and-gold clothing who were in the restaurant had come over to the hostess at the front desk.

He whispered something in her ear, and she changed her tune.

"I'm sorry, Gary, is it?" she asked, looking at the green-haired teenager. "We actually have a table prepared for you. Please follow me."

The group was surprised; they were happy to wait, but for some reason now they suddenly had a table, and the hostess had mentioned Gary's name as well.

"Wait a second, you dumb bitch!" the blond man shouted. "You told me a second ago that there were no more tables, that we would have to wait. We came in before them, and our group is just as large as theirs, so why the hell are they going ahead of us?"

Before the man could cause any trouble, the man wearing black-and-gold stood in front him, making a fist.

"We can easily talk about this outside if you wish."

While they walked to their table, Clem still couldn't help but glance at Gary. Wherever they went in this town, as long as they were by his side, everyone was treating their group differently. It was happening too often to be a coincidence.

CHAPTER 103

WHO ARE YOU?

The hostess seated them at a large oval table off to one side, sectioned off by a little red velvet rope.

It was clearly a seating area meant for VIPs or those who had specially booked it. It was also in the perfect place. They could see the live band, but it wasn't so close to the stage that you wouldn't be able to have a conversation with each other without shouting.

After seating everyone, the hostess was off, and said that a server would arrive soon to take their order.

As quickly as one person left, another arrived to give them complimentary bread and sparkling water, and it didn't seem like something the restaurant did, as their table was the only one receiving these things.

It was safe to say that the group had attracted a lot of attention. Several of them had a star quality about them; they were head turners, and to top it off they had a camera crew and were seated in the VIP area.

The others in the restaurant believed that they had to be quite important people, maybe paying a visit from a higher-tier city.

"I wonder why they are treating us so nice, and gave us this special place? You didn't prepare this in advance, did you?" Rachel asked, looking at Elanor.

"No, I certainly did not, which was bad planning on my part. My guess is it might be the cameras," Elanor explained. "Often when they see that there is a crew with us, places like this will treat us a bit nicer.

"They know that it's a chance to get their restaurant on the big screen and make it more popular."

"I think it might have been because of Gary," Clem said. "Maybe there was another person that he saved in this restaurant. Or someone who is a big fan of his; after all, they did call out your name."

Gary wore a nervous smile.

"I think it might have been the cameras," Gary answered.

As conversation continued, a waiter arrived and the first person he went to was Gary himself, asking him what he wanted.

"I think it's best if you ask the others first," Gary said. "I still haven't decided."

Clem kept giving Gary the side-eye, and each time something happened she was noting it down in her head.

It was clear that they weren't the VIPs; it was Gary. Meanwhile, running through Gary's head was *How did the situation even come to this?*

Little did Gary know that Tyler had played a part, informing everyone, and in turn Burnham Street was informed to look out for the business tycoon Gary Dem.

Nearly all of the restaurants on the street had reserved a table for him and his guests, so no matter what restaurant they went to, Gary would still have gotten the same treatment.

Gary had ordered quite a bit of food for himself; he was an Altered, after all, so the others understood, and they didn't hold back either.

Besides, AJ Entertainment would be paying the bill. Everyone enjoyed the food and the live band, but Gary noticed that one person was enjoying the band more than the others.

Rachel was continuously staring at the band, not focusing on what was happening at the table. At times she also mimed along with the words.

That's right, Rachel is an idol singer, Gary thought.

"Do you want to sing? I think it would be nice to hear you perform," Gary said.

"What a great suggestion! This way Rachel can share her talents with everyone here as well!" Elanor ecstatically said.

Rachel was feeling a bit shy, as she curled her head toward her chest.

"Well, I mean, if they would let me, I wouldn't mind singing," Rachel answered, as it was something she loved to do, no matter what stage there was.

Gary stood up and went to the restroom; on his way back he decided to speak to one of the staff members. If they were going to treat him special, then he might as well use it to ask for a favor, and they gave him the go-ahead for Rachel to go up and sing.

"They said it was okay!" Gary said with a thumbs-up.

An announcement was made, and shortly afterward Rachel took the stage. The group were just about to have their dessert, but their eyes were glued on Rachel.

A song was requested by the band and she soon sang away. When she started to sing, it was as if all of the nerves had left her body.

She looked like a natural as she moved her body, holding the microphone and pouring her heart out.

Gary had sensitive ears, and yet to his ears it still was a beautiful sound, and he could tell she was a truly talented person.

"Okay, Gary, I can't take it anymore," Clem whispered as she scooted over next to Gary.

The others were listening to Rachel or having their own conversations, so she thought it was the perfect time.

"Strange things have been happening in this town all night since we came here. Tell me, who are you? Or what did you do for everyone in this whole town for them to treat you so nice. Did you save ten puppies from a burning building or something?" Clem asked.

Gary smiled at the comment.

"You really want to know the truth? If I told you, you might get a little scared."

"I've seen a lot more than you think; try me," Clem said.

Gary looked back at Rachel as he gave the answer.

"The gang that you see everywhere wearing the black and gold, they are the Howlers, a group that took over Slough and changed everything not so long ago, and I am the leader of that gang . . . does that answer your question?"

CHAPTER 104

PICKED A FIGHT WITH THE WRONG PERSON

Clem and Gary were sitting pretty close to each other, and Clem was staring deep into his eyes after hearing the words that had come out of his mouth, trying to read him, trying to read what was behind those eyes of his.

"I guess you just don't want to tell me," Clem sighed. "I understand, everyone has their own secrets, especially us stars, so we can't let the media and the public know every little detail about us. I guess you will just never have to find out about my secret, then."

With a little show of her tongue, Clem continued to watch Rachel as she performed and the song came to an end. She clapped greatly while cheering on her fellow colleague.

Meanwhile, Gary just couldn't help but smile at her response.

I thought this would be the case, but I guess she didn't even believe me for a second.

Keeping a secret was hard, and there were times when Gary just wanted others to know the truth, but he knew why the secret had to be kept, and the plan that had been set out by Kai.

He was happy to tell Clem the truth because he thought she wouldn't believe him, and if she did, he could just play it off as a joke because the real situation just seemed that unrealistic.

A teenage boy, age seventeen, still not old enough to legally drink, was the leader of a large crime syndicate that ruled an entire town. Even if he was an Altered, that just didn't make sense.

On top of that, it was clear that none of them knew much about the Howlers; they were too busy in their own lives, their own cities, dealing with their own things, but if they also knew that the Howlers were in control of a Tier 2 city, and that it was Notsburg, the story of him being the leader would seem even more unlikely.

It was good to say it at least, Gary thought.

Rachel came offstage and many people asked to take a photo of her. She wasn't famous yet, but since there was a camera crew, and after witnessing her talent, many of them believed that she would be famous one day, and this was their chance to jump at the opportunity.

When she finally came back, everyone gave Rachel compliments on her performance, including Gary.

"You can actually sing! I thought you might be like those other stars that just mime," Gary said.

"I was recruited for my talents; my good looks are just a bonus." Rachel gave Gary a wink as she dove into her dessert.

While they were all enjoying the last course of their meal, the door to the restaurant banged open, causing nearly everyone to turn their head.

When they saw who it was, the staff immediately stood up straight and bowed.

"Who is that?" Rachel asked.

"She looks incredible, and she has an amazing presence as well; she's captured everyone in the room," Spring said.

"Is she a star? If she isn't, should I give her my card?" Elanor said, because she too was stunned.

Wearing a fur coat and a tight dress that revealed the upper part of her cleavage, she walked past everyone, heading straight for Gary's table.

Oh no, Gary thought as he looked at the wall, trying not to grab her attention. *This is the one person that I've been trying to avoid this whole time.*

"I hope you are all enjoying the service!" Olivia said as she greeted the table. "You see, I always like to treat outsiders quite special, and when I heard that you were in the city, I thought it would be best to welcome you this way.

"If you need anything, feel free to ask, as I am in charge of all the establishments on Burnham Street."

Now they all thought they knew why they were being treated so well, and the fact that she claimed to own all the restaurants here just meant she was a very important figure.

When Elanor heard this, her hopes of scouting went down the drain. An actor's life wasn't an easy one, and was likely that this woman was already wealthy.

After her greeting, Olivia didn't stick around; instead, she headed toward the back of the restaurant, but before going through the door, she turned her head and gave Gary a smile.

What was that? Gary thought. *Did she just come in here to give me a heart attack? If she acted like she knew me after saying all of that, what would I have done then? I don't even know how far along Kai's plan is of making me this business tycoon, so I don't even know what I can and can't say.*

Gary was starting to realize the difficulties of being head of a gang, and being so far secluded from it.

"I guess since we're done eating, we should get going and rest up a bit," Gary suggested, wanting to get out of there as soon as possible.

"Right, we should ask for the bill," Elanor said.

But to their surprise, or not to their surprise, the bill had already been paid; according to the staff, it was covered by the owner whom they had seen earlier. If there was one thing Olivia did succeed in, it was getting Elanor on her side.

She thought there were some good people in Slough, and she would make sure it was seen in its best light.

When they stepped outside, the group was pretty tired; it had been a long day, and traveling always took a lot out of them. Some of them were quite used to this, but even they still yawned.

They had parked relatively high up in a multi-story parking structure, because they had two large vehicles. The cameras had been turned off for the day.

"Big shot, where do you think you and your friends are running off to so fast?"

Turning around, they saw the blond man from before, and he wasn't alone; his friends were with him, around ten in total, holding weapons that you could get from a supermarket, like a mop and baseball bats.

Damn it, since we were in a parking structure I thought it was normal to smell others here, and we have the whole camera crew here, Gary thought, blaming himself for not catching it sooner.

Immediately, the guard who was with them stood in front of the group. He was ready to do his job, even though he was a little nervous.

I could take down maybe three of them at most, but with weapons this is going to be a little difficult.

"Why do you have a problem with us?" Spring shouted. "Shouldn't you be taking it out on the restaurant? They were the ones who seated us before you."

"Shut up, bitch!" The blond man pointed his bat toward her. "I saw that smug smile on your face, the look you all gave us as you went to the table. You think you're better than us, right? Well, guess what, there is one thing we can do, and that's beat your ass!"

"I can't believe it." Tyson smiled. "These idiots can't go against the gang here, since they're protecting the restaurant, so they go after us because they think we're easy pickings."

There was a reason why Tyson wasn't scared: he was an Altered as well.

"Get them!" the man shouted, and all of them charged forward; Tyson went right and the guard went left to take out a few of the attackers, but there were still six others running right at them.

"AHHH!" Rachel and Clem screamed, while Spring was still shouting and pointing at them, but Gary quickly ran ahead. He jumped in the air and kicked two of them, chucking them so far back that they crashed into the cars behind them, denting them.

"Oh, that's right, Gary is one of the top students in the AFA, and he is incredibly strong!" Clem said.

It was true, because by the time Tyson and the guard were done dealing with the other two troublemakers, Gary had already taken out all six of them and was holding the blond man by his hair as he knelt on the ground. He had been hit in the stomach, knocking the wind out of him.

"You and all of those who attacked us today are never allowed in this city again," Gary whispered, letting go of the man's head.

"Let's get out of here before we cause a scene," Gary said, and the others were inclined to agree as they got in their vehicles and drove off.

The blond man thought he had gotten away lightly, and he rolled over onto his back, expecting to see the ceiling, but instead, he saw a beautiful woman.

"Am I in heaven?" the man asked.

"Did you not hear what that person said?" she replied. "You messed with a very dangerous person when you should have just gone home. You got off very lightly just getting kicked out of this town—or maybe not."

The woman pulled out what looked like a whip.

"Because I plan to have some fun with you before kicking you out of here."

CHAPTER 105

THE BIG MEET

The group had traveled safely back to the hotel with no problems, and for the first time, they actually felt safer when they saw some people wearing black and gold standing outside.

Never did they think that they would be attacked by the general public and not gang members, and it was starting to become clear that these gang members in particular were integrated into nearly every part of Slough.

The small shops, the food street, and even here in Cipen in front of the luxury hotel, none of the staff were afraid of them. At times it seemed that if there was a problem with the general public, they could rely on the local gang members to take care of it.

They were almost like a police force, but far more reliable. It reminded them a lot of the higher-tier cities.

Gary and Tyson were sharing a room since they were the only two boys. They were lying in their beds not speaking to each other, since they hadn't really seen eye to eye this entire trip.

"Hey, Gary . . . I just want to say something that's been on my mind for a while," Tyson said, staring at the ceiling. "You were pretty cool back there. I thought I was skilled and gifted, and chosen because I was an Altered, but you really showed that there is a huge difference between me and you. "I'm sorry for all the hazing I did to you before; I really thought you thought you were all that because you came from the AFA."

"Hazing?" Gary replied, wondering what Tyson meant by that, and at that point Tyson couldn't help but laugh, because that was when he realized that Gary never even knew what he and Spring were trying to do.

Still, Gary thought it was ironic that Tyson was trying to apologize, when really it was he and Spring who thought they were too good for him, but either way, he was glad that Tyson could admit his mistakes.

"You are a strong Altered yourself, Tyson," Gary said, leaving it at that.

The next morning, it was time for them to leave Slough, and Gary was surprised that nothing happened during the night. He was worried that there would be a knock on his door and a parade of Howlers members would stop by to visit. Or maybe Kai would just come barging in, waving hello.

Yet none of that happened, and they left to return to AJ Entertainment for the second day.

"It was nice to visit your hometown, Gary; I feel like I was able to learn quite a lot," Rachel said with a big smile.

"I guess it was okay," Spring said, staring out the window; she was still shaken up by the surprise attack, and she had not spoken much since getting back on the minibus.

"What will we be doing for the rest of the program? Will we be heading to our own hometowns?" Clem asked.

"I'm not too sure, myself," Elanor said. "I was the one who pushed for you guys to go to Slough. They liked the idea I sold them, but I doubt we will be visiting any of your own areas.

"Today we have a special meeting with the producer who will be in charge of the rest of the program, but don't worry, Big Dave and I will be by your side. It's our job after all," Elanor explained.

Big Dave was their guard, who Gary had to admit was a decent person and strong as well. He had no fear when taking on their armed attackers, which led Gary to believe that he had some experience in that field.

The group had finally arrived back at AJ Entertainment, and the place was just as busy as before. Gary was still wearing the same suit, since it was really the only sharp outfit he had for the TV screen, but it was nice and clean thanks to the hotel's prompt service.

"All right, everyone, we're in a bit of rush here," Elanor said, looking at her watch. "We have a tight schedule, but we're going to redo your makeup and have you look your best before you meet the producer."

They did as they were told, and everything went like clockwork as they entered their dressing room. They were pampered up and made ready.

"If we're meeting the producer, maybe this will be our chance to ask for a program of our own, or more promotion," Rachel exclaimed. "You heard what Elanor said, they have just had a huge injection of funding. I'm sure they're going to be wanting to make big use of the money."

"And to do that, they would need big profits in return," Spring said. "Do you know how much money it takes to break out a new idol group these days? I would say that a TV show, maybe a school romance with low production cost and a star like me, would make the biggest return."

The room was heating up, with Gary honestly not caring for this meeting, but he could see that it was important to the others, who wanted to make this their living. Although Spring wasn't the nicest person, she certainly knew what she wanted, and she looked like the type of person who worked hard to get what she wanted.

When everyone was ready, they took an elevator to the top floors, which housed all the big shots of the company and those who made all of the decisions.

Reaching the twenty-third floor, just shy of the twenty-fifth floor at the top, they stepped out and headed to the meeting room. Elanor gave a quick knock before politely letting them all in.

Three people were seated in front of a single long desk. All of them carried a strong air of power, but Gary recognized one of them.

"Oh, I'm surprised to see you here; I didn't know you were one of our stars," Ash said.

CHAPTER 106

PURE SCUM

When Gary had arrived at AJ Entertainment, he accidentally bumped into a young man who exuded an air of importance. The man was accompanied by guards and his confident posture further confirmed his significance in the organization. Although the encounter was brief, it left a lasting impression on Gary.

"Oh, are you one of the producers?" Gary calmly asked.

"Gary!" Upon seeing the three men, Elanor quickly stepped forward and humbly bowed her head, leaving the others in a state of surprise. Clem instinctively grabbed Gary's sleeve and pulled him to the side, as they both watched Elanor's respectful display.

"You idiot, that's not just anybody. That's Ash!" Clem whispered. "He's the person in charge of AJ Entertainment."

Gary was taken aback to learn that the person running such a large entertainment company was so young; he appeared to be in his early twenties. However, Gary remembered that he too was quite young, and perhaps age was not a barrier to success in the industry.

"Please forgive me, sir. I wasn't aware that you would be present," Elanor apologized politely. "Also, I must clarify that Gary is just a guest and not affiliated with our company as a star or employee. Hence, his knowledge about our business is limited."

Ash smiled, appearing unperturbed by the situation. "No worries, I didn't inform anyone about my arrival either. I just wanted to personally welcome our new talents and share a few words with them.

"You are the future of our company and in order to reach new heights, we must create new stars from the ground up, bigger and better than before," Ash declared with enthusiasm. "Therefore, I have entrusted our producer, Neville Stomper, and one of our directors, Matthew Pearl, to oversee this program and to decide on future projects for both of you.

"You may have heard the rumors that AJ Entertainment no longer holds the majority share in our company, and that is true," Ash confirmed. "However, I will continue to lead this company, and the investment from our partners will allow us to expand and grow even further."

Gary observed the other two people standing beside Ash. He noticed that the producer was wearing sunglasses indoors, despite the lack of sunshine, and a brightly colored shirt as if he were ready for a day at the beach.

The producer's attire and demeanor seemed out of place for the setting. He appeared aloof and disinterested during the conversation.

On the other hand, Matthew, the other man by Ash's side, exuded an intimidating aura that made others feel uneasy. When the new stars arrived, Matthew kept his focus on them, his hairy physique drawing their attention. He wore a V-neck shirt that showed off his chest hair and a pointed beard that accentuated his strong jawline. His curly hair flowed down to his shoulders, completing his rugged look.

Given the amount of hair on his body, Gary couldn't help but feel that Matthew resembled a werewolf more than himself right now.

"It was a pleasure meeting you all, and I look forward to getting to know you better in the future," Ash said, signaling the end of the meeting. As he prepared to leave the room, he gave one last glance at Gary.

As he left the room, Ash couldn't help but ponder about the temporary addition from the AFA. *I didn't bother researching him much, but maybe I should,* he thought. However, first he needed to address the small mess he had created for himself.

As soon as Ash exited the room, Neville stood up and pulled his sunglasses down, glancing toward them. "All female stars, please step forward and do a twirl ever so slowly for me," Neville ordered, his tone oozing with a hint of sleaze. The boys exchanged a glance, uncomfortable with

Neville's request, but the female stars complied, understanding the power dynamics at play and the importance of pleasing the guy before them.

"No, no, no!" Neville shouted, his frustration palpable. "What's with these costumes? Where's the beautiful skin, the long, slim legs? These girls are beautiful and sexy, yet you're not showing any of that. Sex sells, and you have them dressed up like this!" The room fell into an uncomfortable silence as everyone stood frozen, unsure how to respond, except for Gary.

"Is this guy from the 1980s or something?" Gary said, breaking the uncomfortable silence. "It feels like I've stepped into a time machine. Plus, aren't they all aiming for different things? One's an actor, another is a TV presenter, and the third is a singer. This guy seems like a bit of a perv to me, to be honest."

As Neville took off his sunglasses, his eyes narrowed and he glared at Gary, seemingly trying to kill him with his eyes. However, Gary remained unfazed, meeting the producer's gaze without flinching.

Their silent stare-off continued for about half a minute, until Neville sighed heavily and rubbed his nose. "I guess it's safe to say who will be the last pick in everything," he muttered. "All right, this has soured my mood for the day. Just take the rest of the day off; there will be no filming until I call you. You can thank the green-haired boy for missing out on this rare chance."

Gary didn't care about not being involved in much of the program, a fact that Neville had understood from him mouthing off. Rather than punish him in any way, he had left this comment to steer the group's hate toward him.

Eleanor quickly left the room, and the rest followed. They walked down the hallway in silence, until Spring spoke up.

"Why did you have to open your mouth?" Spring said, fury blazing in her eyes. "Did you think this was anything new for any of us? That we haven't heard comments like that dozens of times before? Do you think we don't know what guys like him think, that we just got to meet him because of our looks?

"This was a big chance for all of us, and you might have just ruined what could have been our *only* chance to work with someone like him! WHY? Just because you wanted to be some type of white knight?

"Do you get off on this shit? Do you think doing this type of stuff will get us to sleep with you? Because it won't! Maybe you don't care about this stuff, but we do, so stay out of it!"

Spring entered the elevator and extended her palm out, not wanting Gary to come inside; the others were already in the elevator apart from Big Dave. Gary could see that he wasn't wanted and thought it was best to let them head down on their own and approach them again after they had cooled down.

"That one has quite the mouth on her, doesn't she? Unfortunately, a lot of them are like that," Dave said. "I'm sure you just wanted to do what you felt was right, kid. After all, you got a bad feeling from them two, didn't you? If so, you're not wrong.

"The producer guy is pure scum but he is quite open about it and easy to read; the real one to worry about is the director Matthew. I'm sure you already know, unlike the others, but the guards including myself are a part of the Ashen gang.

"The Ashen gang and AJ Entertainment are run by two people: Ash, who is at the top, and Matthew. As AJ Entertainment got bigger, though, Ash started to run things in the company more rather than the gang.

"In turn, it also means that Matthew has been able to run a few more things. Gary, I'm only telling you all this because I like you. I like what you did back in Slough and saw how you grew up.

"Matthew is a strong Altered, in fact he's the strongest in the gang. However, the loyalty in the gang for Ash used to be unmatched, but slowly it started to change. I have a feeling Ash might have known this, and that's why he sold control over the company, maybe for some outside help, but who knows what he's thinking.

"Either way, I know you are strong, so feel free to get on the bad side of the producer as much as you want, but stay away from the director."

Back in the meeting room, Matthew was licking his lips.

That girl Spring, I liked her, I really liked her.

CHAPTER 107

MYSTERY HOWLERS

The producer, Neville, and the director, Matthew, stayed in the room for a while, as they did need to plan what was the best thing to do for the program considering these new stars.

They had done a lot of things before, but they figured this time it might be interesting to start something new. Yet all of this planning was causing Neville a big headache.

"This is why you should have spent the day with them. We hardly know anything about their personalities, and usually the first day is spent brainstorming," Matthew said. "Besides, it would have given me more time to see our products before trying them."

While they were looking through all the documents, Neville looked at his watch, as he was reminded of something; there was another reason why he had been unable to work with the others today anyway, and the schedule had to be changed.

"I need to get going," Neville said, standing up and putting on a jacket that only came down to his ribs; it was clearly made for style rather than fashion. "Ash asked me to go introduce myself to the Howlers. To see if there was anything they needed."

"The Howlers?" Matthew repeated. "Why would he bother with them? Don't they only own ten percent of AJ Entertainment? the documents said most of the buyout was from a single person."

"Yes, but you should know who the Howlers are and why Ash decided to make a deal with them. Besides, it seems the investor and the

Howlers work relatively close together, but the real one we need to worry about is the Howlers."

The director scoffed at this comment.

"Why should we worry about another gang? Sure, they are strong, but they must be relatively weak after taking over Notsburg, and we have our own pride too. Remember, this whole thing is a partnership, so when you see them, don't be groveling at their feet."

Neville knew that Matthew always acted this way; he was more suited for the gang scene than the entertainment business. The thing was, they all knew about the Howlers and their accomplishments.

No one, not even Matthew, would want to tangle with a dangerous gang, but he needed to keep up the act of the strong guy in the room.

The producer had left, and it didn't take him long to enter Slough. He was traveling with only a couple of guards from AJ Entertainment, since this was meant to be a friendly meeting.

Neville was surprised by everything he saw around him, but at the same time not so much.

I guess this is what happens when a Tier 3 town takes over one of the wealthiest Tier 2 cities. They must have more money than they know what to do with, Neville thought.

I can see why Ash made a deal with them. He must be aware that Matthew has been trying to get more people on his side to try to eventually take over everything, but that will be difficult now that most of the company has been sold to an outside group, especially one that Matthew can't really touch because of their strength.

The problem is, I'm stuck in the middle of all of this, doing both of their bidding and trying to play on both sides. I can't believe what Matthew asked me to do.

Eventually Neville reached the hotel and the three of them were guided inside; he noticed many men in black-and-gold clothing, but there didn't seem to be any guests at all.

Just then three people wearing strange masks over their faces entered the reception area.

"You don't have to worry, we booked out the whole hotel for this meeting," the voice said, and a scarred jaw was visible beneath the mask.

Gesturing, Kai allowed Neville to sit in the reception area, where there were plenty of sofas and seats. At the same time, about fifty Howlers were also present, standing off to the side.

Did he call the whole gang here to intimidate me? Neville thought. Whether it was or wasn't the case, it was working.

"Ash sent me here to tell you how we will be spending your investments, and to give you a business plan showing when you will start to see a return on your investment," Neville said, handing over the documents.

His hand was shaking, he didn't know why, but the masked people were making him incredibly nervous and it was hard for him to breathe. The documents lay on the table, and Kai didn't touch them.

"Thank you for those. I have a question to ask: how is AJ Entertainment? Is everything running smoothly? Are there any problems we should be aware of?" Kai asked.

Neville was sweating more than before. Did they already know about the infighting, or was this a general question?

The truth was that Kai was trying to find out if Gary had caused any problems.

"Everything is fine; if there is anything you are concerned about, you can always contact me or Ash," Neville said.

His body was still shaking, and the words of the director rang through his head. They shouldn't be so intimidated, they both were the same level, and he wasn't in front of a King from a Tier 1 city, so why did he feel this way?

"I have to ask: We have been very open, I have even come here in person showing you my face. Yet you cover yours with a mask. Don't you think it's polite to at least show the face of the leader we are doing business with?" Neville asked.

The blond man in the mask started to laugh.

"This is a rule we have, and the deal has already been made, so that means you have agreed to follow our rules, and besides, I think I should make something clear. Even if you were to see my face, you wouldn't be seeing the leader, because he is . . . having fun somewhere." Kai smiled.

CHAPTER 108

AVOIDING THE PROBLEM

The meeting had come to an end, and when it did, Neville was free to leave the building; as he did. Not a single person followed him.

"What the fuck was that all about!" Neville shouted, as he kicked the air. "They don't respect us at all, they don't even respect me or see us as any type of threat."

Neville turned to the two guards, who were members of the Ashen gang.

"Do you think they were afraid of us, afraid of our power? It was clear as day that they think they are above us, and after I came all the way here to meet them in person, they don't even send out their leader.

"Having fun? What does he even think he's doing!"

Neville continued to complain, more and more, eventually kicking a large trash can outside the hotel. It fell over and caused a mess on the street.

"Ha!" Neville laughed. "Let's just leave this as a parting gift to this shit town called Slough. Come on, let's get out of here."

They got back into the car they had come in, which was a relatively large van, one of the ones that many of their stars used. Neville couldn't wait to get back home. The vehicle started up and went a few feet before it completely stopped.

It felt like someone had slammed on the brakes, causing Neville to nearly fly out of his seat. He had managed to put his arms in front of him in time, stopping himself from getting his face crushed.

"Why did you stop so suddenly!" Neville shouted. "I didn't even have my seat belt on!"

"Sir, I didn't stop. I think we have a problem," the driver said.

When Neville looked through the windshield, he figured out what had happened. Standing in front of the car was a muscular man in a mask, one of the masked men who were in the meeting, with a single hand on the hood of the car.

"He came out of nowhere and just placed his hand on the car, stopping it dead," the driver said.

A number of thoughts were running through Neville's head. For one, something like this wouldn't be possible for a normal human, and no one would have the guts just to jump in front of a car, unless they were confident. It was clear that this person was an Altered.

"Hey!" the masked man shouted. "You should clean up the mess you made before you leave. We don't come to your house and leave a load of shit. Unless you don't want to get out of the car."

With a single hand, the person crushed the hood and started to lift the vehicle in the air. Neville nearly fell to the floor, and the man quickly set the vehicle down again.

"I understand, we'll clean it up," Neville said.

After his one visit to the town of Slough to see the Howlers, he never wanted to run into them again. This was his train of thought as he sadly picked up trash from the ground and placed it back into the bin.

The program had been planned for the new stars of AJ Entertainment, and just as stated, the producer was doing everything he could to make sure that Gary got as little limelight as possible.

They went to multiple locations in the current city as well as surrounding locations, but almost no questions were directly asked of Gary, nor was he given any instructions.

Elanor felt bad for Gary; she was the one who had invited him because she thought she could make him into a big star, but since he had gotten on the wrong side of the producer, it looked like the dream was over.

At the same time, it wasn't just the producer who was shunning out Gary, but several of the others as well. None of them were speaking to Gary, and that included Clem.

Currently, the group was at a beach, the girls in bikinis, the boys shirtless, revealing all. They were to do a set of challenges while answering questions that the public wanted to hear.

It had been a tiring day, and Gary was constantly annoyed.

"Cut, we're going to have to do that shot again! You covered your ass in that last shot! You know what the people want!" Neville shouted.

There were multiple comments like this, and it was quite clear that this was practically a soft porn shoot. Perhaps a lot of what was being filmed wouldn't even be aired but was just for the perv's pleasure. At least this was what Gary thought, but he held his tongue because of what the others had asked of him last time.

When the day had come to an end, they returned to the beach house where they were staying. One could walk out the front door and down a few steps and be standing on the beach. He went out and sat down in the sand looking at the sky.

"The sea smells nice," Gary said, to no one in particular.

"Really? It smells a bit musty to me," a female voice said, as she sat down right next to Gary.

Still in her bikini, but with a large towel wrapped around herself, was none other than Clem.

"Is it okay if I sit here?" she asked.

"It's fine with me, but is it fine with you?" Gary replied, having noticed that all of them were avoiding him.

"I wanted to apologize, Gary," Clem said. "You know, I like you . . . and it's not just me. Rachel and Tyson seem to really like you as well. As for Spring, well, I can't really say anything, but the point is I want to say I'm sorry for avoiding you.

"It's just, you know how important this is for us, and for some reason the producer has it out for you. If we hang around you, there is a good chance it will ruin our chances as well. It's only for a week, in fact only a few more days now.

"I just hope that if we meet after this, we can still talk, and still be friends."

Gary smiled. "I understand. Don't worry, I'm not taking it too personally. How can I complain when I'm on a beach like this, with pretty girls all around me. I'm used to pretty girls avoiding me anyway, so it's not like much has changed."

Clem blushed a little as she remembered seeing Gary's body today on the beach. She found it hard to believe that Gary didn't have girls around him all the time. But she didn't know what he looked like before the big change in his life.

After hanging out for a while, they stood up and started to head inside.

"You go in first; after all, it might be a problem if you're seen with me, right?" Gary said.

"It should be fine," Clem replied. "I came out because the producer called Spring to his room, so I knew he wouldn't be watching me."

Gary paused for a second. Why would the producer call Spring to his room? He started to remember what Big Dave had said—that they should watch out for the director—but in his eyes both of them were scum anyway.

Just inside the front entrance to the large beach house, a central living room branched off to all of the other rooms. No one was there, but Gary was listening in to everything around him, and he overheard an interesting conversation.

"What did you say?" Spring almost shouted, but she didn't just in case the others heard.

"Come on, you should understand," Neville said. "You want to be the lead on your own drama show, right? With this, I can guarantee it for you. All you need to do is spend one night with Matthew, and I'm sure you know he's not just going to talk to you all night."

Spring's heart started to beat faster, and she instinctively took a step back. She didn't know what to say. Getting a role through an act like this?

"I . . . can't . . . I can't do it. I will get a drama with my own skills," Spring said.

Neville stood up, frustrated by the answer.

"Get a role with your own talents? Being pretty and sexy is one of your talents! Think about it, do you know how many people would happily sleep with the director to just get a role, never mind the lead role! Do you think you're special? I'm sure even your mother did something like this!"

"Shut up! I'm not doing it!" Spring shouted back, and headed toward the door.

"If you leave this room, the director has the power to kick you out of AJ Entertainment, and we can spread rumors about you to make sure no agency ever picks you up. Your whole acting career will be over. Just because you didn't want to spread your legs a little."

Spring stopped, her head down, tears flowing down her cheeks. She didn't know what to do, and she was unable to move. That was until she heard a loud crack from the door, the lock broken.

"You? What the fuck are you doing in here?" Neville shouted.

"What I should have done when I first met you." Gary made a fist and punched Neville right in the face, so hard that a tooth flew out of his mouth as his body hit the floor.

CHAPTER 109

REVENGE TASTES SWEET

Blood was running onto the floor from the gap in the producer's mouth. Neville's eyes had rolled into the back of his head.

Crap . . . I really need to start learning to control my strength even when I'm angry. I can't even blame the fact that it's close to a full moon, Gary thought.

"Gary . . ." Spring said, her hand shaking over her mouth, not knowing what to do. It was hard to believe that she was in this situation.

"Don't worry, I did this, this is all my choice, not anyone else's, it was my choice that I hit him and I won't let it affect you in any way."

Gary lifted the producer by the scruff of his neck and shook him a little. Soon his eyes opened and he started to come to. When he saw Gary he tried to push him away, but Gary's strength was enough to hold him there.

"Stop moving!" Gary growled, and remembering the punch to his jaw, the producer stopped there and then. "You asshole, how can a business even operate with you asking someone to do such a thing?

"I'm sure you don't want what I heard to get out to the public. So let's make a deal: you forget about everything that just happened right now. You will never ask any of the girls to do anything like this again, and that goes for you and the director.

"If you do, I will use everything in my power to bring you down, and it will hurt a lot more than it did today. Do you understand?"

The producer almost snarled at Gary as he looked at him; never in his life had someone dared to treat him this way. The Ashen gang, based on his word, would get rid of this guy.

At the same time, the producer had never been hit before. Since he didn't answer, Gary raised his fist; this time it was starting to transform and fur was appearing as well as sharp claws.

Every cell in the producer's body shivered.

"I understand, nothing happened, this will never happen again, just let me go and don't hit me!" Neville cried.

Gary let go and Neville fell to the floor; his body had forgotten how to work properly, he was so stunned with fear. At the same time, Elanor and the others swung the door open and rushed in.

Nearly all of them were in their pajamas; they had been getting ready for bed but had woken up because of the commotion.

"What happened here? Gary, did you hit the producer?" Elanor's voice was shaky. She was more worried for Gary than anything.

Turning around, he headed out of the room.

"He tripped and banged his teeth on the floor; you can ask the producer if you don't believe me," Gary answered.

No one wanted to get in his way; even Tyson stood to the side, while the rest of them tried to figure out what happened.

That night, Neville had told everyone to just clear out of his room, that he wasn't willing to see anyone. They never heard Neville's side of the story, but there was another way the others could find out what happened, since all of the girls were staying in the same room.

"What happened, Spring? What happened that made Gary hit the producer? Did he say something to Gary?" Clem asked.

Spring shook her head.

"Spring, you haven't said anything since you came back in here," Elanor said. "You have to tell us what really happened. Look, this might cause a big problem for you and Gary, and if so, I need to know."

"I think it's going to be okay," Spring said, and she got into bed, pulling the blanket fully over herself to make it clear that she didn't want to talk to anyone. The reason she couldn't speak about what happened was that she was clearly confused herself.

She wanted to shout at Gary, blame him for possibly ruining her chances, but at the same time, she never wanted to be in that situation again, and Gary had saved her from it. Which was why she was unable to clear her thoughts just yet.

In the morning, the group was surprised, and yet not surprised, that Neville had already left. Apparently he had sent a message to Elanor, explaining that he would go ahead without her and decide the final two days of programming ahead of time.

It was nearly the end of their journey. With this, there was an awkward ride back in the minibus, and when Spring and Gary made eye contact, she weirdly asked him a question.

"Are you okay?" Spring asked.

"I was going to ask you the same thing," Gary replied, to which Spring nodded, and they just sat in their seats.

"ARGHHH!" Clem screamed, almost pulling her hair out. "Just what happened yesterday?"

Inside AJ Entertainment, Neville had asked for an emergency meeting, not with Ash, but with Matthew. Because explaining what happened to Ash would be hard to do, and most likely he wouldn't act on it.

Neville wanted payback, and the right person to do that for him was always going to be Matthew.

"So that's what happened!" Matthew slammed his hand on the table. "That damned kid from the AFA, he thinks he's hot crap just because he's a trained fighter. That kid wouldn't survive a second in the underworld."

"What should we do? Should we kick him out of the program?" Neville asked.

"No, that would be too light a punishment, and it would be difficult to edit him out without giving a proper reason. For the last day, let's give him his own special program, one that he won't be coming back from.

"And let's see him try to protect these girls of his. I want all three of them in front of me. It will be a first, but I'm sure I'll be up to the task." Matthew licked his lips once again.

CHAPTER 110

WHERE HAVE I SEEN THIS BEFORE?

The threat that Gary had imposed on Neville hadn't worked for a second. Spreading rumors about what the director and producer were doing. This wasn't the first time they had done things like this, and word had never gotten out.

AJ Entertainment had a pretty good hold on the news and media outlets, and this was because they had to, because of the nature of their business. Their stars were often involved in scandals.

Sometimes the scandal was small, while others were large, but whether AJ Entertainment would try to hush it up was based on how much it affected the business. At times, the group being run by a gang meant that they weren't shy about getting physical.

For the final two days, the group were told that there would mostly be one-on-one interviews where they would be asked questions about their experience, what they had learned from the program, and more.

The producers would even ask some of them to do some voice-overs for the program at certain times. It was pretty standard stuff, and it was made clear that the group was done with moving to different locations, and there was no need for them to travel together anymore.

Which was why Gary hadn't met up with the others. When the next day arrived, Elanor came to his room to talk to him.

"Gary, the producer told me that you have to do some reshoots. Don't worry, they should be small; they want you in studio five, which is on floor one on the outside. After you're done with that, they said you can head back to the AFA," Elanor explained.

She sounded relieved, and she was. During the last two days, she was worried that something would come up, maybe even fake articles about Gary in an attempt to ruin his outside life.

After visiting his hometown she knew he was a good person, and perhaps too good, which was why he needed to get away from the producer as soon as possible.

"I have to go and inform the girls of something as well. It's a shame that we won't all be able to say goodbye to each other, but I think it's for the best if you just head back," Elanor said with a smile, as she mouthed the word *sorry* and left.

Gary had no hard feelings. Elanor was just doing her job; she'd had no idea that things were going to work out this way.

Gary headed to the studio; he had been there before, so he knew the way. It was one where stages could be rolled in and out, and a live crowd could watch the show.

When he was here before, they were using it as a set to record some of the scenes for the program. When Gary entered, he saw the workers wearing black clothes and berets.

There seemed to be a lot of workers here today, Gary thought.

"Elanor told me that I was to come here to wrap up some filming. Is there somewhere I need to be?" Gary asked out loud, not shy at all.

"Sure, just head to the set and wait there for further instructions," one of the cameramen shouted.

Gary did as he was told; the set behind him was currently a restaurant. There were tables, chairs, and a dinner of sorts. He grazed his hand over the table, and then he heard footsteps, multiple footsteps.

"Ah, what a surprise for my last day." Gary smiled as he looked in front of him; all of the men were wearing baggy black clothes, dressed like workers on the studio set. However, it was quite clear that they weren't workers at all.

They all carried weapons, and there were around thirty of them, all different shapes and sizes.

"We know about you," a female voice said. It's owner walked to the front, and behind her a tail swung. It was clear she was an Altered. "The Ashen gang has been ordered to get rid of you. It looks like you have upset someone."

It was easy to figure out who was behind this, but Gary was even more excited that there was an Altered here.

New Quest received
The Ashen Gang has underestimated you. Sending a bunch of crooks and a single Altered
Challenge yourself: Finish them in less than 30 minutes.

At the same time, Elanor had entered the room where the rest of the stars of the program had been placed. Only Gary had been split off, as even Tyson was in the same dressing room as the girls.

"Hi there, everyone. As it is your final day, the director would like to meet with you all," Elanor said.

Somewhere else in AJ Entertainment, Neville was smirking to himself happily, already imagining the trouble that Gary was going through right now. He was in the editing room, looking at the program as a whole, deciding what to cut and what not to cut.

I guess when the news of what happened to the AFA star comes out, we are going to have to cut a lot of him out, to be respectful to him. Neville smirked at himself.

Looking through the videos and the documents attached to them, Neville noticed something.

The group went to Slough . . .

The town's name was familiar, for more reasons than one. Neville quickly remembered why he had been sent there, because of the gang that now had a part in AJ Entertainment, and the horrible feeling that remained in his mouth when he left there.

"But why would they go to Slough?"

Reading the side notes, he realized that one of the stars was from Slough . . . Gary.

Gary is from Slough, and he's an Altered as well. Is this a coincidence?

Neville's heart started to beat slightly faster. He tried to ignore it and started to watch the carefully captured footage, and that was when he noticed that the group was being treated overly nicely.

At the same time, in the background, people wearing black-and-gold clothing, were everywhere, almost as if they were looking over the group.

Neville's hand started to shake as he continued to go through the clips.

Why would the gang be watching over such a person?

Looking into it more, he found more clues. For one, Gary's sponsor in the AFA was the Howlers gang themselves, but on top of that, he recognized the name Gary Dem.

The memo I got this morning about the public shareholders . . .

Neville's entire body started to shake as he fell out of his chair and onto the floor.

CHAPTER 111

STOP THE PROJECT
(PART 1)

Matthew had asked Elanor to call in the other four stars that were part of the program, and they were swiftly making their way to his room. Several of them had many thoughts going through their heads.

They believed that the meeting was to discuss what projects each of them would be working on next, and see if they had any proposals for them. However, one person was quite nervous, looking down at the floor, at her feet, taking one step at a time.

We're meeting the director again, but the producer said that the director asked him whether I would sleep with him to get a lead role in my own program, Spring thought.

She had met the director before, but that was before she was aware of what he was like. There was a chance that the producer had made the request up, but for some reason, she didn't think that was the case.

I'll be okay, right? He won't ask for the same thing. Gary stopped it last time; the producer would never be confident enough to try it again.

Spring had never told the others about what had happened that day, and she was contemplating whether to tell them now. In the end, she decided against it, because there was one thought she was confident in.

I'm not meeting the director alone, the others are with me, so he can't request something from me, even if Gary isn't here. For a second, Spring looked back, hoping she would see a green-haired boy, but he wasn't there.

The group entered the office just as they had before, lined up a few feet apart from each other, standing there politely. Elanor stood at the back and had noticed the strange look on Spring's face.

On top of that, she noticed a few other unusual things in the office. One was that there was a large bed and a few cameras set up.

Since this was an entertainment company that filmed in many locations, it wasn't completely out of place, but it was a bit strange.

"Elanor, there is no need for you to be here; I would like to talk to the young ones on my own, and make sure you don't come back," Matthew ordered with a large smile on his face.

The look in his eyes was causing Elanor's stomach to twirl. She felt like throwing up, but if she stayed longer, she was fearful that something would happen to her.

Doing as she was told, she left the room. She waited by the door, and a few moments later she had heard a click.

Did he just lock the door? All of her instincts were telling her that something was up. The rumors about what the producer and Matthew had done before were coming to her mind. In the past, though, nothing had come of it. That was until now . . .

Maybe I should just go see Ash and see if he knows what is happening, Elanor thought as she rushed toward the elevator.

Back in the room, Matthew had quickly rushed to the door to lock it behind them. Spring's heart was starting to beat faster than it did before, but the others were still unaware of what was happening.

"Don't worry, I just have an important proposal to make to you all while you're here," Matthew said, still standing by the door with a strange smile.

"You see, because of the recent funding we have received, we have room to develop many projects, and I have decided that it is best that we create a project for each and every one of you. "We will be trying our best to promote all of our new stars."

The smiles on all of their faces were beaming, except for Spring.

"I'm sure you have all heard the saying that there is no such thing as a free lunch. In order for each of these projects to go ahead, each of you will be sleeping with me."

For a second, they all thought they had misheard. Even Tyson was quite confused.

"You don't have to worry, I'm not into boys." Matthew started licking his lips.

This sentence made it clear that they hadn't misheard the director.

It's true . . . it's true . . . he really does want us to sleep with him," Spring said as she fell to her knees.

"Director . . . this has to be a joke, right? I mean, something like this can't be legal," Clem said.

"The bed has been set up, and the cameras are there. This will be proof that the deed has been done, and of course if any of you think about telling the world, the video will be distributed, without my face, of course.

"And even if you try to go to the media, the news will be crushed, just like all of you."

"What if we refuse?" Rachel shouted. "What if we leave AJ Entertainment, and we don't tell anyone about what happened? Will you let us go then?"

Rachel was on the verge of tears; she was practically already pleading with the director.

"There's a reason why the door has been locked, and it won't open . . . until I've finished doing what I want with every single one of you," Matthew answered.

CHAPTER 112

STOP THE PROJECT (PART 2)

The director began to lick his lips intensely as he looked at all three of the girls from head to toe. He didn't care that they were afraid; that just made him more excited.

"Now, which one of you girls wishes to go first? I promise to be gentle with the first one," Matthew said.

None of them were in their right state of mind to respond, but there was one person who did.

"Fuck you!" Tyson shouted as he stood in front of the girls. "You disgusting man, do you think just because I'm under your management that I would allow you to do something like this?"

Tyson charged forward, and his body started to transform. After all, he was an Altered, one that had been talented since he was young, which was why he had been picked up.

His face started to puff out a bit, and red fur grew on the sides; his ears changed slightly and a round tail had come out from his bottom. Tyson's Altered form was that of a beast similar to the famous red panda.

This form had brought him to fame; the red panda was already loved, so when AJ Entertainment learned there was a Red Panda Altered out there, they snatched him up immediately.

Despite his lovable appearance, though, just like the red panda he had sharp teeth and claws, a powerful creature that packed quite a punch. With his hand transformed, Tyson threw a punch right toward the director.

I never thought I would be doing this, but you deserve it! Tyson shouted.

But Matthew stopped his fist, and before Tyson could do anything else, he kicked Tyson hard in the stomach, causing him to collapse. Then he shoved Tyson's face into the floor, breaking the floor, keeping his hand on top of his head.

"You people know nothing about the real me, do you?" Matthew said. "Do you even know that AJ Entertainment is really run by a gang, a gang that I'm in charge of? In order to have gotten to the position that we are in now, there were a lot of things that I needed to do.

"Wiping out the competition was one of them, and I was pretty good at it. Just like you, I'm an Altered as well, and one who had to fight to survive, not just become a star and have a cushy lifestyle.

"The reason you guys can live like you do is because of the things I had to do. So don't you think it's only right that I get to do what I want?"

Matthew lifted Tyson's face off the floor, and there were pieces of tile on his face, and blood dripping down from his forehead.

"You're probably wondering why I invited him here too," Matthew said. "It's simple: because I wanted to show you what can happen to you if you don't listen to what I say.

"This is what I can do to an Altered, without even transforming myself. So just imagine what I could do to you, who aren't even Altered."

"You won't get away with this," Spring shouted, lifting her head. "I'll tell my family; they have more power than you think!"

"Ah yes, the famous daughter of a star. The one who lives in a Tier 1 city," Matthew replied. "It's okay, because I'm sure once this video gets out there, you will get plenty of roles. It just might be in a different industry than you would have liked."

In the AJ Entertainment building, Elanor had finally arrived on the top floor and had managed to get a meeting with Ash. She had asked if they could speak in private, and he agreed because she looked so panicked.

She told him her concerns about the girls and what was happening down below.

"I'm worried," Elanor said. "I'm sure you've heard the rumors."

Ash looked conflicted as he reached under his desk and placed a file on the table.

"I have," Ash replied. "I was gathering a case file of all the victims. I was trying to get evidence and was eventually going to pass this on to White Rose. If they found out an Altered was abusing their power like that, they would come here in no time.

"I just needed to make sure I had enough evidence, and that Matthew didn't find out. The thing is, if he's acting this confidently, that means he has enough supporters of the Ashen gang to overthrow me."

Ash felt like he was stuck between a rock and a hard place. His power right now was practically useless; if he went down there now, he wouldn't be able to overpower Matthew, and who knows how long White Rose would take to jump on this case.

In the end, he pulled out his phone and called a particular number. It rang a few times before there was an answer on the other end of the phone.

"I apologize for calling you out of the blue, but I am in a pretty tricky situation. I honestly never imagined I would be calling you so soon for this type of help," Ash said.

Elanor wondered who it was Ash had called so suddenly, who he believed could resolve this situation.

"Trouble always seems to follow us, so this isn't so much of a surprise. Tell us what you want," the voice replied.

Ash was honest as he went on to explain the infighting situation at AJ Entertainment. He said that this didn't affect their deal too much, but Matthew did own twenty percent of the company, and it would be better to get rid of someone of this character.

"I see; you will be happy to know that I agree with you," the person on the other end replied. "The dark side of AJ Entertainment needs to be plucked by its roots, so it doesn't affect us or our investor; we will deal with this."

From overhearing the conversation, Elanor had assumed that this was the buyer, the group that had recently taken over AJ Entertainment and had to have a strong backing for AJ to put so much trust in them, but there was just one problem.

"We need help now!" Eleanor said. "Right now, those girls and Tyson are in there with that monster. How are they supposed to help us *now*?"

It truly felt hopeless, as if there was nothing they could do. That was until the person on the phone spoke up, having overheard Eleanor.

"Don't worry. We already have someone on the inside of AJ Entertainment, and he's very strong."

CHAPTER 113

INTERRUPTED FIGHT

Gary didn't want to admit it, but he had been in this type of situation more than he would have liked: surrounded by people who were attempting to take him out, although unlike before, he didn't feel like his life was on the line.

One of the men threw out what looked like a thick chain. Gary caught it with ease, then pulled on it with such strength that the man fell over as it ripped through his hands, tearing the skin off, and he face-planted onto the floor.

"Be careful! Remember he's an Altered from the AFA, so he's quite skilled!" the others shouted as they all came rushing in. Some of them even had electrified Anti-Altered batons.

Three of them ran toward his side, and Gary quickly kicked the table, sliding it across the floor and sending it crashing right into their knees. The next second he was on the table performing a kick in midair.

He hit all three in the face, crashing their heads into each other and knocking nearly all of them out instantly.

I just have to knock these guys out; I don't need to kill them if I don't have to, Gary thought as he performed a backflip, avoiding more strikes from the others.

He was now behind a couple of them, and he grabbed the backs of their heads and knocked them into each other; he could almost feel the inside of their skulls crush.

Control your strength, Gary!

It was one of the biggest things with him gaining power so fast and going up against other Altered that were able to take the hits.

Turning around, he blocked an electrified baton with his hand. It activated, shocking his whole body, but did next to nothing, as he kicked the man in the stomach and sent him crashing into the tables and chairs and knocking a few of the others over.

Another man tried to kick Gary, who moved to the side and grabbed the leg, then kicked the side of the knee, popping the bone out.

I won't kill you, but that doesn't mean I'll hold back in hurting you, Gary thought.

After breaking the man's leg, he lifted him up with his sheer strength and swung him into another group of people coming toward him.

"How are we supposed to even get this person? He's just too fast and strong! Are all the guys from the AFA like this?" one of them shouted.

These weren't just employees but gang members of a Tier 2 city. They had to have a certain level of strength to even be in the gang, and their weapons were better than most, and yet they were unable to do any damage against Gary.

But the next to strike Gary was the Altered woman who had whiskers on her face, and her hands had grown into what looked like large paws. She struck at Gary with fast jabs.

Moving his head side to side, Gary avoided her assault, and even in the middle of fighting the Altered, he kicked one of the men who tried to sneak up on his side.

It was as if he had eyes all over his head.

Gary was ready to throw a hit back, but just then he felt something vibrate in his pocket. Of all times to get a phone call! Since his opponents weren't too challenging, Gary jumped up on a table and pulled the phone out of his pocket while continuing to dodge hits.

Kai is actually calling me, it might be important, Gary thought as he answered the call.

This frustrated the catlike Altered, and she continued to attack Gary, but almost as if he were the one with catlike reflexes, Gary avoided each of the punches.

"Ah, Gary, are you still at AJ Entertainment?" Kai asked.

"I am, but it seems that I have angered someone here, though, and I'm a bit busy at the moment," Gary said.

"Angered someone? Well, then it might be best if you listen to this, as this is somewhat important," Kai continued.

"Pay attention!" The catlike Altered elongated her claws and swiped at Gary; leaning back, he avoided the strike once again. Even without his Altered form, Gary was far superior to the person in front of him.

"Listen, AJ Entertainment is in a bit of a pickle and they have asked me for our help," Kai explained.

"Our help, why would they ask for our help?" Gary replied.

On the other end Kai smiled.

"There is a lot I need to tell you. The Howlers and Gary the business tycoon have been busy, but I will give you the rundown, as you need to move quickly."

Then Kai told Gary everything, how they had invested in AJ Entertainment, and at the same time what trouble they were currently facing.

Gary stood still, and the cat lady's claw scratched the side of his face, drawing blood.

"I'll deal with it," Gary said, hanging up the phone. His head dropped, and the Altered went in for another strike. Gary grabbed her by the wrist; his hand started to transform, and so did the rest of his body.

"I'm in a bit of a rush now, so I'm sorry but this is going to hurt."

CHAPTER 114

WHO IS HE?

Tyson's body was limp. He was clearly knocked out and his injuries looked pretty bad as he continued to bleed from his head. The only saving grace was the fact that he was an Altered, so it was unlikely that he would die from this type of wound.

Carrying his body with one hand, the director threw it into the corner of the large office.

"Now that the only person who can break the lock is dealt with, it's time for us to get started," Matthew said.

He walked over to the three girls. Each of them was shaking; they were grabbing their own arms, hugging themselves as they looked at the floor, not wanting to believe the situation. In their minds they were repeating a phrase over and over again.

Please, don't pick me . . . don't pick me . . . don't pick me.

"AHHH!" The girls heard a scream, and when the other two looked up, they could see Matthew carrying Spring over his shoulder.

She was kicking and screaming, punching Matthew's back until her fists were raw, but it was doing nothing at all. She truly felt helpless. He threw her onto the bed so hard that her body bounced on it.

"You better be good," Matthew said. "Otherwise, you will be in a lot worse state than him over there."

Crawling onto the bed, Matthew placed his body on top of hers. He cast a deep shadow and a thread of saliva fell from his mouth as he stared down at her.

"I have been waiting for this for a while now. You were always going to be my first pick," Matthew said. "As for the rest of you, you can all blame Gary for getting you involved. It would have only been her if he hadn't caused so much trouble."

"HELP!" Rachel screamed at the top of her lungs. Usually she would have never done that. She was a singer and needed to protect her voice, but if there was any hope out there, maybe someone would be able to hear them.

"PLEASE, SOMEONE HELP!" Rachel continued to scream.

Clem, also not wanting to just do nothing, ran to the door and pulled at the handle with all her might, but it was solid, a high-quality, heavy door with a good locking mechanism that didn't budge at all.

Matthew started to laugh at their pathetic attempts and continued to unbutton his shirt, while something hard rubbed against Spring down below.

Please . . . someone, anyone . . . help me! Spring cried helpless tears as this thought echoed in her head.

Continuing to try to open the door, Clem eventually heard an unlocking sound. Her eyes lit up with hope, and Matthew turned his head to see who it was.

Neville frantically burst into the room, knocking Clem over. He quickly locked the door behind him.

Clem thought the producer would help, but he didn't seem shocked by the scene in front of him.

"Director, sir . . . you have to listen, we're in big trouble!" Neville shouted.

Matthew was moments away from enjoying his pleasure, so it was safe to say that he wasn't happy as he got off the bed and looked at Neville.

"This better be important," Matthew snarled.

"It is, I promise," Neville quickly replied, still panicked. "We messed up, we really messed up. Gary Dem, the student from the AFA, I was doing some research into him.

"Gary Dem from the AFA is from Slough, which is also where the Howlers are from, and on top of that, it's also where our investor is from."

"So?" Matthew asked, scrunching up his face.

"So . . . don't you see? Gary Dem from the AFA is the same Gary Dem from Slough. He is the person who bought out AJ Entertainment. He is the one who owns the majority of the shares of AJ Entertainment, and to top it off, he has a close relationship with the Howlers gang, the gang that took out *Notsburg*!" Neville was practically screaming at this point; his fear was coming through.

Matthew also was quite stunned by this, and the girls were trying to make sense of it. The Gary who had been traveling with them this whole time and who lived in that tiny apartment from the poor town of Slough owned most of AJ Entertainment? How was that even possible?

After Matthew processed the information, though, his initial shock calmed down a little.

"So what? So what if he's from the AFA? It's not like they support him," Matthew said. "And so what if he is some rich businessman. Do you think he has the power to really make the Howlers gang start a war with us? Do you really think a gang would be at the beck and call of a single businessman, all for some shitty girls?" Matthew exclaimed.

As Clem lay on the floor, a memory resurfaced in her head: in the restaurant when she asked him a question about who he really was. She smirked.

Gary didn't lie to me back then. He doesn't just have a close relationship with the Howlers gang. He's the leader.

"ARGHHHH!" A scream came from the other side of the door, and a loud bang followed.

A dent formed in the thick door as the lock was broken and the door went flying, and through the doorway walked the very green-haired boy they were all talking about.

"What the fuck do you guys think you're doing?" Gary asked.

CHAPTER 115

THE FALL OF ASHEN (PART 1)

The door had been flung off its hinges; luckily Clem was still on the floor, or it would have landed right on her, but instead it hit Neville in the back of his head, nearly knocking him out.

In a daze, he managed to crawl out from under the broken door. Turning his head, he rubbed his eyes; his heart was beating fast, and he was struggling to get the words to come out of his mouth as his lips were quivering.

"You . . . y-you . . . it's really you . . . it's Gary Dem, I told you it's Gary Dem!" Neville shouted as if his name were some type of curse.

Gary was full of energy; he had just completed the quest he had received before and come up on the elevator. After learning from Kai what was going on, it took nearly all of his will to not pry open the elevator doors and just climb all the way up himself.

When he reached the floor, the familiar smell of the girl's perfume had wafted into his nose, telling him that he was in the right place. All of the frustration had come out in one punch right as the door unlocked.

He looked around the room; Rachel and Clem both looked like they had lost several years from their lives, their eyes puffy, their hands bleeding. Clem had tried so hard to open the door that she had cut herself, and Rachel felt like she might never get her voice back again.

Then there was Spring lying on the bed; she had a pillow covering her, and her whole body was shaking.

"A camera? I guess I don't even need to ask." Gary tensed his fist and turned to Neville, pointing his finger right at him.

"Didn't I warn you? I said that you were to not touch the girls, and never try this type of shit again! Otherwise you would learn what would happen to you."

Neville scurried off the floor and got up, shaking his head. The anger was being directed toward him, and the look in Gary's eyes told him that this was the most dangerous person he had ever met.

Turning around, Neville attempted to run away; nobody knew where to, since there was only one exit, and it was where Gary had come from, but after he took a single step, Gary reached out and grabbed his curly hair.

His head was yanked back and it felt like the top of his scalp was going to be removed from his head. Now Neville was just staring at the ceiling.

"Please don't . . . please. I'll do anything, I'll leave AJ Entertainment and go into hiding, I'll give you whatever you want!" Neville begged.

Looking at this whole scene, Matthew wasn't afraid. He'd thought something like this would happen one day. There was a reason why Neville did everything he said, and that was because he was easily influenced by fear. It was how Matthew got Neville on his side in the first place.

Neville was more afraid of him than he was of Ash, but from the way he was acting now, he was clearly more afraid of Gary.

Someone else entered the room. With his hands on his knees, he took a deep breath.

"I told you, you should have waited for me," Ash said as he looked up, and now he saw the same scene that Gary had.

A feeling had overcome his stomach; it was swirling about and he felt like he would throw up at any second.

"I can't believe that something like this was going on at my company, the place I made," Ash said out loud to himself.

"Matthew, how did you ever think you could get away with something like this!" Ash shouted.

Since Neville continued to fiddle about and was still moving, Gary pulled on his hair harder, ripping it from his head, and with his hand raised, he then threw his fist down, hitting him right on his Adam's apple. His whole body hit the floor; he had been knocked out.

Perhaps if it had been any other situation, Clem and Rachel would be concerned for the producer; he was so still it didn't look like he was alive anymore. But they honestly couldn't care less about what happened to him, and they wished it were worse.

"Everything that you've done is going to be reported to White Rose, and they will hunt you down and make sure you never get out of a cell for the rest of your life!" Ash said.

Hearing this, Matthew just started to laugh.

"Is this really you speaking, Ash? Is this the Ash who started the Ashen gang with me? Did you forget everything that we have been through together? Did you really throw your past away and change so much now that you have a company?

"Meanwhile, you thought it was fine for me to continue doing the dirty work? Where's the line? Is this too far? I was right, you aren't fit to be head of the Ashen gang anymore, and it seems like a lot of people agree with me.

"Get rid of me? You make me laugh. I will be the one getting rid of you two. I'll force the two of you to hand the company over. It's time to do things the old-fashioned way!"

Matthew started to rip off his shirt, revealing a wide, muscular upper body, and at the same time, his nose started to transform into what looked like a horn, while his skin color was turning gray.

Gary then stood in front of Ash, looking at the partially transformed Matthew.

"You are weak, you're useless, and you're a waste of space on this planet," Gary said. "Even now, you're so useless, you didn't even give me a quest. There is no reason for you to be here."

Gary's body started to transform—his arms, his legs—and he wasn't going to hold back because he wanted to inflict as much pain as possible.

CHAPTER 116

THE FALL OF ASHEN (PART 2)

Gary hadn't known the girls for long, and he didn't know them that well, but his rage was unmatched compared to past situations, and there was a simple reason for this. There were two women in his life who were extremely important to him.

His sister and his mother. For his mother, he hadn't been there, he wasn't able to protect her in time, and he imagined that the same thing could have happened to these girls. Someone could have never turned up, and they would have had a scar for the rest of their life, one that couldn't be seen on the surface and couldn't be removed.

Matthew's upper body was even larger than before, as he had perfectly round shoulders and a rough texture to his skin. From the looks of things, he almost looked like a rhino man.

"Taste my strength!" Matthew shouted as he ran across the floor at great speed pushing off. His head was bent slightly forward with his weight shifted toward the front, and he swung his hand over his head.

At the same time, Gary braced himself; in his head, the image of the fist coming toward him was almost the same as the bag at the academy. At the right time, he twisted his foot and his hips and threw a perfect punch.

Gary's werewolf fist landed on Matthew's rhino fist, clashing against each other, and a cracking noise was heard as Matthew pulled back.

"My hand!" he screamed. "How can this be? My Altered form focuses on pure power!"

Pushing forward, Gary quickly jumped on Matthew. Out of desperation, Matthew threw out his uninjured hand, attempting to hit Gary, but Gary was one step ahead with his own fist.

Matthew was only able to swing his fist a few inches through the air before Gary's own fist pummeled the Altered's fist back. This time, Matthew didn't just think the bones in his hand were broken; he knew they were.

"ARGHHH!" Matthew shouted as he stumbled. "How . . . I am the strongest in a Tier 2 gang, I'm an Altered, and I'm getting toyed around with by a boy!"

Ash was watching in disbelief. He never thought the fight would be so one-sided.

"This is the power of Gary Dem from the AFA! I guess he's not just a businessman."

As Ash watched this display, it suddenly clicked in his head. He had never met the leader of the Howlers before, Kai had said that several times, and yet they trusted this unknown businessman so much.

They supported Gary Dem in the AFA; he was so strong and had so much charisma. Yes, this person in front of them was the leader of the Howlers.

While Matthew stumbled, Gary grabbed his horn.

"This is nothing compared to how you made them feel!" Gary screamed as he used all of his grip strength to snap the horn off to the side.

It was bent at a right angle and blood was now pouring out from Matthew's nose. The pain and the panic were making him fight worse than he had before, but it didn't matter, as Gary continued to pummel him with body blows, one after another.

Each blow was strong, and they were all filled with anger as Gary screamed, hitting him and pushing him back.

"Stop—"

A punch to the face stopped him from speaking and sent him back into the wall; it looked as if Matthew could barely stand at this point.

Gary swung his claw hand and struck Matthew down below, ripping off part of his trousers, and something else was left dangling in place.

"Killing you would be too easy for you. It wouldn't teach you a lesson; you would just simply forget about everything you have done. So I need to give you a reminder for the rest of your life."

With his clawed hand Gary swung again, and in one go *it* was sliced off. The whole thing fell to the floor, and blood was pouring out. Seeing his manhood on the floor, Matthew fainted almost immediately, landing on it.

"You will never be able to do something like this again," Gary said as his body started to transform back to normal, and blood dripped from his hands.

Everyone was stunned into silence as they looked at Gary, as they wondered what had just happened. They thought about thanking him, they thought about saying something, but the words wouldn't come out of their mouths because at that moment, they feared him.

"I'll leave him to you," Gary said. "I'm sorry for everything that happened to you all, and I wish you all good luck in the future."

They all watched Gary walk out of the room, still unable to say anything, and when he finally left, they all felt like they could breathe. They all felt like it was really finally over.

"Gary . . ." Ash said. "You saved this company, but there is still a lot to be done."

Ash's phone started to vibrate, and when he looked, it was the Howlers calling him.

CHAPTER 117

NEVER AGAIN

The incident with AJ Entertainment had come to an end. Apparently, news had traveled fast in the agency as to what had happened. Several ambulances had arrived at the scene, all of them to take the girls to safety.

This caused rumors to swirl around, and quickly everyone working in the industry found out that the producer and director had something to do with the incident. There was no news of what actually happened to the girls, just rumors, but one thing had spread around as a fact, and it was that Ash was the one who resolved everything.

He had somehow managed to find out what Matthew was doing and put a stop to it. The fact that no one could get a hold of Matthew or Neville made them believe that this was the case, but only a few people knew the real truth.

Still, this made those who had supported Matthew quiet down within the company. People knew that Ash wasn't strong enough to take out Matthew on his own, and they assumed that he had done so with some new help.

Regardless, Ash didn't care because he was going to get to the root of it all and make sure anyone who tried to go against him would be cleared out of the company. He would just have to do it slowly.

Right now, Ash was at the hospital, checking a room number with a bunch of flowers in his hands. Forcing a smile, he gave a quick knock before opening the door.

"I hope you guys like flowers, because I brought a lot of them," Ash said.

The second he entered the room, the girls and Tyson sat up in their beds. They made sure their hair looked nice, among other things. It was the normal reaction when they met the head of AJ Entertainment.

"I guess old habits die hard, but you don't have to do that," Ash said, as he walked around handing out flowers to all of the girls.

They looked fine; they didn't have any severe injuries, apart from Tyson who had mostly already healed, but they were here for mental evaluations as well.

"Thank you . . . you didn't have to come out here," Clem said.

"No, please don't say that," Ash replied. "You girls went through something that none of you should have ever experienced."

At that moment, Ash got down on his knees and placed his head on the cold hard surface of the floor.

"I'm sorry, I should have looked out for those who worked for me. Something like that should have never happened. Even now, all I can do is put my head on the floor and ask for your forgiveness."

The scene was something none of them expected to see. Since Ash wasn't the direct cause of the trauma they had gone through, they found it hard to blame him in any way, but they knew it was better not to tell him that, so it was good for all of them.

After a while Ash finally got up from the floor and asked them all about their injuries: the marks on Clem's hand, Rachel's sore throat, and whether Tyson was okay. Finally the last person that Ash went to talk to was Spring, who was affected most by it all.

Before Ash could say anything, Spring was the first one to speak.

"Is it true about Gary?" she asked. "That he is the one who bought out AJ Entertainment?"

None of them had seen Gary since he saved them, and there was a lot they wanted to ask him, and say to him, but they were unable to, and the frustration was unbearable. So Ash was the next best thing.

"It's true . . . but honestly I didn't know much about it either," Ash said. "I knew that it was someone named Gary but never thought it would be him. I did think something was up when I saw his suit, though."

They sat there for a while in disbelief, thinking about the way they had talked to him, thinking about when they went to Slough. In their heads it was starting to make sense. The way he didn't care about money, why everyone was thanking him back then, and the relationship to others in his hometown.

Meanwhile Clem and Ash were having other thoughts, because the two of them knew a little more: the fact that Gary was actually the leader of the Howlers gang. They thought it was best to keep this a secret, as it wasn't an important factor in what happened to them.

Another knock was heard at the door; they wondered who it could be, and guessed it was probably Elanor, but when the door opened, they saw a shade of green past the door.

"Gary!" Clem called out.

He walked into the room, and soon all of them were calling his name.

"Gary, it's really you!"

"You all must be feeling well, to be this energetic," Gary said.

"I'm so, so, sorry!" Spring cried. "I treated you like shit, and you still . . . you . . . you . . . saved me."

She was reminded of all the unjust treatment, the judgment she had given Gary, yet it was because of him that she was saved.

"It's okay . . . I'm just happy I was able to get there in time," Gary replied.

The group talked for a bit, asking Gary a number of questions. How he managed to get his hands on so much money, and why did he even buy AJ Entertainment in the first place? Why was he even keeping it a secret that he owned half of it.

It was hard for him to answer all the questions, and he was looking for a way out.

"Look, the important thing is that none of you have to worry. Ash will continue to take care of things, and he and I have talked. We will try our best to look after you and give you as much promotion as we can," Gary said.

After those words, Gary looked as if he was about to leave the room. They imagined he had to be a busy man, and now they felt like Gary was part of a different world compared to them.

"Gary . . . will we ever see you again?" Clem asked.

With a half smile, looking toward the floor, he answered, "I'll be honest, probably not. I have a feeling that I might get pretty busy soon, and it's best if you all don't get to know me too well."

Clem and Ash understood the real reasons behind those words, and Gary left the room. They all felt as if a part of them were missing, as if they had said goodbye to a dear friend.

Getting up out of his bed, Tyson went to the window and drew the curtain open, and he saw Gary walking toward a car.

Isn't that the same car we saw in Slough? Tyson thought.

Not only that, but there were several people in black-and-gold outfits, the same as the gang they saw all over Slough. As Gary approached the car, the door was opened for him.

"It's nice to see you again, boss." Kai smiled.

"Holy shit!" Tyson's heart thumped as he realized just how special Gary was.

CHAPTER 118

THE HOWLERS' GROWTH

After leaving AJ Entertainment, Gary unexpectedly found himself back in Slough, his hometown that he hadn't anticipated returning to so soon. However, a series of events had led him back.

When Ash had called for the Howlers' help, Kai had already been on his way after informing Gary, just in case anything happened, or more specifically in case there was a need to clean up the aftermath. After all, Kai knew how messy things could get.

With the situation resolved, they decided to head back to Slough and return to the Wolf's Pool Club for a little chat.

"So tell me, how did you enjoy your week as a star?" Kai asked with a broad smile, sitting in his comfortable chair. "Of course, none of what happened at the end will be released to the public, but I heard they've filmed enough to go ahead with the program after the editing is complete."

Gary gave Kai a look that somewhat explained his current feelings. "Why didn't you tell me that you had bought the majority of AJ Entertainment using my name?" Gary slapped his forehead.

He imagined that with that information, things would have been way easier to deal with on the inside.

For one, he would have easily been able to have the producer fired without having to take any action.

"It was a deal with someone I barely knew. I had a good feeling from Ash, but their gang isn't the same as ours, and they were divided. I didn't want to risk that information falling into the wrong hands, and what's better than having a spy on the inside who doesn't even know he's a spy?" Kai explained with a chuckle.

Shaking his head, Gary didn't approve of being used in this way, but he knew that part of the reason Kai kept quiet was because he trusted him. The most important thing was that everything turned out mostly okay. Some people were hurt by these events, but Gary also felt that him taking action should be for the best. If these things hadn't been uncovered, who knows what would have happened.

"Fine, but in the future I think I would prefer knowing these things. Speaking of which, what's your next step in all of this? You seem to be doing a lot, and my time in the AFA is almost up," Gary asked.

"Could it be . . . you think I was waiting for your return to do something big?" Kai asked. "If so, I have to disappoint you. We have been very busy in the background, and a lot of it is thanks to you. There's a lot of business in Notsburg, though it's being handled by Midwak.

"We've also entered alliances with your friends in the AFA, and even the deal made with the Ashen gang and Ash. The Howlers' power is growing by the day. Truth be told, we might have grown a bit too much too fast, so it's best that we don't get involved in any more trouble and focus on increasing our gang's strength for now.

"On that topic, what do you think about us working with a company like NIRV?"

When Gary heard that name, all sorts of thoughts arose in his head. He remembered how he had ended the lesson on the wrong foot. At the same time, there was the contract that said he had to help out whenever they requested.

"As the gang leader, I'm strongly against it. There's something strange about them. If you want anything from them, I think it's best if we talked to Tom, even though I don't want to put him in that situation," Gary replied.

"I thought you might have some issues, but fortunately there are more organizations than just NIRV alone. I agree with your assessment; a company that has ties to most if not all Tier 1 gangs is definitely suspicious. Then again, I have also picked up rumors that claim that NIRV has been set up by the Kings. Either way, getting involved with them would mean unnecessary trouble.

"Still, with the remaining funds, I have asked the others to bring forward the most loyal members of the Howlers. At the next Dark Guild auction, we will be buying as much Altered solution as we can, improving the strength of the Howlers once again."

Gary was finding it hard to believe; the Howlers certainly had come a long way.

"And I have to thank you for something else as well. The Altered won't just be cannon fodder, either, thanks to your teacher, Crowley. Right now, his only Altered student is Austin, but from the way things are looking, he's sure to have more soon."

Gary had considered visiting his old teacher to see how he was doing, but he was happy to hear that he had found a place in Slough. He decided to wait until after his debut match in the AFA before paying him a visit.

"I guess if that's the case, then it should be my time to leave, and I'll be back after my debut match in the AFA," Gary said. "But before I go, what about Marie and Innu? I haven't seen them around much."

"Marie is doing well. She has been training directly under Olivia and attending some of Crowley's classes. She's been coming back with fewer wounds on her body, as I've noticed. I think even you might be impressed by the progress she has made."

Being a werewolf, he did have exceptional growth compared to Altered, but Gary's growth with the system was always beyond what others thought. Even through the small interactions and the quest he had completed back at AJ Entertainment, his skills had grown.

5 Pawn points have been awarded
25 Pawn points in total

"As for Innu, I haven't seen him much. I did check in on him. I gave him funds to set up a new Black Rock Orphanage, sponsored by business tycoon Gary Dem, of course.

"When I met up with Kevin, he said Innu had been coming home late. He hasn't been at the Wolf's Pool Club or hanging around with any of the others, so I'm a little concerned about him. Before you go, I would appreciate if you could meet up with him."

Gary thought it wasn't a bad idea; it wouldn't take long just to drop by. But just as he was about to call, his phone vibrated with a ping, receiving a text message.

"What is it?" Kai asked, seeing the look on Gary's face.

"It's the AFA. They said my debut match has been set . . . but the date is two days from the next full moon," Gary answered.

Kai rested his elbows on the desk and his head in his hands. He'd thought something like this would happen. Fight dates were quite hard to change because of the number of people and amounts of money involved.

"We can't keep running from this situation forever. I've been meaning to do this for a while, but I think it's time that we have another serious talk with Midwak. As someone who belonged to a pack of werewolves, I'm sure he has to have a way to stop this transformation."

CHAPTER 119

A STRUGGLING MEMBER

In the town of Slough, despite numerous improvements, there were still places where one could hide from others. In the alleyway behind a few restaurants, standing at the back, was a single dark-skinned boy. His arms were wrapped from his knuckles all the way to his elbow, while he wore the black-and-gold clothing of his gang. His eyes were closed as he stood alone in the alleyway.

He wasn't letting anything distract him, unlike the times before he had entered the alleyway. The echoes of noise from moving animals or the sound of passing vehicles, as well as the rancid smell from leftover food, used to fill his head every time he came here in the past. But now he was only focusing on one thing.

There was plenty of rubbish and debris on the ground, including leaves that had floated in. They were light, and slowly they started to lift in the air as if being carried. Rather than swaying around, they were slowly levitating in place. The leaves that were moving were only around the boy, while the rest just rustled slightly across the ground. The moment Innu opened his eyes, the leaves started to fall to the ground, carried by the air.

Reaching behind his back, he grabbed the handle of the axe and hurled it into the air. It was a strong, powerful throw. The axe had lit up slightly as he placed his energy inside. It was slicing through the air with ease and going at a fast speed.

In the alleyway, on the wall around twenty yards away, were targets drawn in red spray paint. Next to the markings were several chips in the brickwork. As the axe flew straight, it veered slightly to the right and landed in the center of the target.

He clenched his fists, his whole body shaking as he jumped up in the air. "I did it, I finally did it!" Innu cheered.

This was the reason for his absence from home and from the Wolf's Pool Club. After his teacher had left, showing him his strange powers, Innu was relentless in his training.

His teacher had taught him only a couple of things since he seemed to be low on time, but after that, he just left. But the image of what he could do with this power never left his mind.

Innu was focusing on two types of training. The first was the mysterious power of qi that the teacher had talked about. This was a power that Innu had harnessed himself by accident before, the power that he felt through his body at times when fighting, and at one point had supplemented it into the weapon.

He had learned to control this energy and input a smaller amount into the axe, so it was still more powerful, while also not allowing it to completely drain him. But what he was more interested in was the mysterious telekinesis power he seemed to have. He was able to lift off lightweight objects like leaves off the ground slightly, but that would be useless in a fight. The important thing was that it showed him that it was possible for him to learn this power.

It wasn't something out of a fantasy; the power was real. The next step was learning how to use the power while not in a state of complete focus. At first, he could only use it when closing his eyes, but he got better and better.

He wanted to practice using his power in a practical way, and one way would be if he could influence the direction his axes went. This would trick the enemy and allow him to be more versatile in his attacks.

Several marks on the wall showed that he was able to influence the axe, but not exactly how he wanted. Now he could throw an axe and change its direction with good control, within reason.

It's still not where I want it to be. The next step will be to curve the axe completely. If I can do that, maybe I can move it at the last second if someone tries to block it. Then there is the final step. If I can throw the axe and use its power to return to my hand, that would be ideal.

Throwing the weapon wasn't always the best thing in a fight, since he obtained power from the weapons themselves when holding them. The power would stay in his body a little while after it left, but if his weapon got stuck in a wall or in the enemy, that wasn't good either. Right now, the skill was meant to be a more sure-kill tactic for him.

I wonder if I will ever meet the teacher again. If I went to the Altered Hunters Association or one of their meetings, surely I would see him around then. Unless he's on an important mission, Innu thought. *I bet he would be surprised at what I showed him, and maybe he could give me a few tips.*

Innu was smiling to himself as he imagined the situation, and with great timing, he had received a text.

> **This is Blake. It looks like there is a meeting, and they want you to come as well. This will be good to introduce you to us and also allow you to pick some equipment for yourself.**
>
> **Warning, they might ask us to go somewhere. You are still an apprentice, but at times when they really need people, they ask the apprentices as well. So it's best if you make some excuse to the others that you might be away for a while.**

The text ended there, and it looked like Innu would be going to one of the Altered Hunters Association bases earlier than he thought.

I guess it should be okay. Things have been quiet in Slough for a while, so it might be the perfect time. I just hope no Howlers stuff happens while I'm doing my Altered Hunter stuff. Living a double life is already tiring, Innu thought.

He took a deep breath and looked around the alleyway, taking in the familiar surroundings. He knew that this was only the beginning of his journey and that there was still so much more to learn. But for now, he had to focus on the task at hand and prepare for the upcoming meeting. With a determined expression on his face, Innu headed out of the alleyway, ready to face whatever challenges lay ahead.

CHAPTER 120

UPGRADING THE GROUP

Kai knew that Gary's time was precious at the moment. He couldn't spend long with the group, and the AFA would be wondering just where he was, especially with his debut match booked.

So he decided there and then to send a text out to everyone that he wished to come with him, telling them that they were heading to Notsburg. Of these people, it was truly only the werewolf members of the gang, Marie and Olivia.

"All right, they should all be here in about thirty minutes, and then we'll head off," Kai said.

The good news was the night sky was out, so Gary was currently getting a buff. Meeting Midwak again was always an unpleasant and worrying feeling for Gary.

He knew that the werewolf was the type who would challenge him every month without fail for him to get to the position where he needed to be. Gary originally thought it was a good idea so he could push his own strength to new heights; that way he would always be a step forward compared to his senior werewolf.

The only thing was, since the last time they had met, how much had he improved? He had gained a few stats from the special lesson after eating the crystal. On top of that, he had learned how to use his skills in a more effective way, using the night sky.

Yet there hadn't been a drastic change. In fact, Gary guessed that if the two of them were to go up against each other now, if the sun was out, he would certainly lose. It wasn't as if he could set the time that Midwak would fight him.

I only just beat Midwak at night, and the current class allows me to essentially get twice as strong. Does that mean I have to double my strength in the remaining amount of time?

There was one saving grace in all of this: there was still time. It hadn't been a month since the two of them had fought, so Midwak wasn't able to challenge him. So it was maybe the best time for the two of them to meet.

"Before we go, there is one thing I want to do," Gary said, as he walked over and placed his hand on Kai's shoulder. His head was facing the floor, so Kai was unable to see his expression. "I'm sorry."

"Why don't your words match your expression right now?" Kai asked, as he saw a smile on Gary's face.

Suddenly Kai felt a pain through his body, a jolt in his legs that caused him to fall to the floor.

"Oh, I thought it might not do that since it's not an evolution," Gary said, looking at the struggling Kai.

With twenty-six Pawn points from beating Midwak, taking over Notsburg, and an additional five from completing the timed quest in the AJ Entertainment, Gary had plenty of Pawn points to spare but not enough for him to go to the next rank.

So he decided that it was best to rank up one of the others instead, although the benefits of ranking up weren't much for Gary. For one, the ranking-up system seemed to be a way to create a stronger force.

If Gary had several high-ranking werewolves underneath him who were going out there turning others, then they would be able to produce a higher quality of werewolves, since one was only able to create the same or lower rank.

On top of that, for each werewolf created that was part of the Howlers pack, he himself would gain an additional Pawn point. It almost felt like a pyramid scheme, with Gary at the very top experiencing most of the benefits.

The only thing was, none of them were going out there trying to increase their pack size, so this benefit was practically nil. There were times when Gary thought of it because Pawn points could also be converted into stat points, which would allow him to grow in the quickest way possible, and from the sound of things, the other alpha already had an army of his own.

But it was the fact that a turn wasn't a hundred percent guaranteed, and most likely it meant death to the other person. It wasn't that Gary wouldn't kill, but killing for no reason apart from his own benefit didn't sit well with him.

Still, he used the points on Kai because he wanted to see if he would go through another evolution. There seemed to be two limits to Gary evolving; one was the level and the other was the rank.

The thing was, the other werewolves, at least according to the system, didn't have a level. So the least he could do was improve their rank, and as they got stronger, they were likely to unlock better classes.

The best way to increase the Howlers' strength was by bringing everyone up. He had a few people to choose from. Marie was a new werewolf; she did cross his mind because he wanted to protect her more, but he felt like a way of protecting was to increase their offense.

There was also Olivia, the first person to join the Howlers. Her Hunter Class felt like it was incredibly reliable, and he could only imagine the useful things a class evolution would do with that.

Then there was Kai. He had been affected the most by Midwak's attack, and he had worked the hardest for the Howlers. These things had swayed Gary to pick him.

Your Beta Werewolf's rank has gone up!
Knight >>> Bishop
A new class upgrade is available
There is only one class to choose from
Class upgrade is beginning

On the floor, Kai screamed in even more pain than before.
"Kai, this is all for a good cause," Gary smiled.

CHAPTER 121

A TEAM UPGRADE

Kai writhed in agony, rolling on the floor as he hit the side of his desk, causing a cascade of papers to fall. Gary was concerned for his friend, but he knew there was nothing he could do to alleviate Kai's suffering. So he did the only thing he could do and started to pick up the scattered papers.

"I'm sorry, Kai, I wish there were something I could do to make the process better, but I really have no control over it. Still, I can promise you one thing, you will come out of this better!" Gary said in an attempt to cheer him up, but all he got was a deathly glare from Kai.

Coincidentally, by the time he was done picking up all the paper, the screams of the blond teenager also came to an end. His hand slammed the edge of the table as he lifted himself off the floor.

"You bastard!" Kai seethed, struggling to his feet. "What the hell did you do to me this time, and where the hell do you get off acting so casual about it?" he spat, his eyes blazing with anger. Among the Howlers, Kai was usually the most calm and collected member, but Gary's actions had pushed him to his limits.

"Remember how I grew stronger before fighting Midwak?" Gary said, confusing Kai as to why he would mention this at such a time. "Well, I did what I did because I could feel that just like me, the power inside of you had accumulated to a point where you could get stronger.

"It's hard to explain, but it seems to be a perk I have as alpha, similar to how I can let out howls to make you feel stronger. I could tell that your body was ready to evolve to the next stage so I kinda . . . willed it, I guess."

Gary had never shared the details about the Werewolf System with Kai before, mostly because it was too confusing even for him. After all, filled in a world with Altered, and apparently werewolves and allegedly vampires, the existence of his System seemed to be even more magical. It might also be unique to him, though he would have to ask Midwak about it at some point.

"Since the painful part is over, do you feel any different?" Gary asked while using the system to check out what had just changed.

Superior Gray Werewolf Shapeshifter

When Kai got turned, he received the Unique Class of Gray Werewolf Shapeshifter. I still don't know whether he just had the right physique or aptitude to receive an optimal class choice, or if my Alpha Bite was the reason. Unlike me, he didn't have any evolution paths, though perhaps as a Unique Class his path is predetermined.

Once more Gary wished that his system would have come with instructions, but up until now the trend was that for every new thing he learned on his own, more and more questions would appear. He was slightly hoping for some type of skill that might answer at least some of those questions, but so far the Skill Shop sadly offered no such thing.

All the information he had was the name of the new class. As a Superior Gray Shapeshifter, perhaps Kai could now shapeshift into something besides a wolf, that or perhaps his wolf form had been strengthened. Another possibility was that the inherent trait of a Gray Werewolf had been enhanced by the chance.

In a rare instance of his Werewolf System not keeping mum, it had informed Gary about the trait of Gray Werewolves to grow stronger when in the company of other werewolves, not necessarily from their own pack even.

Shoot, we never really experimented with that, so there's no way to find out if it got improved. This time, we should definitely try to find out just how big the boost of power of a single werewolf is. There is a good chance, if we ever have to clash against one of the other alphas and their pack, that Kai could be a big part of this all.

"The pain is gradually subsiding," Kai said, rousing Gary from his thoughts. The beta werewolf clenched his hand into a fist. "You were right. I can feel the surge of power flowing through me, and it's even stronger than before. It's almost like when I first transformed from human to werewolf."

The power of a werewolf amazed him, but even now as Gary looked at Kai, he saw the scar on his jaw: a reminder of what a moment of weakness could mean for them all. Kai suddenly turned his head, looking at the stairs.

"Seems like the others have arrived."

Gary was caught off guard by the comment, as he couldn't smell the others at the moment. After a couple of seconds, the scent of them finally wafted into his nose, making him smile.

He was able to tell their whereabouts before me . . . His senses appear to be even sharper than mine after this evolution, but should I be happy for him or jealous?

The footsteps could be heard coming down the stairs, and the person in front wearing the tight-fitting black-and-gold uniform turned out to be Olivia. As usual, she had zipped up her jacket right up to her large breasts but not the whole way, still showing off her cleavage.

What was more surprising for Gary, though, was the person who followed after her.

"Marie?" Gary called out, as if to make sure he got the right person.

As soon as he saw her, he was taken aback by how different she looked from the last time they had met. Her hair was no longer in childish pigtails but elegantly tied back in a single ponytail that ran straight down her back. The new hairstyle seemed to suit her well, giving her a more mature and serious look that complemented her piercing eyes, leaving nothing of her old self that used to remind him of a black-haired version of his sister.

He also noticed a change in her demeanor, as if she had become more focused and aware of her surroundings. Her body had transformed as well, gaining noticeable muscle mass in all the right places without looking bulky. Instead, she now had a toned and athletic build that made her appear stronger and more confident than ever before. Just like Olivia, the suit now hugged tight to her skin in a lot of areas.

If I didn't know any better, I would believe they were sisters, Gary thought.

Kai noticed Gary's expression and couldn't resist teasing him. "You're not wrong, Olivia has certainly rubbed off on our Marie," he said with a chuckle.

"Shut up," Marie replied. "I just don't want things to be like before, and now I don't think they will be."

"It's nice to meet you again, Gary." Marie greeted him with a smile.

With all four werewolves gathered together and the car already waiting for them outside, it was time for them to pay Midwak a visit. Hopefully he had a way to stop their full moon transformation; otherwise the town of Slough would have four deadly werewolves to deal with.

CHAPTER 122

THE ONE WITH ANSWERS

The group had returned to Notsburg under the cover of darkness, and the city's lights twinkled in the distance. While Gary wasn't eager to engage in a direct confrontation with Midwak, he believed in being prepared for any eventuality.

The car pulled up in front of the casino, its grandeur as striking as the last time they had visited. The bridge leading up to it and the building's exterior had been restored to their original state, showcasing the owner's wealth and power.

"How long do you want me to wait for you guys?" Tyler asked as the other four headed off into the distance.

"We will update you via phone about what's going on. If you don't hear from us and it's been four hours or more, then it might be best that you just get out of here," Kai ordered.

Tyler's heart sank at Kai's words. At first, he thought it was a joke because of how lightheartedly Kai had made the comment, but as he looked into his eyes, he realized how serious he was. Tyler understood that if there was any force strong enough to take on the four of them the way they were now, then he and the rest of the Howlers wouldn't stand a chance.

As they stepped inside the opulent casino, the Howlers were struck by the blinding lights and deafening sounds of slot machines and chatter. They kept their eyes peeled for any sign of trouble, scanning the crowds of gamblers and guards alike. The masks on their faces concealed their identities, though at the same time they informed the Notsburg members that VIPs had just arrived. One of them was quick to approach them, bowing and addressing them with utmost respect. He led the group through the maze of tables and corridors, avoiding the prying eyes of security cameras.

Carrying on their walk through the casino, they garnered long, hard stares from the customers, who saw see the four masked individuals being escorted and treated as if they were royals. This was standard because the group owned the very casino everyone was gambling in.

"Do you think there's a chance that Midwak would betray us?" Marie asked, not caring about the guide, who stopped for a moment as he listened in on their conversation.

"I don't sense anyone else with him, but Fox and Hunter might be better at noticing if someone is in here," Gary replied, using the code names to make sure their identities would remain hidden.

Kai had proven earlier that his senses were now sharper than Gary's own, though Gary wasn't sure how Kai would fare compared to Olivia's Hunter Class, which specialized in sensing others. Thinking about it made him wonder whether Marie had uncovered any abilities granted to her by her Werewolf Class.

"Betrayal isn't in his best interest," Kai replied confidently. "He certainly doesn't like us, but he's the type to swallow his pride for the sake of revenge. He's accomplished every task I've given him so far, and based on our previous conversations, I can tell that he hates their group far more than ours. As long as we remain his best bet to achieve that revenge, he should at least cooperate with us."

As they approached the hallway leading to the office, Kai motioned for the guide to leave, and the man eagerly complied.

Memories for everyone started to flood their minds as they entered the office they had fought in. It looked a bit different than before, not just because of the lack of corpses.

The decorations of flashy jewels and such had been replaced with a monochrome black-and-white theme. There was also a ton of vintage equipment inside, such as swords, shields, and ancient weapons that looked hundreds of years old.

"I see you have been using the budget that I allocated you quite well?" Kai said, looking at the stuff.

Midwak looked almost bored as he sat in his chair, behind his desk. At first he didn't even acknowledge their arrival, which settled Gary's heart a little, as he took it as a sign that he wasn't looking for a way to get back at their group.

When Midwak finally looked up, his eyes rested on Marie, and a sly smile spread across his face. "I see that you took my advice about increasing the size of your pack," he said, his gaze flickering over the rest of the group before settling back on her. "This will be great for when I become the alpha, though I have to question your choice. If it were me, I would have started with the Black kid . . . could it be that him not being here means you failed to turn him?"

Kai and Gary both made sure that there was nobody else around to overhear what they were planning to discuss.

"Oh, so that's why you came here. I should have guessed by your current entourage." Midwak sighed. "I haven't seen or heard any signs of anyone else daring to attack us or Slough, which means you're here because of a personal problem.

"Go ahead, just tell me what you want. Not like I can stop you from forcing the information out of me anyway, but I do warn you all, things will be much different when I'm in charge."

Gary's mind was in turmoil. On one hand, he knew that as the alpha, he had the authority to alter the pack rules to force Midwak to speak the truth, but on the other hand, he couldn't shake the feeling that something was off.

Had Midwak truly accepted his fate so easily, or was something else going on? Gary knew that he couldn't let his guard down, especially since they were dealing with a cunning opponent like Midwak. Despite the beta's assurance, Gary remained wary and kept a close eye on the situation. He was determined to uncover any secrets that Midwak might be hiding.

"Given that you have been a werewolf for far longer than any of us . . ." Kai was the one to address Midwak, since Gary chose to remain silent for now. "According to what you have told us, werewolves have existed for a much longer time than we could ever imagine, yet they have managed to stay hidden from the public eye. It's difficult for me to believe that their existence has remained a secret if there were mass killings every full moon.

"So there should be a way to prevent us from acting up on the full moon, and I bet you know what it is."

In the worst-case scenario, they could always fall back on the method they had used last time. Unfortunately, it was truly excruciating to endure. Moreover, as their werewolf family continued to expand, there was an increasing possibility that someone would be unable to control or contain themselves, leaving them with no one to blame but themselves.

Midwak finally stood up and walked over to their group, making them flinch for a moment. "That's it? Shit, if that's all you wanted to know, this might as well have been a call. Of course, I know a way. However, I have a feeling that you might not like what you are about to hear."

CHAPTER 123

THE REQUIREMENTS

While in the car on the way to Notsburg, the others talked about what was to come. For one, they had to be careful about the information given by Midwak. Even though Gary could force him to tell the truth, there was a chance that he might miss out on things or phrase them in a certain way that would seem like the truth.

So they were all ready for Midwak to try to frighten them out of this whole thing, and there was a chance that it would be too dangerous for them to do anything in the first place.

"There are a lot of things that people don't know about werewolves that aren't written in books," Midwak said. "A lot of what I'm about to tell you, there is no way to confirm whether it's true. I am simply passing on information."

And with those words, all the credibility Midwak had was thrown out of the window. Either way, they would still listen to what he had to say.

Midwak looked at his arm for a second, and in an instant, it started to change as fur grew all over it, and his hand grew larger.

"The fact that we humans can turn into these types of creatures, don't you think it's strange in the first place? The fact that we are influenced by the moon. What exactly is it that is giving us power, or what exactly is it that is drawing it out?

"None of it makes sense. Say there was life on other planets, ones that have more than one moon orbiting around them. What do you suppose would happen? I'm sure many of you have had these questions on your mind."

Gary was a little embarrassed because he hadn't thought of these things, and what Midwak said had just blown his mind a little.

"The consensus is that this was a type of punishment from above that was brought down on a single human. Could you imagine, in the past, where families and friends lived close together in a confined space? They would have to live with the fact that once a month they would be forced to kill those closest to them. It is perhaps one of the cruelest forms of punishment one can have."

The group was struggling with this already. They could only imagine what would have happened if they had never found out about Gary's method. To what lengths they would have had to go to try to stop themselves.

"However, this punishment was meant only for one man. So is it fair that the rest of us, who have a part of him, should suffer the same fate? No, and the truth is not every werewolf suffers the same fate. For example, I have never once had trouble controlling myself on the full moon. Apart from feeling more powerful, I can stay in my human form and am not forced to hunt."

Everyone's eyes widened when they heard this. Was Midwak telling the truth? If he never had a problem with control, then did that also mean he didn't have an answer for them?

Seeing the looks on their faces, Midwak couldn't help but laugh. "HA-HA-HA! I can see the hope in your eyes vanish. I wish I could leave it at that, but the story doesn't end there.

"What I just told you is no lie, but as I said before, there is something that is passed down from leader to leader, or I should say, alpha to alpha. There is a ritual that can be performed.

"During this ritual, the alpha supposedly has the chance to communicate with the one who looks over us from above, the one who originally put down this punishment and caused us all to be the way we are.

"When making contact with said person, the alpha makes a new vow. A promise between the alpha and the greater power. Whatever this vow or promise is, he and the rest of his pack must keep it and never break it.

"When the ritual is complete, all of those belonging to your pack, whether born into it or forced to join, will no longer have that problem, as this new vow is linked to your pack and only your pack. This is the way to break the punishment given to werewolves and is a responsibility of a werewolf."

The group was silent, and they were, in a way, waiting for Gary to answer. Based on the information they had gained, a lot of what could happen was riding on his shoulders.

Gary was also pleased that the way to control oneself was fairly easy. There was no giant task, or a trial of some sort, or something that every werewolf would have to go through. After this, none of them would have to deal with this problem again.

"This vow." Marie finally spoke up. "You said it's a promise that must never be broken. What happens . . . what happens if someone ends up breaking it, though?"

Midwak sat back in his seat, and in doing so, he couldn't stop smiling, and his shoulders shook up and down.

"I have never seen it happen during my time. Some alphas, like the one I followed, chose to keep the vow a secret. Otherwise, there might be unruly ones like myself who try to break it in order to punish the rest of the pack, but I can tell you the rumors.

"They say one of two things can occur, and it seems to be entirely dependent on what it thinks is worse for the one involved. Either the pack will lose its status, losing its power as a werewolf. They will never be able to transform again no matter what they do, nor be able to be turned by others. They will remember everything they once had, but it will all be lost, and everything taken away from them.

"In a way, you could think of it as a possible cure, something a few werewolves would actually look forward to. Perhaps to scare these off, there is also the second possibility of what could happen. The ones who might have wanted to return to just being human will be punished by permanently turning into a werewolf. What's more, they will suffer from the same condition the full moon has on us without a vow, doomed to live the rest of their lives with an impossible-to-be-quenched bloodlust."

CHAPTER 124

STARTING THE RITUAL?

After hearing the entire explanation from Midwak, Gary was unsure whether he should be happy or not. There were a number of reasons to be frightened by this whole thing. The punishment for breaking a vow seemed quite high.

On both ends, it wouldn't do them any favors. Gary had survived in the underworld and had gotten this far because of his werewolf form, so if that were suddenly taken away, what would he do?

Old enemies such as Ben Clove would be able to take him down, and new ones would always be trying to uproot his position. Then again, the other option didn't sound delightful either.

Essentially, it was no different from a Crazed Altered, when one was unable to turn back, and he was sure that the bloodlust wouldn't be good either.

"I'm sure the vow with this upper being can't be something as simple as never eating sweets again, and the more I think about it, even that would be impossible to maintain," Gary said, scratching his head.

I would be on the edge of my seat every day wondering if someone would eat a sweet by accident, and if I told them about eating sweets, then Midwak would dangle that in front of me.

He could threaten me to force a change to the pack rules; otherwise, he would eat a sweet.

As Gary shook his head, the expression on his face was constantly changing as he went through made-up scenarios, and the others were a little concerned for him.

"What was the vow for your old pack?" Kai asked.

Knowing this would give them an idea of what type of promise they would need to make and would allow them to get the upper hand on other werewolves.

Midwak shrugged. "I don't know. The alpha never told us, and we never asked. Whatever it was, no one had ever broken it in our pack, and as for those before, I can only say they have been rumors but all of that is before my time.

"I don't see why you're all struggling so much. Is it really a big deal to go a bit wild once a month?"

Kai was seriously considering this option. Right now, it was a problem they dealt with monthly, and they did have a solution, but making a vow would cause a permanent problem they would always have to worry about.

"Weren't you an omega wolf for a while?" Olivia suddenly asked as it popped into her head. "If you were kicked out of your pack, did you still have control of yourself, or are you just like us?"

"You got me!" Midwak threw his hands up in the air. It was one of the questions he was hoping they wouldn't ask.

"I said before, from birth I have been in control of my werewolf self, but just as you said, when I became an omega wolf, I was affected just like everyone else. The first turning I experienced before coming to Notsburg wasn't too much trouble, but I am a problem solver.

"Even when joining the Scatterbugs, I had my ways of not causing trouble."

Again, the others felt like it might be best not to ask, but maybe it was a better solution than starving themselves.

"What was it? What did you do every full moon? Did you lock yourself up?" Marie asked. She was the most worried out of everyone.

She had yet to experience a full moon as a werewolf but had been there on the other end when they had attempted to stop the others. In her mind, if the will of the others wasn't strong enough, then what about hers?

Midwak started to laugh again.

"It was an easy solution, at least for me it was," Midwak said. "I just went down to the lower-tier cities. Tier 4 and Tier 5 for a little trip once a month. No one would care, nor would they really notice if they disappeared."

Midwak continued to laugh, and as for Gary, he walked straight toward Midwak while clenching his fists.

"Stop laughing," Gary mumbled.

"Huh?" Midwak replied.

Bending his front knee, Gary threw a fist from underneath and hit Midwak right in the chin. It lifted his body in the air before he landed on the ground. Midwak wasn't stunned but was surprised as he rubbed his chin.

"You fuck!" Midwak shouted. "You come here and ask me for help, and when I tell you things you don't want to hear, you take it out on me! I'm going to rip you to shreds when I get the chance!"

Something had clicked in Gary when he heard that, and it was his own situation. He and his family had been so close to not being able to live in a Tier 3 town and were close to moving down to Tier 4. And from there, maybe their situation would have gotten worse and they would have lived in a Tier 5.

The way Midwak was talking, it was as if their lives were worth less than the others. If he hadn't had a stroke of luck, it was possible that he would be living in fear, scared of someone like Midwak roaming around.

"You guys are screwed anyway!" Midwak shouted. "I know about the ritual, but do you think I even know how to do a ritual in the first place? That is something only alphas know, and someone like you, who knows even less than me about werewolves, will never figure out how to do one.

"So good luck on trying to go down your righteous path."

Standing there, they all felt like Midwak was right. There was now no one to turn to. So what would Gary do with his upcoming AFA match? That was until a ding was heard.

The user has gained knowledge about the Werewolf Vow ritual
Would you like to perform the ritual?

"Ah, system, I'm starting to like you more and more these days." Gary smiled.

The system that was always shrouded in mystery, that sometimes gave Gary quests he never wanted to do at the beginning, and at other times appeared to challenge him, had come through.

The trip wasn't wasted, though; it looks like the information from Midwak was what allowed the ritual to be unlocked, Gary thought.

The others, looking like they had gotten all the answers they could from Midwak, were ready to leave. Knowing full well that they hadn't gotten what they came for, Midwak was smug in his smile.

"It's okay." Gary smiled. "I know how to do the ritual."

For a second, everyone was surprised, including Midwak, but he shook his head in disbelief. It had to be a bluff, after all; it made no sense that Gary would know the ritual. Unfortunately, the others thought the same.

Maybe Gary had just spoken out of annoyance, or maybe he just didn't want to see Midwak so happy. It was understandable, as none of them did.

Rather than explaining, Gary thought it was a lot better to show. Heading back into the center of the room, away from the others, he stood there.

Ritual is being activated

Gary's eyes lit up red, a fierce red, and at the same time, everyone else in the room seemed to react as well. The color of their eyes changed to blue when using their powers. It had come over all of them; they could feel it, including Midwak.

"Damn it, I'm not sure if this is the ritual or not . . . but he's doing something? What is this?" Midwak said, confused.

A circle started to light up around Gary, and inside, there were multiple shapes starting to appear. They were of different colors: red, blue, and yellow. The patterns spiraled and started to move about. A foreign energy coming from the circle started to flow out and enter Gary's body, and with it, an image appeared in his mind.

What is this . . . is this the higher being that Midwak talked about? My stomach . . . it's hurting so much, and the hair on all of my body is standing up!

The image that was appearing in Gary's head wasn't clear. It was almost a sinister black smog, where only eyes could be seen, but the feeling around it, the place it was in, was filled with death. Screams, and pain, and images of torment were going through Gary's head, and he was unsure how much longer he could keep this up.

"A connection . . . but not a strong one." The voice spoke.

From the outside, the others could also faintly hear the voice but were unable to hear what Gary could hear.

Not wanting to waste any time, Gary decided to get right to the point.

"I have activated this ritual to speak with you. I want to make a vow, a promise, and in return for not breaking that promise, to stop our bloodlust and forced turning on the day of the full moon," Gary said.

When he spoke out like this, Gary realized that a lot of the werewolf beliefs that held them together were based on rules. Gary could make a promise with others to mark them. There were pack rules as well, and now this.

"It's as expected . . . It has been a while. I can do that, so state your promise," the voice replied.

Gary probably should have thought about this a bit more before he made the ritual, but he wanted to shock Midwak. What came to mind was a promise that he had made before with Kai, to get to the top of the Underworld.

Would this suffice? Probably not, because it needed to be something that couldn't be broken.

"What type of vow do you accept? What have the others promised before you?" Gary asked, thinking maybe they could learn what the other werewolves knew.

"Vows come in all shapes and sizes. I have been promised to always go against the vampires, a sacrificial vow, an entire kingdom within a set time, and so on through the years. However, in return for you having such power from me, you need difficulty in your life.

"This world needs a balance, and there needs to be a balance to your power. If I take the turning away, something equal to it needs to be replaced, and for you, I think it needs to be even more difficult."

Gary wasn't sure if he was imagining it, but the voice seemed to be almost angry with him for some reason. The tone of voice sounded as if he had done something to annoy it.

"I'm sorry if I annoyed you with my questions. What if I promised to become one of the current Kings in the country within the next five years?" Gary answered.

The voice seemed to be thinking about it.

"That would certainly be a difficult task, and if you broke the promise, then it would mean you would lose everything, and in attempting to do the task, you would make many enemies. I will accept this vow for you, but for your family line you will need to come up with an additional vow."

"Your family has already broken a vow in the past."

Gary hadn't been imagining things. It was true. The voice really was angry with him.

"I don't understand; my family, my current pack?"

"No!" the voice replied. "Did you really think you became a werewolf by chance, when there wasn't even a bite on you? You, the Dem family, have had werewolf blood running in your veins long before you managed to unlock your powers.

"For breaking the vow, I sealed your family's powers away, and yet here you are, in front of me again. After getting your powers back, you have the guts to ask to make another promise with me!"

There was no reply from Gary because he was too stunned by what he had just learned. What was the Dem family? Who knew about this? And what the hell was in that briefcase, then?

Gary had never felt like his family was surrounded in mystery. They had lived an ordinary life without much happening; heck, even their father leaving them had become the norm among families living in poverty.

Now though, learning this information, learning that there had always been werewolf blood running through his body, he started to think, did his father know more? Was there more to him running away? And maybe there was much more significance in the letter that had been sent to Amy.

"I didn't know about this," Gary replied. "So you're saying that I'm the one being punished for someone else's mistake, when I didn't even know about it. Does that sound right to you?"

At first, when Gary saw the dark image in his head, he was unable to talk back like this, but knowing about his family, and only learning about the truth now, had spurred this anger in him.

It was clear that this werewolf blood had to come from his mother's or father's side, and he assumed it had to be his father's. Their mother had always been quite honest with them. Although who knew now, maybe even she knew about all of this but was keeping it a secret.

The fact was, though, that he had turned into a werewolf and had to deal with all these troubles, but there was a chance that the same thing could have happened to Amy. If it did, he wondered just what she would have gone through, the dangers she would have faced, and even if she would have survived.

"I am the one who is in control, I am the one who's in charge," the voice replied. "You were the one who came to me, remember, so it's only right that I decide the rules. So I have made up my mind."

Now it felt like Gary no longer had any leverage in the discussion, and whatever this thing was, it was going to decide the deal for him, and he was right.

"The deal said before, the race of the werewolves was made so there would only be one that led all! There should only ever exist one alpha, and competition among each other is how one grows. In five years' time, there shall only be one alpha!" the voice angrily said.

This meant that Gary's task was now even harder than the vow from before. He had to promise not only to become a King but to topple the other alpha as well. In his mind, while there was no bad blood between the two, there was a chance that maybe they wouldn't have to fight, maybe they could work out something together, but that didn't seem to be the case anymore.

"On top of that, for the second condition. Let's make you suffer a little bit," the voice said. "I want you to remember that at any point I can take your power away, and in order for you to remember that, once a month on the day of the full moon, you and your pack are not allowed to transform into your werewolf selves!"

When the voice spoke, the vow was omitted from the others. The conversation had been made private, so they were unable to hear about Gary's original bloodline or the vows that had taken place.

There was now a big problem with the deal, though; wasn't it just changing the problem into another problem? Now they were unable to change on the full moon.

"Wait!" Gary shouted out, but the power and color from his eyes started to fade.

The circle beneath his feet started to disappear, and the heavy feeling that surrounded the room was going away. Everyone felt less sick; they felt as if they could breathe the clear air once again.

"I guess you weren't joking," Midwak said, standing up with an angry look on his face. He did not enjoy that, whatever that was.

Everyone was taking a few moments to themself, to shake off the strange feeling, while Gary was left with the promises in his head. Looking at the system, he could see that they had turned into a status.

Two had turned into a quest.

New Quest received
Objective 1: Become one of the Kings of the country, controlling a
Tier 1 city
Objective 2: Become the only alpha
Time limit: 5 years

As for the other one, there was a simple message stating the promise.

A vow has been made
The user and members of the pack must not turn into their werewolf
form on the night of the full moon

Based on the words here, it's not saying that we can't fight on the night of the full moon; we just can't transform. Either way, this will greatly diminish our strength. If anyone were to find out about this fact, they could target us, and it's the same if the other alpha found out as well.

"How was it?" Kai said. "Was it a success, did you manage to stop it? Did you manage to make a vow?"

Kai was just looking for a simple answer; he didn't need to know what the vow was because there was a good chance that a certain someone could use it against them. The problem was, Gary had to reveal the truth to everyone.

Because if he didn't, this was a vow that could easily be broken.

"We . . . don't have to worry about turning on the full moon," Gary answered.

The faces of all of those around him reflected full joy, but Kai could tell there was something else Gary wanted to say, and there wasn't a happy look on his face.

"But on the night of the full moon, we have promised that we won't turn into our werewolf selves. Instead, if we do, there is a good chance that we might never be able to turn again," Gary answered.

Gary had stunned the others into silence with his actions before, and he had done it again with his latest statement. They were left speechless, struggling to comprehend the weight of his words.

Midwak's outburst broke the silence that had hung in the air, and he took a step forward, his fists clenched in anger. "This is a joke, right?" he spat out, his voice thick with disbelief. But as he closed in on Gary, something strange happened. Midwak's eyes began to glow an eerie shade of blue, and his movements became unsteady. It was as if some unseen force was taking hold of him, causing him to hesitate in his tracks.

Even if he used all his will, the beta werewolf's body wouldn't allow him to hit the alpha, not until he was able to challenge him for his position again.

Gary's voice was steady as he spoke, his eyes meeting Midwak's in a direct gaze. "I'm not joking," he replied firmly. "The vow wasn't one I made, but one that is being decided on. From here on out, we're not to turn on the night of the full moon."

Hearing the news once again, Midwak jumped from his feet back to where his desk was. Both of his hands were covered in fur as he transformed and slammed them down onto the desk, breaking it in half.

"Do you have any idea what you have done? Thanks to you, *all* of us are in an even worse situation compared to before!" Midwak shouted. "If the other alphas find out about this, then they have a perfect day to attack us all! Just because you couldn't handle one night of bloodlust, you have doomed us all!"

Honestly, Gary wasn't too happy about this either, but it was more for other reasons. Now that this deal had been made, what did it mean for his family? If there was werewolf blood running through him, didn't that mean it was also running through Amy?

According to this being, their family had already been punished for breaking a vow in the past. However, seeing that it had agreed to make a vow with him, would he have to worry about his sister now also being able to turn?

For now, he kept these worries to himself, just like he hid the fact that there was also a second promise, which was to get rid of the alpha in five years. Things were just starting to look good for the Howlers, so now didn't seem like the perfect time to add additional pressure.

"Will you calm down?" Marie shouted. "You're acting like a wild animal. Did you not hear what he said? He wasn't the one who chose to make that vow; it was forced on him!"

Midwak's anger boiled over. "And why do you think that was the case, huh, missy?" he snarled, his words dripping with venom. "Let me tell you, it was given to him because he's a giant piece of shit!" His eyes narrowed as he glared at Gary, his fists shaking with rage. "I promise you, the first thing I'm going to do when I become alpha is get rid of this ridiculous vow!"

As Midwak continued to shout obscenities into the air, his words filled with rage and bitterness, the rest of the group watched in silence. They knew that nothing they could say or do would calm him down in his current state. Finally, one by one, they began to make their way out of the room.

"Hey, Gary, don't kick yourself so much." Kai rested his hand on his shoulder after they left. "We got what we came for; now you can fight in your debut match without having to worry about it. Heck, all of us can eat as much as we want now without having to worry."

"Yeah, and think about it, Gary. Only those in the room know about this. Even without transforming, we're strong enough to fight against anyone who isn't an Altered, and because it affects all of us, we would never say anything that would put us at a disadvantage," Marie said, thinking that even Midwak wouldn't tell the enemy a weakness he had as well.

"Besides, it's one day a month, so that's twelve days a year when we just have to avoid fighting. It's not like we're magnets that attract trouble."

As Olivia followed the group, she listened intently to Marie's words. For the most part, she agreed, nodding along in silent agreement. However, there was one part of Marie's statement that didn't sit right with her. Olivia had never been part of a gang that got involved in so much trouble in such a short amount of time before, and while things had quieted down somewhat, she felt that the danger was always lurking in the shadows for the Howlers.

During the drive back, Gary sat in silence, lost in his own thoughts. The others in the car exchanged glances, unsure of what was going on in his mind. They assumed that he was still preoccupied with the vow that had been made, but little did they know that there was so much more weighing on his mind. The vow was just a small part of a larger puzzle that he was trying to put together.

Tyler just silently did his job and dropped them off at their desired destination. Marie and Olivia got off at Burnham Street first, before Kai and Gary continued toward the Wolf's Pool Club.

They headed inside and down to into Kai's office.

"So now that it's just the two of us again, what's on your mind?" Kai asked as he looked over the papers Gary had collected during his transformation.

"There are a few things that I want to request from you, but I can't really explain why at the moment," Gary answered. "First, I need you to keep an eye on Amy. I mean more than you have been doing already. Tell White to be careful and that she needs to report if she notices anything unusual about Amy. In that case, contact me straightaway."

"That can easily be done," Kai answered. "And for the other requests?"

"I think it's finally time to find out more about the briefcase that started it all. We need to find out where it came from and who Damion planned to deliver it to."

Kai didn't say anything, because he had already been looking into this himself. He had a few guesses in mind, but he didn't want to give Gary an answer until he knew for certain. His guesses were all dangerous people, and sticking their nose in the business of uninvolved parties was just asking for trouble.

"As for my final request," Gary said, his voice steady but laced with emotion. "I need you to use all of the resources at our disposal to find someone very important to me. Contact our allies and ask for their assistance in locating Dean Dem. I need to find my father and ask him about all of this."

ABOUT THE AUTHOR

JKSManga is the pen name of UK-based, *New York Times*–bestselling LitRPG author Kawin Jack Sherwin, whose series include My Vampire System, My Dragon System, and My Werewolf System. His works have sold fifteen million copies worldwide, and several have been adapted into comic books.

RESPAWN YOUR CURIOSITY

follow us on our socials

 podiumentertainment.com

 @podiumentertainment

 /podiumentertainment

 @podium_ent

 @podiumentertainment

www.ingramcontent.com/pod-product-compliance
Lightning Source LLC
Chambersburg PA
CBHW020241120726
47904CB00001B/50